Praise for *Last Night at the Disco*

"*Last Night at the Disco* is a comic gem, told from the perspective of a delusional narcissist with a Jersey-sized chip on her shoulder. Lisa Borders is a very funny writer who knows a ton about pop music and junior high school and bruised egos, and this is one of the most entertaining and psychologically astute novels I've read in quite some time."

—Tom Perrotta, author of *Little Children* and *Tracy Flick Can't Win*

"In *Last Night at the Disco*, Lisa Borders has created an indelibly magnetic and occasionally terrifying heroine. Lynda Boyle is vain, seductive and irresistibly selfish, and she does the Garden State proud, as a comic wonder and the star of this delightful novel."

– Paul Rudnick, author of *What Is Wrong with You?*

"In *Last Night at the Disco*, Lisa Borders has created one of those spectacularly messy narrators whose number you'd block ASAP in real life but whose beguiling voice and misplaced conviction in herself you can't get enough of on the page. The result is a propulsive, funny, and genuinely insightful rock and roll novel with a disco beat. This might be the kind of smart, humane entertainment we all need right now."

—Stephen McCauley, author of *My Ex-Life* and *You Only Call When You're in Trouble*

"After reading this deliciously deranged *cri de coeur*, I hereby declare Lynda Boyle our next great camp icon."

—Christopher Castellani, author of *Leading Men*

"Lisa Borders's *Last Night at the Disco* is as much fun as a night spent boogying on the coke-dusted dance floor of Studio 54, and its narcissistic, beautiful, indefatigable narrator Lynda Boyle should go down in the annals of literature as one of the best anti-heroes ever created. Throughout the pages of this wild and hilarious romp of a book, I alternated between covering my eyes and cheering her on for her terrible behavior. A smart, outrageous, and wonderfully escapist read!"

—Whitney Scharer, author of *The Age of Light*

"*Last Night at the Disco* is a dazzling feat, with its wry echoes of Nabokov's *Pale Fire.* A Jersey girl outsider longs for her rightful place at the glamorous Studio 54, in this deliciously celebrity-studded, disco-and-rock-fueled novel. I didn't want the night to end."

—Patricia Park, author of *What's Eating Jackie Oh?*

"Outrageously funny, deliciously sexy, and sneakily moving, Lynda Boyle's voice is every bit as unforgettable as she'd surely tell you it is, and it makes *Last Night at the Disco* a joy to read. Come for the history of Studio 54 and stay for the subtle send-up of our own glitz-blinded culture. Or come for the catastrophic oedipal triangles and stay for the sweet love story. Either way, there's a strong case to be made that this is the Great New Jersey Novel."

—Yael Goldstein-Love, author of *The Possibilities*

"In *Last Night at the Disco*, novelist Lisa Borders deftly, with cutting humor, explores the impact of ruthless ambition, corruptive casts of fame, and the betrayal of friendship in the competitive music world. A fully entertaining and engaging read from cover to cover."

—*Midwest Book Review*, June 2025

Last Night at the Disco

Lisa Borders

Regal House Publishing

Published by
Regal House Publishing, LLC
Raleigh, NC 27605

ISBN -13 (paperback): 9781646036448
ISBN -13 (epub): 9781646036455
Library of Congress Control Number: 2024951381

Cover images and design by © studiochi.art

Printed in the United States of America

Regal House Publishing, LLC
https://regalhousepublishing.com

For Jeffrey Page, the guy who gets me

"…she always nursed a small mad hope."

– Vladimir Nabokov, *Pale Fire*

Subject: Correction requested re: "Aura Lockhart Inducts Johnny Engel into Rock & Roll Hall of Fame," Rolling Stone #1326, April 2019

From: Lynda Boyle Ross (dancingqueen.54@aol.com)
Date: Monday, April 15, 2019 3:54 a.m.
To: Jann Wenner (jann@rollingstone.com)

Dear Mr. Wenner,

We met twice at Studio 54 in the year or so after the club opened: once on a banquette, where we chatted with Andy Warhol and Brooke Shields, and one brief but memorable encounter in the bathroom. I have especially fond memories of the latter, and trust that you do as well.

The purpose of this email is not to revisit our incendiary past, however, but in reference to the above-mentioned article, which chronicles circumstances well beyond the Hall of Fame induction. I wish to clarify your mention of me, and of my role in launching the careers of Aura Lockhart and Johnny Engel. There are a number of factual inaccuracies in your story, falsehoods that have plagued me for decades. These untruths, I believe, all stem from the same source: A 1980 *New York* magazine article, "Looking for Ms. Goodbar" (with this absurdly sensationalistic subheader: "New Jersey junior high teacher by day, coke-fueled disco queen by night. Where is Lynda Boyle now?") that painted me, my husband, and the events that forced us to leave the tri-state area in terms that were both reductive and unflattering. Rest assured that I don't blame *your* magazine for these inaccuracies; no, I blame the reporter who wrote about me back in 1980, interviewing Johnny Engel, Steve Rubell, three of my former co-workers, a publicity hungry ex-beau, and one of my perpetually jealous sisters-in-law.

Without further preamble, then, the inaccuracies in your article include the following:

I was not fired from my teaching position; I resigned.
I was never charged with any crime.
My husband was also never (formally) charged with any crime.

My other objection to your magazine's story concerns a quote from Aura Lockhart. Aura is on record as saying that the Hall of Fame induction was long overdue, that Johnny was finally getting the recognition he deserved "after his life and career were nearly destroyed." Because I am mentioned in the very next sentence, the implication is that Aura was referring to me.

Imagine the outrage I felt upon reading this! Without me, neither Aura nor Johnny would have the fame they now enjoy; Aura likely would never have escaped that waterlogged hiccup of a town where we first met. My immediate reaction to the article was, of course, to fling my copy of the magazine across the kitchen. As I then began to smash plate after plate from our cupboard, my husband, who had retreated to the safety of the lanai, called out these life-changing words: "Send a correction to *Rolling Stone*, babe. Set the record straight."

But permanently amending the record requires more than a brief iteration of facts. Where to begin? With the weeks or months leading up to the events of May 24, 1978? The year before, when Aura and I met Johnny? Or perhaps with my own origin story.

Like most of the swamp-rat communities lining New Jersey's Raritan Bay, my hometown of Keyhole (a place my high school friends and, later, my students derisively called The Hole) had a pull on its inhabitants that was as strong as the Atlantic's tides. There's a reason Bruce Springsteen wrote so many songs of escape early in his career; it was a rare thing even to make it to the nearby City, as I did in 1969 when I went off to Brooklyn College. The tide rolled me out, and then, six years later, the tide—assisted by my mother, who selfishly denied me the aid my father was more than willing to provide to help support my dream of achieving fame as an East Village poet—rolled me back in. I washed up once again on the shores of Keyhole, and for three years, from 1975 to 1978, taught eighth grade English at my old junior high school.

While it's true that I never tilted the axis of the poetry world as I'd once planned to do—my early work was lauded by none other than the great John Ashbery, a dear mentor who, in a college workshop, referred to the imagery in one of my poems as "painfully exact"—I made my mark in other ways. Had events unfolded differently, I might well have ended up in The City, my acquaintance with Calvin Klein and Bianca Jagger blossoming into inevitable friendships, my visage most likely adorning the cover of your celebrated magazine when my first book of poetry was published to wide acclaim. Perhaps, even, Aura and I would still be close; we'd meet for brunch in Tribeca or Williamsburg or the Lower East Side on Sundays and walk arm-in-arm down Orchard Street, a middle-aged woman and her slightly more mature, more glamorous mentor, two women who, despite a twelve-year age difference, would look more like sisters than student and teacher.

I may have ended up more notorious than famous, but make no mistake: long before Aura Lockhart began commodifying her feminist rage ballads, *I* was the best-known person to come out of Keyhole, New Jersey. It would be impossible to understand my sudden fame without an in-depth accounting of the events of the 1977–78 school year, my last months in New Jersey: Johnny, Aura, meeting my husband, Studio 54, Cher, Halston, *all of it.* I was twenty-six years old and at the height of my beauty, as you may well remember. Does it sound vain, for me to say that I was beautiful? Would you prefer I pretend that I was plain, or average, or oblivious to my own good looks? I was beautiful, had been beautiful since I was eleven, and I knew it. If it helps, I'm now sixty-seven years old and, while I'm often told that I look closer to fifty than seventy, I project more an approximation of glamour rather than glamour itself.

But put aside, for a moment, the ravages of time. Picture it: October of 1977. The cars are huge; the briny air and the nearby ocean, polluted. The Bee Gees and Fleetwood Mac, Electric Light Orchestra and Abba dominate the radio. People still *listen* to the radio. There's a junior high school in a small town on the Central Jersey shore where many of the teachers are young, and searching for whatever would come after the hippie era. Some of us are living double lives in The City. Aura Lockhart is fourteen years old, has been in Keyhole for one month, and things are not going well for her. And my attempts to save her, as you will see, do not go quite as planned.

1

"You're so ugly."

Rest assured, Jann, those foul words were not directed at me. And while I have no idea if you're an Aura Lockhart fan—I, myself, am not; my interest is purely personal—with your vast knowledge of rock music you might recognize that phrase, "You're So Ugly," as the title of one of Aura's early songs, released by her band The Madonna-Whore Complex in 1989. She sang those words repeatedly over thrashing guitars, in the guttural growl that became her trademark.

But back in 1977 there was no musical accompaniment, just that phrase, "you're so ugly," chanted loudly in the grating, sing-songy voice of Keyhole Junior High School's resident eighth-grade bully. I rounded the corner to my classroom, and there they were: the new girl, Aura Lockhart, and the bully, Jody Fromme.

Aura, clad as always in an ill-fitting black leather bomber jacket—too tight in the bust, too blousy in the abdomen—turned to head into the classroom. Jody and her gang blocked the door.

"She stinks as bad as that coat," said one of the other girls, the one sporting the Dorothy Hamill wedge haircut.

"Wait," Jody said in a softer voice. "I can see...her *aura*!" She'd been mocking Aura's name for weeks, her jokes always the lowest of low-hanging fruit.

Aura folded her arms in front of her, light brown hair framing her face in a choppy shag, blue eyes blazing, as she waited for the mercy of the bell. Her demeanor suggested that she was beyond petty junior high school bullshit, that this was at worst a nuisance, an inconvenience; later, her songs and interviews would tell a different story.

"Groovy! What *color* is it, man?" Dorothy Hamill asked in a mock-hippie dialect likely culled from early childhood viewing of *The Mod Squad* or *Laugh-In*, waving her hands around Aura as if feeling for an unseen energy force.

"It's...it's..." Jody closed her eyes. "She's surrounded by a soft brown light. No, deep brown. Shit brown!" Jody and her sidekick laughed loudly; the other dozen or so girls gathered at the door were mostly quiet, some entertained, others terrified they'd be next. "No wonder she smells."

Aura, for the record, did not smell bad. And while that jacket may have been unflattering, she was never ugly. A little chubby, yes, and she hadn't quite grown into her features yet, but she had the presence of an older, more confident—dare I say, more beautiful—woman. It was in the defiant tilt of her head, in the way her eyes shone beneath her shaggy bangs. Jody and her friends felt it too; it threatened them, Aura's magnetism.

Jody had a large, sharp nose and a poorly executed proto-mullet that made her resemble Rod Stewart.

I plowed forward through the crowd.

"Break it up, girls," I said. "The bell's about to ring."

As Jody and her sidekick tried to box Aura in—Jody walking in front of her, Dorothy Hamill pushing from behind—Aura extended her foot ever so slightly in front of Jody's. To a less perceptive teacher, it might have looked like Jody simply stumbled in the rush of students entering the classroom. But I saw what Aura did. As Jody fell onto a desk, turning and flashing her bitchiest look at Aura, I sidled up to the new girl, escorting her inside.

"Smooth move," I whispered in her ear. I was certain she'd heard me, but Aura gave no indication, not even a shrug.

We teachers had been told by our principal not to get too involved in these kinds of incidents, that kids generally worked it out themselves. Today, of course, a school's administration would intervene in this sort of bullying, and everyone would try to figure out why Jody behaved the way she did. I didn't care then, and I don't care now. She was a little cunt whose insults were as uninspired as she was, a girl who most likely fell off the map after high school; good riddance, I say. Even before I made Aura my *cause célèbre*, it was clear which of these girls had something to offer the world.

I stood behind my desk and flipped through my lesson plan. From the corner of my eye I saw Bobby Craig and Johnny Bianchi, whispering and glancing back at Aura. They were plotting something.

"Anything you'd care to share with me?" I asked, moving closer to their desks.

Both boys looked up.

"No, Ms. Boyle," Bobby said. "Just goofin' around." He flashed me the kind of smile men had been flashing me since I was twelve. I knew the boys in my eighth-grade classes found me attractive. Did I use that sometimes, to keep them in line? Of course I did. Everyone who possesses beauty uses it. Those who claim to be above it are not naïve; they are liars.

"I can't wait to hear your poems," I said, a kind lie meant to focus them on the day's lesson.

The assignment had been to write a poem exploring the student's identity. I'd given them examples: Emily Dickinson, Robert Frost, Langston Hughes. And while I had little enthusiasm for teaching in general, I was genuinely excited that day. My students had made art! And by requiring that they recite the poems, I could grade them on the spot—leaving my weekend free for adventures in The City rather than wasting my Sunday trying to decipher a stack of thirty nearly illegible scrawls, red pen at the ready, the suffocating drone of my parents' TV reminding me of how intolerable this life was.

"Okay, everyone," I said. "It's time to read your poems."

A few students groaned. Jody and Dorothy Hamill—Kathi, that was the girl's real name, with an *i*, as if that bit of faux exoticism would make her anything other than a mean girl's sidekick with a figure skater's hairdo—were passing a note back and forth.

"Jody? Why don't you start us off?" I asked.

Jody looked up at me, eyes flashing annoyance. "Oh, I forgot it, Ms. Boyle," she said. The contempt in her tone was unmistakable.

Much of the class giggled.

I glared back at Jody for a moment. Kathi was still engrossed in her note-writing, and I swiftly moved in front of her.

"Give me that, please." I held my hand out toward Kathi.

She looked up, her eyes liquid and panicked.

"That's private," Jody protested.

I ignored Jody and fixed my scariest expression on Kathi, clearly the weak link of the duo.

"Give it to me," I said, "or you can both go down to Principal Singer's office and give it to him."

Kathi and Jody exchanged a glance; Jody nodded, and Kathi offered me the note. In that moment, I had even more contempt for Kathi than I had for Jody. I've never had much patience for followers, the dullest of the dull. Jody was a little beast, but at least she wasn't weak. I took the folded paper from Kathi and tucked it into my leather bag.

"Now," I said. "Jody has a zero for this assignment."

I called on a dozen other kids who dutifully recited their insipid compositions. Then I came to Bobby Craig. I should have been alerted by the wicked smile on his face as he stretched and rose, arching his back so that his *Captain Fantastic* T-shirt rode up and exposed a pinch of lingering baby fat.

He cleared his throat dramatically.

"There once was a teacher named Lynda, whose hot body could get you through winter—"

"Bobby!" I cried out, snatching the paper from his hands as the other students exploded in laughter. Glancing down at the page, I noticed that he'd later paired "rhymin'" and "hymen." I folded the paper into a square and put it in my bag with Jody and Kathi's note.

Bobby remained standing there, staring at my breasts, which I knew looked spectacular in the form-fitting Qiana dress I was wearing that day—fire engine red, my signature color. And though I knew I shouldn't enjoy the attention of a fourteen-year-old, or the fact that he'd made a mockery of the assignment, I did enjoy it, a little. I couldn't help but like Bobby Craig.

"Sit down, Bobby," I said, but I knew I was smiling. Bobby smiled back at me and took his seat.

Aura was the next student up. I expected her to stand, as the others had, but she remained seated in her usual position: leaning against the back of the chair more than actually sitting in it, legs outstretched in front of her, hands fisted in her lap. She sat up slightly and cleared her throat.

"A star," she said, carefully enunciating each word. She paused for a few seconds. "Explodes." She released her fists, fingers spread.

I waited for her to go on. She leaned back into her chair, the wall clock loudly ticking off the seconds.

"That's it?" I finally asked.

"That's it," she said.

Bobby Craig and Johnny Bianchi snickered.

Marisol Rodriguez, the universally acknowledged smartest girl in class, a girl who generally kept her head down and stayed out of any classroom drama, flashed Aura the tiniest smirk of a smile—a clear suggestion that she thought Aura was putting something over on me. I'd deal with that later.

"Do you think three words can constitute a poem?" I asked Aura, knowing full well that there were poets in the East Village who would answer that question with "Yes," and knowing equally well that Aura had simply not done the assignment.

"Consider it a form of haiku," Aura said.

This was the most Aura had said in class in the month since school had started, and I was simultaneously intrigued by her chutzpah and irritated that she thought she could bullshit me. But before I could say anything, Jody spoke up.

"In that case, I have a haiku too," Jody said. She leaned back in her seat, mimicking Aura. "Her head," she recited, then paused, her eyes on Aura. "Explodes."

"Go fuck yourself," Aura muttered.

Now the entire class was "oohing" and laughing, the lesson was off the rails, and I was in the unfortunate position of having to do something about it. Corralling children was such a tedious endeavor, and it was only Monday.

"Aura, Jody—both of you, go to the principal," I said. It might not have been fair, to punish the bully and the bullied, but sometimes, an exhausted teacher must sacrifice what is right to do what is easy.

Aura quickly got up and left the room, her face betraying nothing.

Jody didn't move from her desk. "I'm not the one who swore," she whined.

I motioned for her to get up and ushered her to the door. Even out in the hall, Aura gone, Jody continued to argue her case. I listened for about thirty seconds.

"It doesn't matter what you did or didn't do in class," I finally said, in an eavesdrop-proof whisper I'd perfected in my teens. "I just don't like you."

Her jaw went slack for long enough that I wondered if she'd had a stroke; but then she simply turned and headed down the hall.

As I reentered the classroom, the bell rang.

"We'll hear from the rest of you tomorrow," I called out over the sound of chairs scraping the floor.

I am better than this, I thought as the next class filed in. Just two years earlier, three of my poems were personally chosen by the renowned poet Carlos Barrada for a group reading at the Ninety-Second Street Y—and while, yes, I had slept with Carlos, my reading was a triumph, and I was certain my poems would have been selected even if I hadn't given Carlos what he'd called "the best blowjob in the tri-state area." As I watched some of the lowest-achieving students in the eighth grade of one of the lowest-achieving school systems in the state of New Jersey file into my room, I knew only this one truth: I needed to find an exit ramp from the Garden State Parkway of teaching.

Later that morning I received a cryptic note in my mailbox to report to Dick Singer, the principal, when I had my free period. I knew he'd want to talk about Jody and Aura, of course, but he was usually more direct if it was simply about a punishment. I tried to imagine what else he had in mind to discuss: a merit raise? No, we were unionized and raises were pre-ordained. Praise on the terrific job I was doing? Surely that must be it. I'd described my creative poetry lessons to the parents during our conferences last week. They'd been so impressed that they'd called the principal to express their gratitude!

I entered the main office. Dick's secretary, Patti—a leggy woman of about my age whose huge, teased hair suggested she was either a stubborn hanger-on from the bouffant era or an early pioneer of '80s styling—was on the phone. She looked up, placing one hand over the mouthpiece.

"Head right on in, hon," she said, and her conversation resumed without missing a beat as I slipped into Dick's office.

"Lynda," he said, standing as I entered. It was a gentlemanly pretense; he looked me up and down. I let him take it all in—the cascading chestnut brown hair, the flawless complexion, the hourglass figure—before I sat, demurely smoothing my dress beneath my thighs.

He regarded me with a thin smile on his face, and an awkward silence followed. "You wanted to see me?" I finally asked.

"Yes." Dick cleared his throat. "I received feedback from a couple of the parents following your recent conferences. Just some constructive criticism."

Have I mentioned that Keyhole was not exactly a brain trust? Or the contempt I felt for those who stayed there and spawned—including my two older brothers and my nine cousins? I could only imagine what this "constructive" feedback was.

"I'm always happy to hear something that can help me improve," I said brightly, smiling at Dick and pushing my cleavage ever-so-subtly in his direction.

A tobacco-reeking old letch who was easily susceptible to my looks, Dick blushed a bit and shifted in his chair.

"Several of the parents said they found you to be a bit remote, that you seemed like you cared more about poetry than about their children. And a number of the mothers commented that they thought you dressed too provocatively."

Where to begin here? With the fact that any literate human being would care more about, say, Ginsburg's *Howl* than about the collection of rusty gears and sprockets that comprised most of my students' brains? Or with the jealous rantings of women a decade older than me who'd let themselves go and saw my body as a reminder of what they'd lost?

I decided to tackle the easiest part first.

"Do *you* think I dress provocatively, Dick?' I asked, rearranging myself on the chair.

Dick smiled. "Lynda, between you and me, you'd look provocative in a burlap sack."

I blinked once, slowly. Amateurs bat their lashes too quickly and too often.

"But perhaps you could just dress a little more conservatively, especially when you're meeting with parents?"

"Of course, Dick," I said, thinking that I could always borrow something frumpy from my mother's closet, and realizing in the instant the thought formed that I would rather quit my job than wear one of her hideously sensible dresses.

"I'm more concerned about this perception that you don't care about the kids. I'm sure it's completely unfounded, but perhaps you could volunteer to lead an after-school activity? Befriend a child who seems to need some attention?"

Both of the above suggestions seemed like a colossal waste of my time. But I had the sense that Dick had already devised *my* punishment, and I waited for him to mete it out.

"After talking with Aura Lockhart," Dick said, "I looked over her transcripts. She did well at the school she attended in New York, at least before her father died. I think the transition has been difficult for her."

It was news to me that Aura was from out of state. "Where in New York?" I asked.

"The City," Dick said. "Her father was some kind of poet?"

Some kind of poet? *Some kind of poet?* That could mean anything from the greeting card detritus of Rod McKuen to the brilliance of Kerouac or Corso.

I spun through a mental Rolodex of The City's male poets, trying to remember if any of them had died recently. And then a name flew to the top of my consciousness, flashing, electric, throughout every cell in my body.

Augustus Lockhart.

Augustus Lockhart, infamous in the literary world for his 1969 "I Hate Words" poetry manifesto, friend of the famed New York School of Poets but whose writing was a world apart from theirs. Augustus Lockhart, who had founded the *Sans Mots* reading series in my beloved East Village—readings I had attended with great regularity in college and beyond, readings where I was, in all honesty, the most beautiful woman in the room and therefore left with whichever poet struck my fancy.

Augustus Lockhart, with whom I had gone home once, and spent a glorious weekend, his stamina impressive for a man in his forties.

Augustus Fucking Lockhart was Aura's father.

"Her father was a poet of great renown in certain circles," I said to Dick, as if I'd always made the connection.

"Was he?" Dick asked. "I don't read much poetry."

Of course you don't, I thought. How could a simpleton like Dick Singer understand the rarefied world of a poetry god like Augustus Lockhart? And poor Aura—to lose such a father, at such a young age. And in the greatest indignity of all, to move from The City to fucking Keyhole!

As I considered how dearly young Aura had suffered, I remembered her poem.

A star.

Explodes.

Clearly she *had* done the assignment, with the kind of minimalist flair her father had favored. Perhaps the poem was even *about* Augustus; hadn't he died from a ruptured aneurysm? A star explodes, indeed! O Aura, my grieving tough and tender-hearted genius. How had I not seen it before?

I leaned in toward Dick. "You were saying something about befriending a child in need?"

Dick smiled. "Wonderful! I'm sure you and Aura have a lot in common."

Given that I'd slept with her father, we had more of a connection than Dick ever could have imagined.

I spent the next two days trying to figure out how to approach Aura. This was a child of the East Village, indeed, of one of the East Village's poetry greats; she was Athena, sprung from Zeus's head, and I could not just chat with her about whatever inanities interested most girls her age. Her unkempt nonchalance, that unflattering yet hip jacket that had clearly once been her father's—although I did not remember it specifically, it looked like the kind of thing he would have worn, and I'll admit to a frisson of titillation at the possibility that my own sweet perfume might have nestled in its leather grain!—indeed, her refusal to participate in the hooves-and-lips sausage grinder that was Keyhole Junior High itself, all of it suggested that Aura, the most promising child to enter that school since yours truly, would not be easy to befriend.

By Wednesday I was desperate for both a way in with Aura and a night out in The City; surely shaking my booty on the dance floor would dislodge a brilliant plan from my brain. I had been seeing my current beau for three weeks, and by seeing, I mean fucking. Art had never been to a disco, and it was high time to change that.

I'd discovered gay dance clubs like The Loft and 12 West back when I was still living my East Village dream. I became a regular, enjoying both the music and the challenge; surely you wouldn't be surprised, Jann, if I told you just how often I *did* go home with a guy. During those years, I was at either a club or a poetry reading five or six nights a week. I lived most days on four hours' sleep. O youth!

I continued clubbing on weekends—at the very least—after my tragic move to Jersey. The spring before Aura Lockhart turned up in my class, I'd heard excited chatter about a new club opening on Fifty-Fourth Street.

I went the first week Studio 54 opened, strategically arriving early, when the crowd outside was thick, but not quite the mob scene later immortalized by gossip columnists and TV crews. After watching me dance, Steve Rubell himself invited me to sit in the bleachers, where he was pouring Dom Perignon into paper cups; the club hadn't gotten its liquor license yet. I charmed Steve and made sure to befriend the bouncer. After that, I was always let in.

But when I called Art that Wednesday night and asked him to take me to Studio, he hesitated.

"Isn't that place really hard to get in to?"

"Not at all," I said. Was I aware that there were mere mortals who spent night after night on the wrong side of that velvet rope, women whose dreams were even bigger than their Farrah-flipped hair but who could never make it past the bouncer? Of course. But I wasn't one of them.

"Pick me up at ten," I said, "and wear something sharp."

"Ten p.m.? Lynda, it's a work night!"

I sighed. "Nine-thirty, then."

I could tell he wanted to say no, but what he said was, "Okay."

Three weeks in, I was already fairly certain that things would not work out with Art; but if he continued to bend to my will, he might manage to keep himself in my life for another few months.

The area outside the club was especially crowded for a Wednesday night. As it turned out, Steve was throwing a birthday party for Elizabeth Taylor's Lhasa apso, Elsa. As we approached the throng, Art looked dazed by the sequins, the glitter, the hungry pheromones, and I took his hand and led him through the teeming mob, deftly navigating the angry grunts and sharp elbows from some of the less refined masses. Those outer borough boors were kept away with good reason!

When we were close enough to the bouncer that I could catch his eye, he nodded to me, pulling the velvet rope aside so I could step through. But he put his hands out to stop Art.

"Just her," he said to Art, looking appraisingly at my soon-to-be-erstwhile beau's nondescript white shirt, frayed at the cuffs, and sensible black dress slacks. Art resembled nothing so much as a waiter, perhaps a busboy.

"Let's just go, Lynda," Art said to me.

I made moon eyes at the bouncer, mouthing the word *please* in a way that also suggested a blow job was in his future.

"Just this once," he said, pulling the rope back for Art, who was so dumbfounded, the poor dear, that I had to pull him through.

"You owe me, Lynda," the bouncer called out to me as we entered the club, and I gave him a graceful flick of my wrist in return.

And then we were in: walking the long, grand, mirrored foyer, its arched gold ceiling bathed in soft red light that reflected off the chandeliers, the pulse of bass beckoning me from just beyond the closed double doors. Steve had hired actors in dog costumes to roam the hall, in keeping with the party's theme—but with a Studio twist, each dog was attended by a whip-wielding drag queen dominatrix. I said hello to Glory Whole, who'd been a regular at Studio for as long as I had; Art's eyes widened as she fixed me with a dazzling smile and smacked a six-foot Snoopy just above his little white tail. We stopped near the coat check to pay.

"*Forty dollars*?" Art whined, but I gave him one long lash bat and he handed over two twenties. Inside, I guided him toward the dance floor as the two of us were enveloped by the thrumming music, the flashing white lights, the gold-and-green neon sunray backdrop.

"Let's dance!" I said, already shaking my groove thing to Donna Summer.

Art waved me away and retreated in the general direction of the bar, just as a five-tier chocolate birthday cake was wheeled out. I later saw that it was decorated with paw prints, dusted atop the chocolate icing in what one might assume was powdered sugar, or perhaps cocaine.

Art sulked for the entire night, picking at a slice of cake and watching me like a stalker as I undulated to the rhythm with two beautiful gay boys clad in little more than golden Speedos, and later, Margaux Hemingway. Art begged me to leave at midnight, at twelve thirty, at one in the morning. But I had vowed to dance until my very molecules rearranged themselves, until inspiration struck—and it did, shortly after a raft of balloons were dropped from the ceiling. I watched as a lone white balloon floated down toward a young girl seated on one of the banquettes. Surely no older than my students, the girl chatted animatedly with none other than Liz Taylor—and her dog.

I excused myself to Margaux and made my way up to Liz. As I waited to congratulate her and her canine companion—the circle around that *grande dame* was tight!—I accepted the glass of champagne proffered by a character actor whose name I cannot, to this day, recall, but who starred in many Quinn Martin productions. "Do they usually let kids so young in here?" I asked him, motioning to the girl.

"If they're famous," he said. "She's one of the stars of *Annie*."

As we clinked glasses I thought of Aura, and how she, a daughter of genius, was so much more deserving of that spot at Liz's banquette than some Broadway brat. And what fourteen-year-old girl wouldn't love to be there—long for it, even?

I would introduce Aura to the glittering world that her father could no longer show her—to poetry and music and, of course, to Studio. And Aura, with the contacts bestowed upon her by her paterfamilias—surely Allen Ginsburg, or someone of his ilk, was her godfather!—could help restore me to my rightful place in the poetry world.

It was a bold plan to be sure, audacious in that way any plan worth setting in motion must be. And it might have worked, if only Aura and I had never met Johnny Engel.

2

Four decades have passed since I met, nurtured, bedded, promoted—and was later quite harshly maligned by Johnny Engel. With the exception of watching the Hall of Fame induction, and Hubby's occasional spins of Johnny's old discs when I'm out (something he denies, but I know, I always know), our house is a Johnny-free zone. Imagine my horror, then, when a senescent couple from some godforsaken hamlet in Johnny's home state of Michigan moved in next door last month and began blasting us out of our home: first, with their hangdog vowel sounds as they loudly and uninformedly engaged in political debate; and then, with my once-dear Johnny's music—from speakers I soon discovered they'd placed on their lanai, facing out toward their pool.

If I may, let me provide as much context to this tableau as I can safely share. After many years of moving around, my husband and I have lived in the same house for more than a decade. In the interest of our continued safety I cannot tell you exactly where we're living, except to note that if you'd told twenty-six-year-old Lynda this was where she'd end up, O, the tears that beauty would have shed! Yet we feel safe here, the safest we've felt since our tragic exile from the tri-state area. All this to say: I have broken into the new neighbors' lanai and disconnected their speakers twice in the past three weeks, and will escalate if necessary, as we are not the ones who will move.

These neighbors, we've been told, are retired high school guidance counselors—a tragedy, given the facile conversations we've overheard. Their idiotic takes on everything from skin cancer (they think this melanomatic sun is "healthy") to television (strong opinions on various *Dancing with the Stars* contestants), their reckless posing for selfies with an alligator near the creek at the edge of our cul-de-sac (Hubby thinks if we bide our time we'll be rid of them one way or another)—all of it reminds me of nothing so much as the tiny minds that populated the Keyhole Junior High School teachers' lounge back in 1977.

When I used to party at Studio during the week, the champagne-and-sleep-deprivation hangovers generally lasted well into lunchtime the next day. And so it was after my visit to Studio with Art; morning classes were interminable, and my head was pounding as I entered the teacher's lounge to find it abuzz with the results of the state achievement tests.

Marisol Rodriguez had scored second, and Aura Lockhart, tenth in the entire state in reading comprehension. Marisol was also in the 90th percentile in science and math. Those scores were so unusual for even one student in Keyhole, let alone two, that the educators in Trenton had run the tests through the scoring machine a second time, to be sure it wasn't an error. Or so the gossip went.

"Marisol is brilliant," Dan Wykoski, the shaggy-haired eighth-grade science teacher, said as he poured himself a cup of coffee. "She asked me a question about interplanetary distances the other day that I had to go home and look up."

The other teachers nodded reverently, as I struggled to contain my cynicism. Dan Wykoski spent half of the school day stoned, as did about half of the teachers at Keyhole Junior High; the majority of the faculty were under thirty-five years old. Of course he had to look something up! It was a wonder Dan could remember anything at all.

"There's talk of skipping her right into high school," Peter Ferrari, the seventh grade English teacher, said. "If she were my student, I'd put together special assignments for her." Peter was new to the school, about my age, and unusually clean cut for the times. He tossed a glance in my direction, as if to imply that I wasn't doing enough to cultivate this rare flower in our desert midst.

"A bona fide genius," said ancient Mr. Murton—everyone, even the rest of us teachers, called him that. He was old enough to be my grandfather and wore a bow tie to teach every day.

"She's not a *genius*," I said as I sipped my coffee. My comment met with a sea of scowls. "I mean, Marisol is very bright, yes. But true genius is a rare thing."

I hadn't intended it to sound so sharp, but I couldn't help it; this hyperbole was infuriating. Like Marisol, I had once been a straight-A student in Keyhole. She certainly wasn't the first. Had *my* genius been proclaimed twelve years earlier, in that very teachers' lounge? Why hadn't *I* been skipped a grade or given special assignments?

"So how do you define true genius?" Peter asked.

I was quiet for a moment. "A genius doesn't merely do well on standardized tests," I said. "Einstein failed many of his school subjects. A genius is creative." Although I had racked up every academic award the Keyhole school system could offer me, I never truly felt my genius until I dedicated myself to poetry. It was during those moments scribbling, alone, before first light, my every cell ablaze with its own singularity, that I knew what a rarefied being I was. And I pinned that butterfly of a feeling in my poem, "Things I Do in the Dark—These Poems, These Men (after June Jordan)"—a work whose genius was proclaimed by the eminent Carlos Barrada himself as he read it in my bed.

"How do you know that Marisol's *not* creative?" Peter asked. "Have you given her any creative assignments?" Why was he challenging me so today? I flashed him a smile that usually disarmed men, but couldn't read his expression.

"Actually, I have. She did well, but Aura Lockhart was the one who really displayed a creative spark." A few nods and rumblings followed as they remembered that Aura had earned a top score on the reading portion of the test too.

"Don't get me wrong," I added for Peter's benefit. "Marisol is a very bright girl with great potential. But if we're talking about creative genius, artistic genius, I think that's Aura." Time would prove me right. Marisol eventually became a NASA scientist—impressive for a girl from Keyhole, but sadly destined to live in the Grammy Award-winning Aura Lockhart's shadow.

"Aura's not related to Augustus Lockhart, is she?" Peter asked.

The fact that Peter, a seventh-grade English teacher in a swampy little stew of a town, knew enough about contemporary poetry to have even *heard* of Augustus Lockhart suggested I owed him a reassessment.

"She's his daughter," I said. "And she delivered a poem in class the other day that was worthy of her father's genius."

"You really think Augustus Lockhart was a genius? The guy always seemed like a bit of a charlatan to me. I mean, the 'I Hate Words' manifesto? Come on!"

It was a tragedy, not just for Peter himself but for every student he would ever have, that his thinking was so limited as to be unable to grasp the unmitigated brilliance of Augustus's theories.

"Having studied with his good friend John Ashbery, I see things differently," I said, tossing my shampoo-ad-worthy hair defiantly over my shoulder.

I'd thought this would permanently shut Peter down, but he naively blathered on. "Oh yeah, Ashbery. I have to say, I don't completely get his work, either. But at least with him I feel like there's something there to get."

Before I could come up with the retort to end all retorts, Carla Spagnola, the gym teacher—perpetually clad in a nondescript navy-blue gym-teacher tracksuit—looked up from her yogurt. "I worry about Aura," she said. "Sure, she acts like she's above it all. But underneath that she seems so sad."

The other teachers nodded, as did I. No one could dispute the fact that Aura did not fit in at Keyhole Junior High—and I trust I've made clear by now what a huge compliment that was to her.

"It's that little shit Jody Fromme," Dan said. "She pulled the same kind of crap last year on another new girl. I'm not a violent person. I mean, I protested the war. But I wouldn't mind wringing that kid's neck."

A brief discussion ensued of the ways in which several of us had fantasized about doing Jody bodily harm. These spun out to James Bond-esque ridiculousness; seventh-grade science teacher Tess Boulanger's exothermic reaction experiment was my personal favorite. We all fell silent when Mr. Murton, who had appeared to be napping, looked up and spoke.

"Kill Jody Fromme, and another Jody Fromme will pop up in her place," he said. "I've seen it, year after year. There's always a queen bee."

We all nodded, recognizing this truth.

"I had a talk with Dick about Aura yesterday morning," I said, neglecting to offer the context. "He asked me to take her under my wing."

"That's good," Carla said, "but maybe a group of us should approach him anyway? You can't be everywhere at once, Lynda, and there's got to be more we can do to keep those girls off her back. Who's in?"

All of Aura's current teachers nodded, as well as Peter, who taught seventh grade but apparently sought some refracted glory. I said I'd go with them, too, so I could coordinate our efforts. Aura was my project, after all—not theirs!

"Man, I need a toke before my next class," Dan said. "Who's with me?"

And with that, six of Keyhole Junior High School's finest teachers followed him out to his VW van.

Once the lounge emptied out, when it was just me, Peter, and Mr. Murton, I remembered the note Kathi and Jody had been passing earlier in the week. After I'd removed the plastic wrap from my cafeteria teacher's lunch—tuna salad on a bed of iceberg lettuce, with an unappetizing side of canned peaches—I dug through my bag until I located the paper in a side pocket, unfolding it as I took a bite of my food.

There were two distinct handwritings, and I had to read to the end to correctly assign the writer for each.

Bobby Craig likes you!

Yeah?

He's looking at you! ☺

(Jody was seated directly behind me when Bobby was staring at my breasts. I could see how they'd make this mistake.)

Maybe.

Wanna go to the Monmouth Mall with me and my mom Saturday? We can pick you up.

Okay. Let's invite Aura.

Hahaha.

Really. Let's invite her. Tell her to have her mom drop her at the Bamberger's entrance. Then we'll watch from nearby.

Hahaha your bad!

I wasn't sure what was more pathetic: their planned torture for Aura, or Kathi's incorrect usage of "your." Peter was sitting two seats down from me in the lounge, eating a sandwich he'd brought from home in a little paper bag. I slid him the note.

"Little shits," Peter said. "Is Jody the one who wrote 'your'?"

I shook my head. "Kathi."

"Kathi?"

"Dorothy Hamill haircut?" I realized as soon as I said it that this only narrowed the field to about one-fourth of the girls in the school.

Peter was quiet for a moment. "You taking this to Singer?"

"I guess. I only just read it."

"I'll go with you, if you want."

"Okay." I took another bite of tuna, picked up the note, and Peter and I headed to the principal's office, where Patti informed us that he was gone for the day.

Peter turned to me. "You've got to warn Aura about that note," he said, and I agreed. I had Patti send a message to Aura's next period class for her to see me after school.

Underneath Aura's bravado I sensed a palpable vulnerability, and so, when she was finally in front of me, telling her about the note was harder than I'd expected. Two days earlier she'd started using masking tape to spell out snippets of phrases on the back of her father's bomber jacket. Today's was RAISED ON PROMISES, the final *E* and *S* wrapping around her side. She wore a striped T-shirt that accentuated her chubby abdomen, Levi's that did nothing to flatter her thighs, black Converse High Tops on her feet. All of that with her frosted pink, Lip-Smackered mouth should have been nearly comical, the kind of snapshot she might laugh at now, forty-two years later. But Aura had an inner panache that transformed her questionable sartorial choices.

"You wanted to see me?" she asked.

I needed to gain her trust before I could deliver the news about the note.

"Yes," I said. "I thought your poem was brilliant."

She raised an eyebrow. "Really?" she asked, her lips rearranging themselves into a smirk. "I came up with it while Bobby Craig was reciting that lame limerick."

I realized then how complicated young Aura's psychology was. She had likely convinced herself that the poem was something she'd dashed off at the last minute, when in reality, she possessed her father's genius for profound yet nearly wordless poems. My gift was of a similar nature—verse after verse tumbled from my head, fully formed, requiring no editing at all. Aura and I possessed the same quicksilver mind!

"It would have done your father proud."

She was quiet for a moment, then. I could see the wheels going around behind those blue eyes of hers, reassessing me. "Well, he would have appreciated the silences around the words, anyway."

"Do you write much poetry?"

"Songs," she said. "I play guitar and write music and lyrics with lines that rhyme. My father fucking *hated* the stuff I wrote." She cleared her throat. "Sorry about the swearing."

Looking back on it now, that may have been the first and last time Aura ever apologized for her use of profanity. As an adult she would famously take a male reporter to task for chiding her about her language in a 2005 interview—and I am sure you'll be pleased to know, Jann, that this debacle comes not from your illustrious magazine, but from *Spin.*

"Does Keith Richards swear in interviews? How about Robert Plant? Pete Townshend? Every member of the Ramones? Every member of the Clash? Did Kurt Cobain swear? Hell, even Conor Fucking Oberst swears! The most sensitive singer-songwriter dudes have potty mouths that would set Jerry Falwell a-tremble with indignation, but it's notable when *I* say the occasional 'fuck'? Why? Because I have a vagina? Vaginas aren't allowed to talk like that? It's the twenty-first fucking century. Give me a motherfucking break. *Kind sir.*" The interviewer claimed she snarled the last two words at him.

But in 1977 she was just a fourteen-year-old girl, seeking the approval of her soon-to-be favorite teacher. I waved the apology away, deciding that this was as good an opening as I would get. "Aura, I didn't ask to see you just to talk about your poetry. I wanted to make you aware of the contents of this note."

I handed it to her.

She eyed me warily, then opened it. Aura read quickly, her face betraying nothing.

"*Your*. Ha." She handed the note back to me.

"I just wanted to warn you," I said.

She chuckled softly. "Do those girls think I'm stupid enough to fall for that? I have plans on Saturday. But even if I didn't, the Monmouth Mall is my idea of hell."

O, the quickening of my pulse in that moment, as I realized just how alike Aura and I were. Both of us belonging in The City, both unable to live up to our artistic genius after this banishment to Jersey and its attendant suburban netherworlds.

"I hope your plans involve a trip back to The City," I said.

"I wish. My mom says it reminds her too much of my dad."

"That's—tragic," I said, stopping short of using the words that had first sprung to mind: selfish, provincial.

"Yeah. But there's a silver lining. I'm going to play an open mic in Neptune on Saturday. I might have been scared to do that in The City, but who cares if I bomb in *Neptune*?"

It felt like a further stroke of fate that I was intimately familiar with the open mic to which she referred, that it was, in fact, the place where

Carlos had discovered me, affording me the hope that perhaps there were real poets on this side of the bridge, too. Had the Muses, or the poetry gods themselves, conspired to unite Aura and me? Was it possible that Augustus himself had a hand in this from the great beyond?

"At the Galaxy?" I asked.

Aura's eyes widened. "You know it?"

"I've read my own poetry at that open mic," I said, neglecting to add that I hadn't been back since an unfortunate incident in those early days following my break-up with Carlos.

I expected Aura to ask me about my own work, perhaps even envisioned her reading my "Exile" series and being so moved that she'd pass selected poems along to one of Augustus's powerful friends. Instead, she suggested an outing.

"If you're going Saturday, could you maybe give me a ride? I was planning to hitch but my mom would kill me if she found out."

"Of course I'll give you a ride! It's not the same here as being able to hop on the subway, is it?"

"That's the least of how it's not the same," she said sharply, but then added, "thanks for the ride," and wrote her address down on a scrap of loose-leaf notebook paper.

I picked up Aura on Saturday at her grandmother's house, where she and her mother lived. The grandmother wasn't around; I found this fortunate, since I had little patience for the elderly—and still don't, despite the fact that I'm now approaching seventy. When we first moved to our current "undisclosed location," my husband suggested that we look into a fifty-five-and-over community. Hubby's idea elicited such a stream of profanity from the depths of my soul that he put his hands up in surrender. "Don't go full Jersey on me, babe," he said, but how could I not—the thought of all those wrinkled, ill-kept-up bodies, exposed to varying degrees; or worse, the women who covered their jiggling cellulite in shapeless rainbow-colored muumuus; the inane conversations about the weather, aches and pains, their fucking grandchildren—how could I not get my Jersey up at the idea of such capitulation to the ravages of Father Time's ghastly handiwork?

But back to 1977. As Aura's mother explained to me over coffee, she and her daughter had moved to Keyhole specifically to live with the grandmother.

"I just didn't think I could raise Aura on my own, in the city," Mrs. Lockhart said. "I never expected to be widowed at forty-two, with two children no less."

The way she said it, "widowed at forty-two," the inflection, the sad tilt to her head, suggested to me she'd repeated the phrase many times, for anyone who would listen. Mrs. Lockhart was a frumpy yet surprisingly attractive woman, with blond hair that was not dyed—I could tell, I could always tell—and the same blue eyes Aura had. She wore a sad yellow cardigan and an unironed gray cotton skirt. She'd likely had the clothes since her first political protest in the 1950s; in his youth Augustus was famously outspoken in favor of civil rights, against McCarthyism, and a campus rally was a likely place for him to meet such a dull waif.

That weekend *I'd* spent with Augustus in 1973, I was twenty-two years old, barely out of college, with a wardrobe full of mini-skirts and boots that drove men wild. After looking around his apartment and realizing that he had a wife and kids—a dozen orchid plants blooming in a sunny back room, spin art on a bulletin board, a can of Hi-C in the fridge, a lopsided clay ashtray, clearly made by a kindergartener, around the rim of which an adult had painted *Ceci n'est-ce pas un cendrier*—I'd asked him what his wife was like, since I was utterly disinterested in an anecdote about a child still young enough to drink Hi-Fucking-C.

"As troubled as any poet, but in a much less interesting way," he'd said, and then we'd laughed, bonding in the realization that we were cut from the same mold.

Four years later, sitting in Mrs. Lockhart's mother's (or mother-in-law's) kitchen, I recognized she was a martyr, a common affliction, in my experience, of the maternal condition. No wonder Augustus had needed to step out of the confines of his marriage. But what recourse did poor Aura have? I redoubled my resolve to rescue her.

"Of course you didn't," I said to the Martyr, playing along. "Is your other child older or younger than Aura?"

"Dennis is nineteen," she said. "In college."

So she really had one child and one *adult* child. This woman!

Before either of us could say any more, Aura walked into the kitchen, guitar case in hand. She was wearing a Queen T-shirt tucked into flare jeans with an embroidered rainbow stripe originating at one hip, reaching across her stomach and down the opposite leg; the jeans were popular among girls her age. The ensemble was completed with a clear plastic belt embedded with multi-color glitter and a velvet newsboy cap.

"*That's* what you're wearing?" the Martyr cried.

"Mom," Aura said through clenched teeth.

"I think it looks great," I said. "Love the cap." Objectively, this outfit was a nightmare of early teen fashion—yet Aura once again pulled it off. She'd clearly inherited this flair from her father, not her frumpy mother.

Aura smiled at me as the Martyr attempted an amateur glare.

"Let's go, then," Aura said, and soon, we were off to Neptune.

The Galaxy—in Neptune, get it?—was, at night, a trashy suburban disco. But every Saturday afternoon for the past decade, they'd held this open mic, which was founded by Carlos Barrada. He had moved from The City to Jersey to teach at Monmouth College after his third book of poetry came out. Because the Galaxy's owners were skeptical that poets alone would draw enough of a crowd, Carlos had made the events open to all performers: musicians, writers, actors reciting theatrical monologues.

Before I delve into what happened that day at the Galaxy, I should briefly explain a bit more about Carlos, by way of a short primer on my dating philosophy.

By the time I was sixteen, I'd identified three different qualities in a boyfriend that I found essential, but which never seemed to coexist in the same guy. Enumerating from the least important to the most, there was the #3, the Dependable Guy, the man who'd bring you flowers and charm your mother, one who would come rescue you in the middle of the night if your car broke down and you had to walk half a mile to a pay phone. There was #2, the Guy Who Always Had Drugs, which is self-explanatory. And then there was #1, the Hot Lay: that white whale of a unicorn, a man who gave pleasure as freely as he received it, one who knew exactly what to do with his various appendages and orifices and engaged them in the service of a woman's maximal delight. Sometimes I found numbers 1 and 2 in the same person. Rarely, numbers 1 and 3. But I'd longed for the elusive man who covered all three categories, and I vowed that once I met him, I'd marry him.

Carlos was the first man I'd known who came close to covering all three.

After a blissful six months together, I decided that, despite his refusal to do any drugs harder than grass, he was as close to The One as I was going to find, and I told him I thought we should get more serious. I was twenty-five and nearly every guy I'd dated had wanted to marry me; while only one of them had said this aloud, I could tell, I could always tell. Imagine my shock, my hurt, my all-encompassing rage, when Carlos said I was "fun," but he didn't want to get serious! In that moment, I knew I had been used, used like a common woman. And, yes, I did break many items in his apartment that evening, including an earthenware vase he claimed was an ancient artifact from Peru, but which I'm certain was the kind of knock-off you could buy at any flea market in the Village; and, yes, after I made a few post-breakup clandestine visits to his place, and then at a Galaxy open mic read a poem in front of him called "Things You Didn't Know About Carlos," there had been the threat of a restraining order, as well as a strong suggestion from the Galaxy's owner that I not return for "a good long while." But the fact that Carlos never took legal action against me proves he knew he'd be laughed out of court.

That had all happened the previous year, and the outing with Aura was the first time I'd been back to the Galaxy. If Carlos did turn up that afternoon, so much the better to have Aura with me! His heinous accusations would be risible in the presence of my obvious altruism.

Neither Carlos nor the Galaxy's owner was anywhere in sight that day. Inside the club, after Aura had signed up and learned she'd be going on last, we searched for empty seats. There were several in the front row, and I was pleased that Aura didn't make a childish fuss about being so visible, as some girls her age might. She and I had been born to be seen!

I'd warned her that these afternoons were a bit of a mixed bag, and we exchanged a few eyerolls at the early succession of "talent." A young man with a heavy North Jersey accent who earnestly recited a laughably pornographic poem called "In the Bin." A folk duo who appeared to be emulating early Sonny & Cher, a decade too late. And then a coked-out young woman, dressed primarily in body paint, who repeated the words "Fuck me" thirty or so times, with various inflections. I might have been concerned about how a fourteen-year-old would take all this, but I knew Augustus Lockhart's daughter could handle it.

Nowadays, of course, a teacher wouldn't be allowed to go on any sort of outing with a student. Aura would not even be let in to a club like the Galaxy, despite the fact that alcohol wasn't served until the evening. O, how I miss the swinging seventies! Even the most uptight squares were more relaxed than the average young person is today.

After the "Fuck me" poem I was about to give in to despair when a man around my age took the stage, guitar in hand.

From the waist down, he was clad in ordinary jeans. But above the waist, he was wearing what I can only describe as a mantle of feathers: on his upper arms, shoulders, chest, culminating in wings, of a sort, jutting from his shoulder blades. He even wore tiny speckled feathers in the space between his eyelids and brows.

On most guys this costume would have looked ludicrous. But the man was beautiful. Not handsome; truly beautiful, the kind of beauty that might intimidate a lesser woman: a mane of curly blondish hair (natural), large, deep brown eyes with lush lashes, strong cheekbones and chin, full lips.

"I'm Johnny Engel," the man said into the microphone, and I chuckled a little. Aura shot me a questioning look.

"*Engel* means angel in German," I whispered. "Johnny Angel." She nodded, though she was too young to know the song from Johnny's and my childhood.

Johnny launched into a three-song set, and it was clear from the first few lines that his costume was not the only thing setting him apart from the usual folkie dilettantes at the Galaxy. His guitar had a shimmery sound; there was beauty in it, but an undercurrent of mournfulness too. The lyrics were abstract, closer to East Village poetry than rhyming couplets. It was like nothing I'd ever heard before, and absolutely *not* my cup of tea—why was such a gorgeous young man not celebrating his precious youth by creating songs of joy, songs one could dance to?

Each act in the open mic had a ten-minute limit, but Johnny's songs received such applause that he was given the signal to play a bit longer. This signal—a flashing spotlight—was an honor I'd never received when I'd read there, presumably because I'd refused to fuck anyone involved with the Galaxy's management. They were just so very *Jersey*. But in Johnny's case, I was pleased to have a little more time to take him in.

I knew during his last song, one that he sang full-throated from somewhere deep in his heart, or perhaps his crotch, that I had to have Johnny Engel—if not that night, then soon, very soon. He was clearly a

#1; being a musician, likely a #2 as well. I looked over at Aura and saw that she was transfixed. Johnny Engel was possibly her first crush. How fragile it is, the hummingbird heart of a child!

After his performance, Johnny took an empty seat in our row, just two other people between him and us. Several forgettable performers took the stage after him. But when Aura's name was finally called out, she shrank in her seat.

"I'm scared," she whispered to me, and in an instant she was as insecure as any fourteen-year-old.

"Come on," I said. "'Who cares if you bomb in Neptune,' right?" I motioned toward the stage.

As we were whispering, Johnny Engel himself, quickly assessing the situation, leaned across the people between us. "I was scared too," he whispered to Aura. "I want to hear you play."

Aura shot me a look that was equal parts panic and glee, then picked up her guitar and took the stage.

She performed three songs that day, and, once she relaxed, mesmerized the crowd almost as thoroughly as Johnny had. Her talent was unmistakable, fingers flying along the frets, eyes bright with pain and fury. Aura's voice was more an ache, a frequency of longing; it wasn't as strong or melodic as Johnny's, and her songwriting was in its infancy, but still, her very presence—dare I say, her aura?—was riveting. Only one of the songs she performed that day morphed into anything she'd later put on a record: a rager called "Phyllis Schlafly," which turned up on her 2001 album *The Bitch Sessions* as "Era of E.R.A." While I myself was born with gifts that superseded any need for strident feminism, I was intrigued by Aura's precocious political consciousness.

When she was finished, Aura received thunderous applause from most of the crowd—and a standing ovation from Johnny. I remained in my seat, reasoning that it might be best not to swell the girl's head.

By the time Aura was off the stage, handsome Johnny was mobbed with well-wishers. I ordered us two Tabs and we stood near the bar watching Johnny accept compliments.

"You were great!" I said to her.

"Thanks," she said. "But him—" She motioned toward Johnny.

"Yes, him." We both admired Johnny silently for a moment. "Let's go talk to him," I added.

Aura looked down at her soda. "I don't think I can."

O, this pubescent shyness! Aura would be starting high school in less than a year. She needed to learn how to talk to men, and that moment seemed as good a time as any.

"Just follow me," I said. "Watch what I do."

We sidled up next to the Sonny & Cher couple, who were telling Johnny how "far out" he was—in 1977, the expression was already dated. Johnny caught my eye as the couple gushed; he smiled at me, and then at Aura. As Sonny & Cher went on and on, I realized they were coked up, and that they'd never stop talking if I didn't intervene. I brushed past Cher and stuck my hand out toward Johnny.

"I just wanted to introduce myself," I said in the microsecond that Sonny paused to gulp air. "Lynda Boyle. And you've already met Aura. We both thought you were great."

Johnny smiled and shook my hand—his grip was surprisingly light but not insubstantial—and turned slightly away from Sonny & Cher, who got the hint and crawled back to whatever bridge underpass had spawned them. "Thanks," he said. Then he turned to Aura. "You were amazing."

Aura turned bright red, proving my suspicions that this was her first crush, and that her bravado was razor thin.

"You—those songs," she stammered. "Do you have an album out?"

"Not yet," he said. "I hope to one day. But what about you? How long have you been playing guitar? That was some serious shredding."

She smiled at him. "I started taking lessons when I was eight. My brother was learning guitar, and I bugged my parents until they let me get lessons too."

Johnny smiled. "I'll bet he's not as good as you are."

She shrugged. "He quit after a year. But I kept going."

"Are you still taking lessons, Aura?" I asked. I was certain that Johnny wished for me, the adult woman whom he obviously wanted to fuck, to be part of the conversation.

"Not since we moved."

"And you're a Queen fan too!" Johnny said, gesturing toward her T-shirt, as if I weren't there. "Freddie Mercury is the best vocalist in rock. Period."

"Totally!" Aura said. "I think *A Night at the Opera* might be my favorite album ever. I mean, "39'? 'Love of My Life'?" She sighed ecstatically.

Johnny motioned us both to sit down. "'The Prophet's Song' is incredible too."

"That's my brother Denny's favorite. He says you have to listen to it stoned."

Johnny and I exchanged looks of surprise. "I don't think that's something you should be doing anytime soon," he said in a big-brotherly way.

"No, I'm not really interested," Aura said matter-of-factly.

"Maybe your sister should have a talk with Denny," Johnny said, looking at me.

It took me a moment to catch on. "Oh! I'm not her sister. I'm her teacher."

"Her teacher?" And Johnny—finally!—turned his full attention to me.

"Eighth-grade English. Aura's my best student," I said, my hands on her shoulders. Was it true? Based on her work in my class, no. But Aura's pedigree suggested that it *should* have been true.

"Wow," Johnny said. "You're lucky to have such a great teacher, Aura." He gave me a wide-eyed look that suggested he appreciated more than my educational prowess, and after a few more minutes of pleasantries I asked Johnny for his number, since he seemed too intimidated to ask for mine. Before we left, he plucked a feather from his chest.

"For you," he said to Aura, and she beamed as if she'd been given a dozen roses. But I knew the gesture was really meant for me—to impress me with his kindness. Usually so quiet, Aura chattered about Johnny and his songs the entire ride back to her grandmother's house. I didn't mind her prattling; I knew we'd be seeing more of Johnny.

3

It worked out for the best that Johnny was too shy to immediately whisk me away after his performance at the Galaxy, since I'd completely forgotten I had a date with Art that night. He'd been such a drag at Studio that I'd almost broken up with him on the drive home, but I didn't, because he had money and was always willing to spend it on me. I know *you* wouldn't judge me for that, Jann—but my mother certainly did.

"That poor boy," she said on the night I met Johnny Engel, as Art pulled up and I realized I'd forgotten our date. "You really should stop using him, Lynda. Set him free so he can find a girl who actually cares about him."

"Maybe he thinks he can win her over," my father said. "He likes the challenge." He winked at me.

"But she knows he can't," my mother said.

"So? She's a young woman. It's a free country."

Perhaps I should interject a bit of backstory concerning how it was that I was twenty-six years old and living under my parents' roof. During my lean years in the Village post-college, I was often short on rent. I frequently hit my father up for money; he was more than happy to help, and it's not like my parents couldn't afford it. They were people of simple tastes whose idea of a vacation was a weekend in a Poconos motor lodge, and they rarely did even that; their bank account was fat with money from my father's well-paid factory job. Daddy and I had a spoken pact not to let my mother know about the "little bit of help" he gave me. But the wretched woman eventually figured it out, and that was what led to the teaching job, the forced move back to Jersey. To add insult to injury, my mother insisted I live at home, at first, until I could pay back the money I "owed" them. *Owed* them? I was their child! Had I asked to be brought into the world? The way I saw it, they owed *me*.

Still, I'd settled an approximation of my debt by the end of my first year of teaching. But by then I'd discovered that my parents' home made a great crash pad. Because I had no rent to pay, I could spend my entire salary on clothes and clubbing. The fact that my mother forced this move as punishment and now could not get rid of me was, I knew, a source of torment for her, and so I planned to stay indefinitely.

Art rang the doorbell. Fortunately, I'd dressed up for the open mic in case Carlos Barrada was there, so, with a quick application of lipstick and a vigorous hair brushing, I looked like I was ready for our date. O, to be that young again, when beauty was so effortless!

He came bearing candy for my mother, roses for me—an attempt, I assumed, to make up for his sulking at Studio. Dull as dishwater, as my mother might have said if she ever, even for a second, took my side, but he would make some mousy young thing an excellent husband one day.

"Any ideas what you'd like to do?" Art asked once we were in the car. I did enjoy his deference to my wishes.

"There's a restaurant in The City I've been wanting to try," I said. I'd heard it was terribly expensive.

"Maybe a movie afterward?"

"I'd rather go dancing." When he didn't respond, I added, "We could go to 12 West. You might like it there more than Studio." I knew this was unlikely, of course.

"Maybe another night? You still haven't seen *Star Wars*, and you promised you'd go with me."

Star Wars was not yet the cultural phenomenon it is today. To the young me—Height-of-Her-Powers Lynda, if you will—it was a sci-fi flick for thirteen-year-old boys, and guys like Art: a tween trapped in a twenty-eight-year-old's body. I knew that Art had already seen the movie three or four times; he'd been raving about it since I'd met him.

"Why don't we go see *Star Wars* tomorrow?" I asked. "A matinee?" I was too young, too vital, too beautiful to sit in a darkened theater on a Saturday night and watch some tedious space fantasy while outside, the city brimmed with life.

Art stopped at a traffic light, glanced over at me. "We always do what you want to do, Lynda," he said. "Couldn't we do what I want, just this once?"

"Fine," I sighed, realizing that my mother would most likely get her wish: my time with Art was drawing to a close. I consoled myself with the thought that at least, we'd have a spectacular dinner.

But as it turned out, reservations at that new restaurant were booked weeks in advance. I suggested that Art slip the maître d' some cash, but he either offered too little or bungled the execution. Soon, we were pounding the pavement, searching for another restaurant. We ended up in a dive Italian place; I could have gotten better ziti in any kitchen in Jersey. I fumed through dinner.

"I'm sorry about the restaurant, Lynda," Art said, but he made no offer to alter the movie plans.

Twenty minutes into *Star Wars*, all I could think about was Studio. Soon the early crowd would be arriving, peacocks in their boas, their glitter, their Saturday night personas. The celebrities would show up a little later. I looked at Art, facing the movie screen, his eyes wide with rapture behind his aviator glasses, as he robotically consumed a box of Milk Duds. I excused myself to the ladies' room.

In the bathroom, I examined my face in the pockmarked mirror, wondering if my sallow complexion was just poor lighting or the illumination of my inner despair. How had I landed there? All roads of blame led back to my mother, of course. I shed a few bitter tears. And as I dug around in my purse for a tissue, my fingers located a piece of paper. I pulled it out; on it was written Johnny Engel's phone number.

He had a 212 area code!

I thought of Art, his leisure suits, his shrinking hairline; his consistent refusals, in bed, to go down on me. And then I thought of Johnny: those lips, those cheekbones, the timbre of his voice. I was certain that Johnny was, like me, a creature of the night; as it was only nine-thirty, the odds were good he wasn't out for the evening yet. Could I leave Art there in the theatre, wondering what had happened to me? As I reapplied my lipstick and brushed my long brown hair, a rosy hue returning to my cheeks, the answer came to me with such clarity, it was as if God were speaking directly to me: Yes, Lynda. You *can*.

I quietly exited the theater and walked down the block until I found a pay phone. Johnny's number rang for so long that I was about to give up, when he finally answered.

"Johnny!" I cried, perhaps a little too effusively. After all, he did not yet know that he was my salvation.

"Yes?"

"This is Lynda. Lynda Boyle. We met earlier today at the Galaxy. I was with my student, Aura."

"Oh, of course! It was great to meet you."

"Same here." I paused, deciding how to proceed. "I had planned to call you tomorrow. But I'm calling now because I'm in a bit of a spot."

"A spot?"

"Well, I'm here in The City on a really bad date. So bad that I just left the guy in a movie theatre."

"Ouch," Johnny said.

"I could find a way home, I suppose, but I hate to give up my Saturday night. So I was wondering, Johnny Engel, do you like to dance?" I used my most flirtatious, most seductive voice.

"I guess it depends on the music."

"Want to go to Studio 54 with me?"

He laughed a little. "Isn't that place impossible to get into?"

I suppressed my own chuckle. Did this gorgeous man really think he wouldn't be let in to Studio? "I'm a regular," I said. "And they'll *love* you."

"I don't think that's really my scene," he said, "but I was just heading out to see a band at CBGB. Want to go there with me?"

I'd been to CBGB for a few of their Wednesday night poetry readings; that club and its punk rock scene were definitely not *my* thing. But an evening with the beautiful Johnny Engel, even at a grungy bar rather than the shimmering Studio, was certainly preferable to entertaining myself by placing mental bets on how long it would take Art to consume that last Milk Dud.

"Sure," I said, and soon, I was on the subway, bound for my beloved East Village.

Johnny met me outside the club. He had glitter on his eyelids and below his brows, but was otherwise dressed unremarkably: plain black T-shirt, jeans, tooled leather boots. An ordinary costume that somehow accentuated his beauty. We headed inside and nabbed the last open table.

Before I divulge the contents of my first in-depth conversation with Johnny Engel, let me de-romanticize the CBGB myths that *some* rock magazines—certainly not yours!—have promulgated. Bear in mind that I was no fussbudget, no cleaning-obsessed Jersey *casalinga* like my mother; I'd lived in the Village, waitressed there, read my poetry there. But CBGB was filthy even by Village standards of that era. The table we sat at was wet with beer, dripping off the sides; cigarette ashes mixed in with the sluice. My seat cushion was so grimy-looking that I worried my dress would be permanently stained. The bathroom—I can't even talk about the bathroom. Suffice it to say that, after a used hypodermic needle crunched under my heel, after I peered into a feces-stained toilet whose seat was broken off and propped unhelpfully against the wall, I learned just how much my bladder can endure in one night.

A braless waitress with an unflattering Toni Tennille bowl haircut came by and wiped a filthy-looking rag over the wet table, nearly hitting me with the slosh. She grudgingly took our orders: a beer for Johnny, a gin and tonic for me.

I broke the ice by asking where he was from originally, for Johnny's accent was clearly not of the tri-state area.

"Michigan," he said. "Small town, not too far from Detroit."

"I haven't lived anywhere besides New York and New Jersey," I admitted. In college, I'd occasionally told my classmates that I'd lived in Paris when I was a child; it was true emotionally, if not literally. I *should* have lived in Paris. But I got the sense that wasn't the tack to take with Johnny.

"I hadn't lived anywhere besides Michigan up until last year," he said. "For six years after high school, I worked an assembly line for GM. I wanted desperately to be a musician, gigged on weekends. But I knew I'd never make it the way I wanted if I stayed there."

"That's why most artists move to New York," I said.

"Yeah, but the job I had was plum. Great salary. Amazing benefits. People thought I'd lost my mind to give it up."

"What made you do it?"

"When I turned twenty-five, I realized time was running out. If I wanted to make it in rock, I couldn't wait any longer. I had to try." Johnny sighed. "The band I had in Michigan was glam, or at least, what passed for glam. I moved here to form the ultimate glam band, but the songs I wrote never quite fit that sound. And then last month, glam rock died."

"Glam rock died?"

"Well, Marc Bolan died. It's pretty much the same thing."

The waitress put our drinks in front of us. I took a sip of mine, calculating how best to proceed. I knew nothing of glam rock, but I thought Johnny might enjoy introducing me to his world.

"I don't know much about that kind of music," I said. "Is the band we're seeing tonight glam?"

Johnny laughed. "The Ramones—no. They're not glam." He took a swig of his beer. "But I find their music really exciting. I still love glam, but I kinda think this, what's happening here"—he gestured widely with his arms, toward the grimy tables surrounding us, the emaciated junkie couple making out in the corner, the dingy stickers that covered the inside of the club's walls—"is the future of music."

"Interesting," I said. This poor, deluded man! The future—a much more glamorous future!—was happening a train ride away, at Studio. As if to emphasize this point, a shirtless man who looked and smelled like he hadn't showered in weeks slammed into our table, spilling our remaining drinks. Johnny stood up. He towered over the guy.

"Sorry, man," the guy slurred, and darted back into the crowd. Johnny sat back down.

"The future?" I asked, raising a playful eyebrow.

He smiled and shrugged.

The waitress appeared with two more drinks. "You guys might want to stand when the band comes on," she said.

Johnny thanked her, then looked at me. "I didn't mean to monopolize the conversation. Tell me about yourself. How long have you been teaching?"

"This is my third year," I said. "The teacher thing is temporary for me. I'm a poet. But I wasn't making it financially, and had no choice but to give in to the bourgeoisie for a while."

"Poet and teacher by day, tripping the light fantastic by night," Johnny teased, and I laughed a little.

"You really must come to Studio with me next weekend," I said. "It's not as debauched as its reputation."

"Oh, I don't have a problem with debauchery," Johnny said, and I smiled, thinking I'd clearly found a #1 and a #2, at the very least.

We got up from our table as the floor in front of the stage grew crowded. Four guys in jeans, T-shirts, nearly identical leather jackets and dark hair took the stage. The one on the left snarled and sneered; the lead singer hid behind his hair. Had no one taught them how to perform? Their songs were two-minute assaults, like dodging gunfire. Give me Donna Summer, I thought; give me The Village People. Give me joy and glamour any day over noise and filth. I repeated this like a mantra to myself as I steeled against the onslaught of the band's noise.

Finally, at the point where I thought I would truly have to leave, the Ramones exited the stage.

"What did you think?" Johnny asked.

"It was…different," I said. A guy to my right vomited all over the floor, nearly hitting my shoes. Johnny ushered me away.

"Not your thing at all, huh?" He smiled.

"No," I said. "But I'll come back if you'll come to Studio with me next weekend."

Johnny nodded. "Sure, I'll try anything once." O, the fantasies in that moment!

We left CBGB and found an all-night diner, where we had coffee and pie and talked some more. I'd dearly missed those kinds of nights in the Village: a new conquest, the excited late-night conversation. By the time we left the diner, it was nearly three a.m. The next train back to Jersey wasn't until eight.

"You can stay over at my place, if you want," he said.

O, did I want!

But my evening at Johnny's ended up being a disappointment. We talked for a little while, sitting close on the sleeper couch in his tiny studio. I filled him in on Aura, on how she was bullied at school, grieving the loss of her father—though I kept to myself the special nature of my relationship with Augustus—and how I'd decided to be her mentor. I gave all my best signals, but he never put a hand on my thigh or leaned in for a kiss. By four a.m., he said he was exhausted, and gave me a T-shirt to sleep in. We lay side by side on the thin, hard mattress; it was quaint, nearly Amish. But how to get the Rumspringa started?

I'd never been in a situation like this with a man where he hadn't tried something. What made Johnny so different, so courtly? Was the Midwest like that? Briefly I entertained the notion that he wasn't attracted to me, but I quickly dismissed it. I'd never met a guy who wasn't attracted to me. No, as I drifted off to sleep, I decided that he was simply a gentleman. Even my parents would love him!

The next morning, after breakfast at a diner around the corner from Johnny's place, he offered to drive me back to Jersey. There was a guy in Asbury Park he'd been jamming with, planning to start a new band with. They had a rehearsal that afternoon.

"So that's how you stumbled upon the Galaxy," I said as we crossed the bridge. "I'd wondered."

"Those were all new songs," he said. "I like trying them out in a setting like that, where the pressure's off."

"The pressure?"

"You know," he said, glancing briefly at me, then back at the road. "New York. All the cool people." He flipped on his turn signal, deftly negotiated a lane change.

"Johnny," I said, "You *are* one of the cool people."

He laughed and waved me away with his hand. But I could tell he was pleased.

I knew I had a problem to contend with when I saw both Art's Cutlass Oldsmobile and a Keyhole Police Department cruiser parked in my parents' driveway.

"Oh shit," I said as Johnny pulled up behind the cars.

"What?" he asked. "The police car?"

"Yeah," I said, not wanting to admit that the other car was Art's. I'd made it sound like I'd ditched a bad first date; Johnny didn't need to know additional details. "I forgot to call my parents and tell them I wasn't coming home." I never called them in these circumstances, but I suspected Art had concocted some tale that filled them with alarm.

I wrote my number down for Johnny and told him to call me later. Then I slowly made my way up the walk to my parents' front door. Today, I know, it's called the walk of shame, coming home the next morning in the clothes you wore the night before. But I felt no shame, not even knowing Art was there. What I felt was a profound sense of liberation. I smoothed my dress, which I knew smelled of beer and cigarettes and CBGB, threw my shoulders back and marched through the door.

"Thank God!" my father cried out, leaping from his seat and rushing toward me. "Lynda, sweetie, we were so worried!" He threw his arms around me. I felt a pang of regret in that moment, I'll admit.

"I'm sorry, Daddy," I said. "But you know I don't always come home at night."

"Yes, but Art thought you were kidnapped."

In that moment, I turned from my dear father's embrace to see three faces staring at me. The cop—Tony Cavaletti, my mother's cousin—

wore a bemused expression that barely hid the way he checked me out, as he'd been doing since I was twelve. My mother looked her usual angry, bitter self. And then there was Art, whose wounded puppy expression fueled my growing rage. Who were any of them, to judge me?

"Jesus, Art," I said, formulating a strategy. "Is this your revenge on me for breaking up with you?"

"You two broke up?" my father asked, tossing a stern look in Art's direction. "You didn't tell us that."

"It's news to me," Art said.

"Please," I said to Art, narrowing my eyes. I pushed past him to make my way to my bedroom.

"Lynda, what's that on the back of your *dress*?" my mother called out.

I stopped and gathered the skirt, pulled it frontward and inspected it. CBGB's grease. My best course of action was to ignore the comment, so I continued toward my room, but Art followed me. He grabbed my arm, and I decided to use it to my advantage.

"Let go of me!" I yelled, and both my father and Tony rushed over.

"I'm sorry," Art said. "I just don't understand what happened. She said she was going to the ladies' room, and never came back."

"No," I said. "I told you I didn't think it was working out with us. And I left." I turned my eyes on my father. "Daddy, I had a terrible night, and I'd like to get out of these clothes and take a nap. Can you make him leave?"

My father ushered Art away from me, and I entered my bedroom. Daddy and Tony had clearly bought my story. But as I closed the door to my room, I caught a glimpse of my mother's face. It was the same face she'd used on me when I was nine years old and I'd sworn I hadn't called little Billy Tesoro from down the street a midget. My mother was a witch; she could tell, she could always tell, when I was lying.

I took off the dress and dropped it in my hamper for my mother to contend with on laundry day. I needed to get out of that house, permanently. By the end of the school year, if not before. And I needed to work my charms on Johnny Engel so I could make him part of that equation.

4

As it turns out, our inconsiderate new neighbors here in tropical exile—they of the speakers I had no choice but to disable—have, as a couple, a stark difference in musical taste. She listens to Johnny Engel, Bowie and U2; her husband prefers the kind of "easy listening" favored by dentists' offices—Air Supply, Starship, Kenny G. I honestly don't care what kind of music blasts me from a sound sleep at noon, I just want it silenced. And so my most recent foray onto their lanai included snipping, not just unplugging, a few strategic wires on their ancient Sanyo stereo system. Do they even still make parts for that thing? With luck, I may have bought myself weeks of blissful somnolence.

Our other next-door neighbor is a widower (a divorcé? I haven't bothered to remember), perhaps a couple of years younger than I am, from one of those landlocked states in the middle of the country. Kansas? Iowa? Ohio? His face resembles nothing so much as a potato; sometimes my husband and I refer to him and his pet pug as "Baked and Mashed," but more often we call him the "Pugsub," for he is dominated by his disastrously overbred, barely-able-to-breathe dog.

The pug goes by many names: Michelle. Shelley. Mee-chelle. Ma Belle. These are the sobriquets I've heard the Pugsub call out as the dog runs on its stubby little legs in his fenced-in yard, as he walks it past our home in its pink rhinestone harness, cooing at the tiny beast about its urination and defecation. "Michelle"—the name of his dead or ex-wife, I'm certain, and while my hubby thinks he named the dog in tribute, I'm convinced it was his final revenge—has the black, flat eyes of a serial killer and a perpetual death rattle when it breathes. It is as loathsome a creature as I have ever met—as is its owner.

What, you may ask, is so terrible about a bland man who loves his dog? At least he doesn't blast music at an hour when some of us are still sleeping. But the Pugsub is more than just banal; he is, like many Beta males, awkwardly lecherous. It's in the hopeful inflection of his "Hell-o!"s to me, it's in the way he looks me up and down as he bags Mee-chelle's shit, it's in his awkward double takes when he catches sight of me in a bikini—a frequent occurrence given my still-sensational body and this warm climate. The Pugsub reminds me of no one so much as Dick Singer.

Which brings me back to the Monday morning after my evening with Johnny, my breakup with Art. Before first period, Dick called a brief meeting with every teacher who'd tried to contact him about Aura. Carla, Dan, Peter, and I filled him in on what we'd seen: the contents of Jody and Kathi's note; gym class abuse straight out of *Carrie*; several revolting lougie-hawking incidents; the constant refrain that Aura was "ugly."

Dick shook his head. "Adolescence," he said, waving his hand dismissively. "It wasn't fun for any of us. But now that Lynda is serving as a bridge between Aura and Jody, I'm sure the matter will be settled soon."

A bridge? Had Dick just likened me—glossy-haired, high-cheekboned, voluptuous twenty-six-year-old *me*—to a collection of cantilevers or trusses? And how had my agreeing to look out for our exiled East Village *dauphin* gotten twisted into anything involving Jody?

"Dick, I've only had a few days," I said. "It'll take time to build trust with Aura."

"And with Jody?"

The other teachers and I all looked at each other. *Jody can go fuck herself with a rusty wire brush*, I thought. "Jody doesn't seem to care much what her teachers think."

Dick was quiet for a moment. "It's up to you to make her care." His eyes rested on my breasts for a moment. "But perhaps you're not up for the challenge."

Was this some kind of bullshit motivational technique? I wondered—trying to fill me with rage so I'd go out and prove him wrong?

"Perhaps you haven't spent enough time with Jody to recognize exactly what that challenge would entail," I shot back.

Dick's eyes widened. "Are you suggesting that I don't know how to do my job?"

I was doing exactly that, of course. And I knew that perhaps I should not be testing Dick, what with the recent parents' complaints. But in the two years and two months I'd been teaching at Keyhole Junior High, my respect for Dick Singer had plummeted from zero to negative integers. He was a lazy, ineffectual principal, continually delegating his work to the teachers while he enjoyed frequent afternoons off with whomever among the staff he was fucking at the moment.

"Were you suggesting that I don't know how to do mine?" I asked.

Dan looked more awake than I'd ever seen him, while Carla and Peter regarded me wide-eyed, possibly awestruck at my display of truth to power.

Dick's face grew bright red as I formulated a brilliant save.

"The way you're feeling right now, Dick?' I asked. "That's how we feel every day, dealing with Jody. Habitual insolence. Constant challenges to our authority."

Carla exhaled.

"That was—brilliant, Lynda," Peter said. "She's absolutely right, Dick."

Dick's face went from red to pink, but he eyed me with a wariness that suggested I'd better do some additional damage control. I flashed him a disarming smile and pushed my breasts—my "spectacular breasts," as Carlos Barrada had called them—ever so slightly in his direction.

Dick's eyes lingered on my chest. "Hmm," he murmured, scanning the length of my body. I was wearing one of my more demure outfits—a double-knit shirtdress in my signature red that nipped in sharply at the waist and came to just above the knee. Demure but sexy. As he continued to stare at me, Peter cleared his throat.

"So are you going to talk to Jody?" Peter asked Dick, his voice sharp.

Dick then took his eyes off me—reluctantly—and focused on Peter. "Yes, of course," he said, and turned back to his desk, shuffling papers as a signal we were dismissed.

Outside the principal's office, after Carla and Dan had headed off, Peter turned to me. "That was brave," he said. "Singer is such a creep. The way he was staring at you."

O, what a sweetly naïve man!

"Well, I'm sorry to say it wasn't the first time." I let my voice quiver slightly with feigned outrage, casting my eyes downward to really sell it.

"I'm sure it wasn't," he said. "A beautiful woman like you must be subjected to all sorts of unwelcome attention."

Wonder of wonders—Peter was flirting with me! I sized him up: despite the unfashionably short haircut and the very square clothes, he wasn't bad looking. Tall, which I always liked. Dark, which I always liked. Handsome? Not exactly, but he had a certain presence. He was no Johnny Engel, but he'd make a far more interesting Dependable Guy than Art had.

I looked up at Peter, slowly batted my lashes once. "I'll take that as a compliment."

He blushed then, which I found somewhat endearing, though it did suggest a shyness that meant there was little hope he could be a #1 as well as a #3. My sights were set on Johnny Engel as that phenom who might embody all three categories; but that didn't mean Peter Ferrari wouldn't do for now.

That night, Johnny called to see what had happened with my parents, the police. I told him a version that wasn't far from the truth and asked how his rehearsal had gone.

"Good," he said. "Really good. We're ready to start looking for a bass player and a drummer."

"That's great! I take it you're lead guitar?"

"Yeah," he said. "And vocals."

"Do you know who you want on bass and drums?" I really had very little interest in the other members of his band, but I could play along.

"We're running an ad in the *Voice*. They'll all be stopping by Mike's rehearsal space this weekend. Bass players Saturday, drummers Sunday."

"Sounds exhausting."

"It could be. We're hoping the fact that we're jamming in Jersey won't keep people from New York City away."

It was adorable, the way he said New York City, as if he were still in Michigan and The City was a faraway land.

"So this weekend is out for a visit to Studio 54," he continued, "but I was thinking, maybe you and Aura might like to come check out the tryouts? You could give us your perspective on how the guys sound."

Such a sweet touch, that he invited Aura as well! "I'd love to, and I'm sure Aura would."

"I've been thinking about what you told me, about her dad dying." He was quiet for a moment. "It seems unfair, you know? I'm twenty-five and nothing bad has ever happened to me."

I wasn't sure how to answer that. On the surface, I appeared to have skated through life too. But in reality I'd suffered so many injustices, some at a very young age. One of my earliest tastes of life's cruelty came when I was seven years old, and I desperately wanted a Madame

Alexander doll—specifically, a Cissy doll with a rosebud pink tulle dress and a straw hat whose ribbon matched the dress. I'd seen this doll in the window of FAO Schwartz on a family outing in The City, and I quickly informed both of my parents that I loved the dolly, that I wanted her, needed her, and that, indeed, I might *die* if I didn't get her. It would be the last time I'd communicate a matter of such importance so directly. Cissy was an expensive toy, yes, but my dear father was willing to take an extra shift or two at work to pay for it. My mother—my own mother!—wouldn't let him. She said I had plenty of dolls I barely looked at. When I emerged from the hiding place where I'd been eavesdropping on their conversation, my little lips quivering in hurt and anger, and said, "But I've been such a good girl," summoning tears in my big hazel eyes and focusing them on my father, seeing him melt, my mother had the audacity to repeat four words I'll never forget.

"She's manipulating you, Pat."

I'm willing to concede this point: I *was* manipulating him. But it was a magnanimous manipulation, one intended to help my father do something I knew he wanted to do. Providing for me made my father happy. Who was my mother to deprive him of this happiness? And it's not like Daddy was oblivious. After my mother's heinous statement, he shot back: "She's only seven years old, Maria." And then—he winked at me! That wink said that he knew I was manipulating him; that he didn't care, because he loved me; and that he'd get me my Cissy doll, which, eventually, he did.

And yet, I didn't really enjoy the doll once I got it. My mother took this as evidence that she had been right, that I was spoiled and had too many toys already; but I knew it was because that doll was tainted with her betrayal. How chilling, to learn at such a young age that my own mother was not on my side.

"I've had a few difficulties, but nothing like what Aura has dealt with," I said to Johnny. And I mostly meant it. The thought of losing my sweet father, my only ally, at such a young age—it was unimaginable.

Johnny was quiet for a moment. "So I'll give you the address? The tryouts on Saturday start at noon."

"Sure," I said, jotting down the details. "See you then."

And with that, I had made plans to witness the formation of the critically acclaimed, short-lived but fanatically loved Glow Worm.

I took Aura aside in school the next day and told her about Johnny's offer. She was less excited than I expected her to be.

"I'm not sure if I'll be here," she said. "I'm trying to convince my mother that we should spend the weekend in The City."

"Having any luck?" I asked.

"Not so far." She sighed. "There's a reading Friday night for the final issue of my dad's magazine. I really want to go."

It hadn't occurred to me that *Tongue(less)*, the poetry journal Augustus had founded while I was a student at Brooklyn College, would fold after his death. Would no other poet assume the mantle? I considered how glorious my name might look on the masthead.

"Oh, it's tragic to hear this will be the last issue!"

Aura nodded. "There's a new poetry manifesto of my dad's in it, and one of his former students is going to read it."

A new manifesto? How fortunate that Augustus had put pen to paper before his untimely death! Clearly this event would be the perfect vehicle for me to announce my reemergence in the poetry world. Perhaps I could help rescue *Tongue(less)* from oblivion! My spine shivered with excitement as I imagined the pointed rejections I would write for Carlos's poems.

"I have an idea," I said to Aura. "If your mother doesn't want to take you, what if I go to the reading with you? We could come back that night and still go to Johnny's band tryouts Saturday."

For a second, a smile flickered on Aura's face, and faded just as quickly.

"Why would you do all that with me?" she asked, her eyes narrowed in teenage wariness.

"Why *wouldn't* I?" I asked. "I used to go to poetry readings three or four nights a week when I lived in The City. And I think we can both agree that nothing would be better than to spend a little time with Johnny."

Was it possible, I wondered, that Aura, for all of her genetic cachet, had the harder road of the two of us? How might I have turned out, if I'd not had my father to advocate for my needs? Had my mother had her way, I'd have ended up as excruciatingly dull as she was—married to Art, perhaps, an apron tied around my waist, working to perfect my grandmother Cavaletti's recipe for marinara. I could see Aura's path if her own mother remained her only adult influence: decades of depressing cardigans, dull children with grubby hands and jam-streaked faces, a life of settling, settling, settling.

"You used to live in The City?" Aura asked, looking me in the eyes. Her look was penetrating, and in that moment I sensed her recognition that we were one and the same: poetic exiles, boats against the current, fighting ceaselessly against the death of grander possibilities than current circumstances allowed.

5

The *Tongue(less)* reading was held at that holiest of poetry venues, St. Mark's Church, a favorite haunt during my East Village years. Among the braless City poetesses in their gypsy shawls, silk *Rhoda* scarves covering their hair, I turned heads from the moment I arrived in my red satin jumpsuit, paired with a gold-and-red kimono. Aura wore a shirred white blouse over a maxi skirt made from old pairs of jeans, a dated hippie garment that likely had once been her mother's. It was unlike anything I'd seen Aura wear before; a costume, not an outfit, its beatnik femininity fully negated by the message on her leather jacket: KILL YOUR FATHERS.

It had been more than a year since I'd attended a poetry reading in The City, and I scanned the crowd for familiar faces. Carlos was nowhere to be found—he had little patience for what he called the "pomposity" of the *Sans Mots* poets in general and Augustus in particular—but I saw many luminaries from all branches of the poetry world there. Gregory Corso chatted with Anne Waldman. A circle of people crowded around Patti Smith, a fixture in the poetry scene long before her musical success. Across the room, I spotted Peter Orlovsky with my dear Professor Ashbery.

A number of my exes populated the church's sanctuary, where the reading was to take place. As I'd been in each case the one to cut them loose, I harbored no ill will. But as my young charge and I made our way across the crowded room, I heard a man's voice call out: "Hey, Aura!"

I turned, as did she, and faced an ex to whom I did, in fact, harbor some bitterness: Bryce Bollinger.

Bryce had been my classmate at Brooklyn College. He and I were John Ashbery's most gifted and, of course, favorite students. It was only natural, then, that Bryce and I would start sleeping together during our senior year, and that we'd continue in an on-again, off-again fashion until my mother ripped me from the bosom of the East Village.

For those keeping score, Bryce was a #2 and an above average #1, but definitely not a #3. He was too wealthy and too good looking to be dependable. Heir to a Velcro fortune, he'd been such a lazy student, flunking out of three prep schools as a teenager, that he couldn't get into the kind of Ivies his parents could surely afford, not even with his family's clout. For the record, he wasn't stupid; he simply knew he didn't need to care.

That lack of care extended, unsurprisingly, to the women he dated. Many an evening we'd spent together had been interrupted by some young woman—usually bespectacled, usually a writer, always far less attractive than I—who'd thought Bryce was her "boyfriend" and who discovered to her naïve horror that he had not been faithful. Because I had no interest in Bryce as anything more than an occasional lover, his philandering had no effect on me. But when I'd told him I was moving back to New Jersey and that I'd hoped we could still see each other on occasion, his response had shocked me to my very marrow.

"Sorry, babe," he'd said. "I don't do bridge and tunnel."

Did the fact that we were in my apartment and not his preclude me from lobbing a variety of breakable items at his head? Surely you've already become well-enough acquainted with me to know the answer: it did not.

That was three years ago, and it was the last time I'd been face-to-face with Bryce. Imagine my horror to see that he somehow knew tender young Aura!

"Bryce," I said brightly, as he hugged an unenthusiastic Aura, her shoulders stiff. "This is a surprise."

"The surprise is all mine. How do you two know each other?"

"Ms. Boyle is my teacher," Aura said to Bryce. She then looked at me. "How do you guys know each other?"

I fixed a smirk on Bryce that suggested I might just tell Aura what a cad he was if he didn't tread carefully.

"We went to college together," Bryce said.

"So did you meet Aura…through Augustus?" I asked.

"I'm the associate editor of *Tongue(less)*," Bryce said. "Aura got used to having me camp out in her living room a few times a year as her dad and I worked on the latest issue. Those were fun times, weren't they, Aura?"

Aura said nothing.

"Well, it's great to see you," Bryce said to her, pointedly not including me. "Do you want to say a few words about your dad tonight?"

Aura turned her back to him so he could read her jacket. "I've made my statement."

"'Kill your fathers,'" Bryce said. "That could be interpreted a number of ways."

"It could," Aura said.

I'll admit, I was curious about Aura's intended statement myself. Augustus had espoused a similar idea in the "I Hate Words" manifesto: "Kill your words, kill your father's words, kill your forefathers' words," something like that. She may have been paying homage to her dad, while simultaneously suggesting something a bit darker. Anger at him for dying, perhaps—or anger at the way he'd lived. Augustus had been a legendary slut in the East Village poetry scene, worse even than Bryce, and it was likely a perceptive girl might pick up on such things.

Bryce shifted uncomfortably for a moment, then perked up when a young woman in a yellow chiffon maxi-dress walked by. "I've got to check in with Alessandra about the reading," he said, "but, Aura, let's catch up before you leave!" He kissed Aura on the cheek and turned to Alessandra in one fluid motion.

"He's a dick," Aura muttered after we'd moved away from him.

"He really is," I said.

She looked at me with a hint of a smile. "My dad was planning to kick him off the journal. He called him a 'weaselly little operator.'"

I laughed, my heart light with our shared impression. But before I could offer up an anecdotal nugget of Bryce's weaseldom that might be somewhat appropriate for a fourteen-year-old, Aura's eyes drifted across the room.

"Patti Smith is over there," she said, her tone approaching reverence.

I looked over at the ever-unkempt Patti, noting that she'd never acted upon the kind-hearted suggestion I'd made years ago to use crème rinse and perhaps a curling iron on her flyaway hair. Poor Aura was desperately in need of a better heroine—how lucky for her that she'd found me! "I could introduce you," I said, without enthusiasm.

Aura shook her head. "I've met her. She knows me as Augustus's daughter. But I've never had the guts to tell her what her music means to me." This encounter likely has greater resonance knowing how hard a famous Aura would work, decades later, to help poor Patti revive her flagging career—writing music for her, duetting on a re-release of "People Have the Power" after the 2016 election. I still wish Aura had modeled her vocal stylings on someone with a more pleasing voice, like Debbie Harry.

Before I could reply, the lights flickered several times, a signal the program was about to begin. I looked around for my own figure of reverence, my dear Professor Ashbery. I'd hoped we could sit near him but he was nowhere to be found, and so we took two empty seats near the stage.

A photo of a smolderingly satisfied-looking Augustus, his smile nearly post-coital, was projected onto the stage as a mix of his poems and other pieces from the journal were read by a variety of the scene's luminaries. After an hour, Bryce took the stage to give the audience what they'd really come to hear: Augustus's new manifesto.

"*I...LOVE...words*," Bryce began, punctuating each syllable. The room was mostly silent, save for a few nervous chuckles and one or two soft gasps.

"O, the irony! O, the humanity! This rogue, who declared he hated words!" Bryce paced the length of the stage, journal in hand, delivering Augustus's treatise as if preaching the Sermon on the Mount.

He blathered on about Poetics, about how *Sans Mots* poetry no longer existed, and the new movement would be called *Tous les Mots*. A small contingent seated near us became so animated that their open debate—was the entirety of the new manifesto an ironic counterpoint to "I Hate Words," thus proving the meaninglessness of words themselves and underscoring Augustus's original thesis, or had Augustus truly turned his back on *Sans Mots* poetry?—began to drown out Bryce. A young man among them leapt to his feet and shouted, "Augustus didn't write that! You did!"

"Sit down and open ya mind," a woman with a thick Queens accent called out to the heckler, who sheepishly obeyed.

Bryce soldiered on with the confidence his looks and money provided him, and in the end, the consensus seemed to be that Augustus had, in his final treatise, added a new layer of ironic meaning to his existing poetic theories.

"What did you think?" I asked Aura when it was all over.

She sighed. "Dad would have loved the theater of it."

This kind of cryptic reply might have surprised one who did not understand this teenager's budding genius; but I, Aura's light in the darkness, recognized her need to distance herself from such a poetic supernova as her father.

A star. Exploded.

I dropped Aura off at her grandmother's house shortly before midnight and picked her up again less than twelve hours later. Johnny's rehearsal space was the garage of his bandmate Mike's parents' summer house, and Aura and I arrived just before the tryouts were to begin. We didn't have much time to talk to Johnny, as the first bass player walked in right behind us. Johnny introduced us to Mike, set us up with two stools in the corner.

Aura showed Johnny a notebook she'd brought, a scoring system she said she'd spent the past few days devising. She'd said nothing to me about this on the ride over. I was miffed, but Johnny seemed impressed.

"That's terrific, Aura," he said, looking it over. "You guys are really helping us out."

I peered onto the page. All of her categories pertained to vagaries of musicianship, so I added an important category that Aura had neglected: looks. She and Johnny both laughed.

"That's a really great Les Paul," Aura said, motioning toward Johnny's black guitar, propped against the wall. She approached it, waiting for a nod from Johnny before she picked it up. "Black Beauty, right? '68?"

"Close—'69," Johnny said, exchanging a look with Mike. "You can play it later if you want."

She shrugged and put it back as Johnny turned toward the prospective bass player, introduced him to Mike.

I had feared that I'd be bored that day, but I wasn't. Aura and I had a lot of fun scoring the musicians; my evenings at discos had made me an expert on bass. And we devised subcategories in the looks department which we only noted by acronyms: "WLGON" stood for "Would look great on stage"; "WLGOF" was "Would look great offstage," a designation I added with a wink.

During a late afternoon lull, we all feasted on pizza as Aura and I went over our findings. A guy named Dave—future Glow Worm bass player Dave Spinelli!—was number one in all of Aura's technical categories, and number two in "Would look great on stage." (I didn't rate his offstage looks as high; a little too skinny for my taste.)

"That's amazing," Mike said. "He's our top pick too." He took a bite of pizza, chewed and swallowed. "Though I hadn't thought much about his looks."

Johnny was quiet for a moment. "Aura, how did you learn so much about music?" he finally asked. "I mean, beyond the guitar lessons?"

"My mom," Aura said. "She used to be a classical violinist. But she stopped playing professionally when she got married, and she stopped playing at all when my dad died."

The Martyr, a violinist? It seemed unlikely she'd been featured in any orchestra of note, but it did explain how she'd held an attraction for Augustus.

"Play something for us," Johnny said.

She shook her head.

"Yeah, come on. Play something," Mike added. I sized Mike up: not bad looking, clearly came from a little bit of money. I'd keep him in my back pocket for a rainy day.

"I've never played an electric guitar," she said.

"Oh, my acoustic's in the corner," Johnny said. He got up and retrieved the guitar from its case, put it in Aura's hands. She tuned it a little and strummed softly.

"Don't be shy," Mike said. "It's really cute when girls play."

Aura looked up, the expression on her face unmistakable: she was furious. I had never seen her angry like this before, not even in dealing with Jody; it was thrilling. I could *feel* her anger, and let me tell you, there is no anger quite like the anger of a fourteen-year-old girl. She began strumming ferociously, then launched into a song I didn't recognize. It was one Johnny knew, for he began to sing along with her. She played with gusto, even better than she had at the Galaxy, gaining strength as the song went on. It would not be an exaggeration to say that the music transformed her.

"Shit," Mike said when Aura had finished. "Can you play bass?"

She answered by playing another song. At first, I didn't think I knew it; then it became more and more familiar as she went on. What was that song? As I listened, taking in the look of awe on Johnny's face, I realized where I'd heard it: it was one of the songs he had played at the Galaxy.

"Isn't that one of your new songs?' Mike asked Johnny once she'd finished.

"Aura," Johnny said. "You only heard that song once."

"I have a good memory for music," she said. "I think I screwed up the bridge."

"Oh, I can show you that," Johnny said.

"She only heard that song once?" Mike asked. "Shit."

As I beamed at Aura—she was, after all, *my* discovery—Johnny walked over to her and gave her a hug. "You're amazing," he said, just above a whisper.

As I watched Johnny pull Aura to him, heard his quiet but audible words, I experienced a cascade of questions and emotions. First, I wondered what he was after: could he be attracted to Aura, creepily hitting on a fourteen-year-old girl? Such attractions had ample precedent in the history of rock music, but as I watched them together, I knew it wasn't the case. I'm an expert at sexual attraction, at seduction, and I saw none of that here. If Johnny was developing feelings for Aura, they were those he'd have toward a younger sister, a daughter, even. No, Johnny had simply said what he believed: that Aura was amazing. And in that moment of realization, I felt a pang of jealousy.

It wasn't that I didn't agree. I've already made clear my feelings about Aura's specialness. Given my relationship with Augustus, she was, by extension, family to me. But did Johnny recognize that Aura and I were one, that we shared the same poetic soul? I wanted him to understand that I was amazing too; I wanted the three of us to be amazing together.

But I took the high road and brushed aside those feelings, at least for the afternoon.

A few bass players came in later, but none of them matched Dave. One band member found, we all decided; one to go.

Aura was different on the ride home—looser, less reserved. I rolled down the window, even though it was late October, and the two of us sang along with the radio, at the top of our lungs, to Elton John's "Someone Saved My Life Tonight." Aura never talks about these moments, now that she has chosen to erase me; but that doesn't mean they didn't happen.

I got home in time to shower, change, and go on my date with Peter, the teacher from my school, the new Dependable Guy. Yes, I'm aware I didn't even mention his asking me out, a few days after that meeting with Principal Singer. I'm afraid Peter is a mere footnote to this story, despite the amateurish attempts he would make a few months later, after I'd jilted him, to tank my teaching career. But as is often the case with my lightning-quick mind, I'm getting ahead of myself again.

I stayed over at Peter's that night—he was a B-minus #1, and definitely not a #2 at all—and we slept so late that I almost missed taking Aura to see the drummer tryouts. Peter was impressed that I was spending so much time with Aura, though I kept the details of our outings vague so as not to provide ammunition for the Keyhole Junior High gossips.

None of the potential drummers met Aura's rigorous standards—though there was one guy, Olivier, who scored so high in both WLGON and WLGOF that I slipped him my number, since there was no time to chat him up and I needed to be discreet with Johnny there. Johnny and Mike were equally unimpressed and vowed to hold additional drummer tryouts in The City.

As we got ready to leave, Johnny gave Aura two cassette tapes. Mike and I both looked at the hand-lettered spines: Patti Smith's *Horses* and *Radio Ethiopia* on the first tape, The Runaways and Suzi Quatro on the other.

"I love Patti Smith!" Aura said. We would later learn that she already had both albums. "But I haven't heard of the others. Thanks, Johnny."

Yes, Jann, this was the beginning of Johnny Engel's introducing Aura to the artists that would help her pave her own way to musical success. Would Aura, her first band, and her later solo success ever have existed without all-girl rock bands like The Runaways? And would any of this have ever happened if I had not taken Aura to these band tryouts of Johnny's? One could say that I, Lynda Boyle Ross, am directly responsible for the birth of the Riot Grrl movement—but of course, I would never go so far as to say that myself.

Aura's grandmother met us at the car when I dropped Aura off that night. She was a surprisingly lithe woman, not the hobbled gnome I'd expected.

"Come in for a moment," she said to me. "I'd like to get to know the teacher who's spending so much time with my granddaughter."

I spent the entire walk up the path to Aura's house devising excuses to extricate myself quickly; but the grandmother turned out to be a surprisingly refreshing alternative to the Martyr, who was napping that afternoon. Aura went upstairs and left me alone with "Nana."

"She sleeps too much," the grandmother said of the Martyr as she poured me a cup of coffee.

"Well, I'm sure it's hard for your daughter, losing her husband." I said it merely to be polite: I trust I've been clear on what I really thought of the Martyr's flair for the dramatic.

"She's my daughter-in-law. *Not* my daughter," the grandmother said, in a way that suggested she hadn't entirely approved of her son's choice.

"Oh."

"She's not a bad girl, don't get me wrong," the grandmother added. "I just wish she'd stop taking those tranquilizers."

"Tranquilizers?" This old woman was clearly a well of information.

"She gets them from the doctor."

I nodded. Aura was, in some ways, better off than I'd realized. Her mother may have been a martyr, but at least she spent her days in a drugged-out haze. Aura would have far greater autonomy than I'd had under my own mother's constant sharp-eyed scrutiny.

"That's why I'm so glad Aura has you," the grandmother went on. "She needs someone younger than me who she can turn to." For the record, Aura's grandmother is the only one in that family who ever thanked me for all I did for Aura.

"I'm happy to do it," I said. "Aura is special."

"She is." The grandmother took a sip of coffee. "This musician fellow you're seeing. You think he's a good influence on Aura?"

"Definitely," I said. "He's a really sweet guy. Not your typical musician." Every word of it was true.

"That's a relief," she said. "Aura has an older brother, as you may know, but he's"—she gestured toward the ceiling, where the Martyr was presumably in a Valium trance—"like their mother, I'm afraid."

"Oh." I remembered Aura's comment about her brother's advice to listen to a song high. "You don't have to worry about that. I've never seen Johnny do drugs." It was true, though I suspected that he probably *did* do them, sometimes—didn't everyone our age?

The grandmother smiled. "That's good to hear," she said. "Aura was happy when she came home yesterday. I haven't seen her that happy since before her father died."

"Were they close?' I asked.

"Very. They had some friction when she entered her teens, but Aura was always Daddy's girl."

I'm not one to cry much, but tears sprang to my eyes. I was a Daddy's girl, too, and as I've said before, the thought that I could have lost that dear, sweet man when I was Aura's age was more than I could bear. Without my dad, I'd never have had my East Village years; indeed, I'd never have gone away to Brooklyn College. My tender young life would have been over before it started. As I fought those hot tears, I mourned for the alternate universe me.

The grandmother handed me a tissue. "What a sweet soul you are," she said.

Aura's grandmother understood me as few have.

I went home that night, buoyed by my weekend with Johnny and Aura. The date with Peter, though not hugely memorable, had even served as the perfect intermission—a palate cleanser, if you will. My mother had managed to get that CBGB stain out of my dress, and she'd made lasagna—my favorite—for dinner.

"Tell us about your weekend, Lynda," my dad said.

I gave him an edited version, as I always did, ending with those kind words from Augustus's mother.

"My sweet daughter," Daddy said. "It's wonderful, what you're doing for that girl."

"It is," my mother said. I expected the next line to be some sort of recrimination, or at least for her to narrow her eyes at me, study me, like she was trying to figure out my angle. But she didn't, at least, not that night.

"This lasagna is terrific, Mom," I said, returning the favor.

"As always," my dad said. Then he cleared his throat a little. "Lynda, sweetie, I don't want to pry into your personal life. I know you're a grown woman. But I have to ask you something."

"Sure, Dad."

"When you stay overnight in The City, you still stay with your friend Lola, right?"

Lola was a fiction I'd created in high school, a cover for when I stayed out late with boys; I went so far as to have a boyfriend's sister pose as Lola, so that my parents could meet her. When I went off to college, Lola moved to The City as well. She has been a loyal, convenient friend ever since. At some point during my college years, Mom seemed to catch on to the fact that I was no longer in touch with Lola—or perhaps she even figured out that it had always been a scam. But my dear, sweet father still believed, as a child believes in Santa Claus.

"Of course, Daddy," I said brightly.

My mother made a slight noise in the back of her throat.

"I know you kids think it's a different world, and that my generation's morals are out of fashion," Dad said. "But men still lose respect for women they think are easy. Maybe they shouldn't, but they do."

"I don't let anyone treat me without respect," I said.

After dinner, I sat at the vanity desk in my childhood bedroom and pulled out my most recent poetry notebook. I hadn't made an entry since Carlos Barrada and I had broken up; that selfish egomaniac had not only shattered my heart, he'd murdered my Muse. But that night—thanks to the kind of osmosis that occurs when one has spent a weekend surrounded by other creative souls!—I began to fill the pages. I wrote a poem called "Settling," imagining the dull life I might have had if I'd married Art; I wrote one called "Daddy (after Sylvia Plath)," imagining my life without him. After writing those two poems, I had ideas for several others. I'd gone from not having written for over a year to the promise of an entire collection! I knew then that Johnny and Aura were my Muses: as dear to me as oxygen. Our trio was not only special, it was vital. We'd be written about one day; I felt it as firmly as I felt the pen in my hand, the paper beneath.

6

The day after I cut the wires on our neighbors' stereo here in our balmy hermitage, the local police made a visit to our home. Those midwestern trolls had the audacity to report it as a burglary! Hubby secreted himself in the bedroom after shooting me a fierce look: "One of these days, you're going to get us caught, Lynda," he muttered as he hurried away. But as luck would have it, both officers were male.

I ushered them into our living room, offering lemonade, which they declined. Two white guys in their thirties, one darker-haired, one blond, their accents suggesting they were truly from this godforsaken state and not transplants looking to escape the snow. Starsky and Hutch filled me in on the "break-in."

I nodded, waiting for my cue as to how to play this.

"It seems odd to me," Starsky said, "that a burglar would break in and take nothing, just cut the wires on the stereo." The self-satisfied smile on the cop's face suggested not only that he fancied himself the brains of the duo, but that my neighbors had already pointed the finger at me. In situations like this, a little truth goes a long way.

"Oh, I doubt it was a burglar," I said. "Did they tell you how they blast their stereo throughout the day? Did you see how the speakers were pointed outward?"

The officers exchanged a look and nodded.

"I think everyone on the cul-de-sac has pulled a wire or two loose at least once," I said. "I know I have."

Starsky's eyebrows shot up. "You cut the wires?"

"No," I said. "I once pulled a wire loose, since my polite requests to keep it down were being ignored." A little truth, but not, of course, the whole truth.

"Ma'am," Hutch said, "are you telling us you broke into their house?"

"Of course not!" I said brightly. "They keep their lanai unlocked."

"They said it was locked," Starsky said. "But even if it wasn't, you can't just walk into someone's house and disable their stereo."

"That's what my husband said." This was the point where I really needed to sell my tale of woe. I was wearing a tank top and form-fitting white shorts, and I crossed my tanned legs to get their attention. I may be old enough to be their mother—or, in this backwater, great-grandmother—but I still have terrific legs, and they did not go unnoticed. "But have you ever gone for several nights without sleep? It clouds one's judgment."

Starsky still looked a little skeptical, but Hutch nodded slightly.

"Is your husband home?" Starsky asked.

"Not right now," I said. Hubby was such a worrywart; he feared that we'd be more recognizable as a couple. But I was pretty sure these two wanted nothing more than to close the books on this absurd case. "But you could stop by again tonight, if you like." It was a gamble, but a small one. I smiled brightly.

"I don't think that's necessary," Hutch said.

"Is there anyone else in the neighborhood who you think might have done this?" Starsky asked.

I was quiet for a moment, as if lost in thought. "Well, as I said, it's been a noise nuisance for everyone nearby. You might want to talk to my neighbor on the other side. He's often out walking his darling little dog. Perhaps he saw something." In one deft move, I'd turned their attention to the Pugsub without directly accusing him. How could Hubby ever have doubted me?

The officers looked at each other, then rose in unison. "We'll do that," Starsky said, "and we'll talk to your neighbors about keeping the noise down. If it becomes a nuisance again, call us—don't take matters into your own hands."

I murmured assent and showed them to the door, waited a beat and then headed into the bedroom, where Hubby and I watched from behind the curtains as this less-than-dynamic duo knocked on the Pugsub's door.

"Am I good?" I asked Hubby, slightly miffed that he hadn't immediately congratulated me on my performance.

"The best," he said, and we chuckled as we saw Mee-chelle break free when the Pugsub opened the front door, the tiny beast yapping at the officers, circling and lunging in the air like a graceless ballerina.

After nearly two months of outings with Johnny and Aura—to band rehearsals after they'd found their drummer, Lars; to the Asbury Park boardwalk, where our trio competed at skee-ball; to the Museum of

Modern Art, after Aura and I discovered Johnny had never been—I suggested we take Aura skating at Rockefeller Center. I'd overheard Lars talking with his girlfriend about going there, and in my head I was already planning the cute hat and scarf ensemble I'd wear to attract Johnny's attention.

It was mid-December and Johnny still hadn't made a move on me. I was bewildered, to say the least. None of my tried-and-true seduction moves had worked, and I hadn't even gotten him to Studio yet. I continued dating Peter, but like Art, he danced only reluctantly and so I went dancing by myself most Saturdays, often Wednesdays as well. Sometimes I went home with a guy; sometimes I didn't. But I was never alone at Studio. Regulars like Disco Sally and Rollerena were always glad to see me, along with Steve and Ian, Truman Capote, Warren Beatty, Cher: the list, like the beat, goes on. Everyone who was anyone knew me, danced with me, shared their coke with me. But I wanted to be there with Johnny on my arm. Quite simply, I wanted Johnny.

When we took the skating idea to Aura, she was less than enthusiastic. "Dad always said that was for tourists." But after I prodded her a bit, she agreed to give it a try.

It turned out Lars and his girlfriend, whose name I never bothered to learn, were better skaters than either me or Johnny. They decided to teach Aura some of the basics while Johnny and I sat at a table, sipping coffee.

"So tonight," I said to Johnny, glancing at him over my Styrofoam cup. I'd settled on a red knit cap and a red-and-white-striped scarf; with my white jacket, my dark hair flowing beneath the cap, I knew it was a winning combination. In the large purse I carried, I'd packed the red Qiana dress and some sexy-yet-danceable heels, just in case.

"Uh-oh," Johnny said, smiling.

"You knew this night would come." I gave him one long, slow bat of my lashes.

"Studio 54?"

"Are you up for it?"

"I am," he said. "Maybe dinner first?"

I beamed at him. Finally—*finally*!—this was to be our night.

After we'd been at Rockefeller Center for a couple of hours, I was taking a turn skating with Aura when, gliding near the edge of the rink, I heard her call out: "Denny!" I followed her as she skated over to the side, both of us nearly colliding with the railing as Aura reached out to hug her brother.

Denny had shoulder-length dark hair, the same blue eyes that Aura had, and Augustus's tall, lithe body. He was so good-looking that I had to remind myself he was just a kid—a sophomore in college!—and too young to be a #3, too broke to be a #2, too inexperienced to be a #1. As Johnny skated over and Aura introduced us to her brother, I could see that Denny's eyes were glassy and red—but alert enough to give me an appreciative once-over. He reeked of weed.

"How did you know I was here?" Aura asked.

"I got a call from Nana," Denny said. "She wants us both to come home."

"Is everything okay?" Aura asked.

Denny shrugged. "I guess Mom's freaking out or something."

"Shit," Aura said. "Not again."

Johnny and I exchanged glances as Lars and his girlfriend skated up. I was extremely curious about this attention ploy of the Martyr's, but before I could delicately prod for information, Johnny spoke up.

"Aura, what can we do to help?" he asked.

"Maybe give us a ride back to Jersey? I'm sorry—I know you were planning to stay in The City after this."

Tiny alarm bells went off in my head: what if Johnny decided tonight wasn't the night for dinner and dancing after all, and just dropped me at my parents' house? But then I looked at Lars and his girlfriend and remembered that they lived in Jersey.

"You two are going back there, aren't you?"

"Sure," Lars said, though his girlfriend looked miffed. Ha! Better her evening in The City ruined than mine.

Johnny and I watched as the four of them made their way out to the street. "I'm worried about Aura," Johnny said after they were some distance away. "That kid is stoned out of his mind."

"She's fourteen, Johnny," I said. "And she's with Lars." All the guys in the band were nice to Aura, but Lars was especially kind. He'd told me he had three younger sisters.

"Yeah, I guess," Johnny said. "It's just—she's all alone in the world, you know? Her dad's dead. Her mom's fucked up—I mean, who knows what this emergency really is? And you saw what the brother's like."

"She's not alone," I said. "She has us."

Johnny shrugged. "We're both misfits, Aura and I. In music, and in life."

"You're not a misfit, Johnny."

"I am. You have no idea."

In retrospect, I should have wondered what it was that Johnny was holding back. Why on earth did this gorgeous man fancy himself a misfit? But at the time, all I could focus on was that Johnny seemed to have drawn a line: he and Aura on one side, me on the other.

"I guess we're all misfits," I said, as brightly as I could muster. "Our little trio."

Johnny was quiet for a moment. "Sure," he finally said, but I could tell he didn't mean it.

After Johnny and I went back to his place and listened to a New Wave album from his voluminous collection of obscure artists (it wasn't terrible), after he received a mysterious phone call that, despite my best efforts, I was unable to overhear (jealous girlfriend?), after tacos and two pitchers of margaritas at a dive Mexican place and then an unfortunate visit to Max's Kansas City—the band Johnny took me to see, Devo, wore hazmat suits and neck braces and played music as arrhythmic and off-putting as their look; I spent most of their set trying to get into the back room where I knew Andy and the Factory crowd hung out, and then, when denied, stuffing toilet paper into one of the ladies' room johns and flushing until it overflowed (*no one* fucks with Lynda Boyle!) —finally, FINALLY, we arrived at Studio just before one a.m.

It took me a good fifteen minutes and some heavy elbow play to get the bouncer's attention, but soon, we were behind the velvet rope and inside the club. And oh, had those halls been decked for the holidays—even the bartenders themselves, who wore Santa hats and little else. Johnny got us some drinks, eying the strategically placed red velvet bow on our barkeep's otherwise naked body, and we made our way to the banquettes.

"There you are!" Steve said, giving me his usual warm hug, and slipping some coke and a few Quaaludes in my pocket. "How ya doin'? Who's this?"

"This is Johnny Engel," I said. "Soon to be a rock star."

Johnny flashed a shy smile, but I could tell he was pleased. Down the banquette, Diana Ross was chatting with Elton John.

"Oh yeah? You should play here sometime," Steve said, though his eyes were rolling back in his head, as they sometimes did when he'd taken too many ludes.

"You have bands play here?" Johnny asked, sounding about as aw-shucks-midwestern as I'd ever heard.

"Not really," Steve said, "but for the right act I'd make an exception." He briefly rubbed Johnny's bicep. "What's your music like?" I'll admit to being slightly miffed that he was lavishing so much attention on Johnny and so little on me.

"Hard to categorize," Johnny said, "but the band's really new. We're not ready to play a place like this."

"Well, you let me know when you're ready."

At that moment, a sharply dressed, balding guy I'd never seen before appeared and whispered something in Steve's ear, his appreciative eyes on me the entire time. At least *someone* had the good sense to notice me!

"Gotta go," Steve said to us both. "I'll see you later." Then he turned to Johnny, giving him a long, hard look. "I mean it, stay in touch." He gave him his card—and, I would later learn, slipped him some coke too.

Johnny looked at Steve's card after he'd left. "Wait, so that was the owner?"

"Co-owner." Johnny's naiveté was, at times, adorable. "He liked you," I added. "I knew he would."

Brooke Shields passed by and said hi to me as she made her way over to Elton and Diana.

"You're the queen of this place!" Johnny said.

I smiled. It was true, of course.

Johnny pulled the packet of coke out of his pocket. "Do you do this?" he asked.

"Of course."

"I've never tried it."

O, my dear, sweet, unspoiled Johnny! "Let's go," I said, and I led him to the bathroom.

Johnny Engel on coke was a completely different Johnny. We danced to Thelma Houston, the Village People, Chic. For a rock 'n roll guy,

Johnny could dance! After an hour, drenched in sweat, we took a break and snorted a few more lines. With that much in my system, I had zero inhibitions, and kissed him on the banquette. To my surprise, he kissed me back, fiercely.

I'd seen people have sex, right where we sat, but I found it unseemly. I suggested we retire to the bathroom, where Johnny quickly hiked up my dress and unzipped his jeans; he fucked me hard against the sink, the porcelain cold and smooth as I slid against it. I'd been laid in that bathroom before, but never by anyone I was so desperately drawn to. I wrapped my legs around him and pulled him into me.

We danced some more, then went back to his place and fucked again. By the time we finally collapsed in his pull-out bed, the sun was high and bright.

I fell into a satisfied sleep. Johnny Engel was mine.

7

My first lover was Carmine Bianchi, my middle brother's friend from Navesink, the local community college. With its open admissions policy, Navesink was the only school that would take either of my brothers, given their mediocre grades. While the eldest didn't even last a semester, middle bro—the kind of guy who proudly proclaimed he was "majoring in girls"—managed to hang in there for an entire year before he dropped out and took a factory job. Carmine was a drinking buddy my bro had made during his less-than-distinguished collegiate career.

I was sixteen then, a sophomore in high school, and I generally ignored the guys my brothers brought around to the house; most of them were as jejune as my siblings, six feet or so of barely differentiated protoplasm, their essences held together by Coppertone, canned beer, and Jersey swamp water. My brothers' friends were so interchangeable, so quotidian that, when I first saw Carmine in our family room that fall day, I did a double take.

Carmine could have been a model. He had dark hair, shoulder length, and blue-grey eyes; his skin was fairer than that of the other Italians I knew in Jersey, my own family included. His piercing eyes, coupled with a flawless face and body, had no doubt won him many girlfriends. But when our eyes met that day in 1967, he forgot about the others.

How to describe what *I* looked like in 1967? My father swore I was a ringer for Katharine Ross in *The Graduate*, but really—and with all due respect to both my beloved father and Ms. Ross—I was more beautiful than that. I had won a sort of evolutionary lottery among the two sides of my family: Grandma Boyle's pert Irish nose and large hazel eyes; the sultry Cavaletti lips of my uncles and grandfather (but not my mother, poor unlucky woman); skin that tanned but was also kissed with a faint smattering of freckles; chestnut brown hair, the kind of thick, straight hair that girls envied back then. By the time I was thirteen, I had effortlessly acquired the kind of figure models spend hours a day perfecting, and at sixteen, I passed easily for twenty.

That day in the family room, after Carmine and I exchanged a long, meaningful look, I continued on to the hallway that led to my first-floor bedroom, stopping in the doorway to listen.

"That's your sister?" Carmine asked my brother.

"Yeah," my dim brother grunted.

"What's she, like, a senior in high school?"

"Sophomore."

"Sophomore?"

Dim Bulb was quiet for a moment. "I think." He paused again, and called out: "Ma, what year is Lynda again?"

I heard my mother cease her kitchen activities. Though I couldn't see her from where I was standing, I imagined her looking into the family room, sizing up Carmine.

"She's *sixteen years old*," my mother called out, hitting every word of the last three especially hard.

"Whoa," said Carmine—not the brightest bulb himself.

I feared that would be the end of it—one more missed opportunity to blame my mother for—but imagine my surprise when Carmine was waiting for me outside my high school two days later in his bright red GTO! As he waved me over, I flipped a sheath of hair back from my face, tossed my books in the backseat, and headed with him to his parents' house, where no one was expected home for hours.

I'd been eager to lose my virginity, which I saw as an impediment to the kind of free life of love and adventure I wanted to live, and Carmine seemed to be about the best the Jersey Shore had to offer. Unfortunately, the Pill was still difficult to get back then, but I'd already decided on a birth control strategy—one favored by Catholic girls, if not throughout time, then at least through the latter part of the twentieth century. And I'd practiced on enough bananas and, from our backyard garden, thick, firm zucchini ("hope is the thing with feathers"!) that I was certain I was ready. (How *did* you think I learned to give, as Carlos Barrada proclaimed, "the best blow job in the tri-state area"?) I might not technically lose my virginity to Carmine, but if I practiced at all the other carnal delights, I thought I'd be prepared for real lovers, handsome men of passion and substance. Poets.

Unfortunately, Carmine's foreplay was not at the level of a #1. He was about as unskilled a lover as I've ever encountered; even at sixteen, I could tell, I can always tell. But he did have one thing going for him: he dealt LSD, mushrooms, and speed on a fairly regular basis, and while

I never liked psychedelics, I was always happy, in those days before I'd discovered coke, to do a little speed.

I would have discarded him quickly had he not been supplying me drugs, but since he was, we lasted several months. Unfortunately for Carmine, my brother walked in on us in my bedroom one day—Dim Bulb never grasped the concept of knocking—and though Carmine begged him not to, my brother told our parents. Daddy and cousin Tony, who was then just a few years out of the police academy, paid Carmine a visit at his home in Matawan.

Today, of course, Carmine would likely be thrown in jail and spend the rest of his life on a sexual predators' registry. But he had a few things going in his favor besides the 1960s. For one thing, my parents didn't know about the drugs. For another, I convinced Daddy that we'd done nothing more than kiss. (I say "Daddy" and not "parents" because, at one point during this raucous drama, my mother took me aside and asked me what had really happened. "I saw all those bananas disappear, Lynda," she said. "Either you have a potassium deficiency or you were up to something." Infuriating as she could be, the woman did, at times, have a certain dry sense of humor.)

At any rate, Daddy and cousin Tony told Carmine that if he ever so much as drove over the town line into Keyhole, he'd be arrested and thrown into jail.

"But how will I get to Sandy Hook in the summer?" Carmine asked, referring to a popular local beach, in a response that became a punch line in the Boyle household a few years later, when I was old enough that my father could laugh about it. "Route 36 runs right through Keyhole."

All this to say: I'd had a decade of sexual experience between my unsatisfying encounters with Carmine and my night of hot sex with Johnny, and I'd learned a great deal during those years.

Still, Johnny's morning-after behavior was a surprise to me. I was accustomed to the solicitous delight of a man who couldn't believe his good fortune in having seduced me, yet Johnny displayed nothing more than a casual friendliness. Initially, I was annoyed, but I soon decided this was a midwestern thing and had nothing to do with me. As we sat on his couch nursing quiet cups of coffee around noon, I had a brilliant idea for how to turn the day around.

"Play something for me," I said.

He smiled, that shy Johnny Engel smile that would later make his fans swoon. "Nah." He waved me away with his hand.

"Why not?" I asked. My stomach was awakening to a ravenous post-fucking, post-coke hunger, but I wanted my private concert first.

"Really?"

I nodded. Johnny plucked an acoustic guitar from the corner of the room and perched on the edge of the couch. "Any requests?" he asked.

"Something of yours," I said.

He smiled and launched into a mini concert on the spot. I wish I could tell you which of the songs would become the tunes that made Glow Worm legendary, if not famous in their day. But it's time for me to make an admission that might be shocking.

I never really liked Glow Worm all that much.

Don't get me wrong. I recognized Johnny's technical proficiency, and I loved watching him play. I'm sure you'll agree there's nothing sexier than a beautiful man in the prime of his young life with a guitar strapped on—though when I suggested this to my husband, he teasingly accused me of objectifying men. (My poor beloved has no idea that I've always objectified men.) I may not have been a huge fan of the band, but I knew how special Johnny was; how special it was to be sitting there on his couch, savoring my coffee and the sight, the smell, the sound of him, as he played a little concert just for me.

When he'd finished, I applauded. He smiled shyly.

"Hungry?" he asked.

"Ravenous," I said, with a lasciviousness that made him blush. He retreated into the bathroom to get dressed.

Over a lunchtime breakfast in what I'd come to think of as "our" diner, I asked Johnny whether he was going back to Michigan for Christmas. I'd already resigned myself that it might be the last time I'd see him until the new year.

"Nah. Too expensive."

I formulated a plan on the spot. "Then you should come to my house!"

Johnny looked taken aback. "Oh—that's nice of you." He was quiet for a moment. "In all honesty, I'm not big on Christmas. I was kind of looking forward to doing nothing but practice."

"You can do that at my house," I said. "It'll be crazy. My brothers, their wives, four small kids." (I neglected to mention, as pertains to my siblings' children, the snot running from seemingly every orifice, the perpetually chocolate-streaked, grubby little hands.) "And assorted uncles, aunts, cousins. Grandma Boyle and Nonno Cavaletti. There will be more food than any human being should even look at, let alone eat."

Johnny laughed. "Is your mother a good cook?"

"Exceptional." I had many issues with my mother, but her culinary prowess was unparalleled.

"Okay," he said.

"Terrific! If you want the full Jersey Catholic Christmas experience, come down Christmas Eve for a subversive Midnight Mass."

"How is it subversive?"

"My brothers have been sneaking in a flask of bourbon since they were teens." Johnny didn't need to know that it had originally been my idea—at the tender age of twelve.

He smiled. "Hey, I have an idea. Could we stop over and see Aura on Christmas Day? I think this will be her first Christmas without her father."

Internally, I sighed. Why was it so hard to get this man to focus? But my face, I am certain, betrayed nothing. "That's a great idea—I'll ask my mom if we can invite her family over too." I'd made a quick calculation: that with Aura's entire family there to entertain each other, I could get Johnny alone more easily.

"Any idea what I should get your parents for Christmas?"

This dear, dear man! "You don't have to get them anything, Johnny. They'll love having you over."

"I can't show up empty-handed."

"I haven't done my shopping yet," I said. "I can pick something up for you." I usually shopped on Christmas Eve morning, content with whatever was left—it's the thought that counts, my mother often said, and I liked to test her feelings on that with my gifts to her. But with Johnny coming down that day I might need to get myself to the mall earlier.

"Nah, I'll figure something out," he said.

A gorgeous musician with good manners—1977 Lynda couldn't believe her great fortune! Though 2019 Lynda knows there was more to Johnny than met the eye—at least, than met my eye.

8

"When I was fourteen, my father died, and I went to hell."

Aura pauses, waits for the hoots of recognition to quiet down—she has recited the famous first line from the opening song on her 1994 album, *Nobody's Heaven.*

"My mother, lost in grief, made decisions I had no control over. We moved to a little town on the Jersey Shore, a town where one of the other eighth-grade girls set out to make my life miserable. That town was called Keyhole."

A *Whoop!* escapes from the crowd.

"Oh, I see you've never been there."

She smiles as the audience laughs a little too hard at her joke.

"I was angry—less at my mom than at my lack of autonomy. As a child I had no control over my own destiny; and as a girl, I had fewer unspoken rights than the boys did. The only thing I had that no one could take away from me was my music."

She pauses for a few seconds of applause, something she'd clearly anticipated.

"But even that was frustrating. I wailed on the guitar but was told I looked cute when I played. Or that I made ugly faces when I shredded, that I should *smile more.*"

I love you, Aura! a female voice rings out.

I love you too! Aura responds without missing a beat.

"I was frustrated and grief-stricken and bullied and alone and wondering if I was crazy, thinking that a girl could rock. But then something amazing happened."

She pauses for dramatic effect.

"I met Johnny Engel."

A loud *Johnny!* rings out from the crowd.

"I'll admit, I had a huge crush on Johnny when I first met him. How could I not? He was twenty-five, I was fourteen, and there are lots of male musicians who would have taken advantage of the power dynamic. Some of you are in this room. I see you."

She takes visible pleasure from the scattered nervous laughter in the room.

"But Johnny was a cross between an older brother and the world's coolest dad. He listened to me. He looked out for me. And he's taught me so much—about music, friendship, life.

"I met Johnny at the time Glow Worm was forming. Although I'd watched the band rehearse for months, the first gig I saw was in 1978, and I was blown the (*bleep*) away. That night—it changed me. Even the earliest Glow Worm songs created complete sonic landscapes, shifting intuitively from shimmering and hopeful to dark and mournful. Johnny's impressionistic early lyrics were like mirrors for us outsiders, a place where we could see ourselves.

"The band had only been together for ten months when they recorded *Kandinsky*, recently listed by Rolling Stone as one of the one hundred most influential albums of all time. Critics back then didn't know what to call this new music: Glow Worm had elements of punk but was also melodic and introspective; they had a glam look but only the barest musical echoes of that genre. Legend has it that the term *post-punk* was invented to describe Glow Worm's sound. And bands from The Cure to R.E.M. to My Bloody Valentine to Death Cab for Cutie have cited Kandinsky as an early influence.

"After an unjust hiatus"—Aura looks sharply into the camera—"Glow Worm broke up in 1981, but not before recording the brilliant *Last Night at the Disco*. A rock opera unlike any that had come before, *Last Night at the Disco* built on Glow Worm's sound while lyrically engaging in more straightforward storytelling, memorably creating Micah Fox, a young musician whose rise and fall rivals Ziggy Stardust's. *Last Night at the Disco* tells a coming-of-age story universal enough for Arcade Fire to cite the album as a direct influence on their disc *The Suburbs*, and specific enough that a lot of fans assumed Micah's emotional journey was the same as Johnny's. Was it? I'll never tell.

"If Johnny had helped to create these two masterpieces with Glow Worm and then called it a day, he'd still be a legend. But a few years later, he stunned us all with his debut solo album, *Chiaroscuro*. Building on Johnny's perpetual themes of light and dark, magic and loss, *Chiaroscuro* marked the beginning of Johnny's shift into jangle rock—and that sound, coupled with pioneering videos he conceptualized himself, propelled a string of hits in the eighties and nineties, from 'Galaxy' to 'Viper' to 'Confetti Ball.'

"But even while selling out arenas, Johnny Engel continued to sing from the heart, about identity, pain, fear, love. Without his emotional honesty, I never would have had the courage to open myself up in my own music. And Johnny has accomplished a feat only a handful of other artists have managed: he has continued, for four decades now, to produce deep, uncompromised music, music that somehow speaks to us freaks while also being beloved by millions. Maybe that's because Johnny Engel connects with the misfit in all of us—and helps us to dream of a kinder, more loving world.

"I couldn't be happier to introduce you to my chosen brother, my light in the darkness, my North Star: Johnny Engel."

I've watched Aura's Rock & Roll Hall of Fame induction speech for Johnny at least twenty times now. Every nuance is seared into my brain: fifty-five-year-old Aura looking closer to forty in an airy, frilly dress paired with a biker jacket and Doc Martens. Few women could have pulled off that outfit at her age, but Aura did. She'd clearly had some work done around her eyes; I could tell, I can always tell.

I've stopped and played in slow motion the moment where Johnny walks out on stage and he and Aura hug fiercely. She turns away with tears in her eyes. Aura has always been in love with Johnny; I knew it even back then. The clarity of this moment caught on tape is irrefutable. Aura can call him an older brother or father figure all she wants. She's been in love with him for forty years and can't admit it to herself.

Johnny has been smart enough to let aging do its thing—no creepy facelifts or fillers for him—and as a result, he's still gorgeous. His hair is shorter now, blonder—it looks natural, the grays mixed in. He appears to be in great physical shape, his body toned, and when he smiles on camera, at Aura, his eyes crinkle in a way that enhances his beauty. The men I encounter here in our seaside exile could take a page from him: all the Botox and Rogaine in the world doesn't help a body bloated from a lifetime of bad habits, a leathery face so frozen it can barely smile.

I'll admit that on more than one occasion, my husband has come home from whatever it is he does with his days ("The less you know, the better, babe," he says) to find me weeping in front of our wide-screen television, re-watching the Hall of Fame induction speech. "Fuck them if they don't appreciate you," my beloved hubby says, but it doesn't help.

If Aura hadn't met Johnny, there's a good chance she never would have become a musician; she said so herself. And there's an excellent chance that Johnny's career would have fizzled after his last big hit in 1991 if Aura had not become famous, had not mentioned Johnny as an influence in every interview after her album, *Some Girls Talk*—a feminist retelling of iconic seventies rock songs—became a phenomenon the following year. Johnny and Aura are big parts of rock 'n' roll history and I am directly responsible for bringing them together. Why isn't anyone thanking *me*?

I hadn't heard Aura play any of her own songs since that open mic at the Galaxy, but shortly before Christmas, she brought her guitar into my classroom. We were finishing up a project where students interviewed each other. I'd given them sample questions, including one of paramount importance to the human condition: "What is your greatest passion?" They were required to read the profiles aloud in class that week (no grading at home!).

Jody kicked Aura's guitar case as she made her way to her desk; Marisol, who was seated behind Jody, then shoved her desk into Jody's chair, quite deliberately. The pride I felt! Aura had clearly made a friend, and I was certain that it was because I, Lynda Boyle, had paired them up for this assignment. My little project was working!

"Jody," I said, "are you having some kind of physical issue?"

"Excuse me?" she said in her usual snide tone.

"The way your leg shot out like that. Do you need to go to the nurse?"

The other students laughed, which of course had been my intent.

"I'm fine," she said, her soulless pug eyes boring into me.

"Why don't you present your profile of Kathi now?" I asked.

Jody looked around, an uncertainty in her expression that felt like another victory. Then she rose from her seat, paper in hand.

She read in a monotone as lifeless as her rat-fur hair, a bland description of her "best friend," a girl whose dullness brought to mind cafeteria-produced tapioca pudding, instant oatmeal, vanilla ice milk—that 1970s precursor to frozen yogurt, equally appalling. If there was even the tiniest detail about Kathi that was interesting, Jody hadn't discovered it.

"Kathi Marelli's passion is macramé," Jody read. "She and her mother make belts and purses, like the one Kathi is carrying now."

Kathi held up a ropy-looking creation in a suffocating beige, waving her hand along its base as if she were Carol Merrill in *Let's Make a Deal.*

It was the kind of purse only a mother—my mother—would have loved. "That's fascinating," I said, and I'll admit, I sounded sarcastic. I didn't want to hear about fucking macramé. "Jody, tell us *why* Kathi is passionate about macramé."

"*Why*?" Jody glared at me. "You didn't have that question on the sheet you gave us."

"I don't know why I like macramé," Kathi offered. "I just do."

I allowed myself a lengthy sigh. "Thank you for your report, Jody. Next we have—"

"Umm, Ms. Boyle?" Jody asked. "I wasn't finished yet."

"I think we heard enough," I said.

"That's not fair!" Jody cried out.

"There's a whole section about how my mom and I used to make tie-dye," Kathi added.

"Oh, in that case," I said, perching on the edge of my desk, "please, continue, Jody. Dazzle me with your brilliance."

Was I being cruel? Yes, I was. But there was no one in Keyhole Junior High School more deserving of cruelty than Jody.

"Never mind," Jody said. "You're going to give me a bad grade anyway. You only give As to your pets."

I walked up to Jody's desk and stooped so we were eye to eye. "Perhaps they're my pets because they *earn* As." I gave her a look that unnerved her so, she broke eye contact and stared at her desk.

"Pet *me*," Bobby Craig said, making a cat-like noise in the back of his throat. We all laughed to break the tension—all of us, except for Jody. O, my dear boy Bobby!

"Marisol, why don't you tell us about Aura now," I said.

Marisol spoke, of course, about Aura's passion for music. She told the class how Aura had learned the violin when she was younger but later switched to guitar, describing Aura's own music as "filled with absence." I loved that poetic turn of phrase, and promptly put an A in my grade ledger next to Marisol's name.

"Thank you, Marisol," I said when she was finished. "Aura, would you like to go next?"

Aura stood. She looked around for a moment, her eyes both wary and defiant. Marisol gave her an encouraging look. "I wrote a song about Marisol," she said. "I can just read it as a poem, or I can play it."

"I'd love to hear you play it."

"You didn't say on the sheet that it was okay to do a song, Ms. Boyle," Jody said. "I think you should give Aura an F."

I waved her away with a swish of my hand, dull peasant that she was, and motioned to Aura to play for us. She strapped on her guitar, quickly tuned it, and began to sing about a girl who wanted to reach the stars, who built her own telescope to see the "dazzling lights of the Milky Way." Is this starting to sound familiar, Jann? It was an early version of "Stargirl," now widely seen as a feminist retelling of Bowie's "Space Oddity," from the one and only EP by Aura's first band, Madwoman in the Attic. Not the band, or the song, that made her famous, of course. Even from the various locations of my exile, even as Aura would later callously erase me from her history, I kept up with her career, mail ordering—and later, procuring online—obscure cassettes and CDs from equally obscure places like Seattle. In fact, I may possess one of the only complete Aura Lockhart collections in the country. But I digress.

I wish I could tell you that when she was done, the class burst into spontaneous applause. That even Aura's bullies had to recognize her talent. That Bobby Craig high-fived her, that Jody reluctantly sidled up and apologized. But such a turn in the story would obviously be fiction, the stuff of some idiotic Afterschool Special.

Still, the fact that the room was silent when Aura finished—no spitballs, no mocking wolf whistles, no paper airplanes scrawled with "your so ugly" (sic)—was a testament to her power. Marisol broke the silence by clapping. I joined in. The rest of the class remained quiet.

"That was fantastic, Aura," I said. "Thank you for sharing it with us!"

Just as I recorded an A+ next to Aura's name in my ledger, the bell rang. Buoyed with my success in helping Aura make a friend, I headed straight to Dick Singer's office, to tell him of my triumph.

After I'd left Dick's office with the helping of praise I so richly deserved—not to mention a compliment about the red palazzo pants ensemble I was wearing, with a white cashmere cowlneck sweater and stickpin (the stickpin, a diamond-encrusted *L* that the Dependable Guy I saw just before Art had given me last Christmas)—I ran smack into

Peter in the hallway outside the faculty lounge. I'd been avoiding him, as he'd been trying to pin me down for holiday plans.

"I've been looking all over for you!" he said. "Did you get the message I left with your mother?"

"No! I'm so sorry. She's really absent-minded." I was avoiding Peter, of course, because I planned to spend the holidays with Johnny—but I wasn't ready to give up Peter just yet.

"I was wondering if we can get together sometime Christmas Day. I'd like to give you your gift."

Fuck! Another gift I'd have to pick up in what would most likely be a frantic sweep through the Monmouth Mall.

"I would love to, but we're spending the holiday at my brother's house. It's a fairly long drive." The trick to effective lying is to stay vague; amateurs bog their lies down with too many specific details, easy to torpedo with follow-up questions.

"What about Christmas Eve, then?"

He was sweet, really, such an obedient lap dog. All he wanted was to please me.

"We'll be gone for a few days," I said.

Peter was quiet for a moment, a slightly canine tilt to his head. "Call me when you get back. And pencil me in for New Year's Eve." It was a bold assumption for a man like Peter, and I respected the attempt.

"Sweetie," I said noncommittally, pecked him on the cheek, and sashayed my gorgeous ass down the hall, away.

That night, the phone rang just after my parents and I had finished dinner. I rushed to the kitchen, hoping it was Johnny. It took me a few seconds to place the male voice on the other end of the line: Bryce. Fucking. Bollinger. What did *he* want?

"Bryce," I said. "This is a surprise."

"It was great to see you at the *Tongue(less)* reading," he said. "And how kind of you to take an interest in Augustus's daughter. I didn't know you had it in you, Lynda!"

"I contain multitudes," I quipped, and Bryce chuckled appreciatively.

"We've missed you here in the poetry scene," he said.

Was Bryce sniffing around for a romantic encore? I wondered. I knew that I had looked nothing short of amazing in that jumpsuit and kimono.

We did a little catch-up, and he asked me about my writing. I told him I'd been blocked for a while, but recently had experienced a creative renaissance.

"I'm glad to hear you have new poems," he said. "That's the reason I called. I'm helping to organize the New Year's Day Poetry Marathon this year, and I was wondering if you'd like to read a poem or two there."

Held at St. Mark's Church, the New Year's Day Poetry Marathon was an event that, in a cruel twist of fate, began in 1974—just a year and a half before my Jersey exile. The crème de la crème of the East Village poetry scene gathered there, both on stage and in the audience. The last time I'd gone was in 1976; I'd found it so disheartening, seeing my old compatriots living the life I'd loved and lost, that I skipped the last one.

"I'd love to!" I said.

"Terrific," Bryce said. "Perhaps we could grab a drink afterward."

Ah, there it was—not only had the poetry scene missed me, Bryce Fucking Bollinger had missed me, in the carnal sense. Well, if he thought he was going to get laid after the agony he'd put me through, he was sadly mistaken.

"I'll check with my beau." Was Johnny my beau, to the degree I wanted him to be? Not yet. But it was only a matter of time, and none of Bryce's business.

"Ah," Bryce said. "Of course there's a beau. I hope he treats you well."

"I settle for nothing less," I said, and Bryce laughed.

"Oh, one more thing," he added. "Carlos Barrada will be there too. That's okay, isn't it? Legally, I mean?"

"Legally?" I choked down a curling fury.

"There were rumors, something about a restraining order? That's all over by now, I hope."

I looked around for an object to hurl against a wall. Perilously close was the decorative plate that my mother propped on a miniature easel in the nook between the dining room and the kitchen. It was painted in garish colors, reds and greens and shades of white that approximated a map of Italy. My mother swore it came *from* Italy, though it looked exactly like something you'd see in the clearance bin of Bradlees' Home Goods department. Hurling it against the wall would both alleviate my anger and right the wrong of my ever having to look at that thing again. But my mother would go ballistic, and that would upset my father. Instead I clenched my fists and bit the inside of my cheek, hard.

"There was never a restraining order," I said as calmly as I could muster. "It's amazing, the lies men will tell when they're jilted."

Bryce made a sound in the back of his throat that I couldn't quite interpret. "But you two are okay now, right? This won't be awkward?"

"Not at all," I said, relishing the thought of arriving on Johnny's arm, letting Carlos get a look at the beautiful, talented man I was now with.

"Terrific! See you there on New Year's Day."

"Until then!" I said brightly, and hung up the phone.

I walked into the living room, where my parents were watching *Welcome Back, Kotter.* I sat on the couch next to my father and fumed. The last time I'd seen Carlos was a few months after we broke up, the fourth time I'd been in his apartment uninvited.

How did I accomplish this? I'd had his key duplicated while we were still seeing each other.

I realize how this might sound. And what if I told you that I'd done it before? That in fact, after Bryce jilted me, I'd spent two weeks living in his apartment while he was in the Hamptons and that, as far as I could tell, he'd had no idea his phantom house sitter was *moi*? All I can say is that these men had it coming. Especially Carlos.

I did nothing too extreme at Carlos's place, of course—I'm not crazy! Inside his apartment, I went from room to room, looking for mischief that wouldn't be immediately obvious, as I hoped for him to find many little surprises over time. First I went through his poetry journals and removed random pages, stuffing a few between his mattresses, others in the box of Brillo pads under his sink. His signed copy of Lawrence Ferlinghetti's *A Coney Island of the Mind* I slipped into the crisper drawer in his refrigerator, beneath a browned head of lettuce. As I looked around for a place to hide his favorite writing pen, Carlos's temperamental tortoiseshell cat, Cara Mia, sprang from its hiding place behind a large snake plant, hissing at me.

A brief aside: animals don't especially care for me, nor do I for them. I find their supposed cuteness uninteresting, in much the way I find the cuteness of babies and small children uninteresting. Cats, in particular, recognize me as a rival for others' attention: an adult human who is far more captivating than their little trills or tilts of the head. (For the record, there is no being I could love enough to clean its poop, be it feline, canine, or human. I've made it quite clear to my husband that, if he becomes incontinent in old age, I'll be hiring someone to perform this specific task. He recognizes that our marriage vows do not cover human excrement.)

At any rate, the cat gave me an idea, and I buried the pen in its litter box.

This did not go over well with Cara Mia. As I washed my hands, the cat launched itself onto the sink, hissing and swatting at me. I left the water on longer than I might have, defending myself. That was why I didn't hear Carlos's key in the door, didn't see him until he was already in the bathroom doorway.

The first thing he did was lift the growling cat from the sink, inspecting the animal as if he thought I'd injured it.

"It's fine," I said. "You know it never liked me."

"I wonder why," Carlos said, his voice dripping scorn. He put the cat down and it immediately ran to its litter box, mewling. Ha! The poor dumb creature was trying to tell him, with what little rudimentary brain power it had, that I'd buried his pen.

Carlos proceeded to hurl insults at me, terrible, hurtful words. After I told him I'd given my youth to him—O, the petulant child I was, unaware that I was still so young, so in my prime!—his response knocked the very air from my lungs.

"Lynda, you don't give anything to anyone," he said. "You're a narcissist."

Only a handful of people have had the temerity to associate me with this insult. Yet I sometimes wonder: why does it sting so? Was it Narcissus' fault that his beauty was the most captivating in the land? Why is it so frowned upon to love oneself? Before my husband, my secret fear was that no one would ever love me as much as I loved myself. Why is it so taboo to make this admission?

I don't remember what I said back to Carlos after he used that hateful slur on me. I do remember a threat of the police, of a restraining order if he ever found me back in his place again.

Two weeks later, I discovered that he'd changed the locks—Cara Mia lunging at the front window as I tried in vain to fit my key in the door—and so I decided it might be best to move on from Carlos. Forgiveness, they say, is not for the lout who treated one abominably; it's for oneself. I would forgive, so that I could heal—and not be further victimized by Carlos via our legal system.

As the *Welcome Back, Kotter* theme song played, my mother inanely singing along about dreams being one's ticket out—O, the irony!—my thoughts turned back to the New Year's Day Marathon. Why was I spending precious minutes wallowing in past misery? I should be celebrating! This was the poetry event of the year, and I, Lynda Boyle, had been invited to read. I'd walk in on Johnny's arm, with Aura in tow just to prove to Carlos what a giving person I was, how I was the opposite of a narcissist. He and Bryce would both see the error of their ways, likely making sexual overtures.

1978 would be The Year of Lynda Boyle. It felt so close at hand, so within my reach. I could not possibly have foreseen the ways in which it would all unravel.

9

My very Catholic mother took her greatest glee in the celebration of Jesus's birth—even beyond, it pains me to say, the birthdays of the very children she squeezed from her own womb. Perhaps it was this merry treachery that fueled my skepticism toward Christmas. From the first time I paged through the Sears-Roebuck catalogue at the tender age of six—the "Wish Book," they used to call it, as if the only things one might wish for in life were flame-retardant pajamas or a transistor radio—I recognized the absurdity of this crass commercial holiday. Every year I think that we have reached peak vulgarity, and I am repeatedly proven wrong, as I was last year by the Pugsub, when he chose the day after Thanksgiving to begin his Yuletide onslaught: a Santa hat paired with the Hawaiian shirts he perpetually wore; reindeer antlers and a red-and-white collar with bells for Mee-Chelle, so the creature jingled when it walked up and down the street on its shaky little legs; a giant blow-up Rudolf and reindeer sleigh parked on the Pugsub's front lawn from late November through mid-January, when the red-nosed vermin suffered an unfortunate puncturing accident in the middle of the night.

But knowing that I'd be celebrating with Johnny, I woke up on the morning of Christmas Eve in 1977 with more excitement than I'd felt since I was a toddler—and just enough time to primp for Johnny's arrival.

He pulled up in front of our house that afternoon in his electric blue Monte Carlo. I loved that car, its grandeur so different from the muscle wheels, the bitchin' Camaros favored by the cavemen native to my part of Jersey.

"Whatcha got under the hood?" Dad said to Johnny by way of hello.

"350 four-barrel," Johnny said.

"Must have set you back a pretty penny."

Johnny shrugged. "Before I moved out here, I worked for Chevy in Detroit. I got a deal on it."

They paced around the car, sizing each other up like two boxers at the start of a fight. There was nothing I loved more than watching two men paw the ground as they vied for possession of me. But I also wanted—needed—for Daddy to like Johnny. I decided to step in.

"Dad, this is Johnny Engel," I said. "Johnny, this is my dad, Pat Boyle."

"Nice to meet you, Mr. Boyle," Johnny said, and stuck his hand out.

My dad had a thing about manners. No one in 1977 was respectful enough in his eyes, and he found this to be especially true for people my age. Daddy believed it was largely the fault of the Beatles, that they'd ushered in the current age of disrespect, with their long hair and atheism.

But Johnny had passed my father's test. Dad visibly relaxed, smiled, and shook Johnny's hand.

"You can call me Pat," he said. "I hear you're from Michigan? Whereabouts?" He clapped him on the back as they walked into the house and began a discussion of cars and midwestern values that bored me so thoroughly I almost, but not quite, wished I was out with my mother doing last-minute food shopping at the Pathmark. Eyes on the prize, Lynda, I reminded myself. Having my father like my boyfriend would make everything infinitely easier.

Early Christmas morning, long after the Christmas Eve supper Johnny proclaimed the best food he'd ever had (that charmer!), after our semi-drunken Midnight Mass (Johnny, ever the Boy Scout, passed on the flask), after everyone else in the house was asleep, I snuck into the room where my mother had set Johnny up. It had once been the bedroom of one of the Dim Bulbs, and the requisite sports paraphernalia, along with an old poster of Raquel Welch, adorned the wall.

I was wearing a sheer red negligee and a Santa hat. Johnny was asleep when I crept in, but woke with a start.

"Lynda!" he exclaimed, and I put two fingers to his mouth.

"They'll hear us," he whispered.

"They're deep sleepers, as long as we're not too loud," I said, and began to stroke his chest with my fingers.

He sat up in bed and moved slightly away from me. I was more puzzled than hurt. What twenty-five-year-old man would turn down the thrilling possibility of illicit sex?

"C'mon, Lynda," he said. "Let's respect their wishes. Your mom wouldn't have set me up in here if she was okay with us sleeping together in her house."

"Who cares what she thinks?"

"I do."

Those two words landed on me like a slap. He cared more about my mother's wishes than he did my own? How did she manage such sorcery?

"Don't look at me like that," he said.

"Like what?"

"Like you'd murder me if you had a knife handy."

I was surprised my face betrayed so much of my inner pain; I was usually better at hiding it. Perhaps it was Johnny, dear Johnny, who had found a chink in my armor.

"I'm sorry," I said. "I just thought we could have fun."

"I've had fun," he said. "Your family's great! I just don't want to be disrespectful. It's really kind of them to have me over for the holiday."

It seemed the best way to play this was to hide my disappointment.

"You're right," I said. "I'm a terrible daughter sometimes." I uttered that with a straight face; in a different life, I might have acted in independent films. Those of Warhol, perhaps, or Jarmusch.

He gave me a passionate hug then, and a kiss on the lips. We sparked, as always. But I ended up feeling like I'd been sent back to my own bedroom with a pat on the head. Dismissed.

Being dismissed, as you might remember from the Carlos Barrada story, does not sit well with me.

My brothers, with their retro-coiffed spouses and tedious children, began to arrive around noon. Aura turned up a little while later, with the whole Lockhart clan: the Martyr, the grandmother, and stoner brother Denny. I'd forgotten about Denny, those piercing blue eyes of his. His facial features came largely from the Martyr, but that body, that lithe walk? That was all Augustus. My skin prickled when he said hello.

In previous years I'd found the exchange of holiday gifts to be nearly insufferable: I rarely got anything I remotely liked or found useful, and the children, feral as they were, took forever to claw through the wrappings on their endless mountains of presents. I'll confess that I am generally a terrible gift giver. I have no idea how other people do it, how they can psychically know what another being might want. But that year, I'd decided to try.

Instead of a tortured late-night trip to the Monmouth Mall, I'd taken the train into The City after work one afternoon. There, through various Village boutiques and street vendors, I'd amassed a treasure trove of truly inspired gifts: for Johnny, a tooled leather belt with a guitar etched into the buckle; for Dad, a more conservative belt from the same artist. At the big downtown Macy's, I bought my mother a cashmere sweater in a coral color that, while anathema to me, would flatter her skin tone. For Aura I found a chain-link necklace with a small padlock, like some of the punk girls wore. My mother had promised she'd pick up gifts for Denny, the Martyr, and the grandmother.

The next day I'd done a quick lap through the Monmouth Mall and bought the usual crap for my siblings and their kids.

That Christmas, the gift exchange was far more lively than usual. I could tell that both Johnny and my father were truly thrilled with their presents; when Dad immediately took his belt off to put on the new one, Johnny did the same, causing one of the Dim Bulbs to jokingly wolf whistle, my mother to cluck. Speaking of my mother, she loved the sweater.

"I think this is the nicest gift you've ever given me, Lynda," she said, and while I could tell from her narrowed eyes that she was trying to figure out my angle, I let it pass, buoyed by the lightheartedness of the day.

Johnny handed me a beautifully wrapped gift—my mother gushed over the ribbon, asking where he'd bought it—and inside was a leather-bound journal for my poems. I was, at first, taken aback. The lavishness of the wrapping suggested something more intimate was inside, the kind of gift that would communicate Johnny's intentions toward me. But I consoled myself with the realization that this was a gift for my art, and so was far more intimate than lingerie or, well, diamonds.

And then I saw Johnny's gift to Aura.

It was a guitar, but not just any guitar. This was a beautiful instrument, painted in a metallic mint green that sparkled in the light. He'd tied a big red bow around the neck.

"It was my first electric guitar," Johnny said, handing it to Aura.

"A Danelectro with lipstick pickups!" Aura exclaimed, carefully untying the ribbon.

"Lipstick pickups?" my mother asked.

Aura pointed to the shiny chrome parts—they did, indeed, resemble tubes of lipstick.

"I painted it for you," Johnny said. "If you don't like the color, I can fix that pretty easily."

"I'm so glad you didn't paint it pink," Aura said.

"Yeah, well, I kind of know you."

Aura lunged across the room and hugged Johnny so fiercely that she toppled him over.

I was rendered incapacitated with conflicting emotions as this scene unfolded.

First, Johnny's present to me had been adequate—but if there's anything you know about me by now, it's that I don't settle for "adequate." Aura's was clearly the better gift: larger, more dynamic, a possession that meant a great deal to him, one that he'd lovingly restored for her. I suddenly understood what my mother had meant all those years when she'd uttered the cliché, "It's the thought that counts." His gift to me had likely cost more, but Aura's was by far the more thoughtful.

I kind of know you. What did that mean? How could Johnny know Aura better than he knew me? Internally I shed a few bitter tears. Johnny and I were so clearly destined for each other; he should have been in love with me by then. But it was Aura he doted on.

As I sat on the floor of my parents' living room, a smile fixed on my face while I suffered silently, Denny picked up the guitar.

"This is really cool," he said as he ran his fingers along the frets. "We'll have to get you an amp."

"I brought one of those too," Johnny said. "We'll test it out later."

"*Another* electric guitar in the house?" the Martyr wailed. "How will I cope?" She chuckled as if it were a joke, but oh, I had that Martyr's number.

"The same way you always do," Denny muttered under his breath. If the Martyr heard him, she pretended not to.

After delivering his understated zinger, Denny caught my attention for a brief moment in time. Our eyes met over that electric guitar. I offered him a rueful smile; he returned it with a wicked one. Denny was clearly a boy after my own heart, and the way his eyes settled on my breasts momentarily removed the sting of Johnny's gift-giving betrayal.

That night, Johnny's bandmate Mike was throwing a party at his parents' place in Asbury Park. The rest of Glow Worm would be there, perhaps members of other local bands. I had bought a new dress for the evening, a red sequin shift that I also planned to wear to the poetry marathon. In my bedroom shortly before Christmas dinner, Johnny and Aura in a corner of the family room obsessing about power chords, I gazed upon the shimmering beauty of that dress and imagined turning up at the party that night, arm in arm with Johnny. How jealous his bandmates, especially Mike, would be. The thought made me smile, though every time I heard from the next room Johnny's easy laugh, Aura's soft but strong voice, I was plunged back into despair. There's no denying it: I had started to see her as a rival. But let me explain why.

My parents had, by all accounts, a close bond before I came along. The Dim Bulbs did little to change that; they were barely more than Sea Monkeys, added to water and stirred, requiring little maintenance.

I was a bit more demanding. My parents frequently clashed over my upbringing, or rather, they clashed over my mother's financial and emotional stinginess toward me. When I was fifteen and invited to the junior prom as a freshman, my mother and I had one of our biggest fights (up until then—there were many worse to come!) over my choice of prom dress.

She wanted to buy me a horrendously ordinary frock from that bargain basement of mundanity, Sears: shapeless miles of chiffon in a suffocating pink. But it was 1966 and there were far more fashionable choices out there. I finally saw my dream dress at Bamberger's, a fitted silk gown in a deep, royal purple, inspired by one Oleg Cassini had created for Jackie Kennedy. The problem: that dress cost four times as much as the dress my mother had picked out.

"Champagne taste on a beer budget," my mother had snapped at me in her uninspired way when I told her over dinner about the dress at Bamberger's.

"How much does it cost?" my father asked.

"She doesn't need a designer dress, Pat," my mother said.

"It's not. I said it was *inspired* by Cassini, not an actual Cassini." I'd love to tell you that my mother was dense enough to have misunderstood me. It would, for one thing, explain the shriveled cerebra of the Dim Bulbs. But my mother wasn't stupid at all. I knew immediately what her angle was.

"It's still too expensive," she said. "And it's not even your own prom! Maybe you shouldn't be dating an upperclassman at your age."

She had just employed a sneaky trick that she fell back on when she knew she might lose an argument: appeal to my father's protective streak. My dating life caused him great anxiety, was possibly even responsible for his ulcer. But I knew how to play my mother's game.

"It's the first prom I was ever invited to, Daddy," I said softly. As I fixed a face on him and watched the way he lit up from within, my mother's shrill voice shattered our father-daughter moment.

"If we keep giving in to her, when will it end?"

Daddy was quiet for a moment, and then he turned to her. "It's a dress, Maria. She's a beautiful girl. She should have a beautiful dress."

"There are lots of beautiful dresses at Sears," my mother countered.

I kept my eyes fixed on Daddy.

"I can take a couple extra shifts," he said. "It's no big deal."

"She needs to hear the word 'no' once in a while," my vile mother responded. "You're creating a monster, Pat. Everyone can see it except you."

A monster! Can you imagine being called such a thing *by your own mother*? Hot angry tears sprang to my eyes, even though by then, I'd grown accustomed to my mother's betrayals. My father reached his hand out to me across the table.

"That's right, Pat. Give in to her crocodile tears. Never mind your wife and *her* feelings."

She pushed her chair back as noisily as she could, threw her napkin dramatically onto her plate, and stomped off to their bedroom. How ironic that she often accused me of dramatics; if that's true—and I'm not saying it is—I learned from the best.

After my father followed her, I listened outside their bedroom door with rapt excitement. It was, at first, their usual fight: my mother thought my father was too lenient, too eager to give me what I wanted. He thought my mother was too strict, and too frugal. But on that particular evening, my mother said something I hadn't heard her say before.

"You put us in this position where we're competing with each other," she said. "We're mother and daughter. We shouldn't be rivals."

"You put yourself in that position," Dad said.

But there was a truth that neither of them understood; that I myself had not understood until that moment.

I had been the one to put my mother in that position, to create that rivalry. And by age fifteen I knew, with certainty, that it was a competition I could win.

As I remembered that fight between my parents—one where they barely spoke for a week afterward—it occurred to me that Aura might be more calculating than I realized. That she might be setting up a rivalry with me for Johnny's affection, just as I'd done with my parents, years earlier. No matter. This, too, was a contest I would win.

The party itself was not dissimilar to the kinds of Jersey Shore parties I'd been going to since I was thirteen; that these guys were all musicians didn't erase their Jersey-ness. There was even a former E Street band member there, falling-down drunk and willing to complain to anyone who would listen about how he'd had "artistic differences" with The Boss and parted ways before the band's success.

"Future of rock 'n' roll my ass," he slurred, nearly sloshing his beer onto my red sequin dress.

Johnny and I locked eyes and laughed. It was good for us, being away from Aura, though a part of me longed for Studio's glamour. Those long-haired, unwashed, swampy rock 'n' rollers crowded into Mike's place that night were not at all my type. But Johnny was, and, after Mike broke out some coke, my feelings about the other guests brightened considerably.

Around midnight, an ebullient Mike decided Glow Worm needed to play. I hadn't seen them rehearse in a while and was taken aback by the way their sound had gelled. Johnny's guitar still had that chiming sound, but the bass line was a sinuous, hypnotic thing; not danceable in the way of the funky, pulsing disco I loved, but it did make me want to sway my hips. Rather than the vocal exuberance of the Commodores or the Trammps, Johnny sang with an ache that, frankly, puzzled me. This stone-cold fox of a man had everything he wanted at his fingertips, in particular, the most beautiful woman in the tri-state area: *moi*. What was there to sound so tortured about?

After the short set, as Glow Worm's musician friends crowded around in celebration, I snuck off to the bedroom where I'd seen Mike stash his coke and did a couple of clandestine lines. Johnny caught up with me on my way back to the living room.

"I'm sorry we haven't had much time alone," he said.

"Well, the night is young." I fixed my sexiest pout on Johnny.

He chuckled. "Okay then," he said, and as he leaned in to kiss me I realized, looking in his eyes, that he'd done even more of Mike's coke than I had.

We retreated to a bedroom, where I did the kinds of things to Johnny that ensured any rivalry with Aura was settled. She was a child; I was a woman who could meet his needs. And O, star of wonder, did he meet mine that heavenly Christmas night.

10

On New Year's Day, 1978, I effervesced with the indomitable hope of all grand young creatures. Aura and Denny met me in front of St. Mark's, where we waited for Johnny. I'd been horrendously disappointed that my dashing beau had been "busy" on New Year's Eve; Peter, #3 that he was, had called twice that week, but rather than waste the evening with him, I'd gone to Studio alone. There, I chatted with Calvin Klein as Steve slipped several packets into my purse; in the bathroom, I helped Liza Minelli reapply her false eyelashes. Champagne and streamers popping all around us, I danced with Margaret Trudeau while her six-year-old son—who, unbeknownst to us all, had inherited both his father's political skills and his mother's sex appeal—slept soundly in his bed back in Canada. I ended up going home in the wee hours with one of the few straight bartenders, sparing me an extra trip back and forth from Jersey.

But Johnny, dear Johnny. I had no idea where he'd been when the ball dropped, and I wondered—not for the first time—if there was a part of his life he kept from me. Was there another woman? When he approached us at the entrance to the church, I had trouble hiding my annoyance.

"How was Studio?" he asked as he pecked me on the cheek.

"Fabulous as always," I said. "Where were you?"

"Just got together with some buddies of mine," he said. "We jammed a bit."

"You jammed?" Can you think of anything more absurd—a beautiful man like Johnny saying no to a night at Studio on New Year's Eve to "jam" in what was surely a squalid fifth-floor walk-up?

"Did you work out the bridge in that new song?" Aura asked. She wore black Levi corduroys with a pale blue chenille sweater that matched her eyes, likely gifts from the Martyr. Aura had spelled out PERSON-ALITY CRISIS in three rows of letters on the back of her jacket, each *S* looking more like a Greek sigma.

"Not yet, shred." It was a nickname for Aura that Johnny had recently started using. He motioned to her jacket. "Guess you're pretty into that Dolls album."

She nodded.

Denny caught my eyes and smiled lasciviously. He looked less stoned than usual. What a sweet boy, to want to take this all in. I smiled back, but before I could say anything, Bryce was by my side.

"Lynda!" he exclaimed, placing his hands on my shoulders and air-kissing my cheeks. "How *are* you?" He looked me up and down. "Attractive as always."

Attractive? Given the way I looked in that red sequin dress, it was a weak fucking adjective, and I was certain he knew it. Bryce had always been one for head games. As I introduced him to my entourage, I spotted someone from the corner of my eye, with the kind of sixth sense a lioness has for an antelope.

Carlos Barrada was making his way toward the church entrance.

"Carlos!" Bryce exclaimed loudly. Carlos looked over; his eyes met mine. He turned away and stepped up his pace.

"I think he's embarrassed, Bryce," I said.

"Embarrassed?"

"It's hard on a man's ego, being jilted."

With that, all eyes from my coterie trained on Carlos, who'd been waylaid by a mousy little poetess whose name I could never remember. Bryce hurried to his side and bustled him over, his grip on Carlos's arm appearing to be quite strong.

"Carlos, surely you remember Lynda!" Bryce exclaimed. "We're delighted to have her reading here today."

"She's…*reading*?" Carlos asked, his surprise suggesting I was not worthy of such an honor.

I felt smoke curling through my abdomen, rising in my chest, but I needed to squelch the fire. I would not let him ruin what was sure to be a triumphant moment for me.

"From my new collection," I lied. He didn't need to know that I had neither a collection nor a publisher.

And then Johnny, dear sweet Johnny, did something for which I'll always be grateful. He put his arm around me and introduced himself. And while he didn't come out and call himself my boyfriend, he certainly implied it.

Carlos shook his hand and said to Johnny, in a stage whisper intentionally loud enough for me to hear, "Get out while you can," then whirled around and walked away.

"How's that darling cat of yours?" I called after him.

"What a fucking jerk-off," Denny said.

That dear, dear boy. When he wasn't completely stoned, he always knew the right thing to say.

Our little group made its way to a row of seats near the front of the stage. We chatted amiably as flyers listing the readers were passed out. I felt a frisson of delight as I saw my name right next to Carlos's. All the nights I'd spent in his bed, listening to him name drop—Ginsburg, Ferlinghetti, Berrigan. With this reading, the name Lynda Boyle was added to that pantheon.

I'd arrived! Or so I felt in that moment.

As I pondered the significance of my career, the good fortune bestowed upon Johnny, Aura, and Denny in watching it unfold—they might tell their grandchildren about this day!—I detected motion to the left of the stage, in the wings. I was certain I saw my mentor, dear John Ashbery. Surely he would want to congratulate me!

"I'll be right back," I said, and excused myself to go find him.

But when I got there, my professor was nowhere to be found. I asked around; no one had seen John, and I was about to make my way back out to my seat when I heard raised voices coming from deeper recesses backstage. One of those voices belonged to Carlos. I tiptoed closer to the sound and saw that it was Bryce he was arguing with.

"You'll never organize this reading again," Carlos shouted.

"Oh, come on. In a reading this size, no one will even notice. There are always a few hacks."

"Being a hack would be a step up for her."

"Isn't that a little harsh?"

I wondered who they were talking about, and settled in behind a musty old curtain, secreting myself in its folds. Bryce sounded like he was toying with Carlos. The last time I'd heard that tone in his voice, it had been followed by his eviscerating a woman in our poetry workshop so skillfully that the takedown was a work of art in itself. (My poems in that workshop, it should be noted, filled Bryce with such awe that he only ever uttered one word—"Celebratory!"—before we adjourned for drinks and post-class fucking.)

"Come on, man," Carlos said. "You've said worse about her in the past."

"I hear her work has grown."

"Ha." Carlos was quiet for a moment; then his tone shifted. "Bryce, you know she's a psychopath. Why would you invite her here?"

"Does it make you uncomfortable?"

"Of course it makes me uncomfortable! She broke into my house—repeatedly. She pulled pages out of my poetry notebooks. She buried my Montblanc pen in my cat's litter box!"

As Bryce began to laugh, I hovered in a fugue state, somewhere between the realization that they were talking about me and denial that this could possibly be the case. Hadn't Carlos proclaimed "Requiem for my Youth" to be "an original take on cliché"? Surely he didn't feel I was—I can barely write the hurtful word again—a *hack*.

"Oh man," Bryce said, still guffawing, "you should see your face."

"Fuck off," Carlos spat. I heard him start to walk away and buried myself deeper within the curtain's folds. But Bryce's voice stopped him in his tracks.

"Maybe when I reapply, you'll recommend me for the visiting writer gig at Monmouth."

"What?"

"Your memory can't be that bad," he said. "It was just a few months ago I found out I'd been turned down."

"Are you—Jesus Fucking Christ, are you that petty? I don't have control over those decisions."

"You're the chair of the English Department. I'm sure you could have made it happen. Fortunately, you'll have an opportunity to remedy this oversight in the coming year."

"Seriously? You think, after you brought that she-monster back into my life, that I'll recommend you for anything? I wouldn't recommend you for a job as a janitor! If I have anything to do with it, you'll never teach again."

"She's reading just before you are," Bryce said. "Enjoy!"

I heard some sort of scuffle after that, and the footsteps of a few other poets running toward them. I was still too stunned to move.

This was supposed to be my crowning glory, my poetic triumph, the beginning of The Year of Lynda Boyle. Was it really happening only because Bryce was fucking with Carlos? Tears welled in my eyes. Could

I really be seen as a hack by other poets? Had Carlos and Bryce both lied about my talent when we were dating—perhaps, hard to fathom as it was, simply to get me in bed?

But then the bursts of encouragement I'd received over the years made their way from my subconscious to my conscious mind. A high school English teacher who had praised the large vocabulary I employed in my poems. "It's like an SAT study list come to life on the page," he'd said, while looking at my breasts.

"The introspection here is certainly unencumbered by poetic distance," a female student had offered in my John Ashbery workshop, and, as some in the class chuckled—out of embarrassment that their work was not so clear-headed—John had concurred. "Indeed, there's no distance on the self at all," he'd added, and smiled at me, the rest of the class's failure to comprehend my work a private joke we shared.

And then, of course, Carlos: it was he who'd first told me that my poems needed no revising, after I'd pressed one of my poetry notebooks on him early in our relationship.

"I couldn't make these any better," he'd said, and then, aroused by my talent, began to undress me.

No, the evidence was clear that I was not only worthy of this reading but gifted beyond my years. The only rational explanation for what I'd just overheard was that Bryce had, indeed, been fucking with Carlos, but not in the way Carlos thought. Bryce's final twist of the knife would come when I took the stage, before Carlos, and read work that was so much better than his, so clearly more sophisticated on every level, that Carlos would be reduced to a weeping mass.

It was important for Carlos to know I'd heard him, and for Bryce to be made aware I saw through his ruse. I stepped out from my hiding place, into the line of sight of both men, who by then had been pulled apart. Bryce smirked; Carlos blanched.

I flipped my hair, turned on my heel, and let them get a good look at my spectacular ass before I left. My triumph that night, I resolved, would be grand, and even sweeter than I'd imagined.

After several hours of shattering, soul-baring readings by some of America's finest poets, I took my rightful place on stage to join them. I also decided to make a last-minute change—a poet's prerogative!—and read an older poem along with one of my newer ones.

"This is called 'Requiem for My Youth,'" I said. "I'd like to dedicate it to Carlos Barrada."

Carlos was sitting right in front of the stage, and as our eyes met, he let out a strange, almost strangled sound. Let him squirm, I thought. Let him rue the inspiration he gave you. Let him mourn the Muse you stole from him.

As I launched into my recitation—only charlatans refuse to commit their poems to memory!—I scanned the crowd for my entourage. I expected to see their eyes widen in wonder at my talent, to feel their naked adoration. Instead, what I witnessed was this: Aura slouched into Johnny with a familiarity that I found disconcerting, her hand in front of her mouth. She turned and whispered something to him; he tossed her a sideways glance and a smile, then whispered back. She looked directly at me, then away, appearing to suppress a giggle. What could they possibly have been talking about *during my performance*? To this day, I have no idea, but I was so taken aback by their lack of attention that I nearly lost my place in the poem. Those diamond-cut moments when I'd approached the podium with all eyes on me, my breathtaking command of that stage—it was a *big fucking deal*, and Aura and Johnny were too selfish to pay me the full attention that was my due. The pain I felt in that moment! But as I continued to watch them and wondered at their betrayal, my eyes met Denny's. He was looking at me, really seeing *me*. As I launched into the second poem, we continued to regard each other across the audience. And as I approached the end of the opus, anticipating what I was certain would be thunderous applause, I gave Denny a little wink which caused him to break into a grin. Could I juggle a third beau, without any of them knowing about each other? Denny was a legal adult, sexy in a bad boy way, clearly enamored of me, and definitely a #2. I vowed then and there to find out if he was also a #1.

I performed with unsettling power and strength the riveting last lines of my final poem, "O Me! O Life! (after Walt Whitman)"—"My incandescent pulchritude/my luminous sex-scorched day glo mood/O life!"—and lingered a moment to breathe in the applause. Due to poor acoustics in the church, the reaction was not quite as deafening as I'd expected—such is the terrible, wonderful life of a poet!—but I could tell, I can always tell, that I'd made an impression on every single member of that audience.

11

Perhaps you've been wondering what happened with our cornfed neighbors, they of the ill-timed and insufferably loud music. After that visit from the police we were greeted with glorious silence for several days, long enough that Hubby began to jokingly refer to the incident as "the day the music died." But then on an egregiously sunny Friday, a morning stupefyingly bright even for this fires-of-Hades region, I pulled my satin eye mask off at my usual waking time of noon and discovered an envelope waiting for me on the kitchen table, next to the cup of coffee that my beloved always makes for me when he hears me stirring. Three simple words were scrawled on the envelope: *To our neighbors.* I raised an eyebrow as I poured cream into my coffee.

"Read it," Hubby said, and sat next to me, where he had *The New York Times* spread open. Once or twice a week he drives into a less-provincial city than the one we live in and buys a copy, cash, baseball cap pulled down low. It's one of the rare risky things he does, an indulgence for us.

I sat, took a long sip of coffee, and removed the card from the envelope—shades of pink and lavender, the kind of insipid floral design that adorns everything from curtains to placemats to aprons here in these warm-weather hinterlands.

Sorry we got off on the wrong foot! Please join us for G & T's and soft music on our lanai Friday night at 7. —The Miller's

It was exactly the kind of thing the person who'd bought that card would have written, down to the appalling punctuation.

I shot a look at Hubby.

"The apostrophes, I know," he said.

"And that 'soft music' bit."

"Yeah." He laughed. "I knew you'd pick up on that."

"As if we're some kind of easy listening rubes." I got up and peered through the window into their yard; all was quiet. "If only they knew—"

"You can't tell them anything, Lynda," Hubby said.

"Why would I tell them anything? We're not going over there."

Hubby turned the page of the newspaper.

"Are we?"

He sighed and turned to me. "I think we should. Smooth things over. We don't need any more visits from the cops."

"But I handled that!"

"You did, doll. But we want to stay here, right? So we can't keep feuding with our next door neighbors. It draws too much attention."

I picked up my coffee cup and poor Hubby flinched slightly, uncertain of whether I might fling it at him. Instead I took a long gulp, considering what he'd said. "You're right."

He was quiet, studying me.

"I'll work my charms to keep them in line."

"I hope you mean that, babe," Hubby said.

"I'm nothing if not diplomatic," I purred, and then I slipped the card into the trash so it could get the burial in coffee grinds and eggshells that it so richly deserved.

Speaking of diplomacy, by February of 1978 I was managing three lovers with the efficiency of a bartender at Studio.

There was Peter, whose solid #3-ness was far too reminiscent of the tedium that had been Art. Indeed, it's a function of how disappointed I was by the other men in my life that I'd let Peter linger as long as I had.

Which brings me to Johnny. A life with him would surely not be dull—but would I ever have that life? Months had gone by and I still couldn't get our relationship to evolve beyond the occasional late night, coke-fueled fuck. I saw him less and less frequently, whereas Aura saw him more—they played guitar together on Saturday mornings, jam sessions to which I was never invited. If I was honest with myself, Johnny wasn't even really a #3 (oh, but he was dependable for Aura, anything for our little princess Aura!); he wasn't much of a #2; and about a B-minus #1. If he'd been less beautiful I would have cut him loose long ago, yet I could not ignore how perfect we looked together. I still wanted to believe that Johnny Engel would be mine.

And finally, there was Denny. A solid #2—he dealt weed, shrooms and coke out of his dorm room—Denny had turned out to be a startlingly strong #1 for such a young age, following in the footsteps of his dearly departed father. But unlike Augustus, Denny was voraciously needy. What do I mean by needy? Stoner love poems mailed to my home with such alarming frequency that I raced back from school to intercept the postman before my mother could reach the mailbox. Hitchhiking to my house late at night, too high to finesse sneaking in through my bedroom window, thus forcing me to come up with cover stories for my parents when Denny's antics woke them—a fruitless exercise, at least for my mother.

I knew Denny's obsession with me had reached a fever pitch when he showed up at my school on Valentine's Day and found me in my classroom during a free period. My school! What was wrong with him, I asked after I'd pulled him away from the windows and closed the blinds. We might easily run into Aura!

"I missed you," he said, and I could see his hard-on through his jeans.

Before I continue with this scene, before I describe some of the amazing sexual maneuvers we practiced (most of which I'd learned in the pages of *Cosmopolitan* magazine—thank you, Helen Gurley Brown!), a word about the age difference. By today's standards, some might think that nineteen was too young for me, even though I was only a youthful twenty-six myself. As you surely remember, Jann, back in 1978 no one gave this sort of thing a second thought. When I was Denny's age, I'd had a beau who was in his forties! If helping a nineteen-year-old stoner to become a better lover was wrong, I don't want to be right.

All of that said, I thought it best to keep my relationship with Denny quiet. For one thing, there was Johnny. I didn't even want him to find out about Peter, let alone Denny; though I'd briefly entertained the possibility of such a revelation making Johnny jealous, I decided he was too much of a Boy Scout. Johnny might simply have stepped aside for Peter, thinking it chivalrous; and I had no idea what he'd make of my fucking Denny. And of course, there was my mother, who was already referring to Denny as "that poor boy," as if I weren't the best thing that ever happened to him. (Make no mistake: I was!)

But back to the predicament saluting me that Valentine's Day: Denny and his obvious hard-on, just a desk between us, the walls of my empty classroom festooned with the red hearts and cupid decorations I'd cajoled my mother into making during my first year of teaching. Denny and I didn't dare do it there, but I'd heard rumors of trysts in the basement boiler room. Would the janitor be on his lunch break? What would our cover story be if we were discovered? Just entertaining the thought of such illicitness got my juices flowing, and soon, I was spiriting Denny down the back stairwell, through the double doors, and we were in a corner of the basement, behind one of the ancient, noisy boilers, where we did our part for the school's budget by generating some additional heat, gratis.

When we'd finished up a move that I'd modified from a *Cosmo* tip—I call it the "Snap, Waggle and Pop," and let me tell you, it was the move that would cement my relationship with my husband—I quickly ushered Denny out the back door of the school.

"Can I see you tonight, Lynda?" he asked.

That dear, eager boy! Alas, he could not, for Peter was taking me out in the city that night, to Lutèce, a restaurant he probably couldn't afford but, if he wanted to keep seeing me, couldn't *not* afford.

"How about this weekend?" I asked Denny. Of course, that meant Friday night, since my Saturdays were reserved for Studio, and Denny, though sexy in a shaggy way, was not Studio material.

Denny nodded, but his eyes were cast downward. I gave him a long, lingering kiss, to hold him for a few days.

I arrived home around four p.m. My mother was on me the second I'd shut the back door.

"I need to know right now," she barked, "what you're up to with that boy."

"Peter?" I asked. I knew, of course, that she meant Denny. It was just so much fun to see her squirm.

My mother sighed and wiped her hands on her "Love Is" apron. Surely you remember the cartoons, crudely rendered drawings of a man and a woman my father often referred to as "dirty naked hippies," some cloyingly sentimental cliché written underneath. In the cartoon on my mother's apron, "Love is...bubbling over," the dirty naked hippies were stirring a pot. These cartoons were an atrocious collision of hippie culture and commercialism; when I saw one on a jelly glass in an antique store on the outskirts of the largest city near where my husband and I are now living, I bought it just to take it home and smash it, which I did with some glee, and bemusement from my husband. "That's right, babe, now the seventies are really dead," he said in his usual droll way.

"I'm talking about the drugged-up teenager who showed up here a few hours ago like a lovestruck puppy," my mother said, hands on hips.

I plucked an apple from the bowl on the counter and took a bite of it, knowing my nonchalance, as well as the subconscious echo of Eve and the forbidden fruit, would enrage her. Deliberately I chewed and swallowed before I spoke.

"I've told you, he gets in these—"

"Terrible fights with his mother, I know," Mom said. She untied her apron and tossed it onto the counter. "That's a crock, Lynda. That boy goes to college in The City. When you were in college in The City, I can count on one hand the number of times we saw you during a semester. And they all coincided with your needing laundry done."

"Well, I'm sure you remember the terrible fights we got into. It goes with the age."

"That boy isn't coming home on Valentine's Day to fight with his mother. He's coming here to see you."

I was quiet for a moment as I considered the best way to handle this. I could simply own up to it, reminding my mother that Denny was nineteen—an adult!—and mocking her outdated morality. Or I could fall back on the defense time-honored by politicians: deny, deny, deny. Better yet, I'd tell a half-truth within a lie, my specialty.

"You're right that he's coming here to see me," I said. "He has a crush on me. I'm trying to let him down gently."

She snorted. "When have you ever been gentle with anyone?"

This is the point where an amateur would escalate. My strategy was to feign injury.

"How can you say that, Mother?" I asked in a butter-wouldn't-melt-in-my-mouth quiver of a voice.

"Name me one person you've ever helped out of the goodness of your heart."

I took another bite of apple, chewed and swallowed. "I helped both of my brothers with the papers they wrote at Navesink." She didn't need to know that I'd actually written the papers for them—and that they'd given me cash in exchange.

Her eyes widened in surprise. "But you were in high school then," she said.

I looked at her sideways. "Please. I was in Honors English, and they weren't exactly writing doctoral dissertations."

"I'll have to ask them," she muttered, but I could tell I'd poked a gaping hole in her argument.

"And don't forget about Aura," I added.

"Oh," she said, "you're definitely up to something there. I don't know what it is, but I'll figure it out."

I finished my last bite of apple, set the core on her spotless counter, and retired to my bedroom to dress for dinner.

Peter had, indeed, managed to get us a reservation at Lutèce, so he was already ahead of Art as a much more capable #3. But we were left waiting for nearly an hour after our reservation time, with little complaint from Peter; and once seated, we were stuck at a small table near the kitchen. When I asked him to get the maître d' to switch tables, he refused to speak up.

"It's fine, Lynda," he said. "I don't mind being by the kitchen."

He didn't mind?

"It's just that it's the worst table in the house," I said, taking a sip of the wine he'd selected for us—the cheapest on the list, I'd noted, but was kind enough not to mention. "Giving us this table, it's a sign of disrespect."

"Well, we were lucky to get a table here at all."

"I thought you made the reservation back in December."

"I did. But this is a place where famous people go! We're not celebrities—just a couple of teachers from Jersey."

Surely you know me well enough by now to recognize how this landed—as a punch to the solar plexus, temporarily knocking the wind out of me. *Just a couple of teachers from Jersey*? For a few moments I was unable to speak. What depths had I sunk to, to be dating a man who felt this way? Worse still, it wasn't altogether inaccurate.

I'd gone from being the "It" girl of the East Village poetry scene to a younger version of Maria Cavaletti in three short years, and the one man who might understand my burning desire for fame—Johnny—was closing himself off from me, bit by bit. A montage of my life's injustices flashed before my eyes. The Cissy doll episode. My senior year of high school, when I was kicked off the cheer squad for calling one of my fellow cheerleaders—a girl named Connie who had tragically large nostrils and wore her hair in long dark braids—"Petunia Pig." Was it my fault that the apt nickname stuck, and that a group of girls began affixing Looney Tunes comics to Connie's locker? That some of the other cheerleaders took to oinking at her during practice, then at games, and that this caught on with the fans in the stands, especially fans of the opposing teams? The cheerleading coach, who doubled as the German teacher (I took French, finding it much more sophisticated), had accused me of being the "ringleader," effectively comparing tender seventeen-year-old me to a monster like Jody Fromme. How dare she!

And then there were the lovers who had used me: Bryce, Carlos, perhaps even (though it pains me to say this) Augustus. They'd used me as their Muse, had absorbed the poetry from my soul, wringing the very life-force from my body. In fact, after my triumphal reading at the poetry marathon, I'd sent Bryce a selection of my newer poems for publication in *Forked*, the journal he'd launched in the wake of Augustus's death, and still had heard nothing, six weeks later. His jealousy likely precluded him from accepting my work, and a lesser woman might have been shaken by this, might have seen Bryce as a Ted Hughes to her Sylvia Plath.

But I had far too much self-regard to stick my head in an oven. Men like Bryce and Carlos might try to rob me of my pretty words; men like Johnny might drive me crazy with mixed signals; men like Art and Peter might bore me to tears, but I was still Lynda Fucking Boyle. I was special, I reminded myself; beautiful, brilliant, young.

I sat back in that moment, looking at Peter's very average face and moderately priced suit while all around us, beautiful, powerful New Yorkers sparkled and shone. I saw with utter clarity that the night, and Studio, were calling me. I looked at my watch: it was only eight thirty p.m. Alas, too early for Studio.

So instead of getting up, defiantly throwing my evening shawl around my shoulders, and telling Peter it was over, I simply smiled at him.

"A couple of teachers from Jersey, huh?" I repeated with a soupçon of disgust.

"I didn't mean—"

"It's fine," I lied, then ordered the most expensive entrée, as well as Lutèce's famous flambéed crepes for dessert. When the bill came, I surprised Peter by wishing him a good night, then strolling out of the restaurant and down to catch the E train—quickening my pace outside, in case he followed.

It had been a lovely meal. Whatever my mother thought of me, she hadn't raised a fool.

The Valentine's Day party at Studio was invitation only, and at first, I was turned away by an unfamiliar bouncer. Could this night get any more soul-crushing? I stood by the sidelines, uncertain of how to proceed. But then the gods smiled on me: Steve himself appeared. I waved and called his name to get his attention.

He was with another man, one I had glimpsed before but never met. I sized the guy up: mid-to-late thirties, around five foot nine, dark hair thinning. Physically, he was the epitome of average, the kind of guy I'd have passed on the street without giving him a second glance; but his clothes made a statement. He was dressed in an electric blue silk suit that fit as if it had been custom made. It was an outfit better suited for a rock star than this ordinary-looking, middle-aged man, but I admired his chutzpah. Our eyes met, and in that moment, I could tell—I can always tell—that he was smitten. He whispered something to Steve.

"Lynda!" Steve then cried, and ushered me in.

On the other side of the velvet rope, Steve introduced me. "This is Hal," he said.

Instead of shaking my hand, this unassuming-looking man did something completely unexpected: he bent me over and kissed me on the lips! I realize his actions might disturb delicate sensibilities these days, but this man, this Hal, was a great kisser, and his decisiveness was thrilling.

"Give her whatever she wants," Steve told Hal with a wink as he slipped away, and I understood this to mean drugs as well as, possibly, sex—Steve was so cheeky. Hal asked me if I wanted to do some lines with him. O, did I!

That night, Bill Murray danced with Gilda Radner; Truman Capote and Paloma Picasso sipped champagne with Barbra Streisand and Jon Peters. Studio had been transformed into a red-and-silver wonderland, balloons and hearts and sexy puckered lips, well-endowed cupids hanging from the ceiling, adorning the walls. I only saw it all from the corner of my eye, for I spent the night talking to Hal. He was an accountant who also dealt coke, and he provided both services to Steve. When we finally hit the dance floor we were both tooted up enough to be openly pawing each other, in the way so many of us did at Studio.

The first time we had sex was in the bathroom; Warhol walked in and watched us approvingly. That Andy was such a voyeur! He asked if he could come back with a camera, but we demurred. Afterward, Hal and I snorted more lines and returned to the dance floor, finally leaving the club together in the wee hours.

There was a light snow falling as Hal asked me to come home with him. I was supposed to teach, in Jersey, in three and a half hours. I said yes.

Hal lived in a doorman building on the Upper East Side—clearly the accounting and coke-dealing was serving him well. The building looked conservative on the outside, but the walls of Hal's apartment were full of edgy art, including what I would later learn was an early Mapplethorpe print. I hadn't been in the home of anyone so obviously wealthy since Bryce. But unlike Bryce, Hal had grown up in Queens—the Jersey of the boroughs!—and made his money himself.

When we climbed into bed together, I fully intended to take a two-hour nap and call in sick around six-thirty; but Hal and I crashed hard, and I didn't wake up until eleven. By the time I called my school, I learned that Peter had alarmed everyone with concerns for my safety, and that, in a manner eerily reminiscent of Art, he'd contacted my parents.

When I called my mother, she said, "Your father was beside himself, but I knew you were fine." She hung up just as Hal began to go down on me. His timing, like his stamina, was impressive.

12

We arrived at the home of the "Miller's," they of the dubious apostrophe, at 7:10—a compromise, as Hubby wanted to arrive on time and I refused to send such a message. In their foyer was a lacquered wooden sign, *Mr. and Mrs.* carved into it in the kind of cloyingly perfect script that would give a second-grade teacher a hard-on. There were lots of signs like that: *Another day in paradise* over a sunset background; *You light up my life*, a phrase even Debby Boone must find intolerable by now; others that simply named emotional states: *Gratitude, Serenity, Happiness.* I made a quick gagging pantomime in Hubby's direction as "Mrs." led us to the lanai, where "Mr." was waiting with a pitcher of "G & T's."

"So good to finally meet you!" he said, with an earnestness that reminded me a little of my father. Mrs. handed us our drinks and motioned to our seats. The "soft music" was Fleetwood Mac's *Rumours*, the white noise of the 1970s.

"So where are you from?" Mrs. asked, looking me and Hubby up and down. Her cheekbones and demeanor suggested she'd once turned heads.

"All over," Hubby said. "We've explored every corner of this country." I was certain that only I could hear how practiced his response was.

"Restless spirits, eh?" Mr. asked. "We're more homebodies ourselves."

Mrs. nodded. "So where are you from originally?" She looked right at me.

I didn't blink. "We met in San Francisco during the Summer of Love." It was our fallback response in such situations, colorful enough to steer the topic away from our origins.

"That must have been something!" Mr. said, chuckling a bit. "I was already working by then. Though Patsy here—she was just about the right age."

"I had my own Summer of Love in Michigan," she said, winking at me like we were girlfriends.

I took a long swig of my too-weak drink and began mentally enumerating the ways in which I detested this woman.

"So you're both from Michigan?" Hubby asked.

"Born and bred," Mr. said. "I'm a little older than Patsy. In fact, she was my student—though we didn't get together until decades later."

This immediately pricked my antennae, as it was inconsistent with what they'd told Hubby when they first moved in.

"Sweetie, I thought you said they were both guidance counselors," I said to Hubby in a sugary voice.

"We were both guidance counselors when we retired," Mrs. replied smoothly. "But Gary started out as a high school algebra teacher."

To my mind, her explanation was a little too rehearsed. Was it possible they weren't who they claimed to be? Maintaining our exiled lifestyle required a certain hypervigilance, so I decided to do a little digging.

"Could you tell me where your restroom is?" I asked, catching Hubby's eye in such a way, as I headed back into the house, that I could tell he knew exactly what I was up to.

After the high of Valentine's night with Hal at Studio, going home the next afternoon and facing my parents—my father's questions about where I'd been all night, his wounded puppy eyes, my mother's infuriating scowl—and then to work the following day was a decided let-down. Dick Singer left a note in my box to come see him during my free period; I'd anticipated this and wore a professional but sexy black skirt and stockings that showcased my legs, with a red silk blouse that trumpeted other assets. I studiously avoided the teachers' lounge, hoping I could steer clear of Peter, but he accosted me outside the cafeteria.

"What happened yesterday?" he asked. "Are you okay?"

What was it with these men who couldn't take no for an answer? If a man had ever ditched out on me during a date—not that *that* would ever happen!—I'd understand it to mean that we were through.

"I'm fine," I said.

"Can we go somewhere and talk?"

I was quiet for a moment as I made a mental calculation. If I played this right, I could have four lovers rather than three, as Hal had taken my number—of course he had!—and promised to call. But Peter was so dull, and honestly, juggling three men was already cutting into both my poetry-writing time and my nights at Studio. *Just a couple of teachers from Jersey.* Every instinct cried out: Run, Lynda! Run!

"There's nothing to talk about, Peter. We're just too different."

Peter looked puzzled. "You're breaking up with me? After one disagreement?"

In that moment, I felt a spark of empathy for Peter. I was so good at putting on the brave face, appearing to have a grand time to spare the feelings of the appallingly average. Of course poor Peter was confused.

"You're a nice guy," I said. It was honest, and he had no way of knowing that it was an insult. "But I'm just not ready to settle down right now."

"Settle down?" He shook his head. "Where did you go when you left the restaurant? Where were you yesterday?"

Breaking up with #3s was so tedious: they always wanted explanations, specifics.

"Does it matter?" I asked.

"Yes."

"I went to Studio."

He looked puzzled. "Studio?"

I realized, then, that I'd never even mentioned Studio to Peter. He knew so very little about me.

"54," I said. "I'm a regular there."

I could see him recalibrating his mental image of me. "So what was this, Lynda?" His lips quivered slightly; he looked like he might cry, poor thing. I really did break some hearts in my day!

"It was fun," I said.

He was quiet for a few moments. I watched a series of emotions play across his face and imagined him calculating the price tag of all he'd spent on me in those months: that very expensive dinner at Lutèce, and numerous less costly meals at a variety of establishments up and down the Jersey Shore; the inane bottle of Charlie perfume he'd given me for Christmas—and which I'd tucked in a drawer to re-gift to one of the Dim Bulbs' wives—with apparent obliviousness to the fact that I already had a much more sophisticated signature scent, Yves Saint-Laurent's Opium. A pair of garnet earrings so sensible, so unsexy that he might as well have picked them out for my mother. The evidence was mounting that I was making the right decision in extricating myself from his clutches.

The final emotion that settled on his face was, predictably, anger. So many of my ex-lovers landed there in the end. Think what you will of me, but I promised these men nothing. If they were left angry or wounded, the pain was of their own making.

"Are you seeing someone else?" he asked, an incredulousness in his voice that suggested it was the first time the possibility had occurred to him. Poor Peter. How could he *not* know that I had other lovers?

"The thing is, Peter, I don't plan to stay in Jersey. I lived in The City for years and I'm hoping to get back there soon. I didn't mean to hurt you."

One might notice that I did not utter those two banal words, "I'm sorry"—a phrase that, I'm proud to say, has never, in my sixty-seven years on this planet, passed my lips. I could provide a lengthy treatise as to the origins of my refusal to apologize, how my harried mother offered up constant *mea culpas* in response to the most minor indiscretions—putting too much salt in the manicotti filling, ironing a slight scorch mark into my father's favorite shirt—but in the end, it came down to the simple fact that apologizing was beneath me.

Peter just stood there, his eyes searching mine.

"I have to go, Peter," I said, and touched his cheek lightly before I left, a gesture I'd seen in films and thought looked lovely, but which seemed to harden something in the poor man's bewildered eyes.

Relieved to have that over with, I went straight to Dick Singer's office to talk through my absence of the previous day. Patti ushered me in with a tilt of her head and a pop of her bubble gum.

"That's a gorgeous blouse, hon," she said.

"Thanks, Patti. Love the new highlights!" I motioned toward the ineptly applied stripes of pale blond in her frothy brown bolus of hair. I always let my accent slip back to my Jersey roots when dealing with people like Patti; one never knew when they might prove themselves useful.

Dick looked up as I entered his office. I slowed my pace, allowing him to take it all in: the miles of silky leg, the classic pumps. No one could say my outfit wasn't professional, but it also screamed, "Fuck me!"

"Lynda, sit down," Dick said. He had his stern face on, but I could tell my outfit was registering somewhere in his reptile brain.

"Dick, I'm so sorry about yesterday." I treaded carefully since I wasn't sure how much he knew or didn't know.

"I recognize that unforeseen circumstances sometimes arise," Dick said. "But we need you to call in early so we can get a substitute."

"I understand. It won't happen again, Dick."

He nodded. "Sometimes I think it would be best to have a policy against personal relationships among staff. To avoid situations like this."

"Like this?"

"I assume this was a lover's quarrel, yes? You and Peter?"

What on earth had Peter told him? Had he blabbed my business all over school?

"It sounds to me like Peter has exaggerated our relationship."

Dick raised his eyebrows slightly. "You weren't on a date in The City?" he asked. "You didn't storm away from dinner?"

I sighed. I had, but Dick made it sound so ordinary, a *Days of Our Lives* plot.

"At any rate, it's over," I said.

"That's good," Dick said. "I don't think you understand your power over men, Lynda."

I smiled with my chest and crossed my legs, watching as Dick melted. O Dick, I thought, I understand my power quite well.

"But I hope you know," he added, "that failing to call in again would lead to disciplinary action."

"Of course," I said, though internally I seethed. How dare he talk to me like this? I decided the best approach would be to remind Dick of how indispensable I was.

"On the good news front," I said brightly, smoothing my skirt to draw Dick's attention back to my legs, "Aura Lockhart is doing very well! She seems to have made friends with Marisol Rodriguez, and with the two of them a unit, Jody and her friends have backed off the bullying."

"That's good news, Lynda," Dick said. He was quiet for a moment. "But I'm required, by the terms of your contract, to tell you that a letter of reprimand is going in your file."

A letter of reprimand! Was I supposed to shake in fear? Beg Dick not to? *Oh no, Principal Singer—anything but the letter!*

"Are we done here?' I asked.

"Yes," he said. "But remember, Lynda: I need to be able to rely on you."

"You can, Dick," I said, and stood in such a way that he'd get a good shot of my cleavage before I left his office.

I stayed late after school, tidying my classroom. This was mostly for appearance's sake—proving to Dick what a good little girl I could be—but also, I didn't want to face my parents until dinner time. I sat at my desk and opened my poetry notebook. Perhaps I could use this time for my art!

I began a poem called "A Jersey Shore of the Mind (after Lawrence Ferlinghetti)," amazed that I hadn't come up with such a brilliant premise earlier. My hand and pen flew across the page, and I was grateful, as always, for a visit from the Muse. As I gazed out the window, working on a rhyme—"tilt-a-whirl" and "legs unfurl"?—I caught a glimpse of motion, and a girl's voice. At first I ignored it, but then I recognized the unmistakable, taunting whine of Jody Fromme.

"Stargirl," she caterwauled, "looking at the stars..."

"The stars, the stars," another voice warbled behind her.

I leapt from my desk and ran to the window in time to see Jody and Kathi, with Aura cornered in an alcove outside. Did those stupid girls even realize they were beneath my window? Jody held Aura's guitar case.

"Give it the fuck back," Aura said, lunging at Jody, who tossed the case to Kathi.

"You want it back?" Jody said. "Maybe we should play it first."

Kathi opened the case. "Ooh, fancy," she said, pulling the guitar out, running her hands over the lipstick pick-ups.

Aura made a grab for the guitar; Jody threw the case at her.

"I think it needs a tune-up," Jody said, taking the guitar from Kathi. I assumed she meant "tuning." But then I heard a string whine in protest. It soon was clear she was trying to rip the strings from the guitar.

"Maybe you should smash it, like Pete Townshend," Kathi said.

I watched with rapt attention, fascinated to see how this would all play out. Are you wondering why I had not yet stepped in? Was it that I thought Aura needed to learn self-reliance, to stand up for herself in this unjust world, and was I, in my way, mothering her by refusing to leap to her rescue yet again? Or was I still miffed about her inattention at my poetry reading, for the way she and Johnny were shutting me out? Did I, perhaps, want her to experience what it would be like at Keyhole Junior High School without Ms. Boyle's frequent interventions? I will leave it for you to decide.

Jody lifted the guitar in the air, ready to smack it against the side of the brick building, when Aura leapt on top of her. What a thrill to see! She knocked Jody to the ground and the guitar flew from her hands. But then, Jody ended up on top of Aura, punching at her, with Kathi pulling Aura's hair.

And then it hit me: if word of this incident got back to Dick Singer, I'd look like a fool, having just told him that I'd solved the Jody Fromme problem.

"Stop it, Jody," I screamed out the window. All three girls looked up.

There was no way that little cunt was going to make me a liar.

If I'd run out of the classroom and around the building, they would have been gone by the time I got there. So, in a move as quick and smooth as any of Mick Jagger's, I swung the window open wide and dropped through it, snagging my pantyhose on the brick façade as I hit the ground. A brand-new pair.

And then Jody made a grave miscalculation.

She laughed at me.

"You vile little bitch," I said. My sudden anger was so intense that I left my body, watching from a distance as my hands grabbed Jody and slammed her into the side of the school.

"Ow!" she cried out.

"Oh, does that hurt?" I asked. I held her against the building as she tried to wriggle away.

"You can't act like this," she said, but the smirk was gone from her face. Her lips quivered a bit. Finally, Jody Fromme was afraid. "You're a teacher."

"I'm a teacher who's been pushed too far by you, you hideous cunt."

Kathi began to cry.

"If I ever—and I mean *ever*—see the two of you bothering Aura again, I will *fuck you up*. Do you understand me?" I kept my voice low, but the anger unmistakable.

"Yes," said Kathi as she sniffled in the corner.

I let Jody go.

"You'll get in trouble for this," she said.

"Oh really, will I? It's your word against mine."

"Two of us," Jody said.

Aura then got up off the ground and stood beside me. She didn't say anything, but clearly implied it: two against two. I grabbed Jody by the shoulders and positioned my face inches from hers.

"I don't give a shit about this job," I said. "If you go to the principal, if you give me any grief at all, or if you ever bother Aura again, I will *fuck you up*. Do you doubt me?"

"N-no," Jody said, surrender in her eyes. How easily a weak bully crumbles!

"You're going to apologize to me now," I said. "And to Aura."

"I'm sorry, Ms. Boyle," Jody said, a controlled panic in her voice. "Sorry, Aura."

"Me too," Kathi said quickly.

"Just leave me the fuck alone," Aura said.

Jody and Kathi nodded. I stepped aside, and the two girls quickly ran off.

"Are you okay?" I asked Aura. Whatever her treachery, she was still a part of Augustus and, by extension, a part of me.

"Yeah." She inspected the guitar. "She only broke one string—not too bad." Aura looked up at me. "Holy shit, you really lost it with her!" It was the friendliest, most open she'd been with me since New Year's.

"A petty bully like that," I said to Aura, "doesn't deserve to have any kind of power over you." Aura used that very phrase, "petty bully," in her song "Eighth Grade," a track that, fifteen years after it was first released, became an anthem for disaffected adolescent girls when it was featured in a popular teen film soundtrack. Has Aura given me any songwriting credit, any royalties? The answer is an unbearable shock of a "No."

She nodded and put her guitar back in its case. "Thanks. For everything."

"You're welcome," I said. "And since I may have gone a little too far, it might be best if you didn't tell anyone what happened."

"Sure," she said, though she gave me an appraising look I couldn't quite read.

Aura headed off, the message spelled out on her jacket that day—"REALITY SO HARD"—altered by the scuffle, letters missing, so that it looked more like "LIT SHARD."

I pondered the poetics of the revised phrase as I rounded the corner of the alcove to go back into the school, and ran smack into Bobby Craig.

"Hi, Ms. Boyle," he said, his perpetual shit-eating grin dialed up to eleven. "That was fierce."

"What was fierce?" I gave him my best poker face.

"What you just did," he said.

"I'm not sure what you mean." Could Bobby have witnessed what just happened? If so, he'd purposefully hidden himself.

"Calling a student a bitch and a cunt," he said. "That's probably not allowed, is it?"

I decided to just lay my cards on the table. "Probably not."

"If I go to Principal Singer with Jody and Kathi, that's three against two."

I couldn't figure out Bobby's angle, but I decided to lean into his obvious crush on me.

"Why would you want to get me in trouble, Bobby?" I asked, my voice soft, my breasts pointed in his direction.

"I don't want to," he said. "I just want a kiss."

"A kiss?" Did this fourteen-year-old boy think he could blackmail me?

"Just a little kiss."

Fine, I thought—if his silence could be bought for a kiss, I'd play along. I pecked him on the cheek.

"On the lips," he said. "With tongue."

I was, in all honesty, disappointed in Bobby in that moment. I'd thought he was shrewd enough to ask for, at the very least, a blow job. A kiss with tongue—was that the sad limit of his prepubescent imagination?

I sighed. "Fine," I said. "But not here."

"Where?"

"Inside. Come with me."

There is one thing I've done in my life, and only one, that I think back on and wish I'd done differently. That I could have acted thoughtfully, rather than on instinct. I'll get to that later. The kiss with Bobby? That was nothing. In fact, I considered it a public service to all the girls, the women, he would kiss throughout his life. I taught Bobby a few basic techniques that afternoon, enlightening him that cramming his tongue down a girl's throat was not at all erotic.

I was a gifted teacher, clearly, in a variety of subjects.

A couple of years ago, I searched for Bobby on Facebook and saw that he was a lawyer, still living in Keyhole, married to a younger woman I suspect was a second or third wife. They had a kindergarten-age child, despite the fact that Bobby was in his mid-fifties. The look on his wife's face in their profile photo suggested that she was more than satisfied with her sex life—I can tell, I can always tell—and I, Lynda Boyle, was proud to have played a role in her happiness.

13

Did "The Miller's" have much of a sex life? The pedestrian décor of their house—knickknacks on the tables, cluttered walls, shelves full of cutesy crap—suggested a woman who spent too much time shopping and not nearly enough in the *boudoir.* It was overwhelming, nearly every surface covered, and for all the grief I used to give my mother over her tacky tchotchkes, our modest home in Keyhole was Soho chic compared to this bric-a-brac shack.

As I headed to "the little girls' room," as Mrs. had cloyingly called it, I took in horrors I should never have had to see: Hummels, Precious Moments figurines, a credenza full of Beanie Babies. The wall hangings were equally mundane, likely acquired at a Hobby Lobby or some other nadir of commerce. Just as my antennae twitched at the possibility this house was a little too humdrum, that perhaps "The Miller's" were constructs created by one of the organizations that sought to deprive Hubby and I of our liberty, if not our lives, I found the wall of photographs.

Black-and-white school pictures of Mr., and then Mrs., were displayed in chronological order. A few gaps appeared in the class years, but it was remarkable that both of these people had preserved so many, for all those decades. There's a lid for every pot, my mother used to say, and perhaps there was, for these two had clearly had at least two decades of marital bliss: Mrs. rocked a mid-to-late nineties vest and hat ensemble in one photo, and another, of the two of them flanking Minnie Mouse, was embossed "Disney World Memories 2000." It was all as middle American as Velveeta until I spotted a photo that very nearly made me gasp out loud.

There, just a few frames beyond Mrs.'s last high school yearbook photo—her ironed hair and eyeliner suggesting the late 1960s or early 1970s, meaning that she and I were about the same age (though of course I looked much younger)—was a photo of Mrs., in bell bottoms, a midriff-bearing top and giant peace sign earrings. Standing with his arm around her was—could it really be? Yes, it most definitely was: a young Johnny Engel.

They were on a city street—Detroit?—with throngs of people

around them, likely outside a club. Johnny's hair was shorter than when I first met him, though not short enough to mark him as a square. This was probably during his auto worker days, and he'd found a happy medium length between the assembly line and gigging. I removed the photo from the wall to study it—how could I not?—but just then I heard footsteps coming from the lanai and so I quickly returned the photo to its spot, sprinted to the bathroom, closed the door and flushed the toilet so that anyone who'd come to investigate would think I'd just been taking a particularly long and hard *merde*.

I can't speak to what Johnny's musical performances were like back in Detroit, but I can tell you about Glow Worm's first show at the Galaxy—the one that Aura referenced in her Rock Hall of Fame speech.

The Galaxy had an eighteen-or-over age policy for nighttime shows, as did most venues back then, and I was certain I could make Aura up to look old enough. Denny provided assistance in the form of a borrowed ID from a girl in his dorm, as well as a cover story for the Martyr.

I was certain that his helpfulness was partly a ruse to come with us. I'd been avoiding Denny for a couple of weeks, since our Valentine's Day tryst, trying to cool him off a bit. Free of Peter, I wanted to redouble my efforts toward Johnny—using Hal as an entertaining diversion when needed.

Aura came over to my house around seven, and we began the transformation. I'd bought her an outfit that I thought might help make her look older: Calvin Klein jeans, a top in a sparkling electric blue to set off her eyes, the Candie's shoes all the high school girls wore. I suspected she'd protest at first, thinking it not rock or punk enough; but I had an eye for fashion (in a different life, I might have been a designer of haute couture) and I felt certain that once she tried it on, she'd appreciate the transformation.

"I don't hate it as much as I thought I would," she said, turning in front of my bedroom mirror and taking herself in. I chose to brush off her ingratitude.

"Wait until I do your makeup and hair, Aura," I said. "You'll be fighting off guys Johnny's age."

Aura let out a skeptical snort but turned herself over to me. The trick in such a transformation was a light touch with the makeup: just enough to bring out her features, but not so much that she'd look like a little girl playing dress up. I used my mother's electric rollers on Aura the same way I used them before dates or dancing—to add body rather than curl. When I was finished, Aura could easily pass for eighteen—and a pretty eighteen-year-old at that. Even I was impressed by my own skills.

"This doesn't look like me," Aura said.

"It's you," I said. "Just a better version of you."

"Better?" she asked, the scowl that would become her trademark playing across her face.

"More glamorous," I said. "Which is always better." I pressed a tissue between her lips to blot her lipstick.

She looked at me, then back in the mirror, lips pursed in the kind of sour expression my mother called "pulling a puss."

"I guess it's useful for tonight," she said.

I chose not to immediately respond. I'd just given Aura the keys to a life of lust and attention, a gateway to the adult world—and she'd showed me not an ounce of appreciation for such a profound gift. Perhaps this comes as no surprise, familiar as you must be with the adult Aura's feminist ethos, but I'll admit, I was—am—still puzzled. After she became famous, Aura talked in interviews about using her songs to "deconstruct the male gaze"—clearly a smokescreen for a woman who's not confident in her own attractiveness. Being seen, admired, *gazed* upon is what makes life bearable!

Her lack of gratitude was, frankly, shocking. I had bought her an outfit with my own money, spent an evening transforming her into a dewy beauty out of the goodness of my heart. Does she remember any of that, now?

"Well, I certainly aim to be *useful*," I said, and the look on her face told me she'd registered my sarcasm. "I'll just get dressed myself and we'll be off."

Aura and I were surprised to find a line at the door; how had word gotten out about Glow Worm before their first gig? She gained entrance easily, the bouncer's eyes barely leaving her breasts, outstanding as they were in that top I'd bought her—until, of course, he got a look at mine.

"That guy was a creep," she said once we were inside.

"Who cares?" I asked. "You're here! Oh, Aura, there's a whole world of nightlife for you to explore."

She shrugged, but I could tell as she looked around that she was secretly pleased, to be out in the adult world, mingling with the other creatures of the night.

I sidled up to the bar, Aura behind me. "Want anything?" I asked.

"You mean like alcohol?"

"They think you're over eighteen," I whispered. Surely you remember what it was like back then, Jann, before that group of Puritanical *hausfraus*, terrified their precious babies might drink and drive, caused a mass hysteria that changed the law of the land in the 1980s.

"I—um—what do you think?" She sounded, for once, like the fourteen-year-old she was.

"Have you ever had a drink before?"

She nodded. "Wine with my parents. And beer with Denny."

"Rum and coke, maybe?" I asked. "Or something fruity—a daiquiri?"

"Yeah, I'll try a daiquiri."

With that, I caught the bartender's eye. "Two strawberry daiquiris," I said, and soon, Aura and I had fought our way to the front of the stage and were sipping our drinks, side by side, chatting like friends rather than teacher and student, waiting for the band.

We waved to Lars as we saw him setting up the drum kit, and he squatted down at the foot of the stage.

"Aura, you're not drinking, are you?" he asked.

She shrugged. Lars looked at me.

"It's mostly fruit," I said. "Just one."

He raised an eyebrow. "Take it easy," he said to us both, and disappeared backstage.

At that moment, I felt hands on my shoulders. Denny.

I sighed. I'd known he planned to come, but I was secretly hoping he'd flake out. I'd wanted to use this night to rekindle things with Johnny. Denny's presence here was a complication.

"Hi," I said, removing his hands from my shoulders.

"This daiquiri rocks," Aura said to no one in particular.

As the crowd pushed in on us, Denny slipped his hand into my jeans pocket, massaging my ass. There wasn't much I could do but enjoy it.

There was a band before Glow Worm, an horrific spectacle called Red Tide—an apt name, given that the band members did not appear to be much more evolved than algae. Denny made several runs to the bar for us as we waited for Glow Worm. He later denied it, but I am certain I instructed him to order virgin daiquiris for Aura, grown-up drinks for the two of us. Rest assured I would not have let Aura drink four daiquiris in a row had I known they all contained alcohol—even given my profound disappointment at her lack of gratitude for all I'd done that evening.

Finally, the Red Tide receded and Glow Worm took the stage.

Was it as obvious to me as Aura later claimed it was to her, in that tacky little Jersey Shore bar, that Johnny's band would go on to make one of the most influential albums of all time?

No, it was not.

They had sounded so much better to me at Mike's party—had it been the sweet deception of cocaine's rose-colored glasses? O, the wallowing melancholy my ears absorbed at the Galaxy that night! Even some of the more upbeat, danceable songs were a bit of a bummer. I will never understand why such negativity is attractive to so many critics and fans when so much more exuberant, joyous music is out there. Melancholy is, in my experience, a temporary state caused by the absence of a plan; wallowing is a choice, and it's one that I, Lynda Boyle, shall never make.

But then there was Johnny's physical presence: his glorious mane of hair, those sexy hips, that mantle of feathers. I knew *he* would become famous. Looking around that night, I had the feeling the entire audience had been put under a spell by Johnny. All eyes were focused on the stage. It was so quiet between songs that you could hear the bartender ringing up a customer, the blender whirring. Aura and Denny both looked like they were in a trance.

At Studio, celebrities and the non-famous danced side by side; there was camaraderie rather than idolatry. I'd been given makeup tips by Francesco Scavullo, shared lines of coke with a Hemingway, discussed Ibi*th*a with Bianca Jagger (and I'll admit, I faked my way through that conversation). In short, I'd hobnobbed with superstars and never seen this kind of naked worship.

It was puzzling, to say the least. But I chalked it up to Johnny's charisma.

Halfway through the show, I felt antsy in the crowd, frustrated with the close quarters and the grungy Galaxy regulars. I fought my way through the horde, to the bathroom. There, I sat on the toilet, wondering what my night might have been like if I'd been at Studio. *Snap out of it, Lynda,* I told myself. *Eyes on the prize.* And that prize was Johnny.

It took me some time to get back to the front of the stage. When I finally reached Aura and Denny, the band was gone, the audience clamoring for an encore. Denny was holding Aura up, and when I looked at her face, I realized she was wasted.

"They were amaaaaazing!" she slurred with a sloppy grin.

"Denny, how much did she have to drink?" I asked.

Denny shrugged.

Glow Worm came back out for one more song, a cover of Queen's "'39," a song I knew Aura loved. It sounded different somehow; Johnny had made it his own.

As the band left the stage, Johnny motioned to us, and we made our way to the backstage door. Soon, he poked his head out and waved us in.

"Oh my god, I'm *backstage*!" Aura cried, her disaffected bravado suppressed by the rum.

It was actually a tiny green room adjacent to the stage, as dingy and graffitied as the bathrooms at CBGB. Johnny studied Aura for a moment.

"Is she drunk?" he asked me and Denny.

I looked at Denny. "I told you to get her virgin daiquiris!"

"You did not," Denny said.

"Yes, I did."

Lars studied me but remained silent.

Aura began to spin around in circles like a three-year-old.

"That's a really bad idea," Johnny said, stopping her in mid-spin and nearly toppling her off her Candie's heels.

Lars walked up with a glass of water from the bar. "Drink this, Aura."

I saw a vacant chair. "Why don't you sit down?" I steered her over.

"I'm fine!" Aura exclaimed after downing the water. "You guys were incredible!" Her face was flushed with excitement and rum.

"Did you even hear any of it?" Johnny laughed.

"I heard evvvvverything! That bridge on 'Landscape with Rain'—I need to learn that. And 'Oblivion' sounded so, so good. And "39'! Oh, my beloved "39'!"

I'll give Aura this much: the girl had managed to register every nuance of the show while drunk on her first daiquiris. I was impressed.

Mike popped out from a small alcove off the green room. "Let's pack up," he said. "We can go back to my place and unload first, then maybe get a drink to celebrate?"

Denny helped the guys carry their gear out; Aura and I followed. Out in the parking lot, she was starting to seem more coherent, less drunk.

"Did you have fun tonight?" I asked.

"It was the best night of my life," she said dreamily.

Let me repeat that: I gave Aura Lockhart the best night of her life when she was fourteen—and still she shuns me. And people say *my* generation was self-involved! That's Gen X for you—steeped in irony and devoid of gratitude.

As Johnny brought the last amp out, I said to him, "Should we meet you over at Mike's?"

But before he could answer, Aura let out a little wordless sound, and then, mere seconds later, unleashed an impressively forceful stream of strawberry-red vomit. Johnny steered her to a weeded area next to the parking lot, where he held her hair as she vomited some more.

"Shit," Denny said.

"Shit?" Johnny looked up, Aura still vomiting. "What's wrong with you? Why did you let her drink this much?" He glanced over at me. "Both of you."

"I didn't buy her the drinks," I said. "Denny did."

"Well, you're the fucking grown-up. You should have stopped this. She's fourteen, Lynda."

Now I was pissed—how dare Johnny blame me! "You think I don't know that? She's my student! I never should have taken her here. I was just trying to do something nice for her."

Johnny was quiet for a moment. "I know you were," he said, "but this is a fucking disaster. How are we going to take her home?"

"I'm fine!" Aura squealed, wiping her mouth on the sleeve of her electric blue top.

"You are *not* fine," Johnny said.

At this point, the rest of the band had gathered around.

"Lynda, can we bring her back to your place to get cleaned up?" Johnny asked.

Before Denny, I would have said yes. But my mother had become so vigilant since he'd started trying to sneak in at night; the slightest noise roused her.

"Not a good idea," I said. "Mike, can we bring her back to your place for a while?"

"No way," Mike said. "No way I'm having a drunk underage girl at my house."

Johnny was quiet for a moment. "We'll take her back to New York," he said. "But we need a cover story so she can sleep over."

"I can handle that," Denny said, and he headed over to the pay phone on the wall outside the Galaxy.

"Is your car here?" I asked Johnny. He shook his head no.

"I can drive us all into The City," I said, and I helped him get Aura into the backseat of my car. By the time we got her settled, Denny had returned. "Done," he said. "Can I bum a ride with you?" Johnny opened the door for him, and soon I was driving us all up the Parkway.

Sometime in the late 1980s, a decade after my husband and I had settled into a hellscape state as devoid of culture as the one in which we now reside, but without even the crude pleasures of a nearby ocean, we were able to make a weekend trip to the nearest large city—sadly, two hours away from where we lived. This "city" had as much in common with The City, *my* City, as one of my sisters-in-law, or perhaps my mother, had in common with me—but still, I was grateful for the change of scenery. While there, Hubby and I went to a sad little disco full of crispy-fried, middle-aged swingers. They were white, or at least had started out that way, but looked melanoma-brown, and a decade older than they most likely were.

Yet in the midst of this was a fairly attractive couple who took a fancy to me and my hubby. The man had sandy blond hair, skin that looked tanned but not burnt to carbon. He was a weed dealer who also traded in turquoise artifacts—supposedly Native American, likely fake. His wife was a redhead with fair, pale skin. After we danced with them for a few songs, they told us they were interested in swinging; what this meant, of course, was that he wanted to sleep with me, and he'd convinced his wife to go along with it. My husband and I decamped to talk it over. We both agreed it could be fun, so we went to their place, smoked a little grass, and swapped partners.

I tell this story now not because the guy was an especially good lay (I don't even remember his penis, let alone his name) or because it caused problems in my marriage; it was simply something we tried. My husband has always been understanding about my plethora of male admirers. He adores me but recognizes that a caged bird cannot sing (despite Maya Angelou's assertion to the contrary).

If only Denny and Johnny had been more like my husband, we might have had fun that night at Johnny's. Aura was asleep the second she hit the backseat of the car; Johnny carried her into his apartment and put her to bed on his pull-out. Given the size of his studio, a three-way with Johnny and Denny would have been tricky, but I thought the bathroom might have worked.

Yet there was no way I could communicate to them what the night could be. Denny wanted me, but he wanted me exclusively; Johnny was busy taking care of Aura, who loved him in a way he did not love her. The evening ended with Aura and I asleep on Johnny's bed, Johnny and Denny wrapped in blankets on the floor. No one satisfied, and no one sleeping soundly except for a semi-comatose Aura. Who *did* Johnny love? I wouldn't rest until I understood the mystery that kept him at arm's length from me.

14

Forty-one years later, I had another mystery to solve: that of the connection between "Mrs." and Johnny. I emerged from the "little girls' room" to find her hovering nearby, feigning interest in the placement of one of her Beanie Babies.

"Ah, there you are," she said.

"Burritos for lunch," I said, with a wave of my hand and a calculated little laugh. "Don't go in there." Disarm and deflect; what was once simply a natural talent has become a way of life.

"Oof, I don't touch that Mexican food. Too spicy for me."

I suppressed a smirk as I walked over to the wall of photos. Getting her to talk about Johnny would require a modicum of craftiness.

"I love these old high school photos," I said.

"Well, they certainly date me!" Mrs. let out a forced laugh. "But—we're about the same age, right?"

I shook my head. "I graduated in '82." In truth, that was Aura's year.

"Really? I hope I haven't offended you," she said, though she didn't sound the least bit concerned.

"Not at all." I'd only have been offended if I actually looked my age—and I unequivocally do not.

"Whew!" she said, and pantomimed wiping sweat from her forehead. Despite that community-theatre-level performance, she scrutinized my face like she'd seen it on a wanted poster.

Time to steer the conversation to Johnny. "I love your outfit here," I said, pointing to the photo of her and my once-beloved. "Was that your high school boyfriend?"

"High school and a couple of years after. My first love. Johnny."

"You made a cute couple," I said, playing it cool.

"Actually, you might have heard of him. Johnny Engel? He was just inducted into the Rock & Roll Hall of Fame."

I shook my head, working hard to keep my teeth from gnashing. "Was he in a band I might know?"

"Well, when we were together he had a group called the Detroit

Dazzle. But then he moved to New York and started Glow Worm. After that, he had a number of solo albums. Maybe I'm biased, but I love everything he does."

I smiled. "So you…parted amicably?"

"Oh yeah. He's a sweet guy." She was quiet for a moment. "I was a little sad that he didn't ask me to move to New York with him. I would have gone."

I nodded, an encouragement for her to keep talking.

"But honestly, I don't think I would have liked living there. I mean… have you ever been?" Her eyes trained on me, hawk-like.

"To New York? I've passed through on my way to New England."

"Never spent any time there?"

I shook my head, awaiting her next move.

"Oh. It's just…I visited Johnny there once, after he first moved. It wasn't for me, but Johnny fit right in. You have that kind of New York energy too."

Was that a compliment or a trap? I decided to change the subject.

"I've never known anyone who dated a real rock star," I gushed. "What was he like?" I was looking for the tell, the slip-up, anything that would help me analyze whether her acquaintance with Johnny and recent move next door to us was a bizarre coincidence or something more ominous.

"Like I said, he was sweet. Very talented. Kind of remote, though—in all the years we were a couple I never felt I really knew him. Certainly not the way I know Gary."

O, the restraint it took for me to refrain from remarking that knowing Gary was like knowing a Labrador Retriever.

"Maybe it's a rock star thing." I smiled.

"What kind of music do you like?" Mrs. asked.

"Country, mostly. And contemporary Christian."

"Really?" she asked, extending the long *e* in a tone of disbelief. "I never would have pegged you two as being devout."

"God moves in mysterious ways," I said with a smile, and headed back to the lanai so Hubby and I could begin the extrication process and debrief each other at home.

The Monday after that Glow Worm show, the teacher's lounge was abuzz with a debriefing all its own: Dan Wykoski had been suspended.

The previous Friday, he'd walked over to the high school on his free period and scored weed from a dealer who turned out to be an undercover cop. When I heard how it happened a peal of laughter escaped me; my fellow teachers threw me, as we say today, serious shade.

"Oh, come on," I said. "That level of—*recklessness* (I had wanted to say 'stupidity') is funny."

"He'll probably be fired, and he might go to prison," Carla Spagnola said. "How is that funny?"

"Lynda doesn't possess the human emotions that most of us do," Peter said. "She's devoid of empathy."

I looked around at the women in the room, hoping for some sort of female solidarity, but not one of those bitches came to my defense. Dealing with jealous women has been one of my many crosses to bear in life.

"So every woman who breaks up with you lacks human emotions?" I asked Peter. "That's pretty chauvinistic, isn't it?"

"Not every woman. Just you."

"I let you down as gently as I could, Peter," I said softly, conjuring a hint of a tear.

Old Mr. Murton looked up from his sad lunch of chicken-noodle-flavored Cup-A-Soup, fixing his gaze directly on Peter. "My good man," he said, "this is why work and romance should not mix."

"I'm sure you'll find your special someone soon, Peter," I said brightly, playing on Mr. Murton's sympathy. How magnanimous Lynda is in the face of Peter's inappropriate anger!

Peter gathered his things and headed for the door. "You're a sociopath," he said to me as he left the room.

While I appreciated the support of my ancient colleague, I'll admit I was slightly rattled by how everyone else had lined up against me. Clearly I needed to say something to sway opinion back in my favor.

"I didn't mean to laugh at Dan's predicament," I said. "I was just so shocked. What can we do for him?"

After a bit of discussion, we agreed to take up a collection to help Dan pay for a lawyer. Carla suggested we all visit him now that he was out on bail. With that, Mr. Murton cleared his throat.

"None of you should be seen at his home," he said. "Discretion, my young friends. Discretion."

The room was quiet for a moment as we all took Mr. Murton's warning to heart. At least half of the teachers in that lounge had once identified themselves as part of the counterculture. But now, they were in their thirties, had mortgages, kids. I was certain most of them thought pot should be legal, and that Dan should never have been arrested. They weighed this against the husband, the wife, those bills. Then they began, silently, to throw some cash in a pile; I was more than happy to contribute a sawbuck to cement my status in their good graces. It was decided we'd mail the cash to Dan with an encouraging card signed "from the gang." No signatures.

Back at my parents' house a few nights later, Cousin Tony joined us for dinner. He and his wife were separated, my mother told me before he arrived, and she was hoping to cheer him up with her baked ziti.

I ignored much of the conversation when it focused on Keyhole gossip, my mother's favorite topic; who cared what went on in that dull little backwater? But then my father asked Tony if the police department was working on any interesting cases.

"Well, there's some crazy stuff going on at Keyhole Junior High," he said, looking at me.

"Crazy stuff?" I asked.

"You must have heard about one of your fellow teachers getting arrested for buying drugs," Tony said.

"What?" my mother exclaimed, with a level of alarm that suggested she'd just heard the world would end in the next hour. "One of the *teachers* was doing *drugs*?"

"The science teacher got busted for buying pot," I said.

"*Busted*?" my mother repeated. "You sound like a hippie, Lynda."

I rolled my eyes. "Hippies barely exist anymore, Mother." She was so pathetically out of touch. It was nearly 1980!

"I know people your age don't think marijuana is dangerous," Tony said, "but it's a controlled substance for a reason."

"It's a gateway drug," my father said.

"A gateway to what, Daddy?" I asked, my eyes wide with faux innocence.

"A needle in your arm!" he exclaimed, with such ferocity that I was sorry I'd teased him.

"Lynda, did you know that this other teacher was doing drugs?" my mother asked.

There was only one right answer to that question. "Of course not. I really don't know Dan well."

"There's a rumor," Tony said, lowering his voice conspiratorially, "that Dan isn't the only teacher in that school who does drugs."

Now all three sets of eyes were on me.

"I don't socialize with anyone who works there," I said, which was the truth. "The only teacher I know at all is Peter, and he's as straight as they come." Peter's #3-ness came in handy just then.

"That's true," my mother said. "I can't imagine Peter doing drugs."

"Well, you never know about people," my father said.

I felt grateful just then that I'd never gone out to Dan's van to toke with the other teachers. It's not that I had any compunction about teaching under the influence; I just didn't like pot. Cocaine was my drug of choice, as I've already discussed, and no one else teaching at Keyhole Junior High had the money or savvy to get a hold of any.

"If you hear of anything, Lynda, give me a call at the station," Tony said.

I filed the exchange away like a Get-Out-of-Jail-Free card; something to use as leverage against Singer if the school situation got desperate.

"Sure, Tony," I said, and gave him a smile that I knew caused him to wish, deep down in his crotch, that we weren't related.

But later that night, as I sat in my room trying and failing to write a new poem, I felt an overwhelming sense of unease. It was a Friday night in early March, and I, a nubile twenty-six-year-old, was home with my parents—who were watching the fucking *Rockford Files* in the next room. Spring was around the corner, but my love life had stalled to a near halt. There was Hal, who had called twice since I'd met him, but who was, quite simply, not Johnny; and Johnny himself, who never called, and who I hadn't slept with since Christmas. Denny seemed to have finally accepted that we were over, and while I didn't miss him, I missed all the sex. I was quite literally wasting the best years of my life in this Keyhole purgatory, and I knew I needed to do something to shake things up. I dialed Johnny's number.

"Ah, I'm not the only one spending a quiet night at home," I said coquettishly after he picked up.

"I'm heading out soon to see a band," he said. I couldn't quite read his tone.

"Anyone I've heard of?"

"Probably not."

He couldn't still be upset with me over Aura's daiquiri barf, could he? I decided to appeal to his rock star vanity.

"So, Johnny," I said, "I've been thinking about ways to get your band more exposure."

"Such as?"

What was with these monosyllabic responses? Could it be that he had another woman over there?

"We need to go back to Studio," I said. "We'll remind Steve he promised to have Glow Worm play there."

Johnny laughed. "We're not even close to being famous enough to play there. We only just landed our first gig at CBGB."

"You don't have to be famous if Steve likes you," I said.

"And we don't play disco music."

I laughed. "Johnny, they play lots of different kinds of music at Studio." This wasn't entirely true, but it was certainly less rigid than Johnny's rock clubs were. "Don't you think it's worth a shot?"

Johnny was quiet for a moment. "Why not?"

"Are you free tomorrow night?"

"I can be," he said after a pause.

I chose to ignore the cryptic nature of his response. "So it's a date?"

"Sure," he said, but there was uncertainty in his voice.

I'd told Johnny to dress like a rock star that night at Studio, and did he ever: his trademark eye glitter, skintight gold pants, a pink feather boa dressing up a black T-shirt. He looked more beautiful than ever; more importantly, his gold and pink set off my red sequin dress quite stunningly.

The crowd that night was even thicker than usual, and I had trouble getting the bouncer's attention. Steve finally emerged, peering out from behind the velvet rope. I took Johnny's hand, elbowing the commoners as I pulled him through the crowd.

"Steve!" I called out, but he didn't see me at first. Finally, I saw his eyes settle on Johnny, looking him up and down. He then motioned us to come in.

"Johnny, wasn't it?" Steve said. "So nice to see you back here."

"I can't believe you remember me," Johnny said.

"Would I ever forget a face like this?" He grabbed Johnny's face in his hands. "Lynda, would I ever forget a face like this?"

"Of course not!" I said.

He walked us down the hallway and to the bar, chatting all the while with Johnny. In the din of the club I couldn't hear what they were saying. I was frustrated, but also aware that my plan was working. Steve had taken a shine to Johnny, and it would be easy to get him some sort of show there. And then, in his gratitude, Johnny would finally realize that I was the woman for him.

But when we got to the bar, Hal was there. Hal! Of course he'd be there. I sorted through a variety of excuses for not having called him back as Steve whispered something to Johnny. Soon the two of them were off, Johnny looking back at me apologetically. I was left there with Hal and fixed a bright smile on him. As I started to launch into an improvised excuse—hospitalized mother!—he put his hand out.

"Lynda," he said, "you don't owe me an explanation. We only just met a few weeks ago. You're a knockout, and I expect you to have a rich social life. I'd just like to be part of it."

I believe I've mentioned that Hal wasn't the best-looking guy; he was uniformly average, though a great dresser. But in that moment, his confidence and maturity made my crotch damp with desire. Most of the guys I'd dated would have slinked away with their tails between their legs if they'd seen me walk in with another guy—especially one as gorgeous as Johnny.

"I'd love to see you again," I said, and I meant it.

"Want to dance?"

I nodded.

"A little rocket fuel first?"

We retreated to the bathroom, did a few lines, and soon, we were on the dance floor, shaking our groove things.

Johnny reappeared some time later. Hal and I were still dancing, at peak coke-fueled energy. Johnny joined us on the dance floor, his enthusiasm a sign that he'd done some lines of his own. If Johnny minded dancing with me and another guy, he didn't show it. Could I be so lucky as to have a three-way with Johnny and Hal? Studio had a magic that caused unlikely events to occur with frequency.

Hal and I took a break, Johnny joining us on a banquette. I introduced the two of them, filling Hal in on Johnny's band, and my hope that they could play at Studio.

"Did you talk to Steve about it yet?" Hal asked.

Johnny nodded. "He seems interested. But nothing definite, so maybe he's just like that with everyone."

"Well, not everyone," Hal said. "I think he's taken with you."

I was unsurprised, of course, that Steve would have a thing for Johnny. Whatever one's proclivities were in our daily lives, everyone—and I mean *everyone*!—was bi at Studio. I myself had once participated in a foursome up in the balcony that included two other women, most likely altering the course of their lives. My attraction was almost entirely to men, but could I get it on with a woman, given the right music and dance floor and drugs? Of course I could!

Johnny looked at me. "He took my number. I guess we'll see."

"We'll see Glow Worm down there, performing on that stage!" I cried.

With that, a good-looking guy with a mane of brown curls sidled up to Johnny. Clearly the pansexual magic of Studio was rubbing off on my strait-laced friend.

"Care for a dance?" the guy asked Johnny, who shot a quizzical look at me. He appeared to want to, though it was often so hard to read Johnny.

"Go," I said. "We'll be down there soon."

But Hal and I did more coke, and fooled around, and minutes stretched to hours. Finally, it was five a.m.; the guests were filing out, and, despite looking everywhere, I couldn't find Johnny. Hal asked me to come back to his place.

"I'd love to," I said brightly, but I'll admit to a slight pang of disappointment. Hal was a great guy, but that was supposed to have been my night with Johnny. Somehow, Johnny and I always seemed to lose each other.

15

Had our next-door neighbor really loved and lost Johnny too? Back at our house, I filled Hubby in on the photo, the conversation that ensued.

"I think it's a coincidence," he said. "Those two"—he gestured toward "The Miller's" house—"are just what they appear to be: dull and cornfed."

"It's an awfully big coincidence that Johnny's high school girlfriend would move in next door to us."

"Did he ever mention her?"

I shook my head. "He talked about the auto plant. His band. His family. But I never heard him mention a girlfriend back in Michigan."

Hubby poured two glasses of brandy, handed me one. "Maybe it meant more to her than it did to him."

I took a sip of my nightcap. "Maybe."

"They might have only dated briefly, and she turned it into some big romance after he got famous. Who knows, maybe she was a fan he posed for a photo with, and he didn't know her at all."

"Maybe she was recruited by someone looking for us, as a way to smoke us out."

Hubby was quiet for a moment. "How carefully did you look at the photo?"

I sat down at the kitchen table. "It was definitely Johnny. And definitely her."

Hubby took a seat next to me. "Could it have been photoshopped?"

I took another sip of brandy, letting it swirl in my mouth as I considered this. "I mean, anything's possible. If it was a fake, it wasn't obvious."

"You have a strong feeling about this one, doll?"

"Medium," I said. I'd developed a sixth sense for danger during our years in exile, and Hubby had learned to trust it. "She was trying to get me to talk more about myself. Whether that's because she's trying to figure out who we really are or because she's a lonely twat who's been bored beige by years with Gary, I'm on the fence."

Hubby chortled. "I guess we should investigate further," he said, finishing the brandy in his glass. "You know what that means."

"I do."

He kissed me goodnight on his way to our bedroom. I stayed up a little longer to plot the B&E I'd be committing at my first opportunity, and then I headed to bed, where my still-virile-after-all-these-years hubby was waiting up—so to speak!

Back at Hal's apartment after our night at Studio, I came twice amid an energetic variety of sexual positions—what Hal lacked in looks, he made up for in sheer enthusiasm. We crashed hard around eight a.m. and woke up mid-afternoon, exhausted and starving. I suggested we go to a diner, but he impressed me by cooking: bacon and eggs, with toast and jam, and it was *good.* I told him he'd make some fine woman a great husband one day; it was nothing more than a quip, but he seemed pleased.

Still, it weighed on me that I'd once again lost my shot with Johnny, and when I left Hal's place later that afternoon I decided to stop over at Johnny's before I headed home. Perhaps we could have a do-over. I could go to one of Johnny's rock clubs with him that night; sparks would, finally, fly. And if I was late teaching Monday morning, or missed work altogether? So be it!

I had to ring the bell twice before Johnny finally answered, and even then, he hesitated before buzzing me in. Upstairs, I understood his reluctance: that guy from Studio was just leaving Johnny's apartment.

"I'm Lynda," I said, sticking my hand out to shake. I saw no threat in this curly-maned man; if anything, Johnny's suddenly going bi was a testament to the magic of Studio.

"Clay," the guy said, pumping my hand unenthusiastically before letting it go. *I hope he was better than that in bed*, I thought.

He turned around and looked at Johnny. "Call me," he said, and then, after giving me a bitchy sideways glance, he kissed Johnny hard on the lips before heading down the stairs.

So dramatic, this Clay. Had he thought I hadn't gotten the picture? Please. Clay was probably still giving himself home perms back in Jersey when I was a regular at 12 West.

I walked into Johnny's apartment and fixed him with my brightest smile. "Well, you had a night!"

But Johnny's face was somber, serious. Perhaps that guy had been *terrible* in bed. "I'm sorry, Lynda. I should have told you sooner."

We sat on the couch. "Told me what?"

He motioned toward the door. "That I'm gay."

Gay? O, my dear, sweet, provincial Johnny.

"Everyone who goes to Studio ends up experimenting," I said. "It's no big deal."

Johnny shook his head. "No," he said. "This wasn't experimentation. I'm gay."

I was, in that moment, taken aback. Perhaps Johnny's being gay seems obvious in retrospect—why else would I, Lynda Boyle, have such difficulty enchanting a man?—but it was, after all, 1978. Gay men were out at the clubs; not so much elsewhere, as you surely remember, Jann.

And even with Johnny's admission, I was still confused. I'd always felt certain that any man who thought he was gay would reevaluate after meeting me. Johnny had slept with me several times, so how *could* he be gay? My mind spun.

"But, Johnny," I said. "We had some amazing sex." It wasn't entirely true—sex with Johnny, when I thought about it, wasn't nearly as good as sex with Denny, or Hal—but the man clearly needed some encouragement.

Johnny looked me in the eyes, a piercing look. "Only after I did coke," he said.

Was that true? My mind flashed through all the times we'd had sex. Surely there had been at least one, sans chemical enhancement, that I could use to plead my case? But try as I might I could not think of a single instance. O, how badly I'd miscalculated!

My face must have betrayed some of my feelings, for he said softly, "I really didn't mean to lead you on. I was trying to convince myself I wasn't gay. But you kind of proved it for me."

"Proved it?" Had Johnny—a man I'd always thought so dear and sweet—had he *used* me? My eyes darted in search of an object to break; I struggled to stay seated and not reach for a lamp, or the guitar leaning against the wall.

"If a beautiful woman like you didn't do it for me, then I knew."

Johnny may have meant to flatter me, but it landed like Grandma Boyle's mashed potatoes: heavy as cement, tasteless.

"So I was—an experiment?" I wondered how much force it would take to break that guitar, how many times it would have to hit the floor, or Johnny's head. I'd seen footage of Pete Townshend smashing his guitar onstage, and if a skinny Brit could do it with minimal effort, so could I. My fury might well smash it to atoms.

"No! Not consciously, anyway." Johnny cleared his throat. "Part of the reason I moved here was to be free to…explore my sexuality, I guess. I hadn't planned to date women anymore, like I used to in Michigan. But then I met you."

If I were a different kind of person, I might have found this ironically sweet, and embraced Johnny in that moment. We might have forged a friendship that could have withstood the events that were to follow later that spring. This story might well have been about my chaste friendship with a rock star who would never sleep with me, a beautiful man and a beautiful woman who went shopping for antiques together and gossiped like schoolgirls. Jennifer Aniston starred in a movie like that in the nineties; she played a mousy little thing with no self-esteem who spent her life wishing her gay friend, Paul Rudd, would have sex with her. Surely you can see where I'm going here. I'm the cat, not the mouse. And I'm far more beautiful than poor love-deprived Jen.

In other words, my internal reaction to Johnny's little speech: Fuck *this*, and fuck *you*. I quickly became a white-hot ball of rage.

"You know, if Steve does give you a gig at Studio, it will be either because of me, or because he wants to fuck you," I said. "He doesn't give a shit about your music."

Johnny's face shifted in that moment; his eyes turned steely, and he fixed a hard look on me. "I didn't mean to hurt you, Lynda. But maybe you should leave."

I stood then, my eyes settling on that guitar. It was a beautiful thing, black, with mother-of-pearl inlay on the frets. I knew nothing about guitars, but it was clear that this one was special, and I walked over to it, picked it up, ran my hand along the neck.

"Lynda," Johnny said, his voice taut with panic.

O, how I wanted to smash it! But then I thought of Aura. She had disappointed me in myriad ways, proven herself unworthy of my mentorship, and yet, she was still Augustus's daughter. Her contacts in the poetry world were invaluable. If I smashed Johnny's guitar, there would be no going back. She'd have to take sides, and the side she'd take would be Johnny's.

"You should keep that in a case," I said, leaning it back against the wall and making my way to the door. "It would be a shame if anything happened to it."

I was in a foul mood back home in Jersey that Sunday night, though the dozen roses Hal had sent provided a balm, as did a message from Denny that I chose to ignore, much to my mother's consternation. ("You'd better set that boy straight," she whined.) Blocking out thoughts of Johnny's treachery and focusing on the men who *did* appreciate me, I was in a better mood than I might have been when I went to school the following Monday morning. That feeling was quickly squelched, however, by a note in my mailbox to meet Dick in his office on my free period.

Had Jody and Kathi gone to Dick and told him how I'd shoved Jody, how I'd threatened them both? Equally worrisome, I wasn't wearing one of my best outfits. My mother, in some sort of snit, had refused to do my laundry that weekend. To do it myself would have been a capitulation to her whims, and so I was forced to wear to school that Monday a ho-hum pair of black slacks and a white silk blouse. On my way into Dick's office, I unbuttoned the blouse an extra button—a move that did not escape the notice of his secretary.

"He's in a shitty mood," Patti said, her bright red talon placing a call on hold without bothering to answer the phone. "You want a little Enjoli, hon?"

Patti's taste in perfume was questionable, but she understood me as few have.

I shook my head, thanked her, and entered the weasel's den.

With all my fretting about Jody, it was a relief when Dick told me the real reason for our meeting.

"Several parents called us last week," he said. "There were complaints that you allowed Bobby Craig to present an indecent speech where he begged girls to kiss him."

Was there any truth to this scurrilous allegation, you may be wondering? While it was true that I'd done a unit on public speaking with my classes, and while it was also true that Bobby's speech had begun with the lines, "Ladies, I don't expect to be 'the one,' but I'd like to be the first one—the first one you kiss," and while it was additionally true that Bobby had then recited a series of uproariously funny reasons, including the claim that he was "versed in multiple kissing techniques"—which he was, since I'd taught him myself—I would hardly call the speech "indecent." I and most of the class had laughed heartily at his send-up of the assignment. Even Jody and Kathi had seemed amused.

"It was perfectly PG," I said, pushing my cleavage at Dick.

He moved away from me in his swivel chair, but his eyes landed on my breasts. "Why would you allow him to present something so inappropriate?"

"It was a brilliant satire of the assignment. I was impressed."

"Satire?" Dick blinked at me.

"Yes. The assignment was to deliver a persuasive speech, and Bobby set out to prove that persuasion can be dangerous. Honestly, it was nearly as brilliant as Swift's *A Modest Proposal*." I batted my lashes at Dick and looked for signs that he was buying this.

"One of the parents called it pornographic."

I tried, and failed, to contain a few syllables of laughter.

Dick was quiet for a moment. "Lynda, you're a very young teacher. I know that your generation values freedom, and that you want the students to express themselves." I played with an earring; it threw him off track for a moment. "But this was completely inappropriate as a response to an assignment, and you should have told him so."

O, the tiny minds of Keyhole! I nodded as if I understood.

"It was a judgment call in the moment," I said.

"Apparently, a few of the girls felt uncomfortable."

A *few* of the girls? I wracked my brain for evidence of any child's displeasure that day, and then my mind's eye saw them: Aura and Marisol, sitting stone-faced after Bobby's speech in some sort of budding feminist solidarity.

For the record, I've never identified as a feminist, though I did adopt the convenient "Ms." for my teaching. I was—still am—a twentieth-century girl, beautiful enough to grace the pages of *Playboy* but smart enough to run Hefner's empire if I put my mind to it. Why rail against discrimination or cry foul about discomfort when men are so easy to manipulate? I've never had any trouble getting what I wanted.

Dick, perhaps waiting for me to respond, sighed heavily. It was nearly identical to a loathsome sound my mother often made. "You've been such a valuable member of our staff here," he said, "that I'm concerned about the way you've been stumbling this year."

"Stumbling?" I was not entirely successful in keeping the edge out of my voice.

"The complaints from parents about your attire. That day you were a no-show. The issues with Jody Fromme. And now, this." Dick cleared his throat. "Teachers are usually a little more careful before they make tenure."

O, the bitter laugh I worked to swallow in that moment! Did Dick think I gave a shit about tenure, or that I planned to be there long enough to get it? And given that the Keyhole Police Department seemed to suspect some sort of drug ring was operating out of the teacher's lounge, Dick clearly had his priorities out of order. *Thank God for Cousin Tony*, I thought.

"I'm sorry I disappointed you, Dick," I said, flipping my hair in a sultry way. "But I'm certainly far more careful than the teachers who smoke a joint before class or buy drugs at the high school."

Dick's eyes nearly bulged from his head. "Are you insinuating that Dan isn't the only druggie on my staff?"

Ha! Poor, out-of-touch Dick. "I'm sure I wouldn't know," I said. "But there are rumors."

He sat forward in his seat. "Rumors?"

"Well, my cousin Tony is on the Keyhole police force, and the rumors have gotten all the way to our boys in blue." Silently I congratulated myself on that last phrase; I thought it would resonate with a middle-aged square like Dick.

"I—I really thought this was a one-time thing," he sputtered.

"I have no idea if the rumors are true," I said, "since I don't do drugs myself. But I've had my suspicions."

"Please let me know if you hear anything concrete, Lynda," Dick said, visibly agitated.

"Of course. And I hope we can put my little misstep with Bobby behind us."

Dick sputtered out something that sounded like a yes—I'd really rattled him!—and waved me out of the office.

For the rest of the day, I was nearly bursting with my accomplishment: not only had I turned the situation in my favor, I'd done it not even looking my best. Imagine what I might have accomplished had I been wearing a skirt and heels! Principal Boyle certainly had a nice ring to it, but I really wasn't interested in that sort of job.

Over the next few days, the thought that Aura might have orchestrated the complaints about Bobby's speech nagged at me. She'd been giving out mixed signals for weeks, sometimes friendly, other times avoiding eye contact. As the idea that she might have betrayed me grew in my mind, I decided to clear the air. I'd already been horrifically abused by Johnny; if Aura had done me wrong as well, I wasn't sure what I was capable of.

Rather than have this discussion at school, I cornered her in the hall and asked if she wanted to go to the Galaxy for an open mic that coming Saturday.

"Umm, sure," she said, her eyes darting away from me. Her jacket's message, which she hadn't changed since the previous week: LIFE ON MARS.

"Is something wrong?" I asked. She seemed so squirrely that I briefly wondered if Jody Fromme had been bothering her again.

"No," she said. "It's just that I'm supposed to meet Marisol in the cafeteria."

Marisol, Marisol, Marisol! I was glad she had a friend, but her singular focus was tedious.

"Well, I'm sure she and the cafeteria aren't going anywhere."

"Right."

"So Saturday. Pick you up at noon?"

Aura was quiet for a moment. Something I couldn't quite read was swirling in those blue eyes of hers. But what she said, finally, was: "Sure. Thanks, Ms. Boyle."

16

For days after that dreadful bottom-shelf-gin cocktail hour on "The Miller's" lanai, Hubby and I watched and waited. I'd already learned that it was easy to break into their home through the flimsy screen door. But what I needed to accomplish was more than a simple wire-snipping. Hubby and I had planned a caper that required I enter and exit the house not once, but twice, and so we needed an opportunity when our neighbors were both out.

Finally, we saw them both get into Mrs.'s white Ford Taurus and head off one afternoon. Hubby kept watch out front while I got to work.

The lanai door required just a minute or two of judicious handle jiggling before it popped open. I quickly made my way to the wall of photos, where I took the one of Mrs. and Johnny, frame and all. On the way back, I couldn't help but snoop in the bathroom, since I hadn't had an opportunity the last time I was there. Mr. was on ten different medications, all of them unfamiliar strings of consonants and vowels except for the one drug I'd heard of: Viagra. I chortled to myself, thinking how extremely fortunate I was that Hubby required no such enhancements.

I slipped back through our own lanai door and handed the photo to Hubby. Now it was my turn to watch through the front window while Hubby popped the photo out of its frame so he could examine it. My dear husband had developed many skills during our time in exile; one he'd been perfecting for the past decade involved photo fakes and forgeries, and so he had also become very good at recognizing said fabrications.

After what seemed an interminable time, he called out to me.

"I think it's real, doll," he said.

I kept my watch at the window. "*Think*?"

He walked up to me, framed photo in hand. "If it's a fake, it was done by the absolute best—and I doubt any of the folks looking for us would spend the money to hire the best. They wouldn't have thought we'd get a chance to examine it."

I looked at the photo, Johnny so young and handsome, Mrs. attractive enough by virtue of her youth. It certainly *seemed* to be a faded old photo of the two of them. Was it just a strange coincidence, rather than a set-up, that "The Miller's" had moved in next door?

"Assuming it's real," I said, "could she have been recruited because of her connection to Johnny?"

Hubby shook his head. "Unlikely, unless she also happened to be a cop or a PI."

"It's just so hard for me to believe it's a coincidence," I said. "And the way they were blasting Johnny's music?"

"Coincidences happen," Hubby said. "But if you don't want them to catch us, you'd better get over there and slip it back."

Just as I took it from Hubby and made my way toward the back door, he called out, "Shit! They're home! I'll stall them out front."

When I arrived home from school the Friday after I'd made that date with Aura for the open mic, I was stunned to find she'd left a message with my mother that she couldn't go. Why hadn't she just told me at school? It was as if she'd purposefully tried to avoid me.

I'd been planning to spend that night with Hal, returning the next morning, but suddenly I had the whole weekend at my disposal. "In that case, I might not be back until Sunday," I told my mom as I packed for the weekend. "Tell Daddy I'm staying with Lola."

My mother rolled her eyes. "Who is this Hal, Lynda? Are we ever going to meet him?"

I'd certainly thought about it. I knew that Hal was capable of making an excellent impression on my parents. I also knew that my father would have a fit over the age difference, since Hal was more than ten years my senior, and—no insult intended—looked it. There was also the matter of how his being Jewish might play with my Catholic parents. O, the considerations one had to entertain to accommodate the small, provincial minds of Keyhole!

"You'll meet him when I'm ready for you to meet him." I delivered it with a smile to soften the blow.

But she was in one of her moods. "Does he even exist, Lynda? Or are you still fooling around with that teenager?"

I tossed a hairbrush and my Clairol Herbal Essence shampoo into my toiletries bag. Though the idea of letting my mother spin her wheels held great appeal, I was annoyed that she didn't believe I had another lover.

"Mother, please," I said. "Do you really think Denny has the money to send me roses?" I added to my bag mascara, eye shadow, blush, and my signature red lipstick, along with my toothbrush and Pearl Drops tooth polish.

She was quiet for a moment, considering this. "Well, there's some reason you don't want us to meet him. Art and Peter both picked you up here for your first dates."

"Art and Peter both live in Jersey," I said, relieved to see my red Qiana dress hanging in my closet, clean. My mother had lost her resolve about not doing my laundry. Perhaps I should toss her a bone, I thought.

"He's older," I added. "I'm afraid Daddy will get upset."

Her shoulders relaxed; this was clearly not what she'd expected. "How old is he?"

"Thirty-eight," I said.

"Thirty-eight," she repeated. "What does he do for a living?"

"He's an accountant."

"An accountant? He must make some money."

"He lives in a doorman building on the Upper East Side," I said.

"Really." She sat on the edge of my bed. "Do you like him?"

If she had asked it with any sort of edge in her voice, I might have bristled at the implication that I was using Hal. She knew I could easily date a man I didn't like, especially a man with money; she'd seen me do it before. But that edge was absent. It was a simple question, not a judgment. I folded my sexiest panties and bra ensemble and slipped them into the bag, conspicuously enough to make her react, though she didn't. "You know, I do. I didn't think I would, at first. He's not the best-looking guy. But he gets me." It felt like the most truth I'd ever uttered at my mother.

"That's the kind of guy to marry," she said quietly. "But I don't want to poison your feelings for him by giving you my blessing."

I laughed. Sometimes my mother could be like this, easy with me, and I had to force myself to remember not to let my guard down.

"It's nowhere near that point," I said. "But he's the first guy I've met in a long time who doesn't bore me to tears."

Since Johnny, I thought. The first guy since dear, confused Johnny.

Hal took me to Lutèce that night, and the experience was incomparably different from my night there with Peter. The maître d' clearly knew

Hal; we were seated at one of the best tables in Le Jardin, the main dining room.

"There are private rooms upstairs," Hal said to me after we were seated, "but I like this room better. More action, more excitement."

Clearly this man really *did* get me.

"The night I met you, I was here on a terrible date," I told him.

"Who with?"

"One of the teachers from my school," I said as Hal tasted the exquisitely expensive cabernet sauvignon; he nodded to the waiter to pour. "We had the worst table in the house."

"He didn't grease any palms? What a bum."

Hal talked like this sometimes, using expressions that sounded like they were lifted from a gangster movie. It amused me.

"He thought it was acceptable because we were 'just a couple of teachers from Jersey.' His words."

Hal recoiled dramatically, as if he'd been shot. "And you walked out on him."

"After I ate dinner and a very expensive dessert."

Hal laughed heartily and took a long sip of wine. "That's my Lynda," he said, with great affection.

It was so freeing, being with a man who admired me for the very character traits others harshly judged. Was that the first moment I realized I was officially smitten with Hal? Perhaps.

What a night at Studio that was! No jockeying for position to be sure the bouncer or Steve saw me. Hal was such a member of the inner circle that we went in through the VIP entrance. We danced to the peak of ecstasy, and beyond; at one point, enamored of my moves, Baryshnikov joined us, and I quietly showed him my signature hip shimmy. Lauren Hutton told me she'd enjoyed my work in *The Spy Who Loved Me*, and I realized she'd confused me with Barbara Bach. I rode a high for hours until, exhausted and lounging in the basement, Hal mentioned in passing that Johnny's band was playing at CBGB that night.

If a soundtrack of disco bliss had been playing in my head, Hal's comment felt like a needle scraping across that album.

"Are you sure?" I asked. Johnny had mentioned the gig in passing before we'd had our difficult moment. But I felt certain he'd have invited me despite that kerfuffle.

"They're called Glow Worm, right?"

I nodded.

"I saw it listed in the *Voice*. They seem to be coming up quickly. I told Steve we should host a little showcase for them."

Then it hit me: Aura's canceling on the open mic. Her awkwardness with me at school. They'd conspired to keep me from going to the gig.

"What's wrong, babe?" Hal asked.

I looked around for something to smash, but all I saw was the passed-out form of Peter Frampton on a nearby couch. He looked eminently breakable—not especially tall, and slight of build—but I restrained myself. Quickly I selected the bits of the story I'd tell Hal: that Johnny had confided in me about being gay, and that he and Aura were now shutting me out. Hal didn't need to know of my desire for Johnny.

Hal shook his head. "Their loss," he said. "Wouldn't you rather be here, than at a filthy club downtown?"

I would, of course. I've amply documented my feelings about Johnny's wretched rock clubs. But I also couldn't let them get away with this slight. Not Johnny. And especially not Aura.

"How do you feel about heading over there and catching their set?" I asked. I tried to sound casual, but Hal was on to me.

"Will property damage be involved? Not that I'm averse to that."

"I just want them to squirm," I said.

CBGB was crowded with sweaty, spiky people, and Hal elbowed a path for the two of us toward the front of the stage. Glow Worm had not yet begun their set, but I saw Lars fiddling with an amp near his drum kit. I waved but he didn't seem to see me.

I glanced around at the crowd and quickly spotted Aura—wearing the very outfit I had bought her for that night at the Galaxy!—with Denny, right in front of the stage. I motioned to Hal, and he cut us a path to them. Just as I was about to tap Aura on the shoulder, Denny turned to me. My signature scent, mixed with my own sweet pheromones, had likely tipped him off.

"Lynda!" Denny cried, sounding genuinely pleased to see me.

Aura turned, her eyes made up with thick stripes of black and white eyeliner in the cat-eye style some of the punk girls favored. She'd had the phrase OH BONDAGE UP YOURS! ironed on to the sexy top I'd bought her.

"Hey," she said softly.

"Interesting...words," I said, motioning toward her chest.

"It's a song." To the untrained eye she might have appeared relaxed, but I could see a hint of a squirm.

"I don't think either of you has met Hal," I said brightly, my hand on his arm. "Hal, this is my student, Aura, and her brother Denny."

Hal stuck his hand out to Denny, who simply gaped. The poor boy was still smarting from my rejection.

Aura looked from me to the floor.

"I wish you'd reminded me of this gig, Aura," I said, with just a soupçon of hurt calculated to create gut-twisting guilt.

"I'm sorry," she said, though she didn't sound as sorry as she should have. "It's just—well, you don't even really like Glow Worm, do you? Johnny said you disappeared for most of their set at the Galaxy."

An interesting tidbit—he'd cared enough, at least, to notice that I wasn't watching him that night. Was it possible that Johnny had been hurt by my lack of fawning fandom and was seeking out the company of men as some sort of revenge? I know that women sometimes swear off men in that way—though I, rest assured, never have.

"I love Glow Worm," I said.

Before I could formulate a plan for some well-deserved psychological mayhem, the band appeared. Johnny's stage persona had gotten exponentially more dramatic. He now had, in addition to his mantle of feathers, actual wings, made of what appeared to be ostrich feathers; more eye shadow, more glitter, even a white feather boa.

The crowd at CBGB was as mesmerized as the fans at the Galaxy had been. At one point, Hal whispered in my ear, "Damn, these guys would go over *great* at Studio."

Johnny looked so gorgeous onstage that my heart began to weep anew. Why did he have to be gay, or think he was gay, or whatever was going on with him? How could he not want me as I wanted him?

And why couldn't Hal look more like Johnny?

Yes, looks matter. I was a beautiful woman and I deserved to be with a beautiful man. Some may judge me, but anyone who's honest with themselves has had thoughts like this before. We all overlook something we find unattractive in potential mates: ten extra pounds, a weak chin, thinning hair, a snaggle tooth. Hal possessed all of those attributes, and so anyone who thinks me shallow should keep in mind that I was overlooking a great deal, and that being with Hal when I was still so young and desirable was proof of a profound display of personal growth.

Aura seemed less standoffish toward me after the show; she asked if I knew what had happened to Mr. Wykoski (the students had been told he was on a medical leave!) and so I filled her in. Poor Denny glared at Hal, who responded by looping his arm around me. The dynamic was delicious—I loved it when men fought over me, even if the fight was merely theoretical. But it only lasted for a few minutes before Johnny came out.

He hugged Aura, clapped Denny's shoulders, and then turned to me. I hadn't been able to tell if he could see me from the stage. But of course he had; I am not the kind of woman who fades into a crowd.

"Lynda," he said. "I'm surprised you're here." His mouth was a taut line, his eyes unreadable.

"Well, I couldn't miss your big show!" I said brightly. "You've met Hal, haven't you?"

Johnny nodded and gave me an appraising look. My breezy delivery threw him off guard.

"You were terrific!" I said brightly. "I loved the wings."

"Oh my God, those wings," Aura gushed. "How many hours did we spend gluing those together?"

"A lot of hours," Johnny said.

Had Aura meant to pointedly remind me that I was out of the trio, and they were now a duo? I didn't want to believe, at the time, that she was capable of such treachery. She's certainly capable of it now.

"I'm going to remind Steve about your band," Hal said, cutting the tension. "You guys were terrific."

Johnny looked taken aback. "You really think the Studio crowd would like us?"

"Of course," Hal said. "You have great bass lines."

"I'll tell Dave you said that." Johnny smiled.

I quickly grew bored of this banal chitchat, and decided it was time to go in for—well, if not the kill, certainly the mother of all squirms. "Say, where's Clay?" I asked. "I was hoping to reintroduce myself under less awkward circumstances."

Aura looked from me to Johnny. "Who's Clay?"

Ha! He hadn't come out to Aura yet. This was going to be *fun*.

Lest I seem cruel, rest assured that I would not have really outed him. First of all, I wasn't entirely convinced that he *was* gay. Second, I loved the gay men I'd met in dance clubs: their moves, their exquisite taste, their *joie de vivre*. In fact, if I, Lynda Boyle, had been born male, it is almost certain that I would have been gay; I'd simply have been too fabulous to be a straight man. But Johnny had hurt me, and he needed to pay.

"Nobody," Johnny said. If I'd made him uncomfortable, he gave no indication.

"One-night stand?" Aura asked.

So Aura *did* know?

Johnny shook his head, smiling. "You're too much, Aura."

She rolled her eyes. "You think I don't know what a one-night stand is? My parents were having fights about them when I was five years old."

"Remember that time we saw a trail of long blond hair whoosh out the fire escape as we were coming in the front door?" Denny asked.

"Yeah. I mean, I miss Dad a lot. But I don't miss that bullshit."

I could only think of two blondes in the poetry world who were attractive enough for Augustus to have slept with. Neither was as gifted as I am, poetically or sexually.

"I think he was right about free love, though," Denny said. "It's just that Mom wasn't on board."

"I used to believe in free love," Hal said. "But then I met Lynda."

His timing could not have been more impeccable, for not only had he paid me a much-deserved compliment, he'd inadvertently taken a swipe at the Martyr to boot. Johnny and Aura both looked at me and Hal like they were trying to figure us out. But poor Denny. He trembled with thwarted desire. The stain of his love for me was upon the world!

Hal and I returned to Studio just in time to see the iconic moon and spoon descend from above, the sparkling cocaine trail to the man-in-the-moon's nose reminding us to do a few lines of our own. We danced past dawn, and then did our customary crash. Hal and I spent Saturday afternoon, much of the evening and into Sunday talking in a way we hadn't before: about our lives, about what we wanted from the world. Hal felt, as I did, that the world was there for us to conquer, to take from. Having come of age in the hippie era, when everyone was exhorted to give, give, give, it was such a relief to meet a man who shared my vision. Though we didn't quite know it at the time, we were poised on the brink of a decade that would fit us perfectly—"The 'Me' Decade," a comedian-cum-disgraced senator once called it. The joke was supposed to be that it was a terrible thing, the specter of a decade of hedonism and selfishness. It was anything but. My only regret is that circumstances didn't allow me to enjoy the eighties to their fullest.

Hal revealed to me that while he was an accountant and helped out with the books at Studio, he made his real money selling coke. He'd been doing it for several years; it was what had propelled him from doing tax returns for retirees in Queens to the fancy apartment where we lay in the middle of a white shag rug, half-naked after lovemaking.

I admired his chutzpah, his knowing exactly what he wanted. I told him this.

"I love it when Catholic girls speak Yiddish," he said, and we did a few more lines to fuel another round of lovemaking.

I went back to Jersey on Sunday buoyed by my deepening relationship with Hal, and by my triumph over Johnny's treachery. Awaiting me on the princess desk in my bedroom: a large manila envelope whose East Village return address was stamped with the *Forked* journal's logo (a snake's bifurcated tongue). I ripped the envelope open greedily; surely this was the acceptance I had been waiting for since early January!

But no—my poems had been returned to me. I unfolded the slip of paper tucked inside, thinking that at the very least, Bryce would have sent me a personal note.

Reader, it was a *form rejection*—and (I can barely write the words) a *solicitation to subscribe.*

Bryce had rejected my work and now wanted me to *pay* for copies of his shitty rag?

I lobbed a stapler against the wall, then a hairbrush, then a can of hairspray.

"Everything okay in there?" my father called out from the living room.

"Sure, Daddy," I called back.

But everything was not okay. I read through the rejected poems; they were as brilliant as I remembered. The ferocity of my talent was unsquelchable; it needed, no, demanded to be out in the world. What was I waiting for? Surely my mentor John Ashbery could help me place them in a finer journal than *Forked.* And it was high time I employed a convenient shortcut to get them into his hands.

I picked up the phone and dialed Aura, grateful that she answered. I was in no mood for chitchat with the Martyr or the grandmother.

Aura was monosyllabic at first, but I opened her up by asking about the songs she was writing, and how her practices were going with Johnny.

"Really good," she said. "He's helping me work up a set and I might try to play at Folk City, if my mom will let me."

"That's great!" I said brightly, ignoring the pain it caused me to learn of her and Johnny's continued intimacy.

She started yammering about her songs after that, something about Patti Smith and punk rock and male chauvinism and blah, blah, blah. I barely listened, playing out in my mind the best way to steer the conversation.

"I know what you mean about chauvinism," I said. "I was really taken aback by Bobby Craig's persuasive speech. Sometimes it's hard to know, as a teacher, whether to forbid something or see where it will go."

My calculation was that she would be flattered to be let in on the secret that adults don't always know what they're doing—something that was true for many, though not me. This would both gain me her sympathy and tamp down any further complaints she might want to take to Principal Singer.

"Yeah, it must be," she said. "But with Bobby Craig, it's pretty much a given where it's going to go." She laughed, a good sign.

"That's true," I said. "I've learned my lesson."

"He's no worse than the other boys," she added. "He's just more vocal."

"Boys and men are good at getting what they want, aren't they?" This naked appeal to Aura's feminism would serve as my segue.

"Yes." She sighed. "They are."

"There's such an old boys' network everywhere—especially in the writing world."

"In music too. It's like a hundred times harder for us."

"I think we women have to stick together and help each other, don't you?"

"Absolutely! This is what I want to work on when I'm older."

I had her exactly where I wanted her. "Well, along those lines, how would you like to help a fellow woman out?"

She was quiet for a moment. "Umm. How?"

"I have some new poems that I know are among my best work, but I need to get them in the hands of someone who can help me place them."

"Well, have you sent them to journals? That's what my dad used to do."

"I have. But I fear the old boys' network is conspiring against me."

She was quiet, just a faint static coming through the line.

"I was thinking that perhaps you could get them into my dear former professor's hands."

She let out a long breath. "So you want me to give your poems to Uncle John?"

Uncle John? *Uncle John*? I knew that Augustus and Professor Ashbery had been friends, of course. But to the extent that he'd been given a familial honorific? Given that Aura had such a close relationship with him, I was stunned at her selfishness in not offering to help me earlier.

"Exactly. I just need that foot in the door," I said.

"But he was your professor. Why don't you just send them yourself?"

Why didn't I? In my wildly productive East Village years, I *had* sent my once-encouraging professor poems. Packets of them, popped in the mail as quickly as the ink dried. And yet—it pains me to write this—I heard nary a reply. This sustained lapse in manners was clearly the work of an assistant, a jealous mousy sort who sifted through his mail.

But Aura—surely he'd read poems handed to him by his dear "niece" Aura!

"I'm sure he has many former students who attempt to gain his attention," I said, choosing my words carefully. "But coming from you, with your enthusiasm and our special relationship—it would mean so much more."

She was quiet again.

"What do you think?" I prodded.

"I guess so," she said slowly.

"Terrific!" I recognized that I needed to move swiftly to seal the deal. "I'll give you the packet after class tomorrow. Sleep well, Aura!"

I myself slept very well, knowing that, with my dear mentor's help, my poems would be in *The New Yorker* or *The Paris Review* by summer.

17

On "The Miller's" lanai, there was a wicker table full of magazines and tabloids, the very antithesis of the journals I once aspired to be published in: *Woman's Day*, *InTouch Weekly*, *The National Enquirer.* I brushed past them as I slipped back into our neighbors' home and replaced the photo of Johnny and Mrs., my gloved hands ensuring no fingerprints would be left behind. From outside I heard Mrs.'s voice, pitched higher than normal as she spoke with my husband. I slipped back out before she could put her key in the front door.

Hubby was waiting for me in our kitchen. "All clear?"

"Yes. Thanks for stalling her."

"It wasn't easy. She's in quite a state. Apparently Gary had a heart attack."

I poured myself a glass of iced tea. "How bad?"

"They took him from his doctor's office straight to the hospital. She just came home to pack a bag for him."

"He was on a shitload of drugs," I said. "The medicine cabinet was full of bottles."

"Did you check the names?"

"Of course." This was Investigating 101—be sure the names on the prescriptions matched the subject's alleged name.

"Good." Hubby took a sip of my iced tea. "Anyway, I think this nails it, that they're legit. Or at least no threat to us."

But I wasn't so sure. "She didn't have any prescriptions in her name, though. That's a little weird."

Hubby shrugged. "Maybe hers are all illegal."

We both laughed, and while I was pleased that I'd pulled off our little caper, the thought that something about Mrs. wasn't on the up-and-up nagged at me.

I've learned through bitter experience to feel on guard even when it appears I've triumphed. Back in my twenties I had not yet grasped this painful lesson, and so I floated into work on a jubilant cloud the morning after Aura agreed to pass along my poems. Both Hal and Denny were head-over-heels in love with me; my appearance at the Glow Worm show had smoothed things over with poor confused Johnny; and, with Aura's assistance, I was on the verge of reclaiming my rightful place in the poetry world. On top of all that, it was the first day of spring! My mood was such that I even said a fond good morning to Peter, who scowled in return. 1978—it was, indeed, shaping up to be The Year of Lynda Boyle.

But my mood quickly plummeted when I asked Aura to stay after class and tried to give her my packet of poems. She stood with her arms folded, eying the proffered envelope suspiciously.

"I thought about this last night, and it would be better if you just sent him the poems yourself." Most girls in this situation might have looked at the ground, mustering courage. But Aura looked me in the eyes, defiant.

"We talked about that, Aura. It'll be so much better, coming from you."

"Better for you," she said.

"What?" I felt a heat rising from my toes.

She let out a long, exasperated sigh—likely something she'd picked up from the Martyr. "Better for you," she repeated. "Not for me."

"What do you mean? This is really a small thing to ask, Aura."

"It's not a small thing. I barely see Uncle John or any of Dad's poet friends anymore. It would be weird for me to just call him out of the blue."

I put my hand to my mouth, willing myself to contain the fury unfurling within me. I'd taken this girl under my wing, introduced her to the man who became her musical mentor, had her and her family over to my house for fucking Christmas. Bought her an outfit *with my own money* and helped get her into her first club—and there, I even procured her a strawberry daiquiri. How dare she say no to me! Did she think she could go around using people like that?

Students from my next class were beginning to file in. I motioned her closer to the blackboard, away from the door.

"I understand that it's something you're not used to doing," I said carefully, straining to keep my tone neutral, "but this is how the world works, Aura."

"No," she said, quietly enough that I chose to ignore it.

"It's easy!" I added brightly. "You can just pop the poems in the mail, with a note I'll help you write. Then it's just a quick phone call. I can help you practice what to say."

"No!" Her voice rose now. "I'm not doing it."

The students already in the classroom all looked our way.

"Keep your voice down," I said through clenched teeth.

"You know what, Ms. Boyle? It's really weird, you asking me to do this. I'm not the only one who thinks so. Maybe you should just leave me alone." And with that, she turned and strode out the door, the KILLER QUEEN on the back of her jacket prompting the usual guffaws and pointed fingers.

I'm not the only one who thinks so? Who had she confided in? The Martyr? Johnny? Marisol? My need to smash something was exponential but all I had in front of me were thirty blank-eyed, pimple-faced young teens, and while I wasn't above breaking one of them, I was not yet ready to bring an abrupt end to my teaching career.

My sleep was unsettled that night, full of shadowy dreams where I saw myself as a simple woman, "just a teacher from Jersey," someone whom roguish male poets discarded and ignored. In the dreams, my hair was absent its usual lustrous sheen, my breasts smaller, my waist thicker. I was thirty, then forty, sitting in my classroom with gray-streaked tresses, cutting paper shamrocks from green construction paper to display for St. Patrick's Day, a distant echo of Abba's "SOS" serving as a taunting reminder of my once-promising youth.

I awoke in a cold sweat at two a.m., threw on a silky bathrobe and headed to the kitchen. After downing a glass of water, I realized I needed something stronger, and I pulled my father's Cutty Sark from the liquor cabinet. *The Graduate* was among the limited early morning television fare, and I watched and drank, looking for the resemblance between myself and Katharine Ross that my father insisted upon. With each shot of whiskey, I became more convinced that my looks were far superior. So why was she the actress and I the teacher? When and how would I achieve the fame I so deserved? I drank a few more shots to forget the cruel Fates that had trapped me in the quicksand of the Jersey Shore.

By five a.m. I was able to slip into bed just as I heard my father's alarm go off; his shift work started so early, the poor man. I slept in a state of blank unconsciousness until my own alarm assaulted me an hour and a half later, whereupon I staggered to the shower and headed into a Tuesday morning at school in a precarious state: still a bit intoxicated, while hungover—from both the whiskey and the dreams—at the same time.

I felt like hell all morning, and apparently, I looked it too; both Carla and Tess asked me if I was ill, and Peter, passing me in the hall, smirked and chuckled. Though the chuckle sounded forced, the smirk looked spontaneous, and it sent me in a panicked search for a mirror, the closest one being in the nearby girls' room. The toughest girls from my slowest class were sitting on the radiator in front of the open window, smoking cigarettes; when I entered, there was a flurry of hand-waving, butts tossed outside.

"Don't worry, girls, I'm not here to bust you," I said, staring at myself in the mirror. My skin looked sallow; dark circles creased beneath my eyes. My eyeliner was noticeably heavier on the right eye versus the left, and the part in my hair was askew. Even my red lipstick—something I'd been able to apply with expert precision, sans mirror, since I was fourteen—displayed a Picassoesque asymmetry. What circle of hell was Keyhole Junior High School, I wondered, that it would take my luminous beauty and, in less than three years, reduce me to this? At least Dante's circles were full of passion and excitement. That school was the fucking *vestibule* of hell.

"Rough night?" Rhonda Ford asked, just after she'd practiced a smoke ring. Left back twice in younger grades, she was sixteen, and clearly enjoying the wild abandon of smoking in front of a teacher.

"I just didn't get enough sleep last night," I said.

She smiled, eyeing me in the mirror. "Right. If you give me an A this marking period, I'll give you a couple of Tic Tacs."

I shot her an uncomprehending look. Did she really think I could be bought so cheaply?

"I'm kidding," she said, but she took my hand, turned it palm up, and shook a few Tic Tacs into it, leaning in close to me.

"Alcohol," she whispered. "On your breath."

Rhonda was one of my worst students; perpetually late or absent, only sporadically completing half-hearted assignments. She was a D student only because I sympathized with her unfiltered opinions about what a fascist shitbucket Principal Singer was (her words), and because

I wasn't allowed to give too many Fs. Rhonda had no reason to show me mercy, and yet she had.

Or maybe she was shrewder than she appeared to be.

"Thanks, Rhonda," I said, popping the Tic Tacs into my mouth, and hoping she'd turn in some assignment, any assignment, that term so I could give her a B and complete our transaction.

Aura was absent from my class that morning. Was she avoiding me? I had not yet decided how I'd punish her for her betrayal, but she needed to learn a lesson. Once I was sober and had slept, I reasoned, I'd have a clearer idea of how to exact justice.

Because I did not even remotely have the energy to teach, I divided the class into small groups to discuss the book they were reading, *Call of the Wild.* I divided the groups solely by desk proximity, but because Aura was absent, Marisol ended up in a group with Jody and Kathi. She shot me a "you've got to be kidding" look.

Halfway through the period, as I dozed with my nose in a copy of *Naked Lunch*, Marisol tapped me on the shoulder.

"Marisol," I said, trying to get my bearings. I'd just had a delicious dream about a three-way with Johnny and Ryan O'Neal and I could still smell the faint scent of Ryan's very expensive aftershave.

"Ms. Boyle, Jody and Kathi aren't discussing the book. They're talking about how Jody should get her hair styled."

Anything would be better than that hideous cut she has now, I thought. "Maybe you can guide the discussion," I said.

"I tried. They won't let me."

I looked at her. Could I level with Marisol? Probably not, but I didn't have the energy to keep up this charade.

"Marisol, I'm having a bad day. Maybe you could ignore them and just read?"

Had she ever realized before that I was not just a teacher, but a human being as well? Perhaps not, for she took a step back, seemingly surprised by my admission.

"But I finished that book two weeks ago. I'm reading *The Scarlet Letter* now."

"*The Scarlet Letter*?"

"They read it in eleventh grade, at the high school. I've already read all the books they do in ninth and tenth."

Perhaps you're wondering: was I reassessing the question of whether Marisol was a genius? I was not. Marisol was a by-the-rules girl, reading merely to get ahead, checking off the mental boxes for a college application she wouldn't fill out for several years. She really needed to be shaken out of that complacency.

"Marisol," I said, "read this instead." I handed her my copy of *Naked Lunch*.

She eyed the cover suspiciously. "What's it about?"

"Just read it," I said. "Just have the experience, okay? Read it right now and ignore Jody and Kathi. They're not worth your time."

That last part made her smile. I hadn't thought I'd said it loud enough for those two wretched girls to overhear, but, as Marisol headed to her seat with my copy of Burroughs, they both shot me looks—Kathi wounded, Jody defiant.

I put my head down on the desk and slept openly until the bell rang.

My relief at reaching the time for my lunch period—I was desperately hungry, and by then fully hungover—was shattered when I found a note in my mailbox asking me to go see Dick Singer. There was no way I could face Dick in that condition. I notified Patti that I was going home sick and would need a substitute for the rest of the day.

I headed to a diner I liked in South Amboy, far enough away from Keyhole that I felt certain I wouldn't see anyone I knew. Slumped in a booth in the back, I ordered from a waitress who looked as haggard as I felt. As I was savoring my coffee, anticipating the life-affirming grease of a Florentine omelet and home fries, a woman approached my booth. She looked to be about fifty but was likely only forty. Her mousy brown hair sported stripy auburn "highlights" and split ends like a frayed garden hose. Her eyes were beady, almost feral. She looked slightly familiar. Where had I seen her before?

"Lynda?" she asked, her voice tightly coiled. "Lynda Boyle?" She glared at me.

I nodded. Who was this woman, and what had I done to incur her wrath?

"I'm Beverly Fromme." Jody's mother.

"Mrs. Fromme," I said, my voice dripping honey. "What are you doing out here?" I hoped the coffee would cover any residual smell of alcohol on my breath.

"I'm a stylist at Cheesequake Clip 'N Curl," she spat. "The salon just down the road."

I remembered having passed a strip mall that included a pawn shop and a sketchy insurance agency as well as the "salon" to which she referred, a dreary-looking space with a weather-beaten sign whose logo incorporated a pair of scissors and a lock of curly hair—a helpful pictograph for the illiterate masses. I struggled to keep my face neutral. Beverly Fromme's hair was not exactly a ringing endorsement for her "salon," and she was most likely the culprit behind Jody's unflattering haircut too.

"Oh, I'm not familiar with your shop," I said brightly. "I'll be sure to spread the word!"

She breathed laboriously. "What are *you* doing here?" she asked. "Isn't today a school day?"

Did this woman really think she could taunt me? Amateurs of her ilk held no more significance to me than the seagulls circling the diner's parking lot. "Can I help you with something?" My voice sounded brisk, efficient. But internally, the knives were sharpening.

She took a deep, wheezy breath. "I just want you to know that my daughter told me what you did to her. How you shoved her into a wall. How you swore at her. She's afraid of you, did you know that?"

Afraid of me? Had I really instilled fear in wretched, evil Jody? My terrible morning was showing signs of turning itself around.

"Jody said I did those things to her?"

Bad Highlights Bev nodded, her face quickly shifting from pink to crimson.

"I can't imagine a teacher doing the kinds of things you're accusing me of. Can you?" I offered it in a wounded tone.

"Listen, you can drop that act. My sister Marjorie plays bridge with your mother. I know all about you."

I'll admit that I was thrown a bit off balance with that comment. My mother's close friend Marjorie was—Jody's aunt? And what the fuck had my mother said about me?

"What is it that you think you know?"

"You've been lying since you were a little girl. Your mother could never break you of it. She wanted to take you to a psychiatrist, but your father refused."

A psychiatrist? A *psychiatrist*? And then it hit me, a long-suppressed memory of my mother's treachery: she *did* take me to a psychiatrist! I was seven or eight years old, dressed in an insufferable pink dress—a color I loathed, even as a child. Across from me sat a man in a suit. He wanted me to like him, but I knew instinctively, wise child that I was, not to trust him.

"Tell me what makes you angry," he said.

I had a list, even back then: the olive loaf on Wonder Bread sandwiches my mother sometimes made me for lunch; the cheap Mary Janes she'd bought me at Bradlees after I'd begged for a pair from Bamberger's; the dachshund two doors down from our house that yapped at me, and only me, whenever I walked by; Karen Murphy, a girl in my third grade class who was my only academic rival. She was pale and thin and peasant-faced, undeserving of the accolades heaped upon her by our teacher.

My mother, of course. And my father, at times, for marrying her.

"Nothing really makes me angry," I replied with an angelic smile.

At the time, I assumed I'd played it correctly because I never saw the man again. But after what Bev had said, I couldn't help but wonder: was it my dear, sweet father who'd stepped in to save me from primitive 1950s child psychiatry? O, the debt I owed that man!

"You use people up and throw them away," Bev added. "You go through men like bars of soap."

My mother had specifically accused me of the latter, more than once, absurd simile and all. Between that and the mention of the shrink, Bad Highlights Bev was most likely telling the truth. My *fucking* mother. How dare she? Spouting off to those cloven-hooved ruminants in her bridge club? *Focus on the issue at hand, Lynda*, I thought, and slowly stirred a teaspoon of sugar into my coffee before I spoke.

"Well, you know how mothers and daughters are. I haven't put stock in the things Jody has said about you, so take what my mother said with a grain of salt."

Ha! Bev looked like a volcano about to pop, lava pooling just under her skin. "What did she say about me?"

"Well, your anger problem." She'd pretty much just handed me that one.

"I don't have an anger problem," she screeched.

"No?" I sipped my coffee, wondering if the poor thing would stroke out before we could finish our conversation.

Just when I thought she might reach out a hand to slap me, my breakfast came.

"Listen," she hissed through clenched teeth. "You think because you're young and you have the hair and the body, you can get away with anything. Well, looks are fleeting, missy—in fact, you're looking a little rough around the edges right now. Pretty soon, you'll be forty, with twenty extra pounds for each kid, and no one will put up with your bullshit."

I took a bite of my omelet, chewed, and swallowed. "I don't plan to have children," I said brightly, "so my looks will last quite a bit longer than yours."

"I'm talking to Principal Singer about you," she said. "How dare you talk to me like that."

One of my specialties was delivering icy zingers in a cheerful voice, with a smile. I'd learned in my adolescence that it threw people off-balance, and that later, they would question if they'd really heard me correctly. I leaned in close and fixed her with my best Mona Lisa before I spoke. "You and your daughter are a couple of dim-witted cunts," I said sweetly. "Go fuck yourselves."

She recoiled as if she'd been struck; sputtered for a second; then flew from the diner as if she were on fire. The volcano beneath her surface—thar she blew!

Pleased with how I'd dispatched her, I flipped through the jukebox at my table, put a quarter in, played the Bee Gees' "Stayin' Alive" and Abba's "Dancing Queen," songs that reminded me of my destiny. I was halfway through my meal, savoring my verbal victory when one of her comments returned to me: "Looking a little rough around the edges." Was I? The chrome on the side of the jukebox distorted my reflection like a funhouse mirror.

I thought then about what Jody had told her mother, and about the threat to go to Principal Singer. Would Aura stick with our plan, if interrogated—especially now that she was upset I'd asked a tiny favor of her? I finished my meal quickly. My next stop would have to be Aura's house, where I hoped to reason with her—but if that didn't do the trick, a carefully crafted threat might work just as well.

I knocked on the door, expecting Aura's grandmother to answer. To my surprise, I was greeted by a bloodshot-eyed Denny.

"Lynda!" he cried, ushering me in and giving me a gropey hug.

"You're really stoned," I said.

"I am."

"What are you doing here? Don't you have class?"

He smiled. "I dropped out."

"Out of NYU? Denny, that's a shame."

He shrugged. "I was flunking out anyway." He was quiet for a moment; then his face lit up as if he'd just had a preternaturally profound thought.

"Hey, why aren't you in school now?" He giggled like a ten-year-old.

"I'm playing hooky. Is Aura home?"

"Nah. She's playing hooky too. They all went shopping."

"They?"

"My grandmother. My mother. Aura."

"Any idea when they'll be back?"

"I think they'll be gone for a while." He fixed his barely open eyes upon me. The red surrounding his irises made their blue that much more pronounced. "Come upstairs. I want to show you something." He gestured toward his jeans.

I sighed. "I've seen it before, Denny. I just came over to talk to Aura."

"I have coke."

Although Denny had been a surprisingly good lover, I'd had little interest, since breaking it off with him, in revisiting our sexual relationship. But how could I say no to coke? I was having such a bad day.

Denny and I both did a few lines and, as you might imagine, one thing led to another. I taught Denny a new move that Hal had showed me, something he called TNT; we exploded together, did more lines, and started anew. As we fucked, my failed poet nightmare of the previous night returned to me and so, too, did my anger at Aura. My rocket-fueled brain forgot all about how I needed her to back me up against Jody's accusations, focusing instead on her betrayal. To refuse such a simple request? And after all I'd done for her?

"Let's do it in Aura's room," I said as I rode Denny.

He groaned. "Here is good."

"It'll be thrilling," I said, moving my hips more slowly.

Denny was quiet for a moment. "Maybe on her beanbag chair. A guy in my dorm told me he used to fuck his girlfriend on one and I always wondered if it was as good as he said."

We staggered to Aura's room, connected by various appendages, and I pushed Denny down onto the lime-green beanbag chair. I began to straddle him, but he squirmed.

"That fucking one-eyed teddy bear is staring at me," he said, pointing to a stuffed animal that sat perched on Aura's bed.

We decided to drag the chair to his room. It was surprisingly heavy, unwieldy; we made it halfway down the upstairs hall, naked and panting, before our coke-fueled desire overcame us. I pushed Denny down onto the chair again, straddled him and began fucking him like we were the last two people on earth. Denny reached up for my breasts; I lowered one into his mouth as I continued to pound him.

Halfway down that hall, where we'd given in to our carnal desires, put us right at the top of the stairs, in full view of the front door. Did I realize this when we dropped the chair in that very spot? Not consciously, I assure you—would I *choose* to shock my dear young protégé so, even being as wounded by her as I felt just then? Accident or not, when Aura, the Martyr, and the grandmother came home from shopping, the first thing they saw when they opened the front door was my naked torso, one spectacular breast inside Denny's mouth. Blissfully unaware, his back to the door, Denny moaned with pleasure as I continued to pump him with wild abandon, even after I made brief eye contact with Aura, just until the point where we both heard her scream.

18

Aura's scream—its edge of hysteria, its delicious timbre of shock and betrayal—was all I needed to balance the scales of the wrong she'd done me. I felt certain that once I got dressed, we could talk, mentor to protégé, and work out what she'd say to Principal Singer if asked. As I climbed off Denny his penis slid out of me, making a loud smacking sound that was, unfortunately, audible to our audience.

In Denny's room, the two of us dressed quickly, silently, as we heard the rumblings of an argument brewing below. When we got downstairs, the fight was loud and clear: the grandmother wanted to kick Denny out of her house, forcing him to go back to college; the mother wanted him to stay there but to report me to the police.

"The police? He's almost twenty," the grandmother said.

"Well, it's disgusting. She's Aura's teacher."

"So you want the police to charge her with what? Doing something distasteful?" As I've documented earlier, the grandmother was a fine woman, one who understood the messy nuances of life.

Aura sat in a corner of the living room, wincing as her mother and grandmother battled it out in the nearby kitchen.

"Aura," I said as I entered the room. "Can I talk to you for a moment?"

She fixed me with a piercing look. It reminded me, to my great surprise, of a look that my mother sometimes gave me. It was a look that said: *I'm on to you.*

"Talk to her? Get out of my house!" the Martyr shrieked from the kitchen doorway.

"*Your* house?" the grandmother roared. "Since when is this *your* house?"

"How could I forget whose house it is? You haven't stopped reminding me that we're here by your charity since the day we arrived." The Martyr's voice shook with pent-up rage; perhaps she hadn't taken her Valium that day.

As they went at it, Denny sat down next to Aura.

"I'm sorry, sis," he said. "That must have been weird for you."

Aura shrugged, but her eyes blazed.

From the kitchen: "My son was thinking of *divorcing* you! And now, because he died, I'm living with *Valley of the Dolls*."

"That's a lie!"

"You wish! He told me things, Jeannette. Oh, he told me things."

All this time, I'd never known that the Martyr's first name was Jeannette.

"I just think you should be careful with her," Aura said to Denny, motioning toward me.

"Now, Aura," I said in a tone that I hoped would soothe both Aura and my own nascent anger.

"She'll use you," Aura said to Denny. "She'll pretend to like you and then she'll try to get to Dad's friends through you."

Denny looked from Aura to me in stoner confusion. "Well—I don't really know Dad's friends anyway."

"Neither do I," Aura said, folding her arms and fixing me with a look that might have withered a lesser woman.

"You have no idea what I put up with from that man," the Martyr yelled at the grandmother. "*No idea.*"

"Men have needs, Jeannette," the grandmother said.

"Needs? You think he *needed* the sluts he paraded around under my nose?"

"I don't believe it."

"Believe it. And this one"—she gestured toward Denny, still seated on the couch next to Aura—"is trying to follow in Augustus's footsteps by fooling around with this little tramp." She looked me in the eyes, hands on hips.

This little tramp?

"Men *do* have needs," I said. "You may not realize that I knew Augustus from the poetry scene. He told me a bit about your—troubles."

"That's a lie," the Martyr said, though her lips trembled slightly.

Aura stood. "You knew my dad? I thought you just knew his poetry."

"You're beneath even Augustus's low standards," the Martyr said to me. "When we were walking around the Village, he used to say he could pick up the Jersey stench on a woman a mile away. 'That one has a whiff of the Meadowlands about her,' he'd say."

"Why would he say such a thing?" the grandmother asked. "Augie grew up in Hackensack."

That was news to me; I'd always assumed Augustus was a city boy, his mother's move to Jersey one of those poor decisions elderly people sometimes make.

"And he spent every waking minute he lived in Jersey figuring out how to escape this...*milieu*," the Martyr said. "And its trollops." With the last three words she fixed her eyes, so much like Aura's, directly on me.

What I would say next was, in retrospect, not the wisest move, strategically speaking. But I could not let her get away with assaulting my character. I had to go in for the kill.

"He likely said those things about Jersey girls to deflect suspicion," I said. "By the way, that was a charming apartment you had on Prince Street, especially that back room with all the orchids."

Now the Martyr and the grandmother both stared at me, mouths slightly open.

"You..." the Martyr croaked, but her voice trailed off and she was, poor dear, unable to finish the sentence.

"When were you in our apartment?" Denny asked, the import of what I'd just revealed not yet penetrating his chemically addled brain.

"She was in our apartment," Aura spat, "when she fucked Dad."

The Martyr's hand flew to her mouth; even the grandmother's warm eyes hardened as she looked at me.

Aura leapt to her feet. "Get out," she said to me. "Get out of our house now." She walked into the kitchen, picked up the receiver from the wall phone. "I mean it. Leave now or I'll call the police. I'll say all of Denny's drugs are yours."

"What drugs?" the Martyr wailed.

"My heart," the grandmother said, easing herself into a chair.

I tried to come up with a quick save, a way to get Aura and I back on the same page. But I knew I'd gone too far to fix it in one afternoon, and so I quietly showed myself out.

When I got home, I told my mother I'd left work ill and needed a nap, shutting my bedroom door behind me before she had a chance to answer. Normally I wouldn't have been able to sleep with all that coke in my system, but I'd had so little rest the night before that I fell into stupurous slumbers. In fact, I slept so deeply that when the phone rang an hour or two into my nap, it incorporated itself into a dream where I won the Pulitzer Prize in poetry; on the line was Andy Warhol, calling to congratulate me, with a personal invitation to the Factory. Later still, when my mother's voice roused me, I was confused by the darkness outside and unclear whether it was morning or night. My mother began banging on my door—which I'd wisely locked—until I finally groaned, "Okay, okay! Give me a minute!"

I put my silk bathrobe over my nude body and stuck my head out my bedroom door. "What time is it?" I asked.

"Eight," my mother called. "Come out in the living room."

"Eight a.m.? Why is it dark out?"

"*Come out here*, Lynda."

She had that exasperated note she got in her voice when I'd done something she felt was wrong. I tied my bathrobe and stepped out into it—whatever "it" might be.

Daddy was sitting in his chair, a grim look on his face.

"Oh, eight at night," I said, getting my bearings. "Let me get some water." I was monumentally parched.

After I'd downed a glass, I joined them, sitting on the far end of the sofa from my mother, across from Daddy.

"Lynda, Jeannette Lockhart called here a little while ago."

All this time, my mother knew her name, and I didn't? Unbelievable, the way this woman could ferret out useless information.

"She had some disturbing things to tell us," my mother added.

I was surprised the Martyr would report any of what had transpired to my mother, since it all reflected so badly on her. Had she been selective in the details she'd revealed? I'd tread carefully until I was certain of what they knew. "Mom, you realize she's a Valium addict," I said.

"You have an answer for everything, don't you?" my mother snapped. "Well, Millie confirmed it."

"Millie?"

"Aura's grandmother."

Damn! All these names. My mother was good.

Daddy leaned forward, his grimly creased face rearranging, reddening. "She said you had sex with that boy on a beanbag chair in the hallway, for everyone to see!" He pressed his fist to his mouth, then flung his arm down. "A beanbag chair!"

His eyes burned bright; Daddy had a long fuse, and it appeared I'd reached the end of it. But if the sex with Denny was foremost on his mind, that meant the Martyr hadn't revealed I'd slept with Augustus. I could still defuse this.

"Daddy, do you really think I'd do that?" I worked my most angelic smile on him.

His look cut right through me. "How's Lola?" he asked.

Had my mother told him Lola wasn't real, or was he simply wondering?

"She's fine," I said.

"Let's call her, then." Daddy stomped over to the wall phone, picked up the receiver. "What's her number?"

"Daddy—"

"*What's her number?*" His face was bright red; a vein pulsed in his right temple. I'd never seen him like this. It was time to shift tactics.

"Daddy, I'm sorry," I purred. Certainly I didn't want my sweet father to stroke out! "It's just that times have changed, and I didn't want to upset you."

"How long have you been lying to me? Since you moved back home? Since college?"

Since grade school, I thought, but of course I kept that to myself.

"Pat, it's not her fault," my mother piped in. "It's an illness."

Like an animal that picks up a distant scent of danger, I was alarmed by this turn in the conversation.

"What are you talking about, Mother?" I asked through clenched teeth.

"We took you to a psychiatrist when you were little," she said. "Do you remember?"

I decided to play on my father's sympathies. "I remember a man in a suit, asking me questions. His office was cold. He scared me."

My mother rolled her eyes, but my father winced; I was making inroads.

"He didn't scare you, Lynda. Nothing scares you." She sighed. "That's part of the problem."

Deftly I shifted my approach. "Do you know what psychiatrists were like back then, in the fifties? I'm lucky I didn't end up with a lobotomy!"

A small groan escaped my father's lips. I worked my wounded Bambi eyes on him.

"Dr. Johnston thought you needed treatment," my mother said. "But your father didn't agree."

Dad shot Mom a sharp look. "I still think that was the right decision," he snapped. "A grown man messing around in a little girl's head? But now, you're an adult, honey. Maybe it would be good to talk to someone."

"Talk to someone?" Was this their angle—they wanted me to see a shrink? I suppressed a laugh. Keep in mind that it was 1978; the sophisticates I knew from Studio often saw "analysts," but in Jersey, only crazy people went to psychiatrists.

"A doctor," Daddy said. "Someone who can help you figure out why you do these things."

"What things?" I needed to pin down exactly what they knew.

"What things?" Daddy's face grew red again. "What you did today wasn't enough?"

"Daddy," I said, "you're right that Denny and I should have been more discreet. But if a lack of discretion signals psychiatric illness, then most of our politicians would be in asylums."

"You leave Nixon out of this!" Daddy roared. "The man was railroaded!"

I was pleased to have diverted his wrath.

"It's not just this one incident," my mother said. "Every breakup you have is so dramatic—threats of restraining orders, boys who think you were kidnapped because you just disappeared."

Had she talked to Carlos at some point? How did she know about the threatened restraining order? Before I could answer, my mother leaned toward me, shifting her center of gravity as if readying for a pitch. "Beverly Fromme claims you shoved Jody into a wall." She turned to my father. "Her student, Pat. Her *student*."

And with that, my horrible day had come full circle.

"I may have pushed her out of my way a little more roughly than I should have," I said carefully. "But you have no idea how cruel Jody has been to Aura. She's a mean, heartless girl."

My mother stood and faced me. "So were you," she whispered.

So was I?

The horrified look on my father's face suggested my best play would be to address my mother's treachery. I let seconds tick by as my lower lip quivered.

"I can't believe you just said that to me," I whispered. "My own mother."

My father rose, walked across the living room, and sat down next to me. "Your mother didn't mean that," he said. "She's angry. We both are. I mean, this is a small town, Lynda. You could lose your job."

I wanted to tell him how little of a shit I gave about the town or the job, but I needed him on my side.

"I understand, Daddy," I said. "It's just so hard. What I really want is to be a poet. And it's impossible to be a poet here."

My mother scoffed. "Outside of The City, I mean," I added quickly. "For the connections."

"I know, sweetie," my father said. "But we just don't have that kind of money. I wish we did."

"Don't you apologize, Pat," my mother said. "If she wasn't traipsing around at discos all weekend, she'd have plenty of time to write her poetry."

I ignored my mother, turning toward my father. "Maybe," I said, "if you could just help me a little, I could move back to the East Village."

"Don't fall for it, Pat," my mother warned.

Daddy ignored her. "If you do what we'd like to see you do, then maybe we could help you with that," he said.

"Pat—" my mother started, but my father waved his hand at her.

"What would you like to see me do?"

"We want you to see a doctor or counselor," he said. "Someone who can help you sort things out."

"That's what *she* wants," I said, motioning back toward my mother. "What do you want?"

And then, my father did something that chilled me to my core. In fact, I can barely write the words. He ran his hands through his thinning hair, leaned forward, straightened in his seat, looked me in the eye.

And refused to give in to me.

"It's what I want too," he said. "I worry about you, Lynda. The way you deal with people—you act more like a man than a woman. And I know times have changed, and women are liberated and can burn their bras and all of that, but you know what? *Men* haven't changed. Beautiful girls like you get killed in The City all the time. This life you're living, the way you leave a trail of broken hearts—it's not safe."

"Daddy—"

"Don't 'Daddy' me," he said, his words a cleaver through my heart. "You can continue to live here, and we'll hope that the rumors don't reach your principal. But you have to see a"—he choked up a little before he could get the word out—"*a doctor.*"

I tamped down my outrage as I considered it. If all they wanted was for me to sit in a shrink's office and spill about my life, how bad could that be? I had enough material about my mother for several years' worth of sessions.

"Maybe that's not such a bad idea," I said, choosing my words carefully. "It wouldn't hurt to talk to someone."

"Of course not," my father said, brightening.

"I just hate for you to have to spend your money on something like this," I said.

"You'll be paying for it, Lynda," my mother replied in an icy tone.

I turned and faced her. "I don't make enough to cover that," I said sweetly.

"Yes, you do," she shot back. "You make a good salary, and you don't pay rent. You'll stop going to The City on weekends, buying fancy disco clothes. Then you'll have plenty of money."

I'm sure most daughters have experienced these moments, where your mother says something so simultaneously out-of-touch and condescending that you want to lunge at her and claw her face to hamburger with your manicured nails. *Fancy disco clothes*?

"Are you saying," my voice betrayed a barely controlled rage, "that I'm—*grounded*?"

"You can go out in Jersey and date men here. *Men*," she emphasized, "not boys. If your friend Hal wants to come visit you and meet us, that's fine. But no trips to New York. If you consider that grounded, then, yes, you're grounded."

I stood, inches from her face. "I'm *twenty-six years old*, Mother!"

She didn't flinch. "When you start acting older than a teenager, we'll stop treating you like one."

Many times in my young life I'd wanted to hit my mother, but that moment was the closest I actually came. I pulled my forearm back as if about to deliver a slap. She flinched. The flinch was what I'd wanted, so I didn't carry through.

"Then I guess I'll pack my things and go," I said, my voice quivering with emotion for my father's benefit.

In my bedroom, I quickly got dressed, and began to pack. It took three suitcases to hold all my "fancy disco clothes." I had a sudden inspiration to use that abhorrent phrase for the title of a new poem; returning to the vast well of my art momentarily soothed me.

My mother walked in while I was still packing. "I'll return your suitcases once I get settled," I spat at her.

"That's okay," she said. "Where will you go? To Hal's?"

The truth was, in my shock and rage I hadn't thought about where I'd go. If I wanted to keep teaching—and I would have to, I needed the money now more than ever—I'd need a place to crash in Keyhole at least during the week.

"What do you care?" I snapped, sounding every bit the teenager she believed I was.

"I do care," she said. "If I didn't, I wouldn't get involved."

I zipped a duffel bag filled entirely with "fancy disco" footwear, then cleared armfuls of cosmetics from the bathroom sink straight into my overnight bag.

"What you care about," I said, "is what these Keyhole cunts like Jeannette Lockhart and Beverly Fromme think." I kept my voice deliberately low so that my father wouldn't hear.

My mother's hand flew melodramatically to her heart. "How could I raise a daughter who talks like that?"

"Save it for Father Amato next Sunday," I said, gathering as many bags as I could carry in my first trip to my car. "But while you're in the confessional, don't forget to tell him how you undermined your own daughter's ambitions at every turn."

I left her sitting on the bed, mouth agape, as I took the first suitcases outside. I'd expected my father might get up to help me, but he watched in sullen silence. When I returned to my bedroom, my mother was still there on the bed, the same idiotic, incredulous look on her face. Beyond everything else she'd just said and done, beyond the string of betrayals going back to my childhood, it was that look, the fatuousness of it, the blank-eyed Keyhole-ness of it, that finally blew the lid off my rage. On my way to the front door, I made sure to brush, with the rabbit fur jacket I held folded over one arm, my mother's incomprehensibly prized plate that she claimed was from Italy, sending the garish ceramic disc teetering on its stand and then crashing to the floor, that brightly painted Italian boot landing in jagged pieces on the linoleum.

I drove off quickly but parked two blocks down my parents' street. Where *would* I go? I had no friends in Keyhole, despite having grown up there. One of the Dim Bulbs would probably take me in, but both of their wives hated me, and I couldn't tolerate those shrill, pudding-smeared kids. Would Carla or Tess offer me a room, or at least a couch? Johnny's bandmate in Asbury Park, Mike, would probably let me stay there, but I'd have to give him a blow job, and I found him loathsome. Who in Keyhole was so far down on their luck themselves that they wouldn't know or care about my own rock bottom, wouldn't ask questions, would just acquiesce?

I sat, chewing on my lip, when it hit me: Dan Wykoski.

Smiling with self-pleasure, I dug out a lipstick, applied it perfectly—that nap had done wonders!—and brushed my hair, still big and messy from sleep. Then I drove to a phone booth, hoisted up the dangling phone book, found Dan's address, and drove straight there. After I rang the doorbell twice, he greeted me with a puzzled look, but invited me in.

19

You may be wondering, Jann, what happened with "The Miller's." Were my suspicions warranted, or am I still, as I write this, waiting for the proverbial other shoe to drop? After several days of limbo and a minor argument with Hubby about whether we should pack some bags and take a "vacation," a literal boxful of shoes dropped—leading to the Pugsub making himself useful in more ways than one.

I had ordered, in a late-night bout of insomnia, several sexy pairs from a well-known internet foot emporium. My preference is to shop in person, but the offerings in this part of the country are, in a word, tedious. "It's the twenty-first century, babe," Hubby always says when I complain about our local stores' limited fare, encouraging me to shop online. One night I tried it, and I did indeed find a cornucopia of flamboyant footwear: stilettos in my signature red, gold gladiator sandals, kitten-heels with ostrich feathers, rhinestone platform sneakers.

And so, at my doorstep that morning, an oversized box appeared. With Hubby off doing whatever it is he does to pay for such necessities, I looked around for help—I would not risk breaking a nail myself!—when Mee-chelle began yapping and I knew the Pugsub was nearby. Never one to miss an opportunity, I called out to him.

"I could use a little help," I purr-shouted, motioning to the box.

"Oh, sure, Lola," the Pugsub called back.

Surely you didn't think Hubby and I have been using our real names, all these years?

The Pugsub tied an outraged Mee-chelle to our mailbox and headed up the walkway.

Once he'd carried the box into my foyer, I offered him a glass of iced tea. I'd never extended such a courtesy before; he brightened, and prattled about a recent visit from his daughter and grandson as I poured the tea. But when he pulled out his phone to show me photos, I nearly tossed him out on the spot. I did not have the patience to look at peasant-faced Jessica or Jennifer or whatever 1980s J-name he'd said his daughter had, with hollow-eyed little Jaxon or Jaren seated in her lap, but look I did. O, what these eyes of mine have seen!

Swiftly I returned the phone to him and transitioned to my ulterior motive: information.

"Say, it's been pretty quiet next door," I said, motioning toward "The Miller's." "Have you heard anything about how they're doing?"

"Oh," the Pugsub said, the merriment of a loathsome frat brother in his eyes, "you haven't heard the neighborhood gossip?"

"No! Fill me in." I smiled my most persuasive smile, though it was clearly unnecessary.

"Apparently, they're not really married! Gary had been cheating on his wife for years with Patsy, and they ran off together. From what I heard, he did some cloak-and-dagger stuff to try to keep the wife from tracking him down. Something about a Beanie Baby collection that he didn't want to have to split in half?"

I laughed out loud. I couldn't help it. As the Pugsub fixed me with a questioning look, my laughter intensified. I'd been right—they were hiding *something*! But it was nothing that mattered for Hubby and me. The Pugsub began chuckling along with me like the insipid toad he was. I pulled myself together.

"I'm sorry—it's just, we went over there for drinks one night, and I knew something was amiss."

"I haven't gotten to the best part yet."

I waved him along in the story.

"I stopped by the hospital to see how he was doing. His wife was there! He'd called her to apologize when he thought he was dying, and she flew down from Michigan. Now she and Patsy visit him on a schedule so they don't overlap."

"Wow." I almost felt sorry for Mrs., who was not a Mrs. at all. "Has he decided who he's staying with?"

The Pugsub shrugged. "I got the sense that Patsy might be packing up her things soon."

I took a long swig of iced tea, let the cold liquid rest on my tongue for a moment. "Say, did you ever talk to Patsy much?"

"Oh yeah. She was a chatterer. Plus, you know, the thing with their stereo speakers." He smiled in a conspiratorial way.

"Right," I said quickly, to dash whatever hopes he had of extracting a confession from me. "Did she ever talk about her past? Something about dating a famous musician?"

He rolled his eyes. "Johnny Engel. She mentioned it more than once."

So it really *had* been a weird coincidence. Did I ever have a story to tell Hubby that night!

"How sad," I said. "To be so obsessed with something that happened so long ago."

My antennae had gone up about "The Miller's" partly because of the quirks in their decorating scheme—too much stuff crammed into small spaces, a cutesiness that appeared forced. You can tell a lot about a person by the way they live. Women are accustomed to dolling themselves up, and most do the same for their homes, even if their taste—I'm thinking not just of my neighbor, but of my mother here—is cloying to the point of suffocation. But a man's apartment or house is, even more than his eyes, a window into his soul.

It was clear from the moment I stepped into Dan Wykoski's depressing bachelor pad that he needed help. Pizza boxes sat haphazardly stacked in the living room; the innards of newspapers were strewn around the floor, the coffee table, the arm of the sofa. Empty Budweiser cans were everywhere, crumpled and tossed.

Dan Wykoski was obviously a drowning man, crying out for help. He was fortunate, indeed, that I had come to his rescue.

I filled Dan in on only what he needed to know: namely, that I'd had a fight with my parents and needed a place to stay for a few days until it blew over. I wasn't actually certain how long I would be at Dan's, but I figured he'd be happy for the company.

"Beer?" Dan asked as he headed to the kitchen.

"Sure."

He drank three cans to my one, and in that time, I got him to carry my luggage into the spare bedroom that had clearly once been his office. Filing cabinets that were likely full of lesson plans now sat covered with depositions and copies of legal motions.

"You can just clear this stuff off," he said, attempting to sweep armfuls of papers from the bed, but losing his footing and landing on his ass on the floor. He looked up at me, grinning like an eight-year-old.

Clearly he'd had a few drinks before I got there.

"Dan," I said, "why don't you go to bed? I can handle all this. We'll talk more in the morning."

"Suuuuuure," he slurred, and tried to get his footing, but landed on his ass again.

I helped lift him to his feet, and walked him to his room, where I pushed him inside and shut the door before he could make the inevitable pass at me. While I was often liberal with my spectacular blow jobs, Dan Wykoski was not my type. He was weak, and I'd never needed to use sex to bend weak men to my will.

Once I was done with Dan for the night, I tried to call Hal. If I could stay with him in The City on weekends, this arrangement might be tolerable until I could figure out a better plan. But I got an answering machine—Hal was the first person I knew to have one of those—and I left a message asking him to call me at Dan's number.

I sat on the twin bed in Dan's spare bedroom, running through scenarios in my head regarding how I'd handle things at work. So much depended on what Dick knew. But I was tired; not even my cat nap from earlier that evening helped the bone-crushing fatigue. I was finally crashing hard from all that coke I'd done with Denny.

I set my alarm to call in to work the next morning. I'd already left school "sick"; another day off would really sell it, as well as buy me time. With this short-term plan in place, I quickly plunged into a coma-level sleep that was only interrupted by the insistent buzz of the alarm the next morning.

Once I'd left my message at work, I found my host in the kitchen, a room whose level of filth made it clear that Dan Wykoski had not been raised by an Italian mother. He poured boiling water over Sanka in a chipped black mug. *WNEW-FM, 102.7, Where Rock Lives*, it said in yellow lettering on the side of the cup—a tagline that, in retrospect, was perhaps a defensive jab at my beloved disco music. The absurd Disco vs. Rock debate was at its height in 1978, and post-hippie stoners like Dan tended to be extremely touchy on the subject.

"Do you have any real coffee?" I asked.

Dan shook his head. "I need to go to the store."

I peered into his nearly bare fridge, then his freezer, from which I extracted a container of frozen orange juice concentrate. While it defrosted, I had no choice but Sanka. I winced when I took my first sip.

"Sorry," Dan said. "I didn't know I was going to have company."

I looked around at the grease-splattered walls, the overflowing trash, the beer cans and newspapers that adorned every room of that house.

If my mother were in my position, she'd have taken it upon herself to clean the entire place, as a thank you for Dan's generosity. But what would Dan learn from that?

"Dan," I said, "I'm sure being out of work has been rough, but you can't live like this."

"I know." He rubbed his hands together. "I'm just so freaked out. My lawyer doesn't think I'll go to jail, but you never know."

"Listen to your lawyer," I said. "Look, I'll make you a deal. I'll go out and buy some groceries while you clean this place up. But I mean really clean—from top to bottom, all of that trash out at the curb. I want it sparkling by the end of the day."

I knew I'd sized Dan up correctly when he didn't flinch at my orders.

An hour later, on my way out the door, I turned to him. "Could you give me some money for groceries? I don't have anything until payday."

Dan reluctantly handed over two twenties. *Staying here is going to work out even better than I dared hope*, I thought as I stuffed the bills in my wallet, grabbed my purse, and headed out the door.

My first stop was a diner—this time, one in Atlantic Highlands, as I did not want another run-in with Frumpy Fromme. After a lovely and lengthy breakfast on Dan's dime, I took a walk on the beach. It was a warm early spring day, one that held the promise of summer; the seagulls seemed to cry out to me that I wouldn't be down for long, that a better life was on the horizon. After enough time had passed that I thought Dan might be close to finished with the cleaning, I headed to the Grand Union, bought groceries with what was left of the forty bucks, and drove back to his place.

"Lynda! That was quick," he said when I returned four hours later, a half-filled bag of groceries in each arm. Although Dan was no longer actively smoking pot, he still had that kind of stoner brain where he easily lost track of time.

He'd done a passable job: all of the trash—the beer cans, the pizza boxes, the newspapers—was gone. He'd vacuumed too. But when I put the groceries away, I saw that everything in the kitchen was still coated with a layer of grease, and dirty dishes remained in the sink.

At the Grand Union I'd bought the latest copies of *Glamour* and *Cosmopolitan*; Christie Brinkley was on the cover of both. When would the fashion industry get over its obsession with blondes? I poured myself a glass of Tab and brought it and the magazines to the living room, where I sat on the couch, propping my feet on Dan's coffee table. I could be a blonde if I wanted to, of course, but I refused to capitulate.

"Don't forget to do the kitchen," I said when Dan returned from bringing the trash out to the curb.

He looked puzzled for a moment, as if realizing that I, a guest, should not be giving him orders; but then I promised him a beer once he finished, and, forgetting that he'd actually paid for the beer himself, he did as he'd been told while I thumbed through *Glamour*.

I wore the red Qiana dress to work the next day, knowing that I was walking into a test of my nerve and ingenuity and needing to look and feel my best. I had done a number of things that were potential grounds for dismissal, and I had no idea how much, if any of it, Dick Singer knew. Fortunately, I possessed the improv skills that could get me through all of it, and, after applying some face powder in the car to tamp down my skin's natural glow—I wanted to appear as if I'd been ill, and my color hadn't returned yet—I strode confidently into the school.

When I signed in, the receptionist told me I needed to see Dick "immediately."

"But I have a class first period," I said.

"He has a substitute for your class today. He said he wanted to see you the second you came in."

This wasn't good, I knew. But I reminded myself of how easily manipulated Dick was. *Just stick your tits out*, I thought as I entered his office.

"Go right on in, hon," Patti said, with a sad tilt to her head.

This was definitely not good.

I strode in as if I were walking a runway in Milan.

"Dick," I said, "I'm so happy to be back. That flu really knocked me out."

"The flu, was it?" Dick asked. "It's not really flu season."

"It felt like the flu," I said smoothly. "It took every ounce of strength I had to get back here today." I sat across from him and leaned back with a sigh, as if exhausted from the exertion. "Thank you so much for getting me a substitute today! That was so thoughtful of you."

This clearly knocked him off-axis for a moment. He sat quietly, contemplating my spectacular breasts; I've already communicated what that dress did for them, so no need to revisit it here. But then he tented his fingers in front of him, leaned forward.

"Lynda, a very serious allegation was made against you. I hope it's not true. If it were, we'd have to let you go."

"What's the allegation?" I asked, my mind quickly flipping through the many possibilities.

"There were reports that you were drunk at work Tuesday, the day you left early."

"Drunk?"

Dick nodded. "I heard that you appeared disheveled and smelled of alcohol."

Which one of those rancid little trolls had turned me in? Rhonda Ford? Unlikely—she loathed the principal. Marisol Rodriguez? I doubted it. Marisol had been plotting her escape from Keyhole since she was born, and taking down her eighth-grade English teacher would do nothing in service of her plan. Then I thought of Jody and Kathi. Their faces when I'd told Marisol they weren't worth her time.

"Obviously it's not true," I said. "I'm sure you know that."

Dick sighed. "I want to believe you, Lynda. But there are so many rumors swirling around. Where there's smoke, there's usually fire."

"What rumors?" I asked.

"Two of the mothers swear that you tried to seduce their husbands during parent-teacher conferences. There's been talk of a restraining order in your past. Jody Fromme's mother insists you physically abused her daughter. And now this talk of drunkenness at work."

I decided to tackle the easiest one first—the only rumor that was patently untrue.

"Dick," I said, uncrossing and re-crossing my legs. "Do you really think I'm interested in any of the fathers of my students?"

Dick snorted. "Not really."

"And you can easily check with the police about a restraining order."

"I did. They have no record."

Of course they didn't. Carlos had only *threatened* to do it. But how had that rumor gone so far?

"As for Jody's mother, I have no idea why she's pushing this lie. She confronted me recently and it was, to be frank, frightening." I sighed, as if weary from my recent illness and Bad Highlights Bev's unfounded allegation.

"When I asked Jody, she denied it," Dick said.

Jody had *denied* it? Ha! Blowhard Bev had been correct: Jody really was afraid of me.

"She has more integrity than I realized, not backing up her mother's lie," I said, staring off into the distance as if reconsidering my opinion of Jody. The shift in my gaze gave Dick a chance to ogle me more blatantly, an opportunity he seized.

"I'll admit that last part puzzles me," Dick said. "Jody really hates you. I mean, she told me she hates you. I was surprised she denied the accusation."

"So that just leaves this last allegation," I said, hoping to move the discussion along. "I was not drunk at work, nor was I drinking. I was ill. Whoever made this claim about me was misinformed, or deliberately trying to sabotage me."

Dick stared at my breasts for a good ten seconds, then looked away and sighed. "Perhaps," he said. "But can you tell me why Aura Lockhart came to me this morning and asked to be moved from your classroom?"

Of all the news Dick had delivered, this landed as a gut punch. Of course, I'd known I had work to do in regaining Aura's confidence. But to ask to be moved from my classroom, with no consideration as to how this might affect my job, my position in the school? I found the girl's selfishness and immaturity to be deeply disappointing.

"Did she give a reason?"

"I'm asking you."

It seemed unlikely that Aura had told Dick about my sleeping with Denny, or for that matter, Augustus—teenagers are so easily embarrassed!—so I took a moment to rearrange my dress and calculate the best cover. "I think you know I took Aura under my wing," I finally said.

He nodded.

"Perhaps we got a bit too close. Almost like sisters. And as little sisters sometimes do, she came to see me as a rival."

Dick leaned in closer, his brow furrowed. "A rival?"

"I've been dating a man who Aura has a crush on. Of course there was no real rivalry—he'd never date a child!—but it hurt her feelings. And I probably didn't handle it as well as I should have." So many nuggets of truth in that explanation that it was nearly true in its entirety.

"Oh," Dick said. He appeared lost in thought, as if trying to fathom the unfathomable, namely: women.

"Let me talk to Aura," I said. "I'm sure I can smooth it over. If not, perhaps I can hand her lessons for the rest of the year over to Peter Ferrari, and you can put her in his class." I resisted the urge to smile at the brilliance of this idea: extra work for Peter, and humiliation for Aura at being put into a seventh-grade class. Neither would agree to it.

Dick fixed a look on me: not lecherous, but a more discerning kind of studying.

"And I've learned my lesson about getting too close to my students," I added. "I was trying to follow your direction, but I think I stumbled a bit."

I sat back and waited to see if my subtle shifting of the blame onto him would work. As I watched, he leaned back in his chair, relaxed his shoulders, looked at my breasts again.

"You can go home for the rest of the day today and we'll count it as a regular sick day. Fresh start tomorrow."

I smiled like the good girl Dick wanted me to be—well, in school, anyway.

"But before you leave," he added, "let me call Aura down here, and give you two a few minutes alone to talk things through. We can't move her to another class. I need you to set her mind at ease."

"I will," I said brightly, though I had no idea how I'd accomplish that.

"And, Lynda, I need for things to quiet down. No more complaints."

"You can count on me, Dick," I said, tossing a dazzling smile his way.

20

Before Dick could call Aura out of class, a girl who looked to be about eleven arrived in his office, breathless. Two sixth-grade boys had gotten into a fight, she said; Miss Spagnola had asked her to get help. I'd always found it odd that Carla and so many of the other female teachers still used the antiquated "Miss" or "Mrs." rather than "Ms." It was 1978—we were women, for fuck's sake, hear us roar! What a tragedy for Helen Reddy that I was the only woman who ever took the sentiment to heart.

As Dick ran down to the gym, I relished the reprieve to consider how to handle things with Aura. While I mulled possible tactics, Patti popped her head into Dick's office.

"Hon, do you have a minute?" she asked.

"Of course," I said brightly. Patti was my girl on the inside.

She teetered in on her stiletto heels, shutting the door behind her. Patti's hair had achieved peak Jersey, as high and frothy as was chemically and meteorologically possible.

"Your hair looks amazing today," I said. There was no denying it was a feat of architecture.

"Aww, you're sweet," she said, lightly touching her Aqua-Netted masterpiece. "Dick would kill me for telling you this. But I know who ratted you out the other day."

"Who?" I asked, fully expecting to hear Kathi's name, since Dick had already established that Jody was afraid of me.

"Peter Ferrari."

Peter Ferrari? *Peter Ferrari?* I hadn't thought the weasel-faced motherfucker had it in him! He'd tried and failed to destroy my reputation in the teachers' lounge after our breakup, and now he was setting his sights on my job itself? Bad move, Peter. Bad, bad move.

"I know it's a shock, hon," Patti added. "Some guys are just assholes after you dump them."

It was not a shock, of course, but I decided it best to play out that angle, arranging my expression to one of hurt and bewilderment. "How did you find this out?"

"Well, he stormed in here the other morning, demanding to see Dick immediately. In cases like that, I do a little eavesdropping." She smiled. "The walls are thinner than Dick realizes."

Thank the baby Jesus, as my mother would say, for Patti. And as for Peter Ferrari, my mind was already clicking with plans for a counterattack.

"I tried so hard with him," I said. "But when a guy is terrible in bed, what can you do?"

Patti, gossip that she was, perked right up. "He was bad in bed?"

"Oh, he's so uptight! He has no idea of how to please a woman." I leaned into Patti and lowered my voice conspiratorially. "And he has no staying power."

"Really?"

"He comes faster than a teenager."

Patti grinned in a slightly evil way. "He should have been nicer to you if he wanted you to keep that secret."

"Exactly."

I wondered how long it would take for Patti to spread the impromptu opening salvo in my newly declared war on Peter. Two days, I thought. Tops.

Dick returned with Aura in tow. He and Patti both exited the office, Patti closing the door behind her.

Aura was wearing jeans and a yellow T-shirt with a fluorescent green worm on the front. In small letters beneath, all lower case: "glow worm." Yellow was not her color, but I thought it best to keep that observation to myself.

"When did Johnny get band T-shirts made up?" I asked, to break the ice.

She shrugged. I motioned her to sit down; she shook her head, so I remained standing too.

"Aura, I'm not upset with you," I said, keeping my voice low in case Patti was eavesdropping. "I understand how awkward it was for you, walking in on me with your brother. But I think—"

"*You're* not upset with *me*?"

"I mean, about your asking to be reassigned to a different teacher."

She fixed those blue eyes on me, her look penetrating. "You fucked both my dad and my brother and you're surprised I don't want to be in your class anymore?"

"Keep your voice down," I whispered.

"Oh, you don't want anyone to know that, do you?"

I opened the door a crack and peered into the outer office. Fortunately, Patti was nowhere to be seen.

"I'm sure that was confusing for you," I said.

"I'm not confused. I'm seeing things pretty clearly now. And I'm telling you that you'd better leave my family the fuck alone." Her jaw was set in a hard line, her arms folded, but I saw a slight tremble in her lips.

It was time, I recognized, for a change in tactics.

"Being an adult isn't easy, Aura," I said. "And being a woman is especially hard."

Her eyes continued to blaze as she looked at me.

"The sexual liberation that we women have now? It's great, but it's not without its share of difficulties."

Her body language didn't change but I was certain I saw a slight shift, something softening in her eyes.

I settled into a chair. "When I was in college, we were taught that free love was the answer to everything. It would liberate us. It would keep us from becoming like our parents. Hell, it might even end wars!"

She let out a small, exasperated noise.

"I know, it sounds ridiculous. It *was* ridiculous. But we believed it. And I think maybe, on some level, I still believed it. Until the other day."

She leaned down, searching my eyes, as if she could discern the truth through sheer force of will. It was something I'd seen my mother do.

"I always thought as long as sex was happening between two willing adults, it was a positive thing. A good thing. But I never thought about other kinds of damage that could be done."

Aura pulled a chair up and sat down across from me, her face inches from mine.

"You want me to believe it never occurred to you my mom might have been upset that you slept with her husband? Or that I might be upset you slept with both my dad and my brother?"

I was quiet for a moment, as if mulling it all over. I summoned a few tears to well in my eyes.

"Maybe on some level I did know," I said. "Maybe that was why I wanted to get close to you, to help you through this difficult time. To try to make it up to you."

She shifted in the chair, her back straightening.

"And of course, I wanted to nurture your talent."

She let out a small scoffing sound from the back of her throat. "I told my mom about how you wanted me to give Uncle John your poems. She thinks you've just been using me to get published."

Of course the Martyr would have the worst possible opinion of me! "Do you think that?" I boldly asked.

"Honestly? Most of the poets I know are fucking lunatics, including my dad."

It wasn't exactly an answer, but felt like an opening, so I decided to dive in.

"Aura, let's give it another try in class. I'll give you as much space as you need."

Her look was almost adult in its piercing intensity.

"And if that works out," I added, "maybe we could put this all behind us one day and be friends again." I still had my dreams for fierce young Aura, of course! I longed to see my protégé hobnobbing with celebrities at Studio, becoming best friends with Brooke Shields and those brats from *Annie*. And if the Studio celebration in question were for my first book of poems, published after Aura made just a simple, painless phone call—well, so much the better.

Her entire face contracted and she rose quickly from her seat. "Principal Singer made it clear that I can't leave your class," she said. "But we'll never be friends again, Ms. Boyle. I'll deal with you in school, but beyond that—just leave me alone, okay? I don't trust you anymore."

The clarity and finality of her words might have daunted a lesser woman. But as she turned to leave the office, I saw an expression of confusion on her face that, frankly, pleased me. The adult world, with its shifting emotions and unexpected intricacies, was a difficult place to navigate for most teenagers; her confusion was an opening. My dream of fame for us both might still be realized.

I left Dick's office just as the third-period bell rang. Perhaps a lesser woman would have considered herself lucky, beat a hasty retreat, headed home. But I had a little more work to do that day. I headed straight to the teacher's lounge for what had always been my free period, knowing exactly who would be there: Carla. Tess. Mr. Murton.

And Peter.

I walked slowly, letting the crowded halls thin out, so that everyone would be assembled in the lounge when I arrived. Making an entrance was important. I stood in the doorway for a few crucial seconds.

"And then Danny Fallon yells, 'Your mother swallows,' and Gino Cosella yells, 'Your father would know,' and the next thing the two of them are on top of each other and all the other boys—and even a few girls—are chanting 'Fight! Fight! Fight!' It was crazy." Carla shook her head.

"Any idea what started it?" Peter asked, but before anyone could answer, I swung the door open.

"Lynda!" Tess cried. "How are you feeling?"

"Much better," I said. "I'll be back to work tomorrow. I just had an—*administrative issue* to settle with Dick today." I looked directly at Peter when I said the latter sentence; he shifted in his chair and looked away.

"All settled?" Carla asked.

"All settled," I said brightly.

Mr. Murton, who had appeared to be dozing, peered up at me. "You look well," he said, his expression as inscrutable as that of an ancient sea turtle.

"I feel so much better." I poured myself a mug of coffee, deliberately sat with an empty chair between me and Peter. "You won't believe the crazy thing Dick told me."

Everyone, even Mr. Murton, leaned in closer.

"Oh, but wait, Carla, you were in the middle of a story. Why don't you finish that first?" I can be such a terrible tease!

"Just your typical sixth-grade fight," Carla said. "What did Dick tell you?"

"He said someone claimed I came to work drunk on Tuesday! Can you believe that?"

They were all quiet, Carla and Tess shooting furtive glances at Peter, who sat stone-faced. "Obviously, I didn't come to work intoxicated," I added. "But I'd had a sleepless night the night before."

"Huh," Carla said.

I'd hoped for a little sisterly solidarity from Carla and Tess, an opening to seed information about Peter's irrational vendetta against me. But they sat stone-faced.

"With all the toking that goes on here between classes, it seems especially ironic that someone accused me of being *drunk*."

"No one really tokes between classes anymore, Lynda," Tess said. "Not since Dan got arrested."

Peter was quiet, studying me. A shift in tactics was called for.

"I wonder if the person who accused me was the same person who ratted Dan out to the police," I said. "I mean, it seems likely."

This bit of brilliance on my part fully shifted the dynamic in the room.

"I thought Dan was caught buying drugs," Carla said.

"My cousin Tony is a cop. He told me they received an anonymous tip." Tony had never said that, of course, but it was plausible.

Carla and Tess quietly glared at Peter, obviously wondering if he had ratted Dan out.

"Let's get back to that fight you were telling us about," Peter said to Carla, squirming a bit in his chair, but she didn't answer.

My work there was done; I exited with a swoosh of my red Qiana.

I still had the entire afternoon off, and decided a trip to The City was in order. Not to see Hal; I was irritated that he hadn't returned my call, but not yet enraged enough to cause a scene at his office at Studio. No, I sought some one-on-one time with Johnny. Since we'd smoothed things over at CBGB the previous weekend, I hoped, without Aura around, we could finally get back on track.

I know what you're thinking about, Jann: Johnny's insistence that he was gay. It certainly would have deterred a lesser woman, but I knew, deep in the marrow of my sexy bones, I could sway him if we just had some time alone.

As I walked through Johnny's West Village neighborhood, I realized that I had no idea what he did with his days. He didn't seem to have a job, or at least, he'd never talked about having one. I'd gotten the sense that he'd saved up a wad of cash before he moved to New York—but that nest egg couldn't last forever, could it? O, there were so many depths to Johnny I'd yet to plumb!

Half a block from his apartment, I saw Johnny—beautiful, golden-haloed Johnny—step out of his doorway. I was about to call out to him when another figure emerged, close on his heels. A sour-faced guy with ample curly brown hair, handsome only in the most common of ways.

That guy from Studio. Clay.

They didn't hold hands—such a display would have been rare back then—but there was something about the proximity of their bodies as they walked down the street, a palpable electricity, that told me they weren't just fucking. They were, at least for the moment, a couple.

I slowed my pace until they'd disappeared around a corner. Then I reached Johnny's doorstep, my anger building. How dare he initiate another relationship while our status was still in limbo! At the very least he'd owed me the courtesy of a phone call. What did this Clay have that I didn't have? Besides a penis?

As I stood at the entrance to Johnny's building, contemplating the scope of this betrayal, another tenant headed out, and instinctively I grabbed the door. The frumpy woman looked me up and down as she left.

Grabbing that door had been an impulse, but once I was inside, emotions roiling, my purpose became clear: revenge. I flew up the three flights of stairs to Johnny's apartment and stood in front of his door. But how to get in? I'd picked a lock or two in my day, but Johnny's place had the kind of deadbolt that would not likely succumb to a deftly maneuvered paper clip.

Fortunately, Johnny had only locked the flimsy doorknob lock, not the deadbolt, and I gained entrance relatively easily. I've always felt the hand of Fate in situations like this: the universe was well aware that I'd been ill-treated and helped make it possible for me to settle the score.

I looked around his apartment, considering my options. Nothing so obvious as smashing one of his guitars would do; as with Carlos, I preferred to leave gifts that were not immediately apparent. But the place was so small that my possibilities were truly limited, and then it hit me: smashing an instrument wasn't the only way to ruin it.

I considered keying his electric guitar or prying off the mother of pearl, but again, too unimaginative. My attention shifted to his acoustic guitar, out of its case and propped up against a wall as if he'd just serenaded Clay with it—as he'd once serenaded *moi*.

I threw open Johnny's cupboards, searching for something I could pour into the guitar's sound hole. Honey? Ketchup? Under the sink I finally found an item that I was certain would do the kind of damage my wounded heart demanded: Liquid Plumr. My every blood vessel pounded with fury as I removed it from the cabinet, nearly panting in my need for justice as I raced over to the guitar.

Once I'd poured the entire contents of the drain cleaner into that hole in the middle of the instrument, my steam-heat anger began to quell. I leaned the guitar back against the wall where I'd found it. Would the bottom fall out before Johnny returned home? Or would he pick it up to play and only then realize the magnitude of the destruction? I truly wished I had a hidden camera so I could witness his reaction, but alas, such technology was limited in the 1970s. I put the empty container of drain cleaner back under the sink and let myself out, a spring in my step that told me my revenge had been both adequate and just.

21

Toward the end of my beloved twentieth century, Hubby began doing some work that—well, let's just say it *might* have violated the terms of our agreement with the U.S. government. For my own sake I am not privy to all the details. Hubby was very selective about who he worked with, but one night, he was stunned to run into an old associate from our Studio days: a bartender everyone had called Hot Pants Harry, for obvious reasons.

Hot Pants's pad was in the same lowest-common-denominator state but not the same town where we currently reside. It was, however, in the town where we lived then, and Hubby and I both found this to be an alarming coincidence. We were worried that either my husband's old associates or our government handlers had sent Hot Pants to entrap us. As such, we decided it a necessary risk to meet Hot Pants at his home and get a feel for whether he was setting us up.

Hot Pants's condo was immaculate, yet a bit shabby. The furniture all had a thrift store feel; perhaps he was down on his luck, I thought at first. Two amateurish paintings had a prominent place in the living room. There was a framed photo on the coffee table of a family, a couple with two kids, all of them with light hair, blue or hazel eyes. Hot Pants had thick dark hair, furry brows, brown eyes.

"My brother, and his wife and kids," he said when I asked.

"You don't look much like them," I said.

"I was adopted," Hot Pants said—too quickly and defensively, Hubby and I later agreed.

I nodded. "Could I use your bathroom?"

He steered me in the right direction. On the way through the kitchen, I noticed a cereal bowl with a spoon in the kitchen sink, placed a little too perfectly, designed to make me think he'd had breakfast there.

In the bathroom, my worst suspicions were confirmed when I saw that the toilet seat was down. What man who lives alone puts the toilet seat *down*? I lifted it (carefully, with tissues—no fingerprints), and looked at the underside of the seat. No urine splatter.

What man, I ask you, does not splatter some urine on the underside of the toilet seat?

I flushed the toilet and exited quickly, clutching my stomach.

"Diarrhea," I said.

"What?" Hot Pants asked.

"I'm sorry," Hubby said to him. "I have to get her home. Maybe we can get together soon."

"I don't have your number," Hot Pants called out to us as we forced ourselves to walk, not run, to the car. We took off, Hubby driving erratically around that city until we were sure we hadn't been followed.

"You saved us, babe," he said when we finally felt we could relax. "I knew you'd be the perfect partner in crime."

I smiled, recognizing the truth of this. Do I know for certain that Hot Pants was working for someone who wished to trap us? I do not. But that apartment was certainly not his. If we had to guess, my husband and I both believe it was the Feds, trying to get us to incriminate ourselves about Hubby's recent activities. My husband's former business associates would not have gone to such lengths; if they knew where we were, they'd simply have killed us.

Over coffee at a Waffle House that night—what a sad cross-section of humanity such restaurants draw!—my husband and I talked for hours, eventually deciding to slip the noose of witness protection and go off on our own. Because I had raised strenuous objections to some of the less sophisticated places our handlers had wished to deposit us early on—Okmulgee, Oklahoma? Driggs, Idaho? Can you imagine?—we deliberately chose the kind of place that the Feds might look at and say, "Lynda would never agree to live there."

And thus, the origins of my purgatory. Before purchasing our current home (with cash, *bien sûr*) we spent a good fifteen years moving around from one heartbreakingly unsophisticated little backwater to another within this amalgam of horrors that calls itself a state, all of these plebeian hamlets, including the one where we now reside, the kind of place I'd never want to live.

After the day I destroyed Johnny's guitar, a week and a half passed in a torturous stasis. If Johnny had figured out that I was responsible, he'd given no indication. I checked in with my mother, since Johnny didn't know I was staying at Dan Wykoski's, but she'd received no calls for me—or so she said. Was it possible that an entire bottle of drain cleaner hadn't done much damage? As my curiosity mounted I tried to ferret the information out of Aura after class. But as soon as I began talking, she narrowed her eyes at me and left the room.

And then there was Hal. I'd left twelve messages on his answering machine, the beep before I could leave my next message getting frustratingly longer with each one. At least one of these messages was a wide-ranging late-night diatribe that might well have been considered a threat in a court of law. I was convinced he was ignoring me, and I, much like Glenn Close's unfairly maligned character in *Fatal Attraction*, would not stand for that.

Instead of breaking several more of Dan's cheap jelly glasses, as I'd done that Thursday night to his passive ex-stoner dismay, I took the train to Manhattan right after work Friday and cabbed it directly to Hal's apartment. I entered the lobby, ignoring the doorman and heading decisively to the elevators. My anger generated a heat that actually made my scalp sweat, to a degree I would not feel again until menopause—and let me tell you, having hot flashes in the fucking Sunbelt is a torture far greater than waterboarding. If you've judged any of my actions up to this point, rest assured that I was being systematically betrayed by my beautiful body by the time I was fifty.

"Miss?" the doorman called insistently. "Miss?"

I whipped around. "I'm just going up to see Hal." I trusted the doorman would recognize me, as I'd been there before and was, as I've made clear by now, unforgettable.

"Your gentleman is away on business."

I stopped, looked at him, stepped away from the elevator. "He's… away?"

"Yes, miss," he said. "He's been gone since Monday last week."

"Do you know where he went?" I asked.

The doorman shook his head. "It seemed he left rather suddenly. He told me to hold his mail until he returned."

Perhaps Hal wasn't ignoring me. But why hadn't he told me he was going away? "Could I leave him a note? Do you have any paper?"

"Of course, miss." He handed me a notecard, and an envelope. Both were embossed with the name of the building: *The Bonaire*. I retrieved a pen from my purse.

What to say? I'd told him of my situation, of where I was staying, in multiple phone messages. Was it possible that his machine wasn't working properly? I'd err on the side of caution, for angry as I was, I wanted Hal to find me—if only for the fancy dinners of forgiveness I was owed. I put pen to paper.

Staying with a friend—Dan Wykoski in Keyhole. His number's listed. For a moment, my pen hovered over the notecard as I wondered how much I should reveal. *Miss you. L*

I stood and examined my handiwork. Signing with just my initial lent an appropriate air of mystery. I retrieved my bottle of Opium perfume from my purse and sprayed it in the air, then waved the card through it. The doorman smiled as I slid the scented card into the envelope.

"Very good, miss," he said. "I'll be sure he gets this."

I considered whether to tip him; instead, I gave him the kind of wicked grin that curled men's toes and very nearly induced orgasm. It was clear from the doorman's shy smile in return, the way he coyly turned away from me, that mine had been a far greater treat than a few rolled-up bills could ever have been.

It was now six thirty p.m. on a Friday and I was in The City. There was no way I'd go back to Dan's that night. But where to go next? Standing on the sidewalk in front of Hal's apartment, I had a sudden inspiration and headed for the West Village. Johnny's place. If I could get back in his apartment and see that the guitar was in pieces—or absent altogether—perhaps I'd finally feel a sense of closure on his unsavory treatment of me.

I buzzed Johnny, hoping that he'd be out. To my surprise, he answered: "Be right down." Was he expecting someone? As I considered my options, a teenage boy appeared with a delivery for Johnny from the Chinese restaurant down the street. With a sudden inspiration that flashed in my mind as if placed there by the goddess Nemesis herself, I told the boy to give me the bag. At first, he resisted my attempts to take the food from him, despite my assurances that I'd give it to Johnny; but I handed him a ten, hissed that he'd better leave before he incurred my wrath, and the boy was gone. I put the bag down and quickly reapplied my red lipstick.

When Johnny made it down the three flights of stairs and appeared in the doorway, I was holding the food with a demure smile on my perfectly lipsticked face.

"Oh, *fuck*," he said when he saw me, looking around as if for the delivery boy. "I can't believe you have the nerve to show up here."

"It's on me," I said brightly, proffering the bag.

Johnny took the bag from me, walked down to the curb, and placed it directly in a dumpster.

"Do you think I'd eat anything you touched after what you did to my guitar?" he asked.

I arranged my face into an expression of incredulousness, but inside, I smiled. "Your guitar?" I purred.

Johnny walked back up to the door. "Just cut the act. My neighbor saw you come into the building. She described you down to your bright red dress."

"Well, we're in The City! Lots of stunningly beautiful women come and go at any moment. I'm sure many of them wear red." Perhaps it was cruel to toy with him, but I needed this final bit of satisfaction.

"The thing is, I don't even understand why. What did I do to you that would make you act like that? I'd had that guitar since I was thirteen years old. It might not have been top of the line, but it took me two years of saving money from paper routes to buy it."

Did I feel a pang of regret in that moment, you might ask? Did I envision young Johnny, desperate to rock, slinging copies of the *Detroit Free Press* from his Schwinn to save up for his coveted guitar?

I did not. If he'd wanted his precious instrument to remain safe, he should have treated *me* as well as he'd treated that hunk of wood and string.

"What happened to your guitar, Johnny?" I asked with mock concern. What I really wanted were the details: had it been in lye-soaked pieces when he arrived back home? Did the bottom fall out when he tried to play it?

He ignored my question. "I want to know. Why?"

Could he really be this oblivious? "Hypothetically, whoever sabotaged your guitar might have hoped that next time, you'll end one relationship before you start another."

Johnny was quiet for a moment. "Did you think we were in a relationship?"

We'd fucked on numerous occasions, he'd met my parents, spent Christmas at my home. Did he think I allowed myself to be used, as lesser women did?

I said nothing, but something in my face must have betrayed my emotions.

He leaned against the building. "I told you I was gay. I already apologized to you for not being clearer earlier, but really, Lynda—this is just crazy. I hoped we could be friends after I saw you and Hal at our show, but I think maybe Aura's right."

"About what? Please, enlighten me, Johnny."

"She thinks you're dangerous. What on earth did you do to *her*, anyway? She's really pissed at you but she won't tell me why."

"I didn't do anything to Aura except try to help her," I said, and that, I knew, was true. Was it my fault that she'd taken my liaisons with her family members so personally?

At that moment, the front door opened and Clay stood in the door jamb.

I smiled my prettiest smile at him.

"You!" he exclaimed.

"Johnny threw your food in the trash," I said to Clay. "He's acting really crazy."

"I'm going up to call the police."

"Clay," Johnny said. "It's okay. She's leaving."

"She broke into your place and destroyed your property! She should be in prison." He gave me a bitchy once-over. "You really should find yourself a straight man as soon as possible, Lily Bart."

Had Johnny told him I was an English teacher, or was he showing off, thinking the Edith Wharton reference would go over my head? I could compare him to any number of Gilded Age literary villains, or I could just go in for the kill.

"Do you do that perm yourself?" I asked, motioning to his tightly curled hair. "I can still smell the Toni."

"I would tell you what I smell," he said, "but I was raised with too much civility for that. Perhaps because I didn't grow up in Jersey."

With that, I lunged at him, my perfectly manicured, bright red nails attempting to connect with his pompous face, but Johnny got between us and pushed Clay back inside the building.

"Don't ever come back here," Johnny said, and he—oh, the pain I feel, even forty-one years later, writing these words—*he slammed the door in my face.*

I headed down to the diner near Johnny's apartment, ordered coffee, and considered my next move. The confrontation with Clay had left me surprisingly rattled. For all my liberation, all my insistence that I'd only marry a man who was a number 1, 2 *and* 3, was I just Lily Bart, approaching the hellish age of thirty, about to become an increasingly less beautiful spinster? And where the fuck was Hal? Was he really out of town? Hal didn't seem so spineless as to ask his doorman to lie, but at a fundamental level, most men were invertebrates.

To take my mind off my sorrows I picked up a *Village Voice* from the next table and read through the event listings. Nothing much was happening that night in the poetry world, though my heart skipped a beat when I saw a featured entry: the following weekend, a tribute to none other than the great John Ashbery would be held at the Ear Inn! The preview promised that "a variety of poetic luminaries, including Kenneth Koch" would read their favorite poems written by or for my beloved mentor.

Why had I, one of Professor Ashbery's most gifted students, not been sought out for this reading—at the very least, apprised that it was happening? I felt certain that Bryce—scheming, handsome, infuriating Bryce—was behind this injustice.

I shut thoughts of the reading out of my head as I considered my options that night. I could go to Studio and pick up some charming rogue, crash at his place. But would the Studio experience be as much fun now that I'd been spoiled by Hal's attentions? I'd thought I was getting the VIP treatment until I met him and saw what special treatment at Studio really meant.

My spirits uncharacteristically low, I paid for my coffee and headed to Penn Station, back to Jersey, back to Dan Wykoski's pathetic stoner pad. There had to be a way out of this dismal, ordinary existence—a path to fame I couldn't yet see. I sat sadly on that NJ Transit train amongst an equally dejected cross-section of humanity and prayed to my Muse to reveal that path to me.

My emotional state was still precarious when I woke up the next morning. Wasting my youth at my parents' house was bad enough, but wasting it at Dan's was even worse. I missed the East Village; I missed Studio; I missed Hal; I even missed that scoundrel Carlos. Now that I'd evened the score with Johnny, I allowed myself to miss him too. But what I really mourned was the end of our little trio: Aura, Johnny, and me. Three dazzling talents, banding together in our quest for fame. How could I have been so blind, to not see how unstable they both were?

I sat on Dan's couch, watching him down beer after beer while he passively took in the kind of proletarian sporting event the Dim Bulbs and—it pains me to say it—my dear father often enjoyed watching. There was, still is, nothing less appealing to me than cheering for a stranger's feats of athletic prowess. Why would I waste my time elevating someone else to fame while I sat drowning in Keyhole's swampy purgatory? At the tender age of twenty-six, I'd already given so much to the world: my poetry, my beauty, my *joie de vivre*. When was the world going to start giving back to me? As Dan slumped sideways on the couch and began to softly snore, I was visited by darker thoughts: what if I never escaped New Jersey? What if I never escaped *Keyhole*?

As it stood just then, my only salvation was in my art, and so I went to my room at Dan's to work on some new poems. I had no idea what they would be about, but they were certain to be brilliant; there had to be a way to get these not-yet-written gems to my dear professor, even without Aura's help. That tribute reading, I thought, might provide the perfect opportunity. And then I closed my eyes and had a vision, one of such strength and clarity that I was shocked I hadn't seen it earlier.

I would pay homage to my mentor in a poem cycle; surely such flattery would garner his attention! The Muse grabbed me by the shoulders, and I worked from Saturday afternoon into the wee hours on Sunday, knocking off just as the birds began their incessant chirping and the sky began to lighten. I had four new poems and ideas for several more. O, the excitement!

Panegyric to My Professor: The Ashbery Poems would secure my place in the poetry world; of that I was certain. I just needed to write a few more, so that I could deliver the manuscript to my dear mentor next Friday night—a singular tribute on a night full of tributes. "Uncle John" and his acolytes were in for a grand surprise!

22

I slept well that night and went in to work Monday morning in a decidedly optimistic mood, having hatched my new plan for poetic fame. My cheer was tested, however, when I walked into the teachers' lounge during my free period. Peter and Carla sat with chairs pulled close together, heads bowed, talking quietly as Tess graded a stack of quizzes and Mr. Murton dozed in the back of the room. As soon as Peter turned and saw me, he whispered something to Carla and they stopped talking.

"Good morning, everyone!" I said brightly, my greeting all but ignored save a nod from Tess.

"We should head off," Carla said, as she and Peter both rose. I noticed Carla had bought a new tracksuit, a more form-fitting one in a snazzy aqua. Peter shot me a look I couldn't quite read and attempted a dramatic exit with Carla, which became awkward when his briefcase momentarily got stuck in the door jamb.

I looked at Tess. "Something I said?"

Tess shrugged. "They only have eyes for each other, these days."

I was struck mute for a moment. Peter and Carla? A couple? That could form an unfortunate wedge in my teachers' lounge alliances. "Really? When did this start?"

"I think it's pretty new."

"Hmm." I was quiet for a moment, calculating the best response. "I guess she didn't hear about—"

"She did," Tess interjected. "She said those rumors about Peter aren't even remotely true."

O, the bitter laugh I suppressed in that moment! Poor Carla thought the instant oatmeal that was Peter's lovemaking made for a great sexual feast? The woman clearly hadn't gotten any in a long time.

"Well, I guess we all have different experiences," I said.

Mr. Murton sat up and cleared his throat. "Back in my day," he said, "there were strict rules about dating in the workplace. I think those rules were wise."

And that, it turned out, was something we all could agree on.

Back at Dan's, my mother had left a message: she'd invited us both over for dinner that Wednesday night. Dan was delighted at the thought of a home-cooked meal. I recognized the move as an opening attempt by my parents to insert themselves back into my life.

And still no call from Hal.

Dan shocked me Wednesday night by showering and putting on the kind of dress slacks and shirt he would have worn to teach. He'd even remembered to pick up the bottle of wine I'd asked him to get. Having him look presentable would keep my mother off my back, but I had mild concerns that someone—Dan, my parents—might think we were dating. As I've made quite clear, Dan Wykoski was not my type.

My father chatted amiably with Dan, over chianti and through the antipasto, about the Yankees, about last night's episode of *Laverne & Shirley*. But Daddy ate his manicotti quickly and deliberately, a sure sign that trouble was brewing. Once finished, he pushed his plate out in that way of his, indicating he meant business.

"Daniel," he said. The use of Dan's full name was immediately worrisome. "It's been good of you to allow our daughter to stay at your home while we iron out our family issues. But I'm sure you would agree that the home of a man who's facing criminal charges for selling drugs is not the appropriate place for a young woman."

A sheen of sweat quickly sprung to the surface of Dan's forehead. "I wasn't selling drugs! My lawyer thinks I'll just pay a fine."

Daddy's face reddened. "You were a teacher! You should have been setting an example for youths, not contributing to their downfall."

Dan took a long swig of water.

"If I were on your jury—" Daddy began, but my mother cut him off.

"Pat, never mind all that. Get to the point."

"The point is, we think it's time for Lynda to move back home. We hope you'll agree."

I'd been enjoying the squirminess of it all up to that point. But when my father began discussing me as if I were chattel, well, I realized it was time to set my parents straight.

"Is this what you invited us over for? To torture Dan and speak of me as if I weren't even here? You're unbelievable," I said, looking straight at my mother, since the plan was clearly by her design. Then I softened my gaze and aimed it at Daddy. "I'm so disappointed that you went along with this."

"I'm disappointed that you're living with a felon!" he roared.

"I'm not a felon!" Dan cried. "My lawyer doesn't think I'll go to jail!" But the desperation in his voice betrayed his fears.

"Where I live and with whom is my business, Daddy. Don't talk to Dan about this. Talk to me." I kept my voice controlled, but oh, the rage was boiling. I sensed that whatever garish piece of ceramics my mother had bought to replace the plate of Italy I'd smashed when I moved out could be a casualty of this particular dinner.

My father and I locked eyes and, under my gaze, he began to melt—one thing I could always count on.

"What are you doing with your life, sweetheart?" he asked. "Don't you want to get married? Don't you want to have a family?"

Despite the vexed state my father had gotten him into, Dan let out a brief chortle. He'd learned a few things about me during our time together. But the sound he emitted caused both of my parents to fix their eyes on him, and soon, he began to visibly tremble.

"Could I use your bathroom?" he asked, and I pointed out the way.

"You *know* what I want," I said to my father after Dan had left the table. "My poetry. The East Village."

My father looked down at his plate, ashamed, perhaps, that he couldn't give me those things.

My mother, as always, had no shame. She reached across the table and handed me a card.

Dr. Wendy Silver, psychiatry, it read, with an address in Red Bank. I turned it over and saw that my mother had made me an appointment for four thirty p.m. the following Monday.

As I moved to rip the card up, my father reached out and put his hand over mine. "Don't," he said. "We'll pay for the first visit. Just go. Do it for me."

He gave me his Daddy Face then, the one that used to tell me we were on the same team. But I knew we weren't, for this psychiatrist idea was obviously my mother's, and the fact that he'd used his Daddy Face on me in such a context was nothing short of a heartbreaking betrayal.

"Okay, Daddy," I lied. "For you. I'll go for you." I laid it on thick, hoping to induce some much-deserved guilt.

By the time Dan emerged from the bathroom, pale and sweaty, my mother, deluded in the belief that the magical Dr. Silver would convince me to move back home, had forgotten all her animosity toward him. She handed us Tupperwared leftovers and told Dan to come back again.

It was Daddy, though, who struck the blow that would lead to Dan's asking me to move out, and it was so perfectly timed that I couldn't help but think it was deliberate.

As Dan was putting his blazer on, Daddy wished him a good night. "I should probably tell you," he said, "that my wife's cousin was one of the officers who arrested you. He's been keeping a close watch on your house now that Lynda is living there."

Back at Dan's, I ripped up Dr. Silver's card and deposited it in the kitchen trash bin. An hour and three Budweisers later, Dan asked me to move out, his voice so shaky and eyes so filled with fear that I didn't have the heart to manipulate him into letting me stay.

I asked Dan for a week to figure out somewhere else to live. He agreed, but over the next few days, his drinking got worse; paranoid about being watched, he never left the house. I told him that my father had just been trying to rattle him, that the Keyhole Police Department did not have the money to watch anyone's house twenty-four seven and that Cousin Tony was easily bribable if need be, but none of that relieved him. He just drank more.

Between the drama my parents had created and shopping for a new outfit for the reading Friday night, I never got a chance to write new poems for my Ashbery tribute, but I didn't feel discouraged. I had four masterpieces, and that would be plenty to show my dear mentor just what I was capable of. And while the strapless red dress I bought—a silky, curve-hugging gown with a single ruffle atop the bodice—might not convert the professor over to my team, it would certainly garner the attention of every straight man at that reading.

Sashaying into that bar in my beautiful new dress, a red silk flower in my chestnut brown hair, I felt like a goddess going home to Mount Olympus. O, how desperately I needed to be out of Jersey and living back among The City's poets! Bryce was there, along with a variety of luminaries: the promised Kenneth Koch, Ted Berrigan, Anne Waldman. Feeling utterly at home among my peers, I ordered a whiskey sour at the bar and scanned the room. My beloved Professor Ashbery appeared to be surrounded by young groupies; I'd delight him with my presence (and my poems!) later. I waved at Bryce and his date. They didn't see me, as they immediately moved further into the crowd. But then I spied an even more interesting figure: Carlos Barrada.

He stood in a corner of the bar, leaning in and listening to a talkative woman who gesticulated wildly as she spoke. She appeared to be in her late thirties, or perhaps early forties, ancient to me back then but closer to Carlos's age. Her curly red hair was askew; she wore an Annie Hall shirt, tie, and vest ensemble. How tragic that she didn't have her own sense of style! I quickly made my way through the crowd.

"Carlos!" I said as I came up behind him. He'd been taking a pull on his beer and nearly spat it all out. He whirled around, looked at me, and choked a bit.

"You must be Lynda," the red-headed woman said. "I'm Astrid."

How did she know me? Had she been at the poetry marathon a few months back? I was delighted that my reputation as one of the New York Metro area's premiere poets was spreading despite my lack of constant presence in the East Village.

"Always delighted to meet a fan," I said, extending my hand. Carlos appeared to convulse a bit. The poor dear really needed to take it easy with the alcohol at his age.

"Are you a poet?" I asked Astrid in an act of kindness. If she was a poet, I was certain her work was as derivative as her sartorial choices. But amateurs needed encouragement too.

"Yes," she said. "I'm co-editor of *Double Negative Space*."

I'd never heard of the magazine—most likely a mimeographed little journal. But today's throwaway rag could be tomorrow's hot place to be published. Perhaps it would be worth my while to get to know Astrid.

"Do you have any copies here? I'd love to see one."

She pulled one from her bag: your typical small press affair, stapled in the middle. Carlos was listed on the back cover as one of the contributors.

"Congratulations on another publication!" I said brightly to him, turning my smile up to its highest wattage.

"Lynda," he said, as if finally recovering his ability to speak. "How *are* you?"

"Terrific," I said. "Still teaching, and always, always writing."

"Well, best of luck with it," Astrid said, and then turned away from me, toward Carlos, as if she thought she could dismiss me. This woman needed to know she was not dealing with an amateur.

"Carlos," I said, "what are you doing here? I thought you didn't care for my dear professor's work." Devil that I was, I said it loud enough that two young men to Carlos's left threw him a sharp glance.

"I have a lot of respect for John's work," he said. "It's the *Sans Mots* poets I think are bullshit."

"Ah yes." I took a sip of my whiskey sour. "Well, I doubt Augustus lost any sleep over that."

Carlos studied me for a moment. "Lynda, can we talk?"

I smiled. "Of course we can," I said, and gave Astrid a look of victory as Carlos and I moved into an alcove close to the restrooms.

"I need you to stop," he said before I could utter a word. "Stop trying to contact me. Stop showing up at places where you think I might be. We will never be together again, Lynda, so just—*stop*."

The ego of this man! Thinking I'd gone there to see him, when all I'd wanted was to soak in the precious words of my beloved mentor! O, the anger that grew within me. A number of responses pinged around my brain as I studied Carlos, his facial expression, his body language—he was twisting his torso away from me, as far as he could while keeping his face forward.

Carlos was *afraid* of me!

My path was clear.

I leaned in close, my mouth almost touching his ear. "I'm going to submit three of my best poems to your girlfriend's journal," I said. "And she'd better fucking publish them." Then I straightened up and smiled brightly. "Have a lovely evening!"

Victorious, I strode into the crowd to make my way to my dear, dear Mr. Ashbery.

Poet after luminous poet read my mentor's soul-stirring verse while I studied the room, looking for the best vantage point from which to get my moment with him. Slowly I worked my way to the front, procuring a spot just to the side of the stage. I noticed a young woman waiting in the shadows with a guitar. Would there be music too? She looked a bit punk for this crowd.

Imagine my shock when the young woman shifted into my line of sight and I realized it was Aura. Aura—in whom I'd tried, and clearly failed, to cultivate a sense of seductive style—wearing a baggy red T-shirt emblazoned with the words *Blank Generation*, a black miniskirt she seemed to have carelessly and unevenly cut from something longer, and on her feet—it pains me to even write this—a hideous pair of brown suede Earth shoes that I assume, with hindsight, she was wearing ironically.

I couldn't help but take this nightmarish outfit personally, though she'd had no idea I'd be there. And why *had* she kept news of this event to herself? How long had her own role been in the works?

Worst of all: she was clearly closer to her father's poet friends than she'd let on. She had—I could barely stomach the realization—*lied* to me!

I tried to squelch my growing wrath as Bryce introduced Aura, explaining to the audience that she'd set her father's famous poem, "We (for John Ashbery)" to music.

I was quite familiar with Augustus's poem, as any poet worth her salt would be. It consisted of two lines: halfway down the page, near the left margin, an upper-case *W* turned sideways; and towards the center bottom of the page, a single, lower-case *e*. Scholars have long postulated on the meaning of this poem. Was the sideways *W* really a *W*, or was it actually a Greek sigma? In chemistry, sigma bonds are strong—was Augustus commenting on the strength of his friendship with John? There was general agreement that each letter represented one of the men in this duo of friends, and heated arguments about which man was the sideways *W* (my money was on Augustus) and which was the sturdy *e*.

Aura began to strum. At first she played an instrumental song that, somehow, sounded like two melodies simultaneously. Every so often she would speak the word *we*. But then the tune shifted in such a way that it felt like it was, indeed, going sideways; she said a loud, declarative *W* at the end of that line, to great applause. The tune then righted itself and she spoke, more softly, *e*.

It was a short song, about a minute and a half in length, a tune that has never seen the light of day on any of Aura's recordings. The crowd ate it up, clapping and whistling when she was done. Even in my state of anguish over how cruelly Aura had treated me, I could not deny her budding genius. Or had Johnny helped her with the concept?

"Uncle John" embraced Aura as she exited the stage—oh, the boldness of her mendacity! They were close, as close as he and I once were.

The last two poems of the night were read by my dear mentor himself, brilliant verse that rang gloriously throughout the bar. I waited for the great man to walk away from the microphone, and once he did, I swiftly glided in, even as Bryce was still on the stage, thanking everyone for coming. My mentor and Aura stood surrounded by a small circle of sycophants.

"My dear professor," I said, elbowing an admirer as I enveloped Mr. Ashbery in my embrace. "And, Aura! What a surprise to see you here." I chose not to hug her; she glared at me.

"It's wonderful to see you again," I added, looking directly at "Uncle John."

"I'm sorry," he said. "Have we met before?"

Was he kidding? I'd been his student only six years earlier!

"Lynda Boyle." I struggled to keep the exasperation out of my voice. "I was in your poetry workshop at Brooklyn College."

"Oh yes, that's right. And how do you know Aura?"

"She's my teacher." Aura spat out each word.

The professor nodded. "Wasn't Aura fantastic?"

Aura, Aura, Aura! When was my absentminded mentor going to publicly recognize *my* genius, as he so clearly had in class?

"She was terrific!" one of the hangers-on called out. I knew I had to shift the focus back to myself, and quickly.

"Professor," I said, "this celebration of your art had such resonance for me! I, too, have some recent poems that were inspired by your own work. Would you do me the honor of reading them?"

As I dug in my satchel for the packet of poems, Bryce joined the group. He was clearly drunk, swaying even as he leaned against a post for support.

"What's this?" he bellowed as I retrieved my poems.

"New work," I said, fixing him with a cold stare. "A poem cycle inspired by John's brilliance." For good measure I executed one long, sensual bat of my lashes.

"How fascinating!" Bryce said. "Tell us, what's the title?"

I saw Carlos and Astrid make their way over, Carlos still keeping his distance.

"*Panegyric to My Professor: The Ashbery Poems*," I said, fixing a smile on my mentor and ignoring Bryce.

"How kind of you," Professor Ashbery said, though he made no move to retrieve the outstretched poems. Bryce, however, snatched them from my hands.

"Let's check out Lynda's 'new work,'" Bryce called out. "Should I take the stage and read them aloud?"

"Stop it, Bryce," the professor said.

"Oh my god," he yelled. "The first one is titled 'Self Portrait in a Concave Mirror…'" He then glanced over at his date, a mousy woman I remembered from our college workshop.

"'… *after* John Ashbery,'" Bryce added in a dramatic voice. "Shall I read on?"

Several of the gathered poets guffawed loudly. Aura was silent, her eyes on Bryce. Others looked at the floor. Clearly they were all embarrassed for Bryce, at his drunken grandstanding.

"Bryce," the mousy woman said. She tried, and failed, to retrieve the poems.

"Lynda," Bryce said, swaying slightly in his drunkenness, "I have to tell you a secret." He leaned in close to me; his breath reeked of alcohol. "You're a shit poet."

I laughed in his face, secure in the knowledge of his all-consuming jealousy, aware that we were drawing an even greater crowd. "Is that so?" I asked blithely, shoulders back, my radiantly beautiful body on full display.

"Evvvvvvery one of your poems is a horrendous rip off of some other poet's work," Bryce said, spilling a little beer as he gesticulated. "'After' is supposed to mean 'inspired by,' not 'watch me take a great poem and make it fffffucking terrible.'"

"You're the joke of the poetry world, and you're too *self-absorbed* to realize it," he added.

Why did my lovers all turn on me so? I had a flicker of self-doubt—could any of this be true?—when I remembered, as always, my many accolades. Bryce himself had published me in his own lit mag, back when we were seeing each other.

"Bryce," his date hissed at him. "You're drunk."

"She's right," I said to Bryce. "You must be drunk. Everyone in this room knows my work, the many ways it's been showcased. It's tragic that you came away from our relationship so bitter—"

"We didn't have a relationship! I published you because I was fucking you. That's how you got all your 'showcases.'" He gulped more beer. "Well, except for St. Marks. I did that to get back at Carlos."

I glanced at Carlos, who looked down at the floor. Astrid seemed to be studying the woodwork of the wall in front of her; Aura had been enveloped in the crowd, though I could see her Earth shoes. In fact, everyone gathered around appeared to be studying some part of the restaurant's décor, except for Professor Ashbery, who paid lavish attention to his own hands.

There was a moment where I imagined an alternate reality: one in which what Bryce had said was true, and all the other poets were looking away because they were embarrassed for me. A hideous universe where I possessed the desire to be a great poet but not my prodigious gift for words. A lesser woman might have bought into that reality. In this funhouse mirror world, I might have believed what Bryce had said.

But—thank the gods!—I wasn't in that world. I was Lynda Fucking Boyle, and I could see the situation clearly. Bryce was the asshole I'd always known him to be. And I knew how to deal with assholes.

After flipping through a mental Rolodex of various punishments for Bryce, I went with a classic of elegant simplicity. I walked up to him, inches from his face, and flung the rest of my whiskey sour straight at him. Most of it, including the ice, landed on his forehead. Frothy amber liquid dripped from his eyebrows down to his chin. I plucked my poems from his hands and held them out to John, who wordlessly took them, his mouth agape at my resilience and fortitude.

The crowd parted as I placed my glass decisively on the bar, reached over and plucked a maraschino cherry from the bartender's stash, popped it into my mouth and strode out the door.

Despite my triumph, outside the bar I found myself brooding. Bryce was clearly jealous of my gifts, but the great John Ashbery, who had been so awed by my talent when I was his student, had not even remembered me. How was that possible? If there was one thing I knew with certainty, it was that I was unforgettable.

And worse, I had nowhere to go after the reading. I was in no mood for Studio, not without Hal. It was 10:45 p.m. and my only option was—I can scarcely write the words, even now—heading the hell back to Jersey.

"Fuck!" I screamed at the top of my lungs, standing on the subway platform. "Fuuuuuuck!" I took a deep breath, puffed my chest and cried out again: "Fuuuuuuuuuuuuuuuuuuck!"

This is why I love New York, and why, in my heart, she will always be home: there were at least a dozen people standing on that platform, and no one, not a one, even glanced in my direction. Their solidarity was palpable; they understood my existential dilemma as only New Yorkers could.

23

I am not generally given to mysticism—there's a certain pragmatic streak one acquires from breathing Jersey air at a young age—but I cannot deny that the Fates have often stepped in to smite my enemies or rescue me from life's cruel vicissitudes. For example, that cheerleading coach who got me kicked off the squad in high school? She lost her job at the end of that year when the school board decided to eliminate German as a language offering, deeming a choice between French and Spanish adequate for the few Keyhole High School graduates whose cerebral cortices were developed enough to go on to college.

More recently, divine providence ensured that my neighbors, "The Miller's," were no threat, even going so far as to send "Mrs." packing. A moving van pulled up just the other day and removed a sad hodgepodge of laminated wicker furniture, Ikea debris, and liquor store boxes with newsprint-wrapped belongings peeking out the top. The Pugsub told me that Mrs. had taken an apartment in a less-desirable part of our wholly undesirable town, while Mr. had already flown back to Michigan with his real wife—but not before securing his collectibles and arranging for their transport.

And then there was the Monday after the Ashbery tribute at the Ear Inn.

I still had no idea where I would live. I knew I could probably cajole Dan into another week there, but honestly, the house was getting filthy again, and no nagging on my part seemed to rouse him from the couch. Hal was still MIA and I'd heard nothing from Johnny since our encounter at his apartment—a detail that would be unsurprising for a lesser woman, but I was used to my beauty buying me an abundance of forgiveness.

School, my students, Dick Singer, the teachers' lounge—all of it felt like a rusty anchor mooring me in Keyhole's murky port. I will confess to no small amount of despair as I drove "home" to Dan's place that afternoon.

And when I arrived, it was as if the universe had witnessed my suffering and determined that it was time to intervene.

"Some guy named Hal called," Dan mumbled over his shoulder as he staggered into the kitchen for another beer. "He said you had his number."

It had been a terrible few weeks, but things were starting to shift. I could feel it.

Lynda Fucking Boyle was back.

Hal's call rekindled a flickering flame of hope deep within me, a fire I'd had from birth that told me I deserved the most fabulous of lives. It was because of that flame, its increasing strength, that I didn't call him back for several days. Desperation is about as ugly a stench as one can douse oneself in, and to allow Hal back into my life without some serious ass-kissing would be desperate indeed. No, I waited until Hal had reached his own state of desperation, which came after four more messages, three dozen roses and a singing Candy Gram—sent to both my parents' house and Dan's for good measure.

The roses included a note that Hal wanted to send a limo for me the following Friday night so he could apologize in person; he needed the best address. Now *that* was more like it! I convinced Dan to leave Hal a message with the address of Keyhole Junior High, and to pick me up at three thirty p.m. Not only would I head into the city in style, I'd be the talk of the teachers' lounge for the rest of the school year!

As I packed my weekend bag that Friday morning before school, Dan shuffled up to me, bathrobe open to reveal dirty boxers and a T-shirt, rock 'n' roll coffee mug in hand.

"Umm, Lynda," he said, "do you think you'll be moving in with Hal?"

"It depends on how this weekend goes," I said brightly. "You might want to keep a good thought."

School officially let out at three p.m. Most teachers were there until four, meeting with students, straightening their classrooms or catching up on work. I'd calculated the timing of the limo so that most of my fellow teachers would still be there—particularly Peter and Carla, both of whom always stayed late, eager little beavers that they were. But I couldn't help, when I saw Aura that Friday morning, to pull her aside after class and fill her in on what was happening. Surely a limo ride through Keyhole would smooth any lingering tensions between us!

"You're offering me a *limo ride*?" She curled her lip like I'd tried to give her a months-old tuna sandwich. I saw Marisol waiting for her just outside the classroom door.

"You remember Hal? We had a disagreement, and this is his way of apologizing."

She snorted. "You remember when I asked you to leave me alone?"

I sighed. "I thought you'd be over that by now."

"Over your sleeping with half my family and then showing up at that reading like a fucking stalker? Over your breaking into Johnny's apartment and pouring Drano into his guitar?" I glanced around; fortunately, her voice was low and no one except Marisol was nearby.

"It was Liquid Plumr," I corrected.

"You're a psycho." Aura wheeled around and left the room, she and Marisol quickly making their way down the hall.

My heart raced, a sheen of sweat coating my skin. I felt positively *assaulted* by her words! What made this child think she could talk to me like that? How dare she? Aura was a spoiled brat, infuriatingly ungrateful after all I'd done for her. I'd cut her too much slack; no more. She would not ruin my reconciliation with Hal.

But I *would* deal with Aura later.

As soon as my last class was over, I did a quick change in my office, and emerged wearing a wraparound cocktail dress in a shimmering red-gold that fit my body suggestively and could be removed in one tug of a tie at my waist. Thanks to some strategic hints I'd dropped in the teachers' lounge and in a few of my classes, the entire school knew about the limo, and students and teachers alike hung around to watch Ms. Boyle as she was swept off to The City. I could see the skepticism on Peter's and Carla's faces in particular, the way they elbowed each other. Dick Singer was there too, and his pursed lips suggested he thought such a spectacle had no place at a junior high school. But what was I there for if not to bring a little pizzazz to my students' and colleagues' humdrum lives?

Patti teetered out of the school and stood by my side. "You look gorgeous, hon!" she gushed. "*Love* the gold on you." Patti had swapped out her usual stilettos for bright yellow platform wedges, worn with a kelly green polyester dress that clung to her as tightly as a sausage casing.

"You'd get behind the velvet rope in that outfit," I said. Patti beamed.

It was 3:32 p.m. and I was getting a bit concerned about the hype

I'd created. If that limo didn't show, it would be a personal disaster on a grand scale.

"So now who's this guy sending the limo?" Patti asked.

"Someone I met at Studio," I said, then added, "54."

She nodded. "I never even thought of tryin' to get in there."

"It's not as hard as you think," I whispered, "if you look like we do."

Was Patti a great beauty, and did I really think her my equal in the looks department? Of course not. She was attractive enough for Keyhole, but my dear friend Steve Rubell would have smelled the Jersey on her—that scent of desperation and Aqua Net—and never let her in. Still, she was, as the kids say today, crushing it for a woman who would never leave the Central Jersey shore.

Patti smiled at me and glanced at her watch. I looked at mine as well. 3:35.

I would fucking murder Hal if this goddamn limo didn't show up.

And just as I began to fantasize about the bloodiest ways to extinguish my dear gentleman caller, just as I distinctly heard the phrase "compulsive liar" uttered behind me in Peter's unmistakable tenor, that was when a red stretch limo pulled up, chrome gleaming.

Not a black limo.

Not white.

Red.

Hal had noted my signature color and planned it all for maximum effect. Perhaps even the five minutes of tardiness had been planned.

I was reminded, once again, of the many ways in which Hal and I were a good match. In fact, up until he'd vanished, he'd seemed a promising contender for that elusive status of #1, 2 and 3 all rolled into one man. But after his disappearance from my life, I could no longer count him as a Mr. Reliable. I hoped, at least, he still had lots of drugs.

The limo driver got out of the car, approached the school, and seemed to recognize me.

"Lynda Boyle?" he asked, proffering me a single long-stemmed rose.

"Thank you," I said, turning to face my adoring crowd as I held it below my nostrils and inhaled coquettishly. Would that there were a photograph of that moment! Peter and Carla shrank to the back of the throng.

I glanced over at Patti, who gazed longingly at the magnificent vehicle. She'd been a useful ally and deserved a reward.

"Would you like a ride home, Patti?" I asked.

"Would I!" she exclaimed, and closed the distance to the limo at a remarkably brisk clip for the height of the shoes she was wearing.

Imagine my surprise when I stepped into the limo and saw that Hal himself was in the back, looking sharp in his electric blue suit and a little more handsome than I'd remembered. He poured two glasses of Dom Perignon and offered them to me and Patti.

"To the most beautiful girls in Jersey," he toasted, and Patti beamed.

After we'd dropped Patti off, Hal topped up my champagne. "Should we go meet your parents next?" he asked.

"I think we have a few things to discuss first," I said, eying him sharply.

"So we do. Next time, then." He filled his own champagne glass.

"You seem pretty confident that I'll forgive you."

"I am," he said. "But we can't really talk until we're back at my place."

"We can't?"

He gestured toward the driver. I wondered what Hal had to tell me that would require such discretion.

"All right then," I said. "The Bonaire it is."

The limo dropped us off at Hal's building, and we went into the lobby. The doorman, busy with a phone call, waved to Hal and handed him a stack of mail. Hal peered outside through the glass of the front door, then motioned me to step back out with him. He hailed a taxi.

"What's going on?" I asked after we were both in the cab.

"You'll see," he said. "No questions until we get where we're going."

O, the fantasies my mind concocted in that short car ride! Had he rented out Lutèce for me, complete with a tableside violinist? Or was Andy Warhol waiting for us at the Factory, where a party was being thrown in my honor? How quickly one's fortunes could change! But before I could cook up a third scenario, we pulled up in front of a different apartment building, fifteen blocks from the Bonaire.

"Welcome to the Dakota," he whispered to me after we'd exited the taxi.

"What are we doing here?"

"I live here now."

He took me by the hand and tried to lead me inside, but I stood my ground. "You didn't return my calls for all this time because—you were *moving*?" I asked, heat rising from my toes. The way he'd ignored me called for a far more fraught excuse than something as mundane as changing apartments.

"No," he said. "Come in and let me explain."

The apartment was still full of boxes, many of them open and only partially unpacked. He motioned me over to the couch. At least that luxurious rug was still under our feet.

"Sorry I haven't had time to unpack," he said.

"Can't you hire someone to do that?"

"I don't want any strangers in here."

He got himself a glass of water, downed it, and then offered me one, which I waved away.

"Okay," he said, sitting down next to me. He then proceeded to launch into what I can only describe as a redacted conversation. Surely, Jann, you've seen photos of censored documents, with portions of sentences blacked out? That was what Hal's story felt like.

The gist was this: he'd traveled to an unspecified country to meet with a "business associate." After meeting with said associate, he'd been detained by the local government and questioned. Following that questioning, he was then further detained by his "business associates" and held until they were satisfied that he hadn't named them to their government.

This was, obviously, about his cocaine business. My heart sank at the thought that maybe it meant he didn't, wouldn't, ever have any more coke. And of course, because I was concerned for his safety.

"Does this mean you're out of that line of business?" I asked as gently as I could.

"No," he said. "It just means I need to do business differently."

I relaxed my shoulders. "So why the change in apartments?"

"It's possible the Feds are now watching me," he said. "It's also possible my business associates are watching me. I wanted to make it as hard for everyone as possible." He squirmed a bit. "I'm concerned my old place might have been bugged. This place was thoroughly swept, and you and Steve are the only people who know I live here."

I was honored to be such an insider, one of Hal's few trusted confidants. He opened another bottle of champagne and poured me a glass while I digested the news. Being questioned by a foreign government and then being "detained" for a couple of weeks by his drug-dealing associates certainly qualified as a bone fide emergency; I'd seen *The French Connection*. It was also, I had to admit, kind of thrilling.

"So, what do you think?" he asked as he handed me a champagne refill. "Am I forgiven?"

He was, of course, but it went against my every instinct to tell him so.

"Well, next time you're being held captive by a cartel, I'd appreciate a call," I deadpanned.

"Shhh," he said—he'd studiously avoided using the word *cartel*—but then he began to laugh. It sounded more like a release of tension than a true bemusement.

"There's no one else like you in the world," he finally said. "I hope you know I adore you."

Instead of answering, I decided to show my feelings wordlessly, and Hal, happy to oblige, had me down on that rug within seconds.

24

I didn't notice it until after we'd made love and I lay in Hal's arms: the bruising on his chest, his forearms. I ran my hands down his back and felt welts.

"What happened to you?" I asked, running my fingers lightly over his rib cage, the black-and-blue marks there.

He winced a little, shifted position. "Ah, it was nothing," he said, but the look in his eyes said something else.

"Did they…*torture* you?" I had never before felt as close to Hal as I did in that moment. What had kept this dear man from contacting me? Nothing less than actual, physical torture!

"That's a little dramatic," he said. "It's just that those government officials, my business associates—they can both be a little rough."

"Are we in *danger*?" I asked, unable to hide my excitement. After the spirit-killing humdrum of my Keyhole existence, I thrilled to the idea.

"You'd like that, wouldn't you?" He laughed.

"I'm not afraid of it."

He kissed the top of my head. "I guess there's always that possibility. But I wouldn't have called you if I'd thought I was putting you in danger."

"I laugh at danger," I said, in my twenty-six-year-old naiveté. O, as I write these words, how I miss that spirited girl!

And then Hal stroked my hair, looked me in the eyes, and said, "Move in with me."

My days of living in Dan's filthy pad were over! But it would have been foolhardy to accept too easily.

"I don't know," I said. "It's an awfully long commute from here to Keyhole for work each day."

Hal caressed my collarbones. "Then quit that job. I can give you anything you want. You're too good for that place, anyway."

I agreed with the latter, of course. But it was important to negotiate my own terms.

"I will not be a kept woman," I said, sitting up, feigning offense.

"Of course not." He slid up behind me and massaged my shoulders.

"If you want to keep working there, that's fine. I just wanted you to know that you don't have to."

You might ask: why did I not take the proffered golden parachute, given my previously demonstrated hatred of my job? Was I still uncertain about Hal's reliability? Concerned about getting involved with a drug dealer and wanting to be self-supporting if the situation became dangerous? Was I making some sort of feminist statement?

Bitch, *please*. My reason for keeping my job, at least through the school year, was quite simple: to gloat. I needed to flout my good fortune in the faces of my fellow teachers, regale my students with tales of shopping sprees at Bergdorf's, dazzle the Keyhole hoi polloi as I dressed in Chanel or Diane Von Furstenberg or, in a daring mood, Betsey Johnson. I needed to thoroughly scandalize my mother; I needed for Aura to tell Johnny; I needed for news of my ascendance to reach Carlos Barrada. I needed for Peter Ferrari to rue the day he let a captivating creature like me get away and, given scant options, ended up with a fucking *gym teacher*.

"I'll keep my job," I said to Hal. "At least for now."

"I'll get you a car service," Hal said.

He certainly knew the way to my heart.

After I'd filled Hal in on what had happened with my parents—how they'd kicked me out after misconstruing my relationship with Aura's brother (no need for him to know I'd been fucking Denny!), their insistence I see a psychiatrist (oh, how we laughed!)—we decided it best that the two of us go to Keyhole the next day so my folks could meet Hal, and so I could gather my belongings from Dan's. My body hummed with a post-coital electricity heightened by the very real possibility that I might never live in Jersey again. Young Lynda wished for this with the fervency of a prayer.

In retrospect, I should have heeded Aesop and been a bit more careful with the specifics of what I'd wished for.

Even on short notice, my mother was able to whip up an impressive feast; it was her greatest talent. Yet there was a tension in the air before my first forkful of eggplant parmigiana.

"What was all this talk we heard of you leaving the school yesterday in a *limousine*?" my mother asked while we were still passing the serving dish around. She pronounced every syllable of the word, *lim—o—zeeeeene*, with a palpable level of disapproval.

I smiled at Hal. "He knows how to treat a lady," I said. When I saw my father's face sag slightly—he wanted to give me everything I deserved, I knew, it was my mother who prevented him from acting on his instincts—I added, "Just like you, Daddy."

My mother clucked. I knew her well enough to understand that she'd loathed everything she'd heard about what happened Friday: the spectacle of it, the lack of thrift.

"So, Hal, I hear you're an accountant," my father said.

"I am."

"This must be a busy time of year for you." O, my dear, sweet father, thinking that Hal was an *ordinary* accountant with *ordinary* clients, trying to save the common man a few pennies here and there.

"I just work for Studio these days," Hal said. "Quarterly filings. It's no crazier now than it was in January." Eight months later, Steve Rubell and his partner Ian Schrager would be busted for tax evasion. But that wasn't my dear Hal's fault. Or was it? I've never asked.

"Studio?" my father asked.

"Studio 54, Pat," my mother said. "That *disco* she goes to. You know, like in *Saturday Night Fever*."

Hal and I exchanged a bemused look.

"They seem to do a good business," my dad offered. "I've seen footage on the news of all those people trying to get in." My dear father was thinking entirely in terms of Hal's ability to support me.

"And you're from New York?" my mother asked.

"Queens," Hal said. "But I live in Manhattan now."

"At the Bonaire," I added, so as not to blow Hal's subterfuge, but also, because it sounded fancier than the Dakota.

My mother clucked again.

"In fact, Daddy," I added, looking from my father to Hal, "he's asked me to move in with him. I'll be getting my things from Dan's after we leave here."

"You're going to live in *The City* now?" my mother asked in her Voice of Alarm, which was louder and more nasal than the way she usually spoke. "Lynda, what about your *job*?"

"Mother, please. It's a forty-five-minute commute, if that."

"You're not quitting, are you? In the middle of the school year?"

"You'd never get a good reference after that," my father added.

I sat back for a moment and watched them through Hal's eyes: such provincial people, so pragmatic, so mundane. Later, he said they'd reminded him of his own parents, who I, sadly, never got to meet. The circumstances leading to our marriage didn't allow for it, and besides, Hal said his mother might have "had some problems" with his marrying a *shiksa.* For that reason alone, I'd have loved to meet her—I believe she would have been a formidable opponent! But as always, I'm getting ahead of myself.

"Lynda can work or not work, whatever she wants," Hal said.

My father narrowed his eyes. "For just how long do you plan to live in sin?"

"Daddy," I said.

"Don't Daddy me! If the man loves you, he should marry you."

"Daddy—" I began again, but Hal cut in.

"I would love to marry your daughter one day," Hal said. "All I want is to make her happy."

The sincerity in Hal's voice, in his brown eyes, caught my father off guard. "I'll hold you to that," he said, and Hal nodded.

My mother, of course, could not leave well enough alone.

"I hope you know," she said to Hal, "that making Lynda happy is not easy."

If only I'd had a dagger at the ready! I settled for my eyes, slicing through hers.

"Nothing worth having is easy to attain," Hal said. I felt a stirring deep within me that I'd never felt before—such a new sensation that I did not have language for it. Unsettled, I took a long swig of chianti.

"I like him," my father said to me, as if Hal weren't right there.

My mother pushed her chair back loudly. Her exasperation, as always, felt like a personal victory.

After picking up my things from Dan's—he'd left my bags just outside his front door as if terrified to be seen with me, the poor boy—Hal and I did a quick line of coke each and headed back to The City in his canary yellow Maserati. The delight I felt heading north on the Garden State Parkway in that stylish little car, leaving more and more of Jersey in the rearview, was so great that I didn't even mind when Hal put on the rock station, WNEW.

But my high quickly evaporated when the slightly murky strains of what was clearly a live concert gave way to a song I recognized.

A song of Johnny's. In fact, it *was* Johnny, and his band.

"Hey, isn't that Glow Worm?" Hal asked, and turned the volume up.

I listened in stunned silence. When the song was over, a deejay broke in and said they were broadcasting live from the Stone Pony. How had Johnny gotten his band this much attention, and so quickly? More importantly, how had he done it without me?

"Hey, want to go to the show? I could get off at the next exit and turn around," Hal said, glancing in my direction.

"No." The catch in my voice communicated just a fraction of my pain.

"What's going on?" Hal asked. He slowed the car a bit but made no move for the nearest exit.

"Johnny treated me abominably."

Hal turned off the radio. "What happened?"

How much to tell him? I wasn't in the habit of talking freely about one lover to another. But Hal had a way of making it easy to tell him something close to the truth.

"He strung me along, and then got angry when I confronted him about it." Sure, I'd left a few parts out, but every word was true.

"You know he's gay, right?"

I sighed. "Yes, I know he says he's gay. But in my experience, most guys who think they're gay can swing both ways—at least, after they've met me."

Hal laughed, so heartily that I burned hot as a grill. Sensing the shift in my mood—and not wanting to end up charbroiled—he quickly extinguished the flames.

"I'm sorry, babe," he said. "I'm laughing only because I don't doubt it. If any woman could turn a guy, it'd be you."

I took a few deep breaths. "He's still seeing that creep he met at Studio—you remember, that night we were all there?"

Hal was quiet for a minute. "The guy with the perm? Dark hair?"

"*Home* perm," I said, and Hal smiled. "The worst part is, Johnny never even told me. I went to visit him and caught the two of them together."

"What happened then?"

"We had words."

"Any property damage involved?"

"A little."

Hal nodded. "Musicians. They never know a good thing when they have it."

I fought back a few bitter tears. "It's not just that. I tried so hard to help Aura, and she's not at all grateful. Once she met Johnny, she tossed me aside. Honestly, I feel used by both of them."

The exit for the Vauxhall Service Area was up ahead, and Hal deftly changed lanes and took it. Soon he'd parked the car just to the side of the gas pumps, and turned to face me.

"What can we do to make this right? Do you want them back in your life? Or do you want revenge?"

I can't help but wonder now: was that the point where I thought maybe, just maybe, Hal might be The One? In all my years of dating, I'd missed something important in my cataloguing of men. In addition to reliability, great sex, and abundant drugs, there was a fourth category I'd completely overlooked: #4, The Guy Who Gets Me.

"I want eternal gratitude," I said, looking deep in Hal's eyes. "Especially from Johnny."

Hal studied me for a moment. Then he pulled me close to him. "Doll," he whispered in my ear. "I know a lot of people in the music biz. I'll make sure Johnny understands that if he wants to play at Studio or anywhere else in the tri-state area, he has to kiss your beautiful feet for the rest of his fucking life."

I kissed Hal then, hard, and he ran his hands through my hair, and for a few delicious moments we were making out at the rest stop as cars veered around us to get to the gas pumps. We heard prolonged honking and pulled away from each other to find several muscle cars full of dim bulbs and bulbettes staring at us, some making kissy faces.

"*Nudniks*," Hal said loudly, waving his hand to dismiss them, and we kissed some more. Aware of my audience, I undid Hal's belt and slid my panties down beneath my dress, flicking them onto the backseat as I moved on top of him. The mocking turned to cheers as I rotated my hips, performing my signature spiral move, driving Hal to new realms of ecstasy. I locked eyes with a middle-aged greaser idling his Camaro directly behind us, a guy who was either a little too into *Happy Days* or hadn't gotten the memo that the 1950s were over. I continued to look directly at that greaser as I brought both Hal and myself to climax. In the heady throes of passion I screamed, "Yes! Yes! Yes!" and a chant of "Cum! Cum! Cum!" erupted from the cars surrounding us and I thought to myself, this is it, the life I want to live, a life of passion and sensation and hedonism. That such a breakthrough should occur at, of all places, a service area on the Garden State Parkway—let's just say that the irony, even in the moment, was not lost on me.

25

On the day that a "For Sale" sign went up at the house next door—now vacated by both of "The Miller's"—a news item in *People* magazine caught my attention. "First Woman on Mars?" read the headline. It was about Marisol Rodriguez and her NASA career, specifically how she'd been selected for the upcoming Artemis space mission, which could lead to her being the first woman—possibly even the first human being—on Mars. Never one for hagiography, I skimmed it. But there was a sidebar that caught my eye.

"An Enduring Friendship," the smaller headline read, and there was a photo of Aura and Marisol together at the Johnson Space Center; Aura had been in town for a show and took a tour of Mission Control. The short piece talked about how they'd been friends since junior high, and how Aura had rewritten and was re-recording her early song, "Star Girl," for the Artemis launch.

"Marisol is the smartest person I've ever met," Aura was quoted. "I knew it even back in eighth grade, how special she was. We throw the word *genius* around casually these days, but Marisol is the real deal."

I wondered, of course, if Peter Ferrari had read that news item. If he sat in his clapboard house in Keyhole or a split level in Matawan or wherever the fuck he'd ended up, remembering the conversation we'd had in the teachers' lounge—long before he and I had our ill-fated liaison—when he proclaimed Marisol a genius. I could imagine the smug look of superiority on his aged face. What did he look like now? What did any of them look like—Carlos, Art, Bryce?

I pushed the magazine aside, put on my bikini and swam some laps in our pool to burn off my smoldering ire. *The smartest person I've ever met?* O, the cruelty of how Aura had erased me!

As my body sliced through the pool, I allowed my white-hot rage to be cooled by the chlorinated water. "An Enduring Friendship"—based on what, besides both of them having escaped Keyhole? Did Marisol even understand the depths of Aura's genius? Did the Star Girl comprehend how right I'd been about my once-dear little Rock Girl? And why did they both so stubbornly refuse to give me my due? Surely I was the greatest influence either of them had ever encountered. Was Aura still holding a grudge—because of my free sexuality, or perhaps because of a moment's self-preservation I exercised forty-one years ago? When I get to that story—and it's coming up shortly—will you judge me as well, Jann?

And what the hell was Marisol's problem? I'd given her nothing but straight fucking As when her work in my class was really A-minus at best.

I swam until my lungs could barely take air, until I had to exit the pool or sink like a stone. As I dried myself off, Hubby came out through the lanai.

"How's my girl?" he asked, keeping a safe distance between me and the earthenware pots that sat outside the screen. They had come with the house and, until that day, I hadn't understood their purpose.

"Fuck!" I screamed. "Fuuuuuuuuck!"

"I saw that article about Marisol and Aura," he said. "Babe, you've got to stop reading that stuff. You just torture yourself."

"The smartest person she ever met in her life," I fumed, picking up a pot and smashing it on the concrete next to the shallow end of the pool—nowhere near Hubby, which I thought was quite considerate.

"A genius," I added, a bit more softly, admiring the broken shards.

"Sweetie," he said.

I picked up a large shard of the pot and flung it into the Pugsub's yard with a loud grunt. Mee-chelle commenced her infernal yapping from inside the house.

"Look around you," my husband said. "Maybe this isn't where we'd choose to live if safety weren't a concern. Maybe we don't have the names we were born with. But we've got this house and this pool and we're sitting on a pot of money that we can spend as long as we don't draw attention. We're wanted by the cops *and* the robbers, and we've evaded everyone for all these years. So I ask you, who are the geniuses? Huh?" He waved his hand in the distance between us. "*We're* the fucking geniuses."

My man has always had a talent—dare I say, a genius!—for putting things in proper perspective.

I first began to understand the depth of Hal's brilliance during those six weeks in 1978 that we lived together at the Dakota. Such a short period of time, and yet so consequential to my life! As the month of April gave way to May, I continued teaching, though when the weather warmed I increasingly called in sick. Why schlep down to Jersey when I could spend the day in Central Park, scribbling sonnets in my notebook—or shopping in the Village? Occasionally I ran into John Lennon and his young son Sean on the elevator in our building; once, we shared some plums beneath a weeping willow tree, and I listened with feigned interest to the boy's stream-of-consciousness toddler prattle because his father was *John Fucking Lennon.* I could tell that John was taken with me and so I issued a dinner invitation to him and his wife. When he declined, I read the longing in his eyes. Certainly it was all Yoko's fault.

During this period, I wrote many new poems, including one that favorably compared the prowess of a lover named H. to a previous lover named C. I sent this poem to Astrid's journal even though I hadn't received a response on my previous submission; she was most likely intimidated by my exceptional poetic gifts. I also sent a note to Brooklyn College, to my dear mentor John, apprising him of my new address and phone number. Hal would have flipped out, had he known I'd revealed our whereabouts, but I trusted my mentor to be discreet. Surely the reason I hadn't heard back from him about my Ashbery Cycle poems was that he'd been unable to contact me.

Another glory of that heady spring was that Johnny had done some very satisfying groveling. True to his word, Hal, with Steve's blessing, had set up a short set for Glow Worm at Studio one night in late May. But when Hal reached out to Johnny, he tactfully suggested that the band's career might suffer if Johnny didn't "smooth things over" with me. To torture Johnny a little more, I insisted we meet in person, and so, over coffee at the diner in Johnny's neighborhood, I graciously accepted a mumbled, insincere-sounding apology in the interest of our being able to move on.

As the date of Glow Worm's performance at Studio neared, as that magical last day of school—June 16!—was a mere three weeks away, I found my job surprisingly tolerable. Feeling beneficent, I created new lessons for my students, lessons that occasionally resulted in *more work for me*; I even ignored opportunities to torture Peter. With my life in The City so full, I lost interest in Aura, and we reached a détente. I treated her like any other student, and she stopped casting hateful looks in my direction.

Jody Fromme had been mostly quiet in class that spring, and to reward her for not being a loathsome pain in my and everyone else's asses, I gave her Cs for D+ work. Was it the knowledge that my job at Keyhole Junior High was now wholly voluntary that made it so much easier to bear? Had Hal and our endless, star-studded nights at Studio softened me in some way? Whatever the reason, I might have sailed along like that to the end of the school year, or at least until the night of the Glow Worm show, had Jody not reverted to form one day in class.

I'd asked my students to write about their lives forty years in the future. What would the world be like in 2018? What would their lives look like? I'd told them to dream big.

Most of my pupils had only the narrowest visions. Mundane jobs, dim-witted kids, houses with picket fucking fences. Bobby Craig broke the monotony with his tale of becoming an intergalactic porn star, his movies projected in 3D on the surfaces of moons so that his "throbbing manhood" could be shown to scale.

Instead of imagining herself an astronaut, as she came to be, Marisol wrote about the technology she thought we'd have. Telephones with view screens, robots working assembly lines, cars that drove themselves. As it turns out, she was right about a lot of it, but honestly, her essay would have been better suited for a technical journal. It was *such* a snooze.

Then Aura read her piece. Instead of 2018, she chose 1988, ten years in the future; as always, my East Village vixen bent the rules to her liking! She envisioned herself getting a Grammy Award for album of the year, and then played us one of the songs she said would be on the album.

No doubt you are well aware that Aura didn't win a Grammy until much later in her career, although her breakthrough album, *Some Girls Talk*, topped every critic's poll in 1992.

But back in my eighth-grade class, she launched into "Pretty Good for a Girl," a song that never made it onto any of her albums. How I thrilled to her send-up of Johnny's bandmate Mike, and his dismissive comments that previous fall! O Aura, godmother of woke twenty-first century feminists, the little sister I might have had—does anyone else remember you with such complicated tenderness and rage?

As I closed my eyes and sat cross-legged on my desk, swaying to Aura's delicious take-down of the male rock star ego, as I luxuriated in the sound of her guitar, I heard a few scattered laughs and opened my eyes. Jody sat cross-legged on her own desk, eyes closed, smarmy grin on her face, swaying and flipping an imaginary sheath of hair.

Jody had not been mocking Aura. She was mocking me.

When I picked up the stapler from my desk, I had no intention of throwing it at Jody. It was my rage, or rather, my outrage that catapulted the metal instrument through the air; how dare this swamp rat child, this collection of cellular detritus, mock *me*! I feel certain that anyone in my position would have done the same. Self-preservation is hard-wired into us, and to have let Jody's mockery go unpunished would have extinguished my very soul.

Fortunately for Jody, she opened her eyes just as I lobbed the stapler, and she managed to duck out of its path. It landed squarely on Kathi's desk. Her eyes grew large and liquid, as they always did when she realized she or Jody had gone too far.

"You could have killed me with that!" Jody screeched.

Aura continued to play and sing, which delighted me no end.

"My hand slipped," I said. "Shhh." I motioned to Aura.

"You threw a *stapler* at my *head*," Jody said, "and you think I give a shit that your little pet is singing?"

"Principal's office," I said. "Now."

Jody stood, looking around at her classmates. Aura, sensing a storm brewing, finally stopped playing. "You tried to kill me," Jody said, "and you're sending me to the principal's office? Great! I can't wait to tell him what you just did."

Perhaps I should have been more concerned, but my contempt for her was unwavering.

"Shoo," I said, flicking my fingers toward the door. "We have work to do here."

What a cheeky young thing I was!

I was not entirely surprised, though, when I received a note to report to Dick's office for a grilling later that day, and I was not surprised by the grilling itself. It was the usual huffing and puffing, interspersed with lecherous glances: "Inappropriate, you need to set an example, these accusations are serious, blah blah blah."

I told him Jody had exaggerated, that the stapler had slipped out of my hands. And that I was, frankly, disturbed he was taking the word of a continually disruptive student over mine.

"You're on the brink, Lynda," he said, and informed me of a scheduled disciplinary hearing that, apparently, not even my spectacular breasts could get me out of. If only I'd worn the Qiana that day!

Still, as I told Hal the story over drinks at Studio that night—o, the hangover I'd have the next day!—and even as he suggested I quit, I refused to give up. It was the principle of the thing, I said. Anything I'd done to Jody she'd richly deserved.

"She's wretched," I added, within earshot of Andy Warhol.

"Who are you talking about?" Andy asked.

"A dreadful, provincial little parasite in my class," I said.

"Lynda's a teacher," Hal added for Andy's benefit.

Andy took me in with those piercing eyes of his for a few long seconds.

"What do you teach?" he asked.

"Eighth grade English."

He looked straight at me for another few moments. "I find that *fascinating*," he finally said, and yawned in an exaggerated fashion, and asked Hal if he had any more coke.

"No," Hal said. And then he pulled out his stash and offered me a line, right in front of Andy.

Titillated by how Hal had chosen me over one of Steve Rubell's darlings, I pushed the coke away, undid Hal's pants and blew him right there on the banquette, with no attempt at discretion. Midway through the blow job, Hal at half-mast, I looked up and saw that Andy was still watching us. I proceeded to give him a show that he surely took to his grave.

A few days before Glow Worm's showcase at Studio, Denny resurfaced, waiting for me outside my school. O, handsome Denny! I hadn't seen him since our beanbag rendezvous.

After a few minutes of surprisingly lucid chitchat—had Denny cleaned himself up?—he asked if I could get him on the guest list for the Glow Worm show. Johnny had already put Aura on his list, Denny said, but their mother wouldn't let her go unless Denny accompanied her. I suspected this request was less for Aura's benefit and more because Denny had missed me, but still, I was happy to pass it along to

Hal. Aura would owe me, and that debt would tip the scales back in my favor.

It should have occurred to me that Aura would have asked Johnny to put her brother on the list if Denny's story had been true. But I didn't think about that until much later.

26

I haven't been back to Manhattan in decades, but I've seen photos of the sad, sanitized spectacle it's become. Times Square has gone from peep shows and porn to a garish "family values" monument: tourists stuffing their faces at Olive Garden and Red Lobster, neon Disney mouse ears looming above the ticket line as entire families clamor for the slow death of a *Frozen* matinee. Studio 54 itself now houses a respectable theatre company, and CBGB only exists as a restaurant at Newark International Airport. Greasy spoons and luncheonettes have made way for the bland ubiquity of Starbucks and Panera. This is the wretched story of every city in America, of course, but New York City—The City, *my* City—is the only one that matters.

Take a moment to picture Midtown Manhattan in the late spring of 1978. Curbs lined with enormous cars, sporting hoods so flat and wide people sat on them to light a smoke or for a brief conversation. Whiffs of car exhaust and sewage, grease from nearby diners overpowered by designer fragrances that, in turn, competed with our pheromones, all of these atoms pinballing headily through the air. Freed of the need for winter coats, the hopefuls that lined up outside Studio showed off their bodies: for the women, a graceful arch of back, a well-chiseled collarbone, large, firm breasts, the curve of a tight ass. Men wore silky shirts snug enough to cling to muscles, buttons undone, pants tight—bulges, one would hope, not artificially enhanced. On the night that Glow Worm played, there were even more drag queens and glam types than usual clamoring to get in; I realized then that Johnny had a following, and not just with the rock dudes.

When Hal and I pulled up—I in a gold lamé jumpsuit and glitter stilettos I'd bought just for this night, a clutch purse held by the most delicate gold chain on my shoulder, and Hal in a spectacular blue-and-gold brocade suit that I'd picked out for him—our magnificence was so palpable that the crowd parted before us like the Red Sea. I felt godlike, my head high, my chestnut hair thick and luminous as I tossed it, finally living the life I'd been born for. The bouncer greeted us warmly and ushered us behind the velvet rope.

Just inside the doorway, at the front of the long, mirrored hall that led to the dance floor, the bar, *the action*, there was a seven-foot-tall poster of Johnny—not the entire band, just Johnny, naked, his nether regions covered by two tastefully draped feather boas. My shy Michigan boy had certainly come out of his shell! As Hal and I took in the poster, Steve stopped by.

"That's amazing, right?"

"It is," I said. "Who shot that?"

"Dick, of course," he said, meaning Avedon.

This was three years before the photographer famously wrapped a different kind of boa—a snake—around Nastassja Kinski. Dare I say that Johnny was far more gorgeous than she?

"He's got a spark, that's for sure," Hal said, gesturing toward the poster. I wondered, did it bother Hal that Johnny and I had been lovers? I considered squeezing his hand in a gesture of intimacy, but restrained myself, devilishly enjoying seeing him off balance.

"You discovered him, didn't you?" Steve asked me.

"I did," I said. "Last fall. Playing an open mic at a tiny club on the Jersey Shore."

Steve laughed. "That's the great thing about this city, right? A guy goes from playing for free at a crappy little club in Jersey to a showcase at Studio in less than a year. A couple of guys from Queens"—he motioned to himself and Hal—"wind up the ringmasters in a celebrity circus. This is the best city in the world!"

I'll admit it, I was peeved. How dare Steve not give me my due? As my eyes roamed for an object to smash, as I seriously considered clawing that gorgeous poster of Johnny, Hal squeezed my hand.

"The most gorgeous, brilliant woman on the fucking earth moves in with a *schlemiel* like me," Hal said, and even though Steve gave me a slightly bitchy once-over, my anger evaporated in the wake of Hal's adoration. Hal recognized my worth, my very *destiny*, and, armed with his admiration, I was ready to go into the fray, into the throbbing, pulsing bass and lights just beyond the entrance.

Hal and I went down to the basement, where the band was getting ready. Much to my delight, Mr. Home Perm was nowhere in sight. Lovers quarrel, perhaps? Johnny was dressed in a pale pink catsuit and white platform boots, his angel wings propped in a corner—I couldn't see until later, when he was onstage, that he'd had new wings made, and that they were spectacular. The six of us did lines, of course. As Hal had provided a generous quantity, I popped what was left of the coke into my purse, for later.

Steve's partner Ian stopped down and he and Johnny chatted for a moment about the details of the short stage show. It was unlike anything Studio had ever done, having a full live band; the excitement would have been palpable even without chemical enhancement.

Johnny was standoffish toward me at first, but the coke loosened him up.

"You seem happy, Lynda," he said after Hal left.

"I am." I was quiet for a moment, contemplating the spectacular journey that had brought me to that night. "For so long, I thought the life I wanted was in the Village, collecting crumbs of approval from the poetry world. But that was nothing compared to this!"

Johnny smiled, a tight-lipped, enigmatic smile I couldn't quite read.

Hal popped his head in.

"We should go get a spot near the stage, doll," he said, motioning toward me. I kissed Johnny lightly on the cheek and wished him a good show. That was the last time we ever spoke in a civil manner.

I spotted Aura and Denny in the crowd near the stage, and Hal and I made our way over. Denny gave me a weak, distracted hug, looking around with an alertness that was unusual for him. At the time, I dismissed it as his wonder at being inside the hottest club in the world.

Aura wore a white button-down shirt with a black menswear tie—perhaps one that had belonged to Augustus?—tucked into black straight-leg jeans. Although she lacked the glamour I'd encouraged her to project, I had to admit she'd developed a certain panache. Her only acknowledgment of my presence was a sideways glance. She took a sip of her drink. Not even a "thank you"—such an arrogant child! She clearly needed a verbal spanking.

"I hope that's not a daiquiri!" I said brightly. "I'd hate to see you barfing through the show."

She glared at me. "I no longer accept drinks from strangers." But she didn't mind accepting the gift of being on the guest list at Studio—and whose doing was that if not mine?

"Aww, come on now, ladies," Hal said, before I could lob another spoken word grenade. "This is going to be a great night. Let's bury the hatchet, eh?" He put one arm around each of us.

But before Aura or I could react, Denny motioned Hal aside.

"Can I talk to you for a minute?" he asked. I assumed he sought drugs.

"Sure," Hal said. He kissed me on the cheek. "Be back in a bit." The two of them disappeared into the crowd.

Aura and I stood there in an uncomfortable silence. Debbie Harry brushed by me as she made her way toward the stage; I nodded, and she flashed a smile in return.

Aura looked at me. "Do you know her?"

"Debbie? Sure." We'd danced together just a week earlier, with one of the lesser stars of *Welcome Back, Kotter.*

Aura studied me, her blue eyes penetrating. "I can't figure you out."

I considered this a great compliment. Doesn't every woman strive to cultivate an air of mystery? There was so much I could teach Aura, if only she would let me. Perhaps this was an opening to talk frankly.

"Oh, Aura," I said. "If you could set aside your upset over my—personal life," I chose my words carefully, "we could have a grand time together."

She was quiet, her expression unreadable. I forged ahead.

"You, my dear, are destined for greatness, but your biggest obstacle is your mother. She will destroy your uniqueness, if you let her."

Her eyes widened, and her face took on a teenage sneer. "My mother," she said, "is doing the best she can. Her husband treated her like shit when he was alive, and then died and left us with basically no money. You don't know anything about us, me and my mother."

"I do," I said, "because my mother is just like yours. A martyr. You and I are so much alike, Aura! You can't see it, but I can."

She made a scoffing sound and took a long swig of her drink. "You and I are nothing alike, Ms. Boyle," she said. "*Nothing.* I have no idea what made you fixate on me or decide we were the same or whatever, but my god. Just stop! I came here to see Johnny. To see Glow Worm. I'm glad you helped him get this showcase. But that's it. I don't want anything to do with you. And once school lets out, I really hope I never see you again."

This happened forty-one years ago, and yet the anger that consumed me in that moment ran so deep, it feels, as I write these words, that it's happening all over again. I longed to fling my drink at her; I longed to scream until she cowered in terror; I longed to do more. The elegant chain on my purse, I thought, might be strong enough to strangle a delicate young neck. But as I stood there, flames shooting along every nerve in my body, the lights went down, three-fourths of Glow Worm took the stage, and I was forced to swallow those feelings, to swallow Aura's cruel and ungrateful words. That fire swirled inside my chest, just waiting for its release.

After everyone except Johnny had taken their instruments, a catwalk lowered from the ceiling, and a figure, obscured in smoke, slowly became visible. Johnny clearly looked like a rock star now. The new angel wings—an enormous pair covered in silvery feathers—were unforgettable. Glitter adorned his eyelids and his cheekbones.

Aura tried to move away from me in the crowd. Did she think she could escape my wrath so easily? I matched her every step and delighted as I saw her squirm.

Still, I tried my best to put her heinous words out of my mind; I'd been looking forward to that show for weeks and I wouldn't let a bitchy little teenager ruin it for me. Glow Worm began with a cover of Donna Summer's "I Feel Love," which Johnny sang from the catwalk, suspended above the rest of the band. Although he was mainly a rock fan, he connected with the song, delivering it with gusto to the wildly dancing crowd, all of whom were quickly, I was certain, turned into fans. Once that song was over, the stage area went black for a few moments; then a spotlight revealed that the catwalk was gone, and Johnny was onstage with the band. They began to do a short set of their own songs, though they'd clearly chosen the more danceable tunes. The crowd was enraptured.

Four songs into Johnny's set, an enormous quantity of golden glitter fell from the ceiling, covering band and audience alike, and I wanted to revel in the perfection, the glorious beauty of the moment: these people I loved or had once loved, this place that was my spiritual home, all of us literally sparkling, our most luminous selves revealed. Yet I could not shake the pain of Aura's betrayal. After all the gifts I'd bestowed upon her, after quite literally plucking her from the swamps of Jersey, recognizing her worth, introducing her to my world, for her to speak to me as she had? Mine was an anguish second to none. Tightly held as I was there in the bosom of the crowd, I longed to physically express my rage.

And where the fuck had Hal and Denny gone?

I was in the free fall of an ever-deepening internal firestorm that threatened to unleash itself directly on Aura, consequences be damned, when the house lights came up, the music stopped, and several uniformed police officers swept onto the stage. One of them grabbed the microphone and announced a raid. For a moment, I thought it was part of the show. A raid? During Johnny's set? O no, no, *no*.

I looked around wildly for Hal, but he was nowhere to be seen.

Johnny and the band filed off the stage. Patrons headed for the front exit like there was a fire, celebrities slipping quietly toward the VIP door in the back. But those of us near the stage were, unfortunately, caught up in the raid. We were sectioned off and funneled to the main entrance, where cops flanked the door. I lost sight of Aura, but then spotted her just ahead of me in the crowd. I was a few patrons away from a stern-faced and tragically coiffed policewoman when my heart nearly stopped as I remembered it: that baggie of cocaine in my purse.

O, how I hated to waste good coke! But I had no interest in being arrested, for I knew that I would not do well in prison, robbed of life's carnal pleasures. As we were marched to the entranceway, I saw a celebrity who I shall not name—but who I will tell you was on a popular sitcom at the time, and who never became anywhere near as famous as her male co-star—slip a baggie from her own handbag into the pocket of the man next to her. She may not have been the comic genius her co-star was, but that gal was certainly adept at self-preservation! To my left was a drag queen in a tight, sparkly dress that appeared to have no pockets. Just ahead of me was Aura. Wearing jeans.

Before you judge me, consider this: Aura was fourteen. The police were unlikely to believe the coke was hers, I reasoned, and even if they did, she'd be treated as a minor. Her family was already a mess, so a little more Lockhart drama couldn't possibly make a difference. Denny would be blamed, of course. She'd emerge unscathed, with a great story to tell interviewers when she was famous—though, curiously, I've found in my research that she doesn't talk about it much, at least not directly.

I, on the other hand, was twenty-six years old. My job didn't matter to me in the slightest, but my parents would shit themselves if I was fired—or arrested! I knew I'd never hear the fucking end of it from my mother. And what kind of repercussions might my arrest have on Hal, his business? I could end up in Dan Wykoski's position, praying to a God I didn't believe in to deliver me from jail.

It's not like I made a conscious decision to slip the coke into Aura's pocket. It just happened. One moment my hand was on my purse's clasp, then on the baggie; the next, it had expertly tucked the drugs into Aura's back pocket, my touch so light that she barely registered a jostle—and, as she flinched and glanced over her shoulder, her eyes, expecting some lecherous man, met mine.

Before I could read her expression, I was assaulted by a raft of plumage. The feathers blocked my sight, the force of them nearly knocking me over. When I'd righted myself, I realized I'd been hit by one of Johnny's angel wings. He'd plucked the baggie of coke from Aura's pocket but, alas, I and two uniformed police officers both saw him drop it to the floor.

"How could you do that, Lynda?" he hissed at me as one of the cops pulled him, and the coke, aside. "Planting this on Aura?"

I shrugged and feigned innocence, watching as the few celebrities who hadn't made it to the back exit quickly peeled off and away. I tried to follow them, but that female officer grasped my wrist—much harder than was necessary.

"You have no lawful right to detain me," I said through clenched teeth. The paparazzi had appeared, most likely trying to get shots of celebrities for Page Six.

"That cocaine was hers," Johnny said to the officer who'd taken him aside. He pointed a wing at me.

"ID, please," the policewoman said to me. I sighed and retrieved my license.

She looked at my name and called another officer over. The two of them examined my license and talked with heads bowed.

"I'd like my ID back," I said, loudly, for the benefit of the crowd. "I've done nothing wrong."

"We'd like you to come with us for questioning," she said, her hand still around my wrist.

"Questioning about what?"

"About how you tried to plant coke on one of your *students*," Johnny called out.

"We'll get to that at the station," the policewoman said.

"What is this, the USSR?" I bellowed, channeling my father and his

Red Scare overreactions—though in this case, I was wholly justified. "I've done nothing illegal. You'll take your hand off me, now."

Perhaps because of my extreme beauty, we drew a bit of attention, the officer and I. As she slapped handcuffs on me—handcuffs!—at least one flash distinctly went off near my face. I looked to my left and saw Johnny being handcuffed as well, Aura standing next to him, her eyes wide with concern. Denny was nowhere to be found; Hal, I assumed, had escaped out the back.

As the policewoman ushered me past Aura, Johnny's eyes met mine. The top third of one of his wings had broken off in the scuffle.

"Don't let her get away with it," Johnny said to the female cop, nodding his head toward me.

My captor stopped for a moment to confer briefly with the other cop, providing me a moment to do damage control.

"Johnny, I don't know what you think—"

"Save it," Johnny said. "I *saw* you."

And with that, the officer turned me away from Johnny and led me down Fifty-Fourth Street, to the Midtown North police precinct.

27

My questioning at the police station was, to be frank, less rigorous than I'd expected from New York's finest. They seemed much less interested in that baggie of coke and who it had belonged to than they were in Hal and his business. When asked where I lived, I gave my parents' address, but they somehow knew that Hal and I had shacked up. One of the officers, apparently trying to scare me, said that Hal was being questioned by the FBI at that very moment. How my heart ached for my love—first interrogated and beaten by another government, by his business associates, and now this!

Would it be off-putting if I revealed that my lacy panties became moist at this point in the questioning? Not that I was turned on by Hal's suffering; it was the proximity to danger that got my juices flowing. I felt even more alive in that police station than I had at Studio.

"Do you think I need a lawyer?" I asked the male officer in my sexiest voice. I sat back to give him the full view of all my gold-lamé glory.

He and the female officer exchanged glances.

"Well, that's up to you," he said. "But we can't help you once you bring a lawyer in."

"Really? I'm certain my cousin Tony always said to obtain legal counsel if one is being questioned. The stories he's told about interrogating suspects!"

"You have a cousin on the job?" the female officer asked.

I nodded.

"What precinct?"

"In Jersey."

They left the room for a few minutes, and two plainclothes officers came back. Perhaps from the FBI? To this day I have no idea. They asked more questions about Hal, questions I couldn't answer—because he'd been wise enough to shield me from every detail of his business. Partway through these questions, it occurred to me that Hal had been with Denny at the time of the raid.

"What about Denny—Dennis Lockhart?" I asked, hoping to take the heat off Hal a bit.

They looked at me with equally blank faces. A little *too* blank, I thought.

"You don't know who he is? He was with Hal when your officers burst in."

"Did you hear of anyone by that name?" one officer asked the other with the kind of feigned nonchalance one might expect from an actor in a Keyhole community theatre production.

"No," the other said.

Perhaps this act fooled the common criminal, but it did not fool me. The last-minute request to be on the guest list, Denny's looking around nervously when we encountered him, his asking to do business with Hal: it hit me then that Denny had set Hal up. When had Denny been arrested for his own drug dealing, and struck this devil's bargain to deliver Hal to them? I had to acknowledge a surprised admiration: I wouldn't have believed him to have the smarts for such treachery.

"Just so you know who you made a deal with, Denny sells drugs to college kids, many of whom are minors," I said.

They looked at each other and left the room, confirming my theory.

The officers in uniform returned. I asked to see Hal several times and was refused. As the same questions were repeated for the eighth, ninth, tenth times, my titillation gave way to ennui.

By three a.m. I had had it. If they had grounds to arrest me, I reasoned, they would have already done so. I took a calculated risk.

"Either arrest me," I said, "or let me go. I'm finished with this petty little exercise." I cleared my throat for effect. "I demand a lawyer."

Seeing that I was firm in my resolve, they chose to release me—with an admonition not to leave the tri-state area. I took a taxi back to the Dakota, hoping that Hal would be waiting there for me, fearing that he would not.

Hal was not home, but the light blinked on the answering machine: a message from Hal himself, for me. He said that I should go to Keyhole and teach that morning like it was a normal day. I should pack a bag, he said, and stay with my parents for a few days.

"I know you don't want to go there," he added, "but do it for me. I'll be in touch as soon as I can."

And, he said, don't take the car service.

Did he not know that I'd been questioned too? Could he not at least have asked how *I* was doing? I got undressed and brewed some coffee. I had no interest in driving to Keyhole that morning, let alone staying with—horror of horrors—*my parents*, but Hal was adamant on the message. Where was he now? How was he? What if the FBI really had something on him, and he went to prison? My irritation dissipated as I imagined losing my VIP status at Studio, as well as that apartment, the car service, that *life*.

And Hal, of course.

I decided the smartest play would be to do exactly as he'd asked.

I arrived at school to find a note from Dick Singer asking me to see him immediately. On my way to Dick's office, I passed Bobby Craig and a few of the other boys from his class.

"Foxy jumpsuit, Ms. Boyle!" he called out, and they all laughed. Another boy from a younger grade wolf whistled as I passed him farther down the hall. I'd gotten nothing but a nap the night before and was wearing one of my demurer dresses—yet still, I was driving the young men wild! Buoyed by the adolescent libidos revving all around me, I strode confidently toward Dick's office.

When I got to Patty's desk, she motioned me in with a sympathetic look.

"I'm sorry, hon," she said.

It wasn't until I sat across from Dick and he tossed a copy of the *New York Post* at me that I understood what had happened.

Drug Bust at Studio 54, the headline blared, and there, on the front page, was a photo of me—and a stunning photo at that!—in my gold lamé jumpsuit, being led away in handcuffs. My spectacular breasts rested just above the headline. I took a brief second to note that Bobby Craig was right: it *was* a foxy jumpsuit.

"This isn't what it appears to be," I began, but Dick put his hand out.

"Save it for the disciplinary board," he said. "You're suspended until your hearing." He couldn't resist one more lascivious look at my breasts. "You should expect to be fired."

Fired? *Fired*? I started to work up a righteous lather before I realized that I *longed* to be fired! That it was something I'd dreamed about for the past three years of Keyhole purgatory—a release from this horrific limbo, a rebirth into the rest of my life. My parents had certainly seen the cover of the *Post* by now, so there would be no reasoning with them;

Aura and Johnny would likely never forgive me. I had no idea what was happening to Hal, but I knew one thing for certain: he was my future, and Keyhole was my past.

"You can't fire me," I said to Dick, "because I quit."

"Thanks for simplifying the matter," Dick said.

I stood. Began to turn. I might have simply walked out of the office then and there, had his eyes not made one more up-and-down sweep along the length of my body.

I whirled back around to face him.

"Do you think I'm resigning to simplify your job, you disgusting old letch?"

He pushed back in his chair, eyes wide.

"What, you thought I didn't notice? All the lingering looks at my breasts? The way you practically drooled when I leaned forward? You're a male chauvinist fucking pig, and I *played* you."

"I—"

I leaned over the desk, inches from his face, my breasts now taunting him with their unavailability.

"What did you think, that I'd fuck you some day? Or blow your shriveled dick under that desk? Maybe you thought I'd do that to keep my job. 'Oh no, Principal Singer, anything but the disciplinary hearing, please!'"

I laughed in his face. He tried to push his chair back more, but it was already against the wall.

"When I'm done with you, you'll be the one brought before the disciplinary board, not me!"

His face blanched.

It was an empty threat; I had no plans to fight for my job, or to orchestrate his downfall. He wasn't worth my time. But I greatly enjoyed seeing him squirm in the moment.

"So," I said. "I will send you a letter of resignation, which you will accept. You'll tell everyone this was a mutual parting of the ways. You will not gossip about me in town. If a whiff of any of this gets back to my parents, I'll make sure you and Dan Wykoski are next to each other on the unemployment line. Or in prison."

His jaw was still slack as I made my exit. I wondered idly if he'd had a stroke but didn't care enough to check.

Patti was waiting for me just beyond his office.

"You're my hero," she said.

O, my dear, sweet Patti!

"I'll miss you," I said to her, "and only you."

Was I the talk of the teachers' lounge for the rest of the school year? Did it stretch into the following fall? Am I still discussed forty years later, the stuff of legend? At the risk of sounding immodest, I am certain the answer to all those questions is a resounding "yes."

After resigning from my teaching job, I headed to my parents' house to deal with whatever fallout was waiting for me, and to use their phone to try to track down Hal. My father's car and Tony's police cruiser were both in the driveway when I pulled up.

"Lynda!" my father cried as I walked through the front door. "Maria, Tony—she's here!"

I'd expected to be berated, but my dear father was simply relieved that I wasn't in jail. He really did love me like none other—or perhaps, like only one other.

"How did you get out?" Tony asked. "I've been working my contacts in Manhattan, but they couldn't find a record of your arrest."

I sighed. "They never arrested me," I said. "Just questioned me. It was a raid on the club, and I just got swept up in it." I made big eyes at my father. "I didn't do anything wrong, Daddy."

"Then why were you in *handcuffs*?" my mother asked, brandishing a copy of the *Post*.

I did a brief mental calculation, and yes, fact mixed with fiction was called for here. "I got in an argument with the officer because they were trying to arrest Johnny," I said.

"Johnny was there?" my father asked.

"His band was playing. Aura was there too."

"At that disco?" my mother wailed. "Oh, Jeannette will be beside herself."

"She was there with Denny," I said, to ensure that I wouldn't be blamed. "Most likely they just questioned her and let her go."

My mother tossed the newspaper onto the kitchen table and sat down, her head in her melodramatic hands. "How will we ever live this down?"

"Maria," my father said, "just be happy that she's home safe, and not rotting in a jail cell with all those junkies and hookers."

I could have played my parents against each other, but in that moment, I had an unexpected soupçon of sympathy for my mother. She'd done everything society had told her to do; for her trouble she'd gotten two sons with moldy cheese for brains, and a daughter so extraordinary that looking at her was like looking directly at the sun. Two extremes, when what she'd really wanted was something in the middle.

Perhaps it was some sort of ESP, a sense I had that I'd never return to Keyhole after that day. Perhaps it was just that I fully saw the tragedy of my mother's life in that moment—not as something to react against, but truly *saw* it for the sad spectacle it was. I did not forgive her, of course—could a lifetime of sabotage ever be forgiven? But for that brief mote of time, I chose to let her off the hook.

I pulled a chair out and sat down next to her.

"Mother," I said, gesturing toward the newspaper. "People might talk about me, but they can't deny that Maria Boyle has a gorgeous daughter."

She flashed me a stern look of disapproval but couldn't hold the mood. A smile cracked through.

"I wish," she said, "that I had more of your self-confidence. And that you had a little less."

I chose to take the remark as an acknowledgment of her failure at sabotaging my specialness, and gave her what appeared to be a badly needed hug.

"Well, I guess I can get back to the station now," Tony said. "Stay out of those discos, okay?"

As he was leaving, we heard a knock on the door. Tony opened it.

The sun was in my eyes; it took me a moment to realize that the man standing there in dark sunglasses and a baseball cap was Hal. Just beyond him, a black car with darkened windows sat idling in front of my parents' house.

"Babe," Hal said.

I fell into his arms, realizing only then that I'd been holding in check a storm of roiling anxieties, and now felt a kind of relief I'd never experienced before.

I'd been worried—truly worried—about Hal.

What a brave new world, to have such emotions in it!

After chatting for a few minutes with my parents, he asked if we could go into my bedroom to talk. And that was when he made me an offer I couldn't refuse.

Hal told me everything then: how he had organized crime ties, and how he had as much to fear from them as from the cartels. How Denny had indeed set him up—apparently Denny had been busted weeks earlier—and how the FBI had enough on Hal to put him in jail for life, or at least, until he was too old to enjoy life. How they'd offered him a deal: witness protection, if he testified against everyone he did business with.

"But I can't go into witness protection if it means losing you," he said.

"You mean you're choosing prison—just so you can see me?" My mind immediately spun with lascivious outfits I could wear, files I'd insert into bakery-bought cakes.

He smiled. "Only if I don't have a better option."

And then he got down on one knee.

"You're the one, doll," he said, looking me in the eyes. "I've been waiting all my life for you. You're drop dead gorgeous, but it's so much more than that. You're smart and scrappy, not afraid to bend the rules, to get your hands a little dirty—figuratively, I mean." He took my hands in his. "You know what you want, and you find a way to get it. And you're fucking impossible to figure out sometimes, so I'll never get bored."

I laughed in exactly the way I'd always imagined I'd laugh when a day like this came: a heady, knowing, Katherine Hepburn kind of laugh.

"I'm sorry I don't have a ring," he said. "But I promise I'll get you the biggest, most gorgeous rock you've ever seen. If you'll marry me. And come on the lam with me."

"On the lam?"

"Witness protection. Initially they'll put us in some crappy town in the middle of nowhere. I can't lie to you, doll, it might suck at first." He lowered his voice. "But I have a few tricks up my sleeve."

"What kind of tricks?" I was titillated by the cloak-and-daggerness of it all.

"The Feds will take most of my money and force me to get a Working Joe kind of job. But I've got money hidden that they'll never find. A *lot* of it. We won't dare access it at first. But once things settle down, we'll get a hold of that money, and live like fucking royalty."

"How long do you think that will take?"

Hal sighed and shifted to his other knee. "A couple of years. We'll have to live a middle-class life until then. But I promise you, that pot of gold will be waiting. I will always, always take care of you."

I sat back on my childhood bed, that bed that had been mine up until just a few months ago, and considered Hal's offer. It provided an escape from Keyhole, yes—but to where? Somewhere worse? Could there really *be* anywhere worse?

"Would we ever be able to go back to The City?" I asked.

"Probably not, doll," he said. "I know I'm asking you to give up a lot."

He was, of course, and my mind wandered to other possibilities. If I found a way to stay in New York, could I make it on my own? Could I meet another Hal?

But then I looked at him, really looked at him, as he was looking at me. Most people gazed my way and saw a beautiful face, a body worthy of a Fashion Week runway. Certain expectations went with that; I became their fantasy. And when I didn't live up to the image they'd created, they turned on me, as so many of my lovers had: Bryce, Carlos, Peter, even Johnny. In that moment, I knew that Hal really saw me, saw all of me. He *loved* the things about me that others loathed. He was that elusive #1, 2 and 3 but he was even more: he was also a #4, a Guy Who Gets Me. And that, it turned out, was the most important category of all.

I knew in that moment that I would go with him. I had never loved before, and in all honesty, I wasn't certain that I loved Hal, even then. But I *wanted* to love him, and I knew that I would blossom in the light of his adoration. I had burned bridges from Jersey to The City and back; if I didn't go with Hal, I'd have to move to some other, lesser city to rebuild my life. Philadelphia, maybe, or Los Angeles. I saw with utter clarity that Hal's was not only the best offer on the table right now; it might be the best offer I'd ever get.

"I love you," I said, and it didn't feel like a lie. "Let's go get married and disappear."

And, with nothing more than a simple "goodbye" to my parents and Tony—because Hal had made it clear we could not fill them in—I left my childhood home on his arm and sashayed down the flagstone path toward that waiting car, climbing decisively into the backseat without so much as a glance over my shoulder, never to be seen in the tri-state area again.

❧

Jann, I trust that I've done a thorough job of clearing up the haunting inaccuracies I noted at the beginning of this missive, while also gifting you with the story of the century—the twentieth century, that is. What a relief, to finally divulge these details after carrying them deep within me for all these years Hal and I have been on the run. We've lived in parts of America no New Yorker should ever have to see, from one-stoplight farming villages to zombie mill towns to strip mall suburbs that could almost have been Keyhole, but without the redemption of the beach and the nearby City. My disappearance has allowed Johnny and Aura—and a few reporters with more ambition than talent—to control the narrative for decades now. With repetition, their biased and, dare I say, sexist interpretations of me became enshrined as fact.

But that Rock Hall of Fame induction was like Proust's madeleine, the vivid memories it evoked whispering in my ear: *it's time for the world to hear your story, Lynda*. In fact, I am willing to grant you an exclusive as long as you publish, word for word, every morsel I've written here.

I look forward to your swift reply.

Sincerely yours,

Lynda Boyle Ross

-----------Forwarded Message----------

Subject: Undeliverable Mail Return to Sender (Failure)
Date: Monday, April 15, 2019 3:55 a.m.
From: (MAILER-DAEMON@aol.com)
To: dancingqueen.54@aol.com

Sorry, we were unable to deliver your message to the following address:

jann@rollingstone.com

The email account that you tried to reach does not exist. Please try double-checking the recipient's email address for typos or unnecessary spaces.

Subject: Re: Correction requested re: "Aura Lockhart Inducts Johnny Engel into Rock & Roll Hall of Fame," Rolling Stone #1326, April 2019

From: Lynda Boyle Ross (dancingqueen.54@aol.com)
Date: Monday, April 15, 2019 4:14 p.m.
To: Jann Wenner (jann@rollingstone.com)

Dear Mr. Wenner,

I am at a loss to understand your far-too-swift reply to the *tour de force* you had the inconceivable good fortune of receiving early this morning. Who is this Daemon—your assistant? Surely neither he, nor you, could have read my life story in *one fucking minute*.

I realize that we were only briefly acquainted, but our connection alone should pique your curiosity enough to clear a few hours in your schedule—which I suspect is not all that busy these days, as it's obvious you have this Daemon replying to your correspondence. I'm sure your assistant's interventions free you for the kind of day-drinking I've been doing since reading his short-sighted reply, but he is likely too young and ill-informed to recognize literary gold when he sees it.

Does this story not have every possible ingredient for publishing success? Sex, drugs, rock 'n' roll *and* disco? New York City in all its gritty late-seventies glamour? A spectacular young beauty at the center of it all?

Perhaps Daemon is older and savvier than I give him credit for, and his reaction is colored by the misplaced anger toward me that I realize still simmers in pockets of the rock world, especially among Glow Worm fans—rumors that I suspect Aura is behind. Rest assured it is not my fault that Johnny spent a year in prison for that bag of cocaine he dropped. Nor is it my fault that I had a new identity and was unavailable to corroborate his story when he went to trial. Had he simply let events unfold as I'd intended them, young Aura would have received a slap on the wrist, if that, and he'd never have been arrested.

For the record, I didn't even know Johnny had gone to prison until years later, when I read an article about the making of Glow Worm's second album. And I didn't know about his fans' anger toward me until I stumbled upon an internet message board dedicated to the band, where I learned that many of the group's most ardent admirers referred to me as "Yoko."

Blaming me for the brevity of Glow Worm's career is, of course, absurd. Is it my fault that prison changed Johnny, that he wrote a dark rock opera when he got out, and that after they recorded it, the band broke up? In fact, many of the very fans who pin Glow Worm's demise on me also say that *Last Night at the Disco* is their favorite album of all time. One could say that Glow Worm's magnum opus would never have been created without me. But I would never go so far as to take credit for it myself.

I even found a small dark corner of the internet that holds me culpable for the political career of Rep. Dennis Lockhart (R-Idaho). Given that I've had no contact with Denny since 1978, how could I possibly be responsible for the way he took Augustus's liberal politics and free love theories and spun it all into a far-right libertarian ideology after moving to Idaho in the early 1990s? My pussy may be head-spinningly amazing, but it is decidedly apolitical.

Perhaps my anger at Daemon's disregard for my magnificent story is unfounded here. Maybe he recognized my name and decided not to read on out of concern for my husband's and my safety. I will admit, when Hal finally cajoled me into revealing why I'd mixed a pitcher of martinis for lunch, he expressed exactly such concerns, in delightfully colorful language. He also believes that you and Daemon never received my e-mail, that it "bounced around the goddamn internet for fuck knows who to see."

"Jann sold *Rolling Stone* a couple of years ago, Lynda," Hubby added, reading Daemon's message. "Whatever his email address is, that ain't it."

But I know you well enough, Jann, to intuit that you'd never give up being involved with your crowning achievement, your *raison d'être.* While Hal sits on his own computer making plans for where we'll move next—he is, at this very minute, obtaining falsified documents through an "encrypted server" and suggesting that we might be leaving the country!—I have resolved to give you one final opportunity to read my story and recognize its historical and artistic significance.

Thus I am resending my previous email, and attaching a selection of my finest poems from the one notebook I had with me when Hal and I left the tri-state area. As I stopped writing poetry after we went into witness protection—what is the point of getting published if one cannot see one's given name up in lights?—they were all written in the 1970s, but I assure you they hold up as classics.

If I do not hear from you in a timely manner, I will seek other publishing venues, perhaps with some names and facts obscured at Hubby's insistence. I may also pursue legal action regarding the falsehoods about me in the article referenced in my previous email. In short, Mr. Wenner, it would serve you well in multiple ways to address these matters *immediately*.

Perhaps you think you can ignore me? I trust you saw how well that went for Michael Douglas in *Fatal Attraction*. I don't mean to frighten you, and I would certainly never boil your bunny.

But I am Lynda Fucking Boyle, and rest assured that I am *not* going away.

Acknowledgments

First and foremost, I'm grateful to Jaynie Royal and everyone at Regal House Publishing. It's been a joy to work with this fabulous house, and I feel fortunate that *Last Night at the Disco* found a home with them.

Eternal appreciation and affection to my agent, Esmond Harmsworth, who believed in this novel even when I wasn't sure about it, and whose astute editorial eye made it so much better.

For crucial feedback at various draft stages, a huge round of thanks to: Christopher Castellani, Shalene Gupta, Ron MacLean, Cynthia Borders Nunez, Patricia Park, Whitney Scharer, Judy Casulli Tan and Anna Williams.

For research and background on Studio 54, Jenny Goldman, Victoria Leacock Hoffman and Calliope Nicholas tirelessly answered my detailed questions. The excellent 2018 documentary film *Studio 54* also provided a wealth of information.

Special thanks to Sonya Larson and Patricia Park for their help with the title.

Portions of this novel were written at the Blue Mountain Center, Millay Arts and the Virginia Center for the Creative Arts. I'm grateful for the support of these organizations, whose residencies help sustain my creative life.

Finally, love and gratitude to my partner, Jeffrey Page, whose kindness and patience are a remarkable and welcome counterpoint to my high-strung, anxious nature. And a special shout-out to our cats, Clarence and Neko, whose antics bring us joy on a daily basis. I love our little family and I'm grateful to Jeff for all he does to help keep it running.

Acknowledgments